DOOMED—

꧁꧂꧁꧂

The door of the small cell clanged shut behind Seagryn the powershaper, and the key was turned. He spun around to throw his weight against it, but the door was solid metal.

Seagryn slumped to the floor, feeling breathless. Then he noticed that the torch in the wall bracket behind him was flickering, and he realized the reason. There was no ventilation in the room, except for the little air that came through a tiny slit at the bottom of the door—enough to slow his dying, but not to prevent it.

No problem, he told himself. He'd just take his tugolith form . . .

And be crushed to death! The cell was too small to contain a huge tugolith, and, since it had been carved out of rock, its walls would certainly not burst outward.

There was no way the magic of the powers he could shape would save him. And without such magic, he was doomed to die of asphyxiation—slowing, lingeringly, but inevitably!

THE
FAITHFUL
TRAITOR

Book Two of
Wizard & Dragon

Robert Don Hughes

A Del Rey Book

BALLANTINE BOOKS • NEW YORK

A Del Rey Book
Published by Ballantine Books

Library of Congress Catalog Card Number: 91-93047

ISBN 0-345-36090-7

Manufactured in the United States of America

First Edition: March 1992

Cover Art by Romas

TO MY TWO EDITORS—
GAIL AND LESTER.

✖✖✖✖✖

TABLE OF CONTENTS

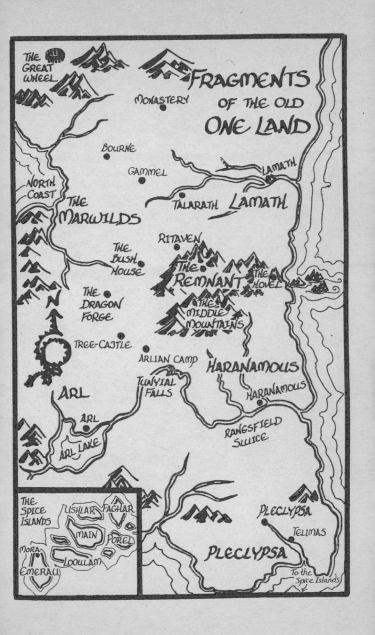

Chapter One

❊❊❊❊❊

FIERY SUNSET

A blue flyer darted past him as Seagryn rode up the long lane to the mansion he shared with his wife and her father. He smiled as he watched it go and leaned over to scratch the side of Kerl's neck. "Did you see that, Kerl? Don't you wish you could move that fast?" Kerl said nothing, of course, being a horse of few words, and Seagryn sat back in his saddle and grinned up at the trees.

The summer had been remarkably pleasant: always warm, but only occasionally hot. He turned to gaze between the tree trunks at a lush green field, where a breeze rippled waist-high stalks of grass. Insects skittered everywhere, adding the chatter of their wings to the whisper of the wind that stirred the afternoon air. Seagryn's nose tickled and his eyes watered, but he would not trade this Lamathian lane for any other place in the old One Land. This was home, and he'd been deprived of it long enough to learn truly to appreciate it. Since the humiliating day when he'd first taken his altershape in public, Seagryn had grown wise in the ways of manipulating magic. But no magic could compare to this simple joy—riding home to Elaryl under a canopy of trees.

She had grown so much in the last year. On the day of their marriage she'd been far more concerned with the state of her blond hair than with his state of mind. Her beautiful blue eyes had focused only on the flowers and the frills. But now she seemed to direct most of her attention to what he was thinking, how he was feeling, what he was planning . . . in fact, curiously so.

1

Then again, Seagryn told himself, how else could she act? After all, he did possess that terrifying ability to transform himself into a monster—a horned tugolith, complete with that beast's oddly sweet stink. And she knew he tended to take that altershape only when attacked or enraged or under pressure of some sort. Little wonder that Elaryl kept a regular check on his state of mind.

He *had* wondered lately if she was trying to hide something from him, but whenever such thoughts occurred he scolded himself for being overly suspicious. While on the road, he had needed to be suspicious in order to survive. His powershaping abilities had made him a prominent figure in world affairs and had provided him some powerful enemies. But Seagryn was home at last and well loved by the people of Lamath. If Elaryl was hiding anything from him, he felt confident she did so for his own good—

The sound of rapid hoofbeats climbed above the volume of the summer rustle that had masked them. They came from behind him, and Seagryn, suddenly concerned, reined in Kerl and frowned over his shoulder. The rider never slowed. The lane was wide enough to permit six horses to ride abreast—or one tugolith—and the man's sleek mount dodged Kerl to the left and raced on toward the mansion. Seagryn watched him go, realizing now that this was a messenger dispatched from the capital with some news for his father-in-law.

"We'd better hurry, Kerl," he muttered, spurring the flanks of his stolid steed. "This looks important; if we don't hear it straight from the messenger, we'll never learn what it's about. Old Talarath certainly won't tell us." Kerl responded with a businesslike canter; but if Seagryn wanted any more than that, he was out of luck. Kerl knew his rights.

Talarath was a member of the Ruling Council of Lamath, headed by Ranoth himself, and this rider wore Ranoth's livery. The Council sent regular reports from the capital each week, but Elaryl always seemed to have something for Seagryn to do whenever they arrived. He'd once asked Talarath, "What was the news?" But the old man had only snorted and growled back, "Are YOU on the Ruling Council?" Seagryn wasn't, of course. But he had been privy to many of the Council's recent dealings with other powers and he had a personal stake in the course of events. If this was news of the dragon, then it concerned him deeply, for Seagryn had played a rôle in making the two-headed beast and was solely responsible for loosing it on the world. But even if the news did not concern him, Seagryn was determined to hear it. This was not the normal day nor time for the weekly messages to arrive, and the horse and rider moved at emergency-level speed—a pace not matched, unfortunately, by his own mount.

"Kerl," he grumbled, "come ON." The gray horse ran several steps to indicate his spiritual willingness but gradually slowed back down to a trot, obviously hoping Seagryn wouldn't notice. Seagryn spurred him again. With a deep sigh, Kerl pushed himself forward into an unenthusiastic gallop.

The courier was already inside the mansion when they finally arrived—and Elaryl waited in the doorway with a radiant smile. Seagryn jumped from Kerl's back and walked quickly toward her, returning her smile in the hope that she would let him slide past her. When she immediately blocked his path he realized there wasn't a chance.

"Did you have a good ride?" she murmured, slipping her arms up around his neck and punctuating her question by nibbling his ear.

He craned his neck to look beyond her down the entryway. "Beautiful. Did you see a messenger from Ranoth arri—"

"For Father," she interrupted, shifting to his other ear and screening his view.

"Passed me on the road. Seemed to think it was urgent—"

"They always do. All messengers have an inflated sense of self-importance." She slipped her arms down around his waist now and flattened herself against him, tipping her head back to plant her chin against his. "Do you love me?"

"You know I love you," he answered. No chance of hearing the messenger now. She was deliberately preventing him from—

"How do I know?" Elaryl pouted prettily, subtly shifting her hips against him. He felt her hands dropping down from his waist to clasp around his thighs.

On the other hand, if the news was *truly* important he'd hear it eventually anyway . . .

Kerl watched the couple disappear inside the mansion, then trotted off toward the stable to put himself away. He had enough sense to know he wouldn't be needed again this afternoon.

Summer sunsets were spectacular when viewed from the rooftop of the rebuilt House of Talarath, and Seagryn and Elaryl had taken to eating their evening meal there in order to enjoy them. They seemed even more pleasant whenever Seagryn contrasted their silent beauty to the equally silent tension of dinner in the formal dining room. Talarath's mood always set the tone of meals in the great hall, and the old gentleman was surly far more often than he was not. Seagryn wondered about that occasionally, since, to his knowledge, things were going well in Lamath. He usually attributed his father-in-law's foul spirits to his own presence. Talarath had seemed to care about him years ago, when he was the old man's student. But a student is quite different from a son-in-law, Seagryn realized; besides, the events of the last year had put their relationship under quite a strain.

Just a glance at this building reminded him how much. While a beautiful house, it was also quite new. On the day of his wedding to Elaryl, an attack by Marwandian raiders had forced Seagryn to take his tugolith shape. Quite without noticing, he'd proceeded to knock the old house down.

He'd been banished, then, from Lamath for being a user of magic and had only been restored to his homeland by an unprecedented act of the Ruling Council itself. He'd earned his restoration, Seagryn thought grimly as he watched the clouds turn pink. He'd helped provide the raw materials for the making of the dragon, which Ranoth and Talarath had believed was a good idea at the time. But it had cost him. The thought of how a gentle female tugolith named Berillitha had sacrificed herself for him still brought an enormous lump to his throat, and he expected to live with the guilt from that act forever. But, as Elaryl always reminded him, he'd done his best to save her at the time . . .

Seagryn frowned. "Does the sky look a little more red tonight than usual?" he asked.

Elaryl looked up from her plate and followed the direction of his gaze. "No." She shrugged, but he happened to glance at her eyes, and they said something entirely different. Suddenly she laid her fork down. "I'm not really hungry," she announced. "Let's go for a walk."

Seagryn took another bite and chewed it thoughtfully. "Strange. You were eating with great appetite a moment ago."

"Was I?" Elaryl shrugged. "Oh—out of habit, I suppose. Come on—walk with me." She stood up and extended her hand, but Seagryn remained in his chair.

"What is it?" he asked.

"What's what?" she replied, sounding rather annoyed—and far too quickly for the situation. It assured him that something was, indeed, amiss.

"What is it that you're hiding from me?" Seagryn asked.

"Hiding? Why would I be hiding anything from you?"

"He knows, Elaryl." Talarath spoke from behind him, and

now Seagryn did get up. Neither he nor Elaryl had heard the old man coming up the stairs.

Seagryn faced Talarath and shook his head. "No, I'm afraid I *don't* know," he said quietly.

"Not the specifics, perhaps. But you *do* know that my daughter has been attempting to keep something from you." Talarath turned his accusing gaze on Elaryl.

She appeared uncowed by him. "Father, if you'll permit me, I had planned to explain it all fully to him in good time—"

"Events have their own pace, my dear. I've honored your wishes as far as I've been able, but eventually national concerns outweigh even family promises."

"What events?" Seagryn asked, his voice flat. He'd turned to look back at the sunset, but he no longer noticed its uplifting grandeur. Instead, it filled him with an aching loneliness, a feeling he'd often experienced at dusk on the open road. It seemed to say to him, "Others have their places of rest and are settling into them right now. But you, Seagryn, are a wanderer. You have no place that is truly yours . . ."

"Did I not hear you noticing a red tinge to the western sky tonight?" Talarath asked, his voice taking on a bitter edge. "Have your eyes not smarted today? Did you not smell the smoke? If the wind were blowing toward us, I fear we should be covered with the ashes, for your friend the dragon has been visiting Lamath and has left a dozen villages in cinders!"

" 'My friend the dragon,' " Seagryn echoed Talarath mockingly, his smile utterly without humor. "Meaning I'm to blame for its existence."

"Meaning you aided in the making of the beast. Meaning you engineered its premature release. Meaning you rode upon its back and are the only person with whom it's ever conversed whom it did not subsequently digest!"

"Father, that's not fair and you know it!" Elaryl shouted, walking around to put herself bodily between the two men.

"Talk to the refugees streaming out of the Western District about what's fair, Elaryl!" Talarath snarled.

"It's not fair to try to shift the blame for all this to Seagryn! He only did what you and the rest of your accursed Conspiracy agreed needed to be done—"

"The project wasn't completed—" Talarath began.

"Oh, and the dragon would have been far nicer if it had been? I was *there*, Father, remember? *There* in that dismal cave, listening to the beast scream while your precious sorcerer Sheth tortured it!''

''Your husband did not allow the process to run its full course—''

''You *believe* that, don't you?'' Elaryl screamed at her father, and Seagryn noted with an odd detachment that this was the most enraged he'd ever seen her with anyone other than himself. As they argued, he turned to look to the west, imagining he could see tiny puffs of smoke on the horizon.

''You really do believe that, if Seagryn hadn't interfered with Sheth's plan, Vicia-Heinox would have been controllable! Father, I've always known you were a stubborn man, but I've never believed you were a fool!''

''Silence! I will not hear such disrespect from you in my own house!''

''I am *not* your little girl anymore, Father,'' Elaryl answered, more quietly but no less dangerously. ''This is my house, too, and my life, and I *will* make my voice heard in matters that affect myself and my husband—''

''What do you want me to do?'' Seagryn interrupted, his voice still expressionless. The other two looked at him, uncertain which of them he was asking.

Talarath seized the opportunity first. ''The Executive Committee of the Ruling Council has met in Lamath—''

''You mean Ranoth has decided on his own,'' Seagryn said sarcastically, but Talarath continued on anyway.

''—and sent the request that you go to the Western District and investigate the situation there.''

''Investigate the situation!'' Elaryl snarled in disgust. Seagryn had to chuckle at the words himself.

''What did Ranoth mean by that, exactly?'' he asked, and Talarath's neck reddened.

''The request means what it says! We need you to go and investigate the dragon's destruction, and—and—''

''Talk to it?'' Seagryn supplied.

''If it will talk to you, yes!'' Talarath roared, his eyes snapping. ''Perhaps you could assume that stinking 'altershape' of yours! You've proved yourself capable of knocking down buildings while wearing it! Presumably its thick hide would provide you some protection against the dragon's flames!''

''Vicia-Heinox doesn't shoot flames,'' Seagryn murmured. ''The dragon focuses attention upon an object and somehow creates heat inside it.''

"There, you see?" Talarath gestured with his long arm. "You're the expert who can aid us in our dilemma."

"But Father, this isn't fair!" Elaryl said again, returning to a theme Seagryn assumed had been frequently argued between them in his absence. "You refuse to put him on your Ruling Council because he's a magic user, but when you run into a problem you can't solve, you want to send him to do your dirty work!"

"I remind you, daughter, that it's you who has discouraged contact between the Council and your husband ever since your return from the Marwild forests. Besides—any attempt to elevate him to a Council rôle would be met with violent protest. You know as well as I do his current reputation among the people of Lamath."

"What reputation?" Seagryn asked, as they glanced at him in surprise. When neither answered, he asked, "What *is* my reputation with the people?"

"It's . . ." Elaryl began, but her voice trailed off.

"It's not good," Talarath finished for her but didn't elaborate.

"So I gathered." Seagryn nodded, failing to keep the bitterness out of his voice. He turned to look out over the parapet again, but, although the light was fading, he could see no fires on the horizon. "And whose fault is that, I wonder?"

"Your own," said Talarath.

"The fault lies with your Conspiracy!" his daughter countered, and they fell to arguing again.

Seagryn no longer heard them. He thought of a place far to the northwest, a village in the Western District called Bourne—his home village. Was it among those that had suffered the dragon's burning? For reasons of his own, he'd not been there for many years. It appeared he would be seeing it again soon. It no longer mattered who won the debate behind him; from the first mention of the dragon, he'd known that his summer idyll had ended. A monster had been loosed upon the world, and yes, he had loosed it. To free the beast had seemed the right thing to do at the time. His affection for Berillitha had demanded it. "But I can't very well just let you burn Bourne, can I?" he asked the purple twilight.

"What?" the arguing pair asked him in unison, and Seagryn shrugged and turned to look at them.

"I'm going to bed. I have a long journey to begin in the morning, and the very thought of it exhausts me."

He didn't know how long the argument continued, but it was some time later when Elaryl came drifting into their bedroom.

She held a lit lamp designed to disturb his slumber as well as to illuminate her white-lace gown. "Are you asleep?" she asked.

He hadn't slept at all—how could he? The thought of pretending sleep crossed his mind, but he discarded the idea immediately. Elaryl was very persistent when she wanted to talk. "Not really."

She set the lamp on the table and came to sit down beside him. "You don't have to go, you know."

He looked up into her face—that achingly beautiful face he and all the other students had so admired from the choir loft—and sighed. "Yes, I do."

"You don't. It's not your business—it's not your fight."

"Elaryl," he murmured. "How can you say that?"

"You did your part—and more! They just want to use you!"

Seagryn studied the flickering lamplight on the ceiling. "I've got to go, love. The Western District is my home."

"This is your home!" She lay down beside him and slipped one arm beneath his head to hug him tightly to her. "Those people don't care anything about you! They wouldn't even recognize you after all these years!"

"It's my fault, Elaryl. I did turn the dragon loose."

"Sheth would have loosed it eventually anyway, and you know it!"

"I don't want to argue," he murmured, enjoying the closeness of her touch. He reached around to pull her up on top of him and kissed her cheek, but her eyes weren't on him. Her gaze was turned inward upon her own thoughts. He lay back on his pillow and waited for her to express them.

"I don't understand why they always do it—why *you* always do it," she corrected herself, including him in the indictment.

"We always do what?" he asked, wishing he didn't have to hear this right now but knowing he had no choice.

"This is supposed to be the land of faith. Everyone always talks about the One Who Holds All Power. Yet you clerics always act as if the outcome of the world depended entirely upon you. You act as if the Power is nothing other than a convenient myth, a magic word you can use to justify whatever you decide you want to do!"

"Umm," he nodded, partly because there was some truth in what she was saying, but partly, too, because if he made no comment now she would only get angrier and demand some further response from him.

"Why can't you just wait? This plan is my father's idea, and

Ranoth's—why can't you wait until the Power speaks to you and tells you to go battle the dragon?''

He thought for several moments before responding—not because he didn't know how he felt, but because he didn't know how best to phrase his answer. The fact was, he'd known all along this night was coming. He'd managed to conceal it from himself this long because he couldn't abide the thought of leaving this face, these eyes, this precious spirit, these pretty little thighs . . .

"I'm trying to talk to you seriously," she scolded.

"I know," he grumbled, gliding his hands back up onto her back. "You want to know why I can't wait for the Power to speak. I guess we have to face the fact that perhaps that's already occurred."

She leaned her head back to gaze at him. "Has it?"

"Events move at their own pace," he quoted her father to her, and Elaryl rolled her eyes. "That's true, Elaryl. And gifts of power—abilities like mine—bring responsibilities."

Elaryl groaned and rolled off him. "So you're going to be our savior now, is that it?"

Her sarcasm didn't offend him. "Dark knows," he murmured.

"Yes," she said to the ceiling, "he probably does. Did he tell you so?"

Seagryn visualized for a moment the charming young face of his friend Dark the prophet. He realized he missed the lad. "Dark never tells me anything if he can avoid it."

"I wish you'd avoided him," Elaryl grumbled.

Seagryn chuckled. "Jealous?"

"Well, he *has* spent far more time with you than I have since our wedding day."

"Never by my intention, my love, I can assure you. I've never found Dark; he's always found me, and it's impossible to escape him, since he always knows exactly where I'm going to be long before I know myself." Was it possible, Seagryn thought to himself, that even now the young prophet waited for him somewhere along the road to the Western District?

"But why you?" Elaryl demanded, truly angry now. "Do you think so much of yourself that you feel no one else could deal with this beast the way you could?"

"It isn't just that," he muttered, wishing they didn't have to fight on this last night together. He wondered how long he'd be gone. It struck him, then, that he'd really not considered the possibility that he might not return. Obviously, Elaryl had.

"Then what is it? This—this monster is destroying villages,

devouring people, ruining the countryside! What makes you think you can go find the thing and change its behavior with a wave of your hand?''

"I—don't know."

"I'd guessed as much," she snapped, sitting up in bed and folding her arms across her breasts.

Seagryn propped himself up on an elbow and reached out to trace the curve of her back. She jerked aside once, but when his hand returned she let him stroke her without comment. He already missed her terribly. Why was he going?

"There is the guilt, you know . . ." he murmured.

"About loosing the dragon on the world?" she asked. "Or about causing that female tugolith to be incorporated into the beast?"

Seagryn thought about it. "Both, I guess." Evidently he'd said the wrong thing, for Elaryl bounded off the bed and stalked angrily to the door. There she stopped and turned around to glower back at him in the lovely glow of the lamplight.

"While you're feeling guilty, why not add to the list some guilt about leaving *me*?" Elaryl slammed her way out.

Talarath had certainly used heavy doors in rebuilding this place, Seagryn thought to himself. He felt certain that sound had been heard in every part of the mansion. He didn't sleep well at all . . .

Elaryl's mood was much subdued in the morning as she watched him roll a few belongings and store them in a leather bag. Her attitude hadn't changed; she was just controlling it better. "Don't take Kerl," she half suggested, half ordered. "Take one of the stronger horses."

"There's not a stronger horse than Kerl in the stable, but I'll not be taking any horse. I can cover more ground faster in my tugolith shape than I can on horseback."

She looked as if she wanted to argue about that, too, but restrained herself. "You'll need to eat. I've asked the kitchen to prepare several meals to carry with you—" She stopped herself and gave him a sidelong glance. "But since you'll be in bestial form, I guess you'll be able to grab a bite along the way. An occasional fellow traveler along the road, perhaps?"

Ignoring her, Seagryn shouldered his bag and walked down the steps toward the great hall. Several packages sat on the head table, prepared for his journey at Elaryl's order. She had followed him, and watched silently as he stored them in his bag. "How will you carry it?" she muttered.

"On my horn," he said, giving her an artificial smile. "It has a large strap—see?"

Talarath overheard them from the stairs and walked into the great hall to join them. Seagryn could tell at a glance that his father-in-law knew what had transpired between his children and was trying hard to hide his elation at the outcome. Seagryn wondered if Talarath might not be just as pleased to hear the news that the dragon had consumed him as to learn he'd somehow restrained the dragon.

"The Land of Lamath is deeply grateful for your sacrificial spirit, Seagryn," Talarath began with great formality.

"I can't handle that," Elaryl said as she wheeled around and headed for the door. She stopped when she got there and turned to look back at Seagryn, her blond hair hiding half of her face. "I hate what you're doing," she announced loudly enough for everyone in the common room to hear. "But I love you." Then she was gone.

Talarath watched her go, then looked back at Seagryn and shrugged his shoulders as if to say, "Women—who can fathom their moods?"

Seagryn ignored the look and answered Talarath's statement with a mocking formality of his own. "I'm pleased to know that 'the Land of Lamath' thinks so highly of me. And I would be grateful for any support 'the Land of Lamath' might lend me—although of course, I expect none."

Talarath frowned—which looked far more natural on his craggy face than that deeply appreciative expression he'd been forcing onto his features. "Why do you say that?"

"You've openly declared me a hero, Talarath. You've restored my right to live among my own people, despite the fact that I'm a magic user. You've even accepted me into your own home. But I can't say you have welcomed me. I wonder sometimes what you talk about in your private councils of state. Do I make a convenient dumping ground for all the troubles that plague 'the Land of Lamath' today? Well, you can tell 'the Land of Lamath'—if you should ever chance to address it on the issue—that Vicia-Heinox was never my idea. I go to deal with the dragon for my own reasons and none of yours."

Talarath raised himself to his full height as Seagryn spoke—a long way, for he was tall—and glared down at his son-in-law as he so often had when he'd been a teacher and Seagryn a mere student. "You want everything on your own terms, don't you,

Seagryn? You always have.'' He clucked his tongue reprovingly and added, "You'll never change.''

Seagryn smiled. "On the contrary. I'm going to change right now.''

"What do you mean?'' Talarath asked. Seagryn just looked at him. When he suddenly comprehended what Seagryn meant, his eyes grew huge, and he sprinted for the doors of the great hall, shouting, "Not in here! Please! I *implore* you, not inside the house!''

Seagryn gleefully hoisted his sack upon his shoulder and left the mansion by the front door. A moment later an enormous, thick-skinned beast departed the estate toward the northwest, wearing a leather satchel on his single tusk.

The trip to Gammel would have taken until nightfall on horseback—and doubtless until midnight on Kerl. In his tugolith shape, Seagryn made the journey by midafternoon. As soon as he saw the charred skeleton of the village in the distance, he took his human form again. Then he hoisted his burden and walked on into what had once been a town, his green eyes moist with dismay. He'd not been there long when he saw a wrinkle-faced old woman shuffling toward him through the ashes, trying to conceal a long stick behind her back. She hardly looked friendly. Then again, glancing around at the destruction, he could easily see why.

There was not a single house left in the village—only a few individual walls that stood against the sky, looking resolute but lonely. Seagryn had lodged in Gammel on his way eastward to Lamath long years ago, and remembered it as a charmingly ordinary little village. Its people had not been particularly friendly toward him, but then, that was the western way. A westerner himself, Seagryn would have been wary of them had they been otherwise. That's why he thought little of the harridan's mistrustful gaze. He was certain now that she was trying to sneak up on him. He sighed, turned away, and surveyed the damage behind him. Vicia-Heinox had certainly been thorough.

A thatch-roofed, cross-beamed inn had occupied the place where he now stood. It had been a grand building by the standards of Gammel and too expensive for the penniless student he'd been at that time. He could certainly lodge within its charred timbers tonight. Glancing around at the terrible wreckage so aggravated his guilt that he felt deserving of censure and scorn—perhaps even of the blow to the head this strange little woman seemed ready to inflict upon him. Almost—but not quite.

* * *

Pilany noticed the young man standing on the far side of the scorched village around the middle of the afternoon. He was just standing there, looking about. He didn't move, and he didn't weep. He made her suspicious. Of course, most things made Pilany suspicious. She had to admit it, and she did so to anyone who would listen. But announcing her suspicions to others didn't make her any less suspicious of the scoundrels! She knew how to deal with them, too.

This man was dressed in clerical green and wore that disgusting expression she associated with anyone educated in the east. A mudgecurdle from the Ruling Council, no doubt. He'd come to investigate the destruction of Gammel and report back to those thieves in the capital. Well, Pilany was having none of that. She had a good, heavy cudgel that had survived the fires undamaged. She'd already put it to good use braining a couple of looters from the neighboring towns. Nothing would give her greater pleasure than to plant a big knot on some cleric's noggin, and this fellow's would do as well as any. Pilany realized, though, that she was going to have a hard time sneaking up on him with all the houses burned almost to the ground. She hid her club behind her back. Starting to whistle, she angled across the wreckage toward him. Soon as she got close enough, out would come the stick and she'd smack him—just like that. He'd never know what hit him!

Pilany couldn't believe her good fortune when the fool turned away, just as she was getting into range. She took a good hold of her cudgel and charged forward swinging!

"Drat," Pilany muttered under her breath, for the fellow had proved nimble for a cleric and had skipped aside, kicking up a cloud of black ash that rose almost to her waist. The weight of the club carried her all the way around, and Pilany had to stop a moment and get her bearings before she could take another swipe. But she didn't give up easily. She went for him again, this time raising the stick over her head to bring it crashing right down on his skull—

"Margnarel!" Pilany swore as her stick embedded itself harmlessly in the spot he'd just vacated. More ashes spewed into the air, filling her nose and lungs, and she had to back away and cough for a moment. She cleared her throat, then squinted her eyes and peered through the fine black dust to try to spot him again.

"Haagh!" Pilany shouted, and, despite her age, leaped backward a good two yards, the cudgel frozen in her hands. For now she faced no government cleric, but an immense monster—and the glistening point of its single huge horn was pointing right at her heart!

They stood frozen like that for several moments before Pilany slammed her stick to the ground and shouted, "Well go ahead and stick me then! But I warn you—I'll make a bony dish going down your gullet and I swear I'll do my best to give you indigestion!"

"I have no intention of sticking you, and much less of eating you." The great nostrils flared wide in a sniff she could actually feel. "Pardon my saying it, but you smell anything but appetizing."

Pilany frowned and sniffed herself. "Really? Perhaps that's what discouraged the dragon. I'd thought I talked him out of it."

"You *talked* to the dragon?"

"I certainly did. Hard doings, too, what with him having those two heads and all, because you can be talking to this head over here, and then that long neck snakes around and the other head is right behind you, and then you don't know which head to talk to, and I got the impression that they don't always get along."

"Who?"

"The two heads."

The tugolith nodded, and Pilany eyed his horn with great concern. "In fact, that's why I'm not at all nervous talking to you," she said nervously, "because you only have the one head. But that is one powerfully threatening horn, I'd have to say, and the dragon didn't have that; so, if you don't mind, I'll just—edge—back here a way." The woman put another two yards between herself and Seagryn's horn, then began glancing around for the quickest route of escape.

"And the dragon didn't eat you?"

She shot the beast a disdainful frown. Evidently this thing was as stupid as it looked. "Would I be standing here talking to you if it had?"

"Of course not." The monster chuckled self-consciously, which surprised her. It seemed a rather subtle expression for a dumb beast. Maybe it wasn't so stupid after all. "Excuse my asking, but what are you?"

"I'm a tugolith," the beast grunted, its thoughts apparently elsewhere. "Did the dragon eat anyone?"

"Only those who tried to talk to him. Excepting myself, of course."

"Was that—many?"

Pilany growled in irritation. "Why? Are you writing a report?'' she asked sarcastically. "I'd like to see you hold a stylus in that foot—'' As she gestured down at the tugolith's enormous feet, something occurred to her. "Say, what happened to that cleric fellow? Are you standing on him?''

"I am him.''

"No you're not,'' she grumbled.

"Who tried to talk to the dragon?'' the beast asked. "And where is everyone else? Can you tell me what happened here? It's really very important that I know.''

Pilany studied him reflectively, one bony hand rubbing her jaw. "If you are really this cleric fellow, why don't you turn back into him.''

"If you'll promise not to brain me with your stick, I will.''

Pilany waved off his comment. "You're safe with me,'' she told the enormous tugolith. "I promise not to hurt you.''

Seagryn did feel more comfortable back in his human form again. But as he changed, he wondered why he hadn't simply cloaked himself in a curtain of invisibility instead of taking his altershape. He guessed he'd been living in Lamath too long. Powershaping was considered such outrageous behavior in the land of faith that he hadn't used his abilities in months. He realized he'd better get his magical imagination back into practice quickly if he expected to deal with a hungry dragon . . .

"Why were you trying to hit me?'' he asked as he walked back toward the woman.

"I thought you were from the Ruling Elders.'' Pilany sniffed, scratching herself. "I just don't care for those scoundrels much.''

Seagryn raised his eyebrows and nodded slightly. "There's one thing we can agree on. I don't either.''

"If they didn't send you, then why the green gown?'' Pilany asked, cocking her head to look at him suspiciously. "Why all the questions?''

"I'd like to prevent any more villages from being charred to cinders—''

"And just how are you going to do that?'' she snapped, her fierce old eyes glaring into his. "He's a *dragon*, for goodness sake! He's going to burn things, he's going to eat people, and nothing's going to stop him, because he's too big and too powerful and too fast!'' Seagryn blinked. Pilany certainly spoke frankly. "Now, if you want my thoughts on the matter, it's that mudge-curdle Seagryn you ought to be looking for.''

"Why?'' Seagryn asked, his mouth going suddenly dry.

"Why?'' she croaked, echoing his question back at him scornfully. "For *vengeance*, that's why! He's the traitor who let the beast out of its cave, isn't he?"

"Yes," Seagryn murmured, his eyes shifting down to his feet.

"There's nothing to be done about this dragon, you can mark down my words on that. We'll have to learn to live with his visits. Be like watching out for blizzards or tornadoes—you know they're going to come, sometime, but you hope, if you watch them closely, that maybe you'll survive. Still, it'd do a whole lot of people a whole lot of good to make the one responsible for the twi-beast suffer! This Seagryn fellow ought to be chopped in two and fed to the thing, one half to this head and the other half to that! Although somehow I think—"

Suddenly she was racing away through the ashes, moving with remarkable swiftness for a woman of her apparent age. Seagryn looked up after her in surprise. Had something startled her? Had it dawned on her somehow that he was the person she vilified? And was she now running away from him for fear of his alter-shape? He strained to make out her muffled parting shout. "Just remember not to talk to it!"

He watched her scuttle on, stirring up a plume of ashes behind her, and tried to make sense of her words. Not to talk to—? Then he felt the shadow cross him and understood.

Vicia-Heinox, the two-headed dragon, was in the air above him.

Chapter Two

✕✕✕✕

LIGHT SNACK

Hᴀᴅ he been spotted?

Seagryn instantly cloaked himself. It was the first trick he'd learned from watching Sheth, and it would protect him long enough to dodge the dragon's attack. He raced away from the spot where he'd stood, expecting the shadow to swoop down upon him at any moment. Once he felt certain he'd reached a safe distance from the place, he filled his lungs with a deep draught of courage—and not a few ashes—and turned his gaze to the sky.

Vicia-Heinox wasn't looking at him with either head. They were instead looking at each other, wings flapping the air erratically in a halfhearted effort to stay airborne while they argued. The beast seemed to be in a quandary about where to go next. Seagryn could barely make out the words of the debate.

"I want to go back to the cave where I spent last night."

"I do not! I am hungry, and there is nothing to eat in that cave."

"I cannot understand how I could still be hungry! I've gobbled persons until my stomach wants to pop. When I think of all the weight I've put on in the last week alone—"

"And it's been marvelous! I can't remember a more entertaining group of suppers!"

"I can't remember much of anything at all . . ."

"But then again, what's to remember?"

"Where I came from, what I'm doing here. . . ?"

17

"I came from the place where dragons are made!" Vicia shouted at his other head impatiently.

Seagryn knew the dragon as well as any man could. Only the gallant sacrifice of Berillitha had kept him from becoming a part of it himself. And by their conversation, he could easily tell that this more arrogant speaker had once been the foul-spirited Vilanlitha.

"I live, I fly, I eat—why do I need to ask why?" Vicia's kettle-sized nostrils hissed as he sucked in a deep breath. "I smell that lovely odor of a charred human habitation and I think to myself, 'What could be lovelier than a barbecue?' "

"All I can smell is myself," Heinox responded.

"Exactly!" Vicia enthused. "My fragrance fills all that I survey!"

"I stink, therefore I am."

Seagryn listened with growing confidence. He had once ridden through the sky atop this Heinox head and had managed to control the beast by getting its two personalities to argue. If he could just talk to the thing, perhaps he could convince Heinox, at least, to reconsider its behavior. Feeling bold, Seagryn dismissed the spell that had cloaked him and revealed himself to the dragon.

Vicia-Heinox apparently didn't notice. "Why am I so indecisive?" Vicia snarled. "I never used to have this much trouble making decisions!"

"I don't remember that . . ." Heinox said.

"And I get so tired of talking to myself all the time!"

"I don't talk to myself all the time," Heinox corrected. "Often I talk to my dinner."

"Now there's a thought! I'm going to go find a meal to talk to!" Vicia announced, and one wing flapped. But Heinox wouldn't cooperate.

"I don't think I could eat another thing . . ."

"Hello!" Seagryn called up at the twi-beast, but obviously not loudly enough, since the dragon continued to debate. "Down here!" he called. Still the heads argued. "Listen to me!" Seagryn shouted, but it was no use. No one could make himself heard over two such powerful voices. To roar loudly enough for them to notice him, he'd need the lungs of a tugolith—

But of course. Once again Seagryn took his tugolith shape and bellowed at the sky.

"What is that?" the dragon said to itself as both heads turned to scan the ground below.

"I—don't know what that is," Heinox said thoughtfully. "But I must confess it looks very familiar to me."

"It certainly does. I have the feeling that I've seen such a being before—somewhere." Vicia looked at Heinox, a wicked glint in his eye. "I wonder if it talks!"

"If I'm thinking what I think I'm thinking," Heinox groaned, "I'm going to have one enormous bellyache . . . ." Then the green dragon spiraled down from the sky to talk with the waiting tugolith.

As Vicia-Heinox settled its mansion-sized bulk into the ashes of this once-prosperous village, Seagryn started having second thoughts. "A bit late for that—" he told himself, and cleared his throat.

"Did you bellow?" the Heinox head asked.

Before he could answer, Vicia added, "Can you talk?"

"Of course I can talk," Seagryn said.

"Wonderful!" the elated Vicia said. "How do you taste?"

"How do I what?" Seagryn frowned. He found Vicia's question disconcerting. Who wouldn't?

"You must understand," Heinox explained quickly, "that I only eat those who talk to me."

"Why?" Seagryn demanded, and Heinox looked with uncertainty at his other head.

"I—don't exactly know . . ."

Vicia did. "Good talk, good food—they just go together!" he said cheerfully. "But I've never eaten anything like you, so I wonder how you'd taste. What are you?"

Did the dragon really not know? Seagryn had been impressed to this point with the beast's vocabulary. After all, Vilanlitha and Berillitha had talked like children. Had the incredible spell that had merged them into one somehow doubled the beast's intelligence as well? Seagryn had to believe so, and that was worrisome. He'd found tugoliths very susceptible to suggestion. An intelligent dragon would be less so . . .

"I asked you what you are," the dragon repeated in a threatening tone—but this time it was Heinox who spoke. Seagryn had been regarding these heads as separate beasts. He reminded himself that they were now one and probably becoming more so every day.

"I'm a tugolith—at the moment."

"A tugolith," Vicia mused. "Never heard of such a thing . . ."

". . . that I recall," Heinox finished.

"Are you certain?" Seagryn asked. Being shaped into a dragon had apparently wiped the beast's mind—minds?—of certain memories. Which memories? What did Vicia-Heinox remember? Could Seagryn use these memory gaps somehow to change the beast's behavior? "What *do* you recall?"

The dragon frowned and looked itself in the eyes. "Tugoliths are nosy creatures, aren't they?" Heinox observed.

"Perhaps they're tasty as well . . ."

Which returned Seagryn to that most important question of all—that is, how was he to keep the beast from eating him? He decided to try and change the subject. "Do you remember Sheth?"

He'd evidently succeeded. Both heads jerked around to stare at him.

"Sheth," one head murmured quietly as the other snaked forward to peer at him eyeball-to-eyeball.

"What do *you* know of Sheth?" Heinox demanded menacingly.

"I know that he made you," Seagryn said, and both heads suddenly recoiled back as if he'd thumped them each on the nose.

"Made me?" Vicia howled.

"Sheth didn't make me, he tormented me!" Heinox screamed.

"I've looked long and far for this Sheth," Vicia roared. "I've destroyed cave after cave. I will find him eventually, and when I do—"

"—I will rip him limb from limb and devour him!"

"Slowly, of course." Vicia smiled wickedly. "Savoring the taste of his flesh."

Heinox had glided around behind and now pulled right up beside Seagryn, one eye barely a handsbreadth away from his own. "What do you know about Sheth? Do you know where I might find him?"

Seagryn shivered involuntarily. He had no love for Sheth, of course—and the dragon did speak the truth. Sheth had tortured Vicia-Heinox into becoming the monster that now ravaged the world. Perhaps Sheth deserved to be rent to pieces and chewed slowly. But standing this close to the razor-sharp teeth that would do the rending, Seagryn didn't wish that on anyone. "I—don't know where he is."

There was a long moment of pause. Then Heinox said quietly, "I think you're lying."

"No, it's true!" Seagryn blurted out defensively. "I've not seen him since you have!"

The dragon frowned again, and now both heads rose above

Seagryn to look itself once more in the eye. They then sank down to either side of him, like a pair of enormous pincers ready to clip off his head. "How do you know when I saw him last?"

He saw no purpose in hiding his identity any longer. "Because I was there, on top of you!" In an eyeblink, Seagryn took his human form again. "I'm Seagryn!" he proclaimed.

The heads jerked apart in surprise. Both heads just stared at him for a moment, then each began to move closer, examining this tiny human standing between them.

"So?" Vicia murmured. This was not a response Seagryn had hoped for. As he mentally catalogued his magical options, Vicia added with a wicked grin, "I know how people taste . . ."

"Seagryn," Heinox breathed quietly. "I know you. You sat on top of me. How could I forget!" The Heinox head popped into the air to smile into Vicia's puzzled gaze. "This is Seagryn! This is the wizard who freed me!"

Now Vicia shot up into the sky, and Seagryn realized that while Vicia-Heinox had looked enormous from the vantage point of a tugolith, to a human he was unimaginably huge. "Seagryn!" Vicia thundered. "He's the wizard who made me!"

Seagryn's relieved smile at having been recognized suddenly froze on his face. He'd made the dragon? The dragon thought he, Seagryn, had made it?

"I've been looking all over for you, too!" Heinox rumbled, moving back down to stare at him with a very accusing frown. "Why did you leave me?"

Oh dear, thought Seagryn. When he glanced back over at Vicia, he felt worse. That head had settled his chin into the ashes to peer petulantly at him, a pout on his leathery lips. Oh dear, he thought again. "You, ah—you think I made you? Have you told anyone that—ah—that you think I . . ."

"I've told lots of people!" Heinox said, and Seagryn's heart sank. No wonder his reputation among the population of Lamath had suffered so . . .

"Of course, I then ate them all." Vicia cackled.

"You left me!" Heinox whined, genuinely hurt. "I was confused, and I didn't know how to fly, and I fell into the snow, and then you left me! One minute you were on my head, and the next you were gone!"

Vicia frowned, obviously puzzled. "You weren't on my head," he mused.

"Yes, you were!" Heinox corrected vehemently. "And then

you were gone! Vanished!'' Heinox' immense eyes squinted at Seagryn threateningly. "You'd better not ever do that again.''

"Ah—yes. Well.'' Seagryn suddenly felt very small and very lonely. As he glanced around in confusion, he spotted his satchel, and it reminded him of Elaryl. He started to walk toward it.

"Where do you think you're going?'' Vicia snarled, rising up off the ashes.

Seagryn froze. "I—need to get my things. They're—in my bag.'' He pointed tentatively. "Right there.''

"Very well.'' the dragon begrudged him, and Seagryn walked the few steps to pick it up. But as he did he was very much aware of the fact that the two heads were gliding around behind him until their noses almost touched. Vicia-Heinox had encircled him within a scaly wall.

"All this conversation has made me hungry,'' Vicia told Heinox, who responded, "It sure has.'' Both heads swiveled around to look at him, and jaw-to-jaw they asked this same question in unison. "Where are you taking us to eat?''

Seagryn clutched the knobby ridges at the juncture of Heinox' head and neck and implored the Power for inspiration. His improvised plan to influence the dragon somehow had succeeded far beyond his wildest expectations. He evidently had enormous influence over Vicia-Heinox. Now what was he to do with it?

They soared over the Lamathian landscape. The wind wrestled with him, shifting its grip all around his body in search of the hold that would prevent his being tossed from his perch. It stung his eyes and stole his breath, and all this at the very moment when he most needed his wits about him. What to suggest? The dragon was waiting!

Vicia flew above and a little behind him. "Just point,'' that head roared, "and I'll go there.'' When Seagryn glanced around, all he could see were those giant, flared nostrils. He tried not to look behind him much. "Just point!'' the dragon rumbled again.

Point where? In the first place, he didn't want to let go with either hand, even for a moment. He'd sneaked one or two glances below him and had immediately been sorry. This was far, far different from his first ride on the dragon. Then he'd felt exultant, for he'd just freed this beast from the power of a horrible wizard. It had been new then, an unanticipated thrill—and he hadn't known, at that point, just how painful landing could be.

Now he knew. He'd been up here before, and it was a long way down. Besides, this time he had a lot more to lose. He thought again of Elaryl. How could he have been so stupid as to leave her this morning? Up here splashing through the moist clouds, he remembered when he'd promised himself he would never leave her again. Why is it, he wondered ruefully, that when you become comfortable, you forget all the really important promises you've made?

"Where am I going?" the dragon screamed, and Seagryn struggled to think of some suggestion. He could hear Talarath's instructions in his mind. "Get the dragon out of Lamath! Let it eat Marwandians—or Haranians—or Pleclypsans! Let it gobble the Armies of Arl! Just get it out of Lamath!" And Seagryn wanted to take it out of Lamath. But how could he sacrifice those other nations just to save his own? What made the people who lived on this particular plot of earth more special or worthy of protection than any other?

It was a beautiful piece of ground, that was certain. As he grew more confident of his perch, Seagryn glanced down with less terror and more appreciation. He was curious to see what, if anything, a person could recognize from this height. That first time he'd flown, it had been over the untracked forests of the Marwilds, far to the southwest. Now they soared above orderly lands—neatly cut squares and rectangles of every shade of green. In just a few weeks, these fields would be yellowing or returning to brown under the harvesting scythes. In this early, summer evening, though, they were green—emerald, mostly, like the color of the priestly tunic he wore—

Vicia suddenly whipped around in front of him to stare him in the eyes. "Where?" the dragon demanded.

"Ah, ah, ah—" This was very troubling. It was as if the thing flew backward! Once again Seagryn racked his mind for a solution that might prevent any more human deaths. Then he spotted a patch of brown dots upon a field down to his left and asked Vicia, "Have you ever eaten mooser?"

"Mooser," Vicia mused.

"They're delicious—even I can vouch for that! They don't have that delicate sweetness you get with stippled-stag, but since they move in herds you could eat several at once. And they'd make a substantial mouthful—not like a puny little person."

"Mmm." Vicia nodded eagerly, his eyes glowing. Saliva sprayed back from his knifelike teeth as he asked, "And these moosers make good conversation?"

Oh. Yes. There was that. "They . . . say . . . 'moo' a lot . . ."

Vicia frowned. " 'Moo'? What does that mean?"

"I . . . gather it means quite a lot to another mooser," Seagryn tried lamely, but Vicia was having none of it.

"I like to talk to my food," the dragon explained, his unblinking gaze never leaving Seagryn's face.

"That *is* going to be a problem," Seagryn mumbled to himself. He could tell by the way the sun was setting they were flying to the northeast, and on beyond those distant, jagged mountains they would come eventually to the land of the tugoliths. The thought raced through his mind, but he just as quickly discarded it. Tugoliths could indeed talk—but the idea of loosing this slavering nightmare upon those tender creatures was beyond comprehension—worse by far than letting Vicia-Heinox consume Lamath. Seagryn gazed below him again at those beautiful farmlands of his own Western District. Then he wondered—what were the chances of turning a dragon into a vegetarian?

"WHERE?" Vicia screamed in his face again, more loudly than ever, and by now he hovered close enough that Seagryn got sprayed by the spittle. Squinting his eyes against it, wincing in pain at the ringing in his ears, Seagryn did at last let go with one hand to wave the dragon away. Vicia evidently took it as a direction, for he immediately turned forward again, and Seagryn heard him shout, "There!" Moments later they were dropping from the sky, and for the first time Seagryn could see the ground directly in front of them—and the village. He could tell at a glance where they were.

He hadn't been home in a long time, but things never changed quickly in the Western District. The city tower looked exactly as it had on his very first day of school. Not a single merchant along the main street had painted a shop since the day Seagryn left for the capital. Bourne. He'd directed the dragon to burn Bourne.

"No! Not here! Not here!" he shouted—he wailed it, really— but the wind tore his words away and they never reached the dragon's ears. He guessed that probably wouldn't matter anyway. Vicia-Heinox was hungry, and right below them a crowd of dumbstruck farmers stared upward at them in shock—easy pickings for a monster with an appetite. Out of the corner of his eye he could see Vicia licking his chops . . .

Beside the tower was the village green, a tree-lined park that belonged to every Bournean citizen. Children raced across it during the daytime, and in the night it was the meeting place of youthful lovers. But activity on the greensward reached its peak in the late afternoon, as farmers who'd finished their daily tasks met to lounge along its grassy banks and lie to one another. The sun had burned hot in Bourne today, driving the lads from the fields a little earlier than usual, and the crowd that gathered under the shade trees seemed larger than any Seagryn could remember. It diminished quickly, however, as the dragon swooped low over the village. Certain of the merchants who had drifted out to join their customers for a cool drink suddenly found reason to dive back inside their shops. Mothers grabbed children and raced away, horses spooked and galloped down the avenues with their riderless wagons still attached. But the farmers, the heart of Bourne, the stalwart, faithful believers that made up the backbone of Lamathian society, just stood staring up at the dragon with open mouths, reminding Seagryn of the moosers they had left behind in the fields. And that gave him an idea.

The dragon glided around and came in toward the tower across the field. It flew low and more slowly. Suddenly the ride became very bumpy and Seagryn realized the beast was no longer flying, but running. Then it stopped and raised its two heads high above the slack-jawed watchers until Seagryn realized he sat at the level of the city tower's spire. He looked down—and saw that every eye now stared at *him*.

What a curious feeling. Seagryn had dreamed years ago of arriving home in spectacular triumph, but he'd thought more along the lines of a parade when he finally became a Ruling Elder. This was certainly more dramatic—and tragic, too, if he didn't do something about it soon! He looked down at these faces, adult versions of the boyish faces he'd once known, and shouted, "Don't talk to it! It won't eat you if you won't talk!"

Much of the crowd had had the good sense to disappear while they had the opportunity, but a group of men stayed clustered together beneath him for reasons Seagryn knew too well. Put simply, they didn't believe this was happening. Dragons had never just dropped down out of the sky onto the Green of Bourne, and they had no reason to expect that such a thing could happen today. They were practiced skeptics, these men. They required demonstration before they would believe a new thing to be true, and they hadn't seen anything demonstrated yet. Besides—wasn't that Seagryn up there on top of one of those heads?

"Seagryn?" a broad-faced peasant called up to him. "Is that you?"

"That's him," Vicia said warmly. Then he ate the peasant.

Now *this* was a demonstration a man could believe in. The farmers all screamed and scattered.

Seagryn covered his face and shook his head. Then he shouted again, "Didn't I tell you not to *talk* to it?"

Heinox rolled his eyes up to look at him. "Why are you telling them that?"

"Because I don't want you to eat them," Seagryn said flatly as he watched Vicia gobble up a bald-headed fellow who stood there pleading for him not to.

"Why not?" Heinox asked.

"They're my friends," Seagryn said as Vicia plucked a poor unfortunate out of the tree he was trying to climb and tossed him high into the air. The man never hit the ground. "Were my friends," Seagryn corrected himself.

"What's a friend?" Heinox asked, and somehow the question prodded Seagryn into action. The dragon's ears were as big as he was—huge, leaflike things—and now he grabbed one of Heinox' ears and began to shout into it.

"This is a waste of your time! I know these people, and there aren't enough interesting conversationalists here to make more than a between-meal snack!" This was, to be sure, true. The farmers normally didn't say much to one another. Even their best stories they told slowly and with an economy of word choices that had once threatened to drive Seagryn mad. Now he felt grateful for it. It could prove their salvation. But he had to get this monster back into the sky and away! "Let me take you instead to a city— a *vast* city, with thousands upon thousands of people, many of whom talk for a living! Come on, Vicia-Heinox! Get up! Get up from here!"

Vicia still slithered up and around and underneath his body, pursuing fleeing peasants. But apparently the people of Bourne had finally gotten the idea. No one was saying anything, and Vicia was understandably furious. When he tried to slalom down a row of trees after a particularly nimble farm boy, he found himself in a predicament that only added fuel to his fury. The only way to untangle his neck from the line of trunks was to back out, and Vicia didn't back out of anything. It was trapped, and somewhere in the vestiges of its shared memory Vicia-Heinox remembered being trapped somewhere in a cave and a wicked little power-shaper hurting it . . . In panic, Heinox launched the massive body skyward, and Vicia was forced to come free—not, however, before smacking alternating ears against the entangling tree trunks. He flapped out the way he'd gone in.

The dragon was furious. And it had the means to give vent to its rage: With that ability that Seagryn attributed to Sheth's original dragonmaking spell, the two heads locked their vision onto the city tower, and it immediately burst into flames. Vicia-Heinox scorched the green, then the offending trees, and finally set fire to the whole block of thatch-roofed, double-storied shops before winging its way up into the clouds. All this time it was shouting at Seagryn, calling him the most awful names it could remember. Fortunately, Vicia-Heinox' memory was short—and in response to Seagryn's shouted directions, it turned to fly south at high speed.

Once the dragon was gone, the people of Bourne burst into activity. The whole town was aflame. Racing to find buckets, they formed a line down to the stream and began passing water from man to man up to the main avenue. Twilight came, and soon they found their best illumination for the task in the very fire they fought to douse. Some pitched water up at it, others pulled the contents of the shops out into the streets before the flames could crawl down to get them, but every able-bodied citizen of the village did his or her best to lessen the fire's impact.

All except one man. Yammerlid stood at the south end of the greensward, staring up into the sky. He had followed the flight of the horrible beast until it became less than a dot in the purpling night, but still didn't move from his spot. "Seagryn," he grunted. To him, the word was a curse.

Yammerlid had known Seagryn all his life. Boyhood slights left unresolved had festered into an adolescent rivalry. Yammerlid had played a part in the events that had driven Seagryn from Bourne, and in the aftermath his childish feelings had ripened into a grown man's hatred. Yammerlid was convinced that Seagryn had ruined his life. He'd waited impatiently through the years for Seagryn's return, carefully planning his vengeance.

But now Seagryn had come and gone again, leaving even more ruin in his wake! On a dragon he'd come, just to heap more humiliation upon Yammerlid! The man howled at the sky in frustration.

Far behind him, across a field now gone black under a moonless night, his own boyhood home was burning. Yammerlid didn't watch it. Let it burn. He'd be leaving this place first thing in the morning, for he now understood his destiny. He'd heard tales of cadres forming all across the land with the sole purpose of carving the heart out of the dragonmaker. He'd heard rumors that the traitor was Seagryn, but he'd never really believed them. Now that he knew for certain, he couldn't wait to join one!

"Seagryn," he whispered up at the darkness, "Yammerlid's going to kill you—and when I do, you and the whole world will know it was me."

Chapter Three

✖✖✖✖

GROOM'S NIGHTMARE

Nebalath had visited the Paumer House palace in Pleclypsa many times in his life. He was old, after all, and he'd had a long— if not always warm—relationship with Paumer the Shrewd. So when he received a secret plea from the merchant's daughter, Uda, to visit her in Pleclypsa, he knew exactly the spire upon which he would appear.

Nebalath could appear anywhere he chose. As the foremost wizard in the old One Land, he had the ability to cast himself to distant places, arriving instantaneously—and often quite dramatically as well. He alone of all wizards had perfected this ability! Well, Sheth could do it, too, of course, but Nebalath had given Sheth the idea. It was necessary, however, that he know exactly where he was going. Nebalath had never cast himself into a well or a wall before, but he imagined such an experience would be horrible. Let others experiment with the possibilities of casting themselves blindly: He'd not become an old wizard by being an idiot. He would play it safe.

The secretive messenger had told him Uda's plea was urgent but knew nothing else about it. Why would the girl call him? They had met, certainly. He had, in fact, nominated her to take his seat on the ridiculously named Grand Council for Reunification. Grand Council indeed! It was a conspiracy of the powerful, nothing more, and Nebalath's suggestion that a mere slip of a girl replace him upon it had been an insult calculated to show Paumer his disgust for the entire idea. He'd known nothing about her, save that she was just a child. He knew little more about her now.

But he *did* know that young Miss Uda had snared as her swain a friend Nebalath held very dear. Dark the prophet was no more a man than Uda was a woman, but no other prophet of this age could equal his gift for foresight. Whatever Dark said would happen, happened. Nebalath had personally witnessed that truth a hundred times over. Though widely separated by age, the unique gifts of the two men had bound them together as fast friends. And Dark had confided to Nebalath months ago that he was destined to marry Uda—whether he liked the idea or not. Nebalath jumped to conclusions in the same way that he cast himself—only when he was reasonably certain that he knew exactly where he would land. This morning he felt it safe to assume that Uda's plea for help involved young Dark in some way.

Nebalath stood on the top of the Imperial House of Haranamous and announced that he was traveling to Pleclypsa. He recognized that anyone watching would think he was crazy, but anyone watching probably wouldn't be able to hear the castle's reply, either.

—This House has never been there.

"That's rather obvious, isn't it? You've never been anywhere but right here."

—Feeling a bit testy this morning, are we?

"I don't like being awakened in the middle of the night."

—You don't like being awakened at all, the Imperial House corrected.

"When you get older, you find it's much more difficult to get back to sleep when you've been routed out of bed before the sun comes up!"

—This House is much older than you are.

"Yes, yes," Nebalath grumbled, "but that just proves my point. Old Nobalog woke you up centuries ago and you've not been able to get back to sleep since!" Nobalog had been a wizard who'd lived in this castle long before the One Land splintered into Fragments. He'd been a very capable powershaper—Nebalath had never heard of any other who'd actually brought a structure to life.

—This House considers sleep an utter waste of time.

"You think I don't know that?" Nebalath groused. "Since you're the one who's constantly waking me up at all hours?"

—The courier from Pleclypsa told the gateman his message was urgent. This House assumed you would want to know that.

"Yes, well. We shall see how urgent it really is," the old wizard said as he wrapped his cloak about him and began to visualize that particular spire of Paumer's palace where he planned to appear.

—Are you certain where you are going? the House inquired. Because it is the understanding of this House that the mistress of that palace is particularly given to—

Nebalath disappeared from the rooftop of the Imperial House with an audible snap.

—remodeling . . .

"Help!" Nebalath yelled as he clung desperately to a trellis thirty feet below the point in the air where he had materialized. "Help!" he repeated as he saw servants clad in Paumer's distinctive red and blue livery scurrying about below him but not doing anything. In fact, it appeared to him all they were interested in was getting out from under him! "Get me some help!" the wizard demanded, which only added to the speed with which they scurried—not to their efficiency. A moment later, a recognizable face showed itself below him—they had gone to fetch Kerily, Paumer's socially active wife—the mistress of the manor. All things considered, Nebalath would have preferred a ladder.

Kerily frowned at first, but this brightened to a smile when she recognized him. "Why, Nebalath! I must say, this is quite a surprise."

"I'm rather surprised myself," the magician called down through gritted teeth. The trellis was quivering, and he had no alternative but to quiver along with it. "I thought there was a tower here!"

"Oh!" Kerily laughed, and her laughter was a trilling, delightful thing—or would have been to anyone not in danger of plunging to his death. "That's why you're up there! Well, of course, you're exactly right, there was a tower there! But we had to have it removed, you see, for the wedding. We needed a canopy right here—we'll cover it in pink and pale blue, incidentally, which I expect will set the gowns off nicely. And of course, the trellis will arch over the canopy, decorated with flowers to match, imported from the spice islands. That is, if the trellis is still standing," she added, just a hint of criticism in her voice. The structure had just given a loud snap, and Nebalath felt himself drop at least a foot before it caught again. "You don't think you could get off of it, do you?" Kerily asked, adding brightly, "I don't believe it was constructed to support the weight of a wizard . . ."

Nebalath was prepared to make a very rude remark when it

suddenly struck him that if he could cast himself up here from a hundred miles to the north, he certainly could cast himself the mere sixty feet down to the courtyard beside her. Quietly berating himself for being an old fool, Nebalath disappeared with the same distinctive snap with which he'd departed the Imperial House— and reappeared beside Paumer's wife in the marble courtyard below. She whirled in surprise to face him, then smiled. It had been some time since he'd last seen her, and there was something different about her— Oh. The hair.

This week Kerily's hair was copper colored and curly. No one could quite remember what it had been last week, least of all Kerily herself. What did it matter, anyway—that was last week. And next week? Why, that mattered even less, at the moment. It would match the color of the dress she wore to the gallery gala, of course—but she hadn't yet decided what color that would be. Kerily said she couldn't remember what color her hair had originally been. "I was bald, of course," she liked to joke. "Aren't most babies bald?" She *did* wish sometimes she could change the color of her eyes, too. Then again, she thought it might be a trifle disconcerting to peer into a mirror and see something other than blue gazing back at her. Kerily's blue eyes were legendary— Pleclypsan poets had written odes to them, and painters had struggled to match their hue on canvas. And to be honest, they were really the only eyes Kerily trusted. When she gazed at herself in the mirror, she believed she saw her only true friend. Nebalath had been around her enough to realize this. He wasn't surprised by the suspicion in her voice when she trilled, "The wizard Nebalath! So happy you could drop in."

"I'm rather happy I thought of it myself," he grumbled, "since there appears to be a shortage of ladders about."

"Oh, but there are ladders simply everywhere around this house—ladders, scaffolding— Why there's even a scaffold in the kitchen, especially constructed for the chef to decorate the cakes— we expect to need fifteen of them, monstrous things, but plans seem be changing daily, so it's a bit difficult to say. The guest list is unbelievable! I never knew I had so many friends until I started to write them all down, and, of course, we had to invite all my husband's business associates, which, as I'm sure you know, includes just about the whole world. But I have a plan," she added brightly, tapping the side of her head, "and the way I have it worked out, the cream of artistic Pleclypsan society will not have to spend a single moment listening to that boring business talk. May I ask you something?"

"Hmm?" Nebalath said, suddenly realizing he had faded out somewhere in the midst of the wedding cakes. "Yes?"

"Why are you here?"

"Oh! Yes. Well, I was sent for."

She frowned prettily. "Did—*I* send for you?"

"I believe it was your daughter who did that."

"Oh," she said meaningfully, raising her eyebrows and dropping her voice in disapproval. "May I guess? Does it have something to do with that boy of hers?"

"I don't know."

She leaned forward and half whispered, "Did you know he sleeps all the time?"

"No," Nebalath said.

She straightened back up and nodded her head. "He sleeps all the time."

"May I see him?" the wizard asked.

"Certainly!" she said, smiling brightly once again. "I believe he's in the azure room. No, no, not there!" she shouted suddenly, thoroughly confusing him until she rushed by him and he saw she was talking to a group of servants who were lugging in a large ceramic pot. "Over there!" she pointed, and he watched as they changed course, wrestling it toward the new location. He recognized their expression—they were expecting her to change her mind again as soon as they got it into place.

He waited for her to finish; but as soon as she did, she bolted across the courtyard and into a corridor through a pair of ornate double doors. He was evidently on his own. He caught the eye of one of the servants and asked, "The azure room?"

"Which one? She's got four . . ."

Nebalath nodded. "Perhaps you could just show me each?"

The house of Paumer in Pleclypsa was not really the house of Paumer at all: This was Kerily's place, reflecting in every way her personality. The Grand Council had met here three times, and on each occasion the walls had been a different color, the floors covered with a different tile, and whole rooms altered to fit some new aesthetic function. Paumer had once joked that, if the arts in Pleclypsa continued to expand, he would be pushed right out of his house. Since their last meeting here that had indeed happened; all business functions of the House of Paumer in this region had been shifted to another building on the south end of the city, closer to the Telimas Corridor. And Paumer himself had moved out— he made no secret of the fact that he preferred to dwell at what

he called his hovel—a mountain mansion far removed from Pleclypsa and his wife's hobbies.

Nebalath noticed that most of the rooms they passed through
had been turned over to wedding preparations—one appeared to
be overgrown entirely with a jungle of lace, another was crammed
with long tables where scribes labored busily over stacks of cards.
This place would drive him mad, Nebalath decided, and he wondered how Dark could endure it. Then again, perhaps the boy
wasn't enduring it . . .

"Here's one of them," the servant mumbled, motioning with
his arm as Nebalath looked inside. A score of seamstresses looked
up at him wearily from billows of yellow and blue fish-satin.

The wizard frowned. "Is there an azure room with a bed in
it?"

"Upstairs." The servant sighed; but as they turned to go,
Nebalath came face-to-face with Uda.

"Good morning," she said with subdued appreciation. "I
knew you'd come."

Nebalath stiffened with discomfort. He recognized that tone of
voice—people used it with healers all the time. But he was no
physician! "Something's wrong with Dark?"

"You knew!" she gushed, and Nebalath's discomfort grew.
"Come on," Uda said. "I'll show you."

Only the central tower of the house had been razed. There were
several others, and Dark's chamber appeared to be at the top of
one of these. Nebalath had to puff to keep up with the girl; she
was young, and she moved with that protective purposefulness of
a woman in her mothering mode.

This was quite a contrast to the girl he'd first met on Paumer's
portico at the hovel palace. She looked the same—slight build,
straight black hair hanging almost to her waist, and intense eyes.
But evidently she'd learned some things since then—odd how
quickly children grow up, he thought to himself as they reached
the last landing and she led him into the room.

Dark lay on the bed without cover, his knees tucked under his
chin and his arms clasped tightly around them. He faced the wall—
which was, indeed, a rich azure color. "He's been this way for
days," Uda whispered.

"Asleep?"

"I guess so. His eyes are closed—he moans aloud, as if in a
dream, but I can't seem to wake him. And he clutches his stomach
and rolls back and forth as if he's hurting somewhere." She looked
at him, eyes filling with tears. "Is he going to be all right?"

"In time for the wedding?" Kerily added from the doorway behind them.

Immediately angry, Uda whirled around to face her. "Mother! I told you to stay out of here!"

Kerily floated on in, totally oblivious to her daughter's command. "Is he? We've had healers in to look at him, but they can't do much good, of course—his being different and all . . ."

"Mother!"

"Relax, darling, I'm just talking to Nebalath. I'm certain he understands the uniqueness of our situation—"

"Far more than you ever will!" Uda shouted, but she was addressing Kerily's back now, for her mother had moved in right beside Nebalath and turned her pretty face up to smile into his.

"My daughter doesn't give me credit for knowing anything, but then, I felt the same about my own mother." She glanced away as if in thought, then back up at him. "Of course—I was right about mine . . ." she purred, and Nebalath couldn't prevent a smile from appearing on his face. Suddenly serious, Kerily continued. "You do understand, don't you, Wizard?"

"Understand what, exactly?" He glanced over Kerily's head at Uda.

The girl obviously felt outmaneuvered by her mother—and who wouldn't, Nebalath wondered in dismay—but she wasn't giving up. "If he has any sense he understands that all you're concerned about is getting the wedding off on schedule. 'Flawlessly, of course,' " she added, in perfect imitation of her mother's voice.

Kerily's gaze never left Nebalath. "She's a delightful child, isn't she? But legitimately concerned—the boy does appear to be sick, but not with anything we understand. It was a wonderful idea for her to call you—"

"You told me not to," Uda corrected.

"—and we are deeply appreciative of your coming, of course," Kerily continued. "But do you think you can help us? I had wondered, myself, if we didn't need to call that Ranoth fellow—the religious one? From up in Lamath?"

"He's the Ruling Elder of a nation, Mother." Uda said. "I doubt if he makes pastoral visits of this distance at a moment's notice, even upon the summons of the House of Paumer."

"We don't know until we try . . ."

"Besides," Uda continued, turning to Nebalath, "we already know Ranoth is scheduled to attend a meeting of the Grand Council someplace in the Marwand in the next few days."

"Call it the Conspiracy, dear." Kerily smiled. "Everyone else does."

"Father hates for people to call it that."

"Just one more reason to do it! Right, Wizard?" Kerily winked at Nebalath.

"I've called it a conspiracy for years," the powershaper muttered, "so you'll get no argument from me." He peered at Uda. "In fact, didn't I recommend to your father that he replace me on the Council by making you a member of it?" The young woman nodded. "And didn't I hear that he did so?"

"He did." She shrugged.

"Indeed he did," Kerily chortled bitterly. "We've had more than one family discussion about that act of lunacy, haven't we, darling!"

"It caused a lot of problems," Uda admitted. "My brother Ognadzu broke with my father over it and left the family."

Ognadzu, Nebalath thought to himself, trying to remember the brother's face. He did recall a son of Paumers being seated on the Conspiracy just before he'd left it. He'd been furious about it at the time. But he couldn't remember what the young man looked like. "People have always underestimated Ognadzu," Kerily said quietly—almost as if she was warning him . . .

"What about Dark?" Uda asked him flatly. "Do you have any suggestions?"

Nebalath turned his head to look back at the prophet. Dark tossed and turned upon the low bed, as if seized by a nightmare from which he couldn't wake. Nebalath wanted to help him but didn't know how. "I don't know if Ranoth could aid us or not. I don't have much patience with the people of faith—" Turning to look again at Uda, Nebalath said, "If I remember from the Conspiracy's discussions, neither Ranoth nor Talarath cared much for the boy . . ." Uda nodded. "So I doubt they would give you much help. If you think a believer in the Power is needed, I suggest we contact Seagryn."

"Seagryn!" Kerily said, her pretty eyes widening. "The dragonmaker? Why, there's not a more hated man on the face of this earth than Seagryn! He certainly didn't make the guest list." She smiled and started to let her laughter trill out again before interrupting herself to add reassuringly, "You did, of course . . ."

"Dragonmaker?" Nebalath frowned. "I thought Sheth had made the dragon?"

"He did." Uda nodded. "But I can't convince her of that. I was there, but she won't believe me."

"Your father was there, and he says Seagryn made the monster. You want me to call your father a liar?"

"Father knows the truth as well as I do," Uda said wearily. "He only says that because the Conspiracy wants Seagryn to bear the blame." She shook her head at Nebalath. "We've had this discussion before, too."

Nebalath looked around the room. Like every other room in this palace, it had a light, airy feel, as if at any moment it might tear itself away from the house and fly back up to reassume its rightful place in the sky. Whatever one might say about Kerily, she certainly had a flair for decoration. But when it came to Dark's welfare, he thought, allowing his gaze to drift back down to the restless boy, her daughter Uda was the one he trusted. "We need Seagryn to look at him. He may be a believer, but at least he's got some sense about him, and he knows more than a little about shaping the powers." He looked back at them. "That's my suggestion."

He'd taken sides, obviously. While Uda appeared grateful, Kerily now looked as if she'd suddenly whiffed the taint of some unpleasant odor. "Well!" she said, summoning with effort her brightest smile. "Perhaps the two of you can somehow work that out." She took notice at last of a servant who stood waiting patiently in the doorway, and seemed grateful for the interruption. "Yes, what is it?"

"Your cat, milady. I think perhaps you might want to come. . . ?"

"Oh all right," she grumbled graciously. "Always some new crisis." Kerily smiled at Nebalath as she started out of the room but stopped in the doorway to look back at him. "I do hope that you can have him up and around by the wedding date—and that this Seagryn fellow will be gone by then." A moment later they heard her heels *clack*ing down the stairs.

Now that they were allies, Uda moved closer to him. "He looks so sick . . ."

"Do you know where Seagryn is these days?" Nebalath asked.

"The last Dark saw of him he was heading toward his father-in-law's palace—he married Talarath's daughter, you know."

"Did he?" The wizard nodded, raising his eyebrows. Perhaps he remembered hearing that before, but the information hadn't stayed with him. "A wizard in the House of Talarath. That should be interesting."

"I'd have sent for Seagryn before now if my mother had let

me,'' Uda murmured. ''I'll dispatch a messenger to Lamath immediately.''

''Don't bother,'' Nebalath said, flipping a speck of dust from his robe. ''Talarath lives in the Rivers Region, and it would take a messenger five days to get to him. I'll go there myself this afternoon—after I drop by the Imperial House for a snack.''

''Thank you,'' Uda said, gushing again. That attitude gave him the powerful urge to disappear. Suddenly she frowned. ''How do you know so much about Lamath?''

Nebalath chuckled, and a far-off look came into his old eyes. ''Have you never noticed the similarity between my name and the names of the Lamathian leaders you know? You see, I was born in—''

A heart-stopping scream suddenly rocked through the Paumer palace, having roughly the same impact as a peal of thunder from directly overhead. The two stared at each other, then bolted out the door and down the steps. They both knew without speaking that it had come from Kerily, out in the new courtyard.

''My cat!'' she shrieked when they arrived at her side. With tears streaming down her cheeks, she pointed upward to the trellis upon which Nebalath had made his arrival. There was a cat up there, all right—a cat such as Nebalath had never seen before. He was used to cats being brown, gray, or yellow striped. This cat was striped, but with bands of brilliant jungle green on a lime background. It was also twice the size of a normal cat—and the trellis was cracking under its weight. Nebalath could sympathize . . .

When he looked back at Kerily, he immediately wished he hadn't. Her eyes pleaded with him. ''Go get it,'' she begged. He was stunned.

''What?''

''Please go get it for me! You can pop right up there, grab it, and pop right back down here, just like you did this morning!''

He stared at her. This woman believed the entire world was in her employ! ''Milady, I am a wizard, not a—''

''Please! It's going to break, and he'll be crushed—hurry!''

Nebalath looked up, sighed, and disappeared.

He was hanging in midair, regarding a rather large cat who looked back at him balefully with violet eyes. ''Violet eyes?'' he said. Then he grabbed it, disappeared, and returned to Kerily's side.

''Here is your cat, milady,'' he growled, pushing the furry beast into Kerily's arms quickly lest it scratch him. As she took it gratefully, he noticed that, despite its size, it appeared to be more of a kitten than an adult. As Kerily nuzzled the cat against her cheek, it turned again to gaze at him, and once more he was startled by those violet eyes. They seemed to—recognize him. "I've never seen such an animal," he marveled. "Where did you get it?"

"The spice islands," Kerily said in the cloying little girl's voice she apparently used with the beast. "You came from the spice islands, didn't you, sweetheart? Yes! All the way on a boat! And Paumer gave you to me to make up for being such an idiot, didn't he? Yes!" She was trying to get the cat to look at her, but it seemed more interested in Nebalath. The wizard cleared his throat and looked over his shoulder at Uda.

"Your father apparently likes to give exotic pets. Didn't he gift you with a tugolith, once?"

Uda tossed her long black mane. "Yes." She snorted. "A tugolith that is now part of a world-consuming dragon."

"Hmm," Nebalath mused. Then he angled his head a little to the right and leaned it onto his chest—and was gone.

The dragon grew tired at last, and Seagryn breathed a quiet hallelujah. They'd been flying around all night—whether in circles or not, Seagryn couldn't tell. It was dark, after all, and they'd not chanced across any of the larger cities that would have been lit up enough to be visible. He considered that fortunate. While he had promised the dragon a city to eat, he had no intention of actually guiding Vicia-Heinox to one. His last clear vision before the cloak of night had fallen had been of his home village in flames, and he was still in shock. Bourne had been so distant for so long that he'd almost come to regard it as more a memory than a real place. To descend out of the sky on dragon-back—head, really—and depart the same way, leaving the place in ruin . . . It just didn't seem possible. The whole episode had been so dreamlike he had to struggle to convince himself it had actually happened.

And yet it had happened. People he'd known from childhood had been swallowed by this monster. Others who could tell stories about the kind of student he'd been had seen his face clearly and identified him. He comforted himself with the thought that it could have been much worse. Hadn't Gammel been reduced to cinders by the dragon's visit? His presence had minimized the carnage in Bourne. But that wouldn't alter the perception his old neighbors now had of him. He could never go home again.

At the moment it seemed unlikely he would ever have the

chance. While the dragon seemed to care for him—the Heinox head, at least—Seagryn realized that could easily change. Although he needed to steer the twi-beast away from major metropolitan areas, he knew if the dragon became too hungry, he could become a most convenient snack.

There was also the problem of maintaining his perch. What if he fell off? This had been a long, wearying day, and several times he'd caught himself dozing. He couldn't see it, but he felt it reasonable to assume that the ground was a long way down. He'd already decided that if he did fall, he would change into his altershape before he hit. He hoped that his tugolith body might bounce better, but he realized that might just cause him to splatter over a much larger area. Better, he told himself, just not to go to sleep.

And if he did get down safely, what then? He knew the old woman in Gammel had spoken for hosts of others in wishing upon him the most painful kind of end. The tragedy in Bourne would certainly add to his notoriety. He was already hated—he would soon be hated with greater intensity, with more detailed vehemence, by people who had never laid eyes on him and who knew him through nothing more than his name. Someone would certainly try to kill him. He was surprised they hadn't tried already.

He no longer wondered why Elaryl had worked so hard to keep events from him. His summer idyll in the house of Talarath had been the dream—this was the reality of his life. But Seagryn did wonder why he no longer felt any sense of self-revulsion. Why, instead, did he feel somehow elated to be plunged once more into the midst of happenings that would shape the destiny of the old One Land? It was as if he had been taken out of the barn and harnessed once more to do useful work. If indeed he was the only person Vicia-Heinox would listen to, then here upon the dragon's head was exactly where he belonged: Counseling, cajoling—ultimately controlling. If he could only stay awake . . .

"I need to sleep," Vicia called over, his voice rising above the sound of the wind.

"I've been telling myself that for hours!" Heinox grumbled peevishly, and Seagryn felt the beast descending. He tried to peer below but could really see nothing in the inky black. Tugolith eyes were weak, he knew from experience. How could this dragon see any better?

"Where am I?" Vicia called, just before the twi-beast crashed into the ground. Seagryn clutched at the wrinkle of dragonscale and clamped his legs around Heinox' neck as they bounced and skidded along through some kind of vegetation.

Heinox waited until they'd come to a full and complete stop before announcing, "I'm down."

"That hurt," Vicia complained, and Heinox agreed, but the dragon was really too sleepy for conversation. What did it matter where they were, anyway? They were no longer in the air. Moments later both heads slept.

Seagryn had a little more trouble. It had been months since he'd slept anywhere but in the wonderful bed he shared with Elaryl. He felt certain sleeping on the ground again would take some getting used to. Besides, something was troubling him—something he couldn't name. He strained his weary mind to bring it to consciousness but felt himself fading. Despite his discomfort Seagryn just couldn't keep his eyes open . . .

Chapter Four

✕✕✕✕

DRAGON'S PET

Seagryn woke with a start, fully aware of what his mind had been struggling to tell him. "It didn't need to happen," he gasped aloud. He could have protected Bourne from burning, if only he'd been thinking as a powershaper!

In the shaper wars that had been waged constantly in the One Land prior to its breakup, wizard after wizard had learned to apply to whole armies the ability to cloak themselves from view. In his first skirmish, Seagryn had done so intuitively—in his first major battle he had hidden an entire fleet of Haranian ships from Sheth and the approaching Armada of Arl. Had he thought, he could have simply prevented the dragon from seeing Bourne—

What he'd learned about shaping the powers had come less from other wizards than from his own experience. In fact, Nebalath had once told him that no shaper could teach another how to shape. But he did remember one piece of advice the old powershaper had given him the morning of that first battle. "Shaping is manipulation of powers, of perceptions, of objects, of outcomes, or of persons by an act of the will, and everyone does it to some degree. Some of us are just better at it than others. The essential gift of the true shaper is imagination. Free yours, Seagryn, and *use* it!" Seagryn covered his eyes, crushed now by an enormous burden of guilt. Why had he not applied his imagination to the rescue of Bourne?

He struggled to his feet. Every muscle of his body felt the soreness of yesterday's long travels—most especially his backside

and his fingers. Riding a dragon was no easy task. And yet he
hardly noticed the physical pain for the mental anguish that preyed
upon him. He shook his head in dismay, only marginally aware
of the long, light-brown hair that hung down over his face. He'd
obviously overvalued the contribution he could make through his
abilities. As a wizard, he was an utter failure. What good was the
gift of powershaping when he didn't have the sense to use it?

"I'm hungry," a menacing voice growled behind him, and
Seagryn turned suddenly to face the dragon's two heads. He'd
slept last night within a ring formed by the necks of Vicia and
Heinox—extremely secure quarters, he reasoned, as long as one
was on friendly terms with the beast. As he pushed his hair back
out of his eyes, Seagryn thought regretfully that he was, indeed,
on good terms with this monster—too good. He needed to do
something about that.

"I said I'm hungry!" Vicia growled again, more loudly.

Seagryn said, "I heard you."

"You promised me a feast!" the dragon accused—or Vicia did,
at any rate. Heinox appeared to be still asleep.

Seagryn knew, now, what he would do. He would ride the
dragon everywhere, pretending to show it new feeding places
while ensuring that the beast ate no one. "If you'll wake up your
other head we'll get started."

Heinox opened the eye closest to Seagryn and gazed at him.
"What other head?"

"Oh. You're awake."

"Of course I'm awake," Vicia snarled. "I've been talking to
you, haven't I? Climb on and show me this city!" The dragon
was *not* in good humor.

Vicia-Heinox was in a far worse mood five days later when,
despite crisscrossing the countryside again and again, he hadn't
spotted a single person to engage in dinner conversation.

"Where are they?" the dragon screamed. "It's as if every human habitation has disappeared from the face of the earth!"

"It does look exactly that way," Seagryn agreed, clinging
grimly to his perch. By now he'd grown accustomed to this spot
behind Heinox' ears. It seemed to have shaped itself to his body—
or was it the other way around? He could see that his fingers had
started to wear grooves into the scales of the wrinkle he gripped.

"You're not keeping your promise!" Vicia roared.

"But I am," Seagryn argued calmly, telling a half truth. In
fact, they had flown over numerous cities, one at least twice. But

each time, Seagryn's better eyes had spotted the buildings before the dragon did, and, by a combination of distractions, confusions, and cloakings, he had managed to shield each city from the twi-beast's view. Thus they had soared twenty feet above the spire of the tallest building in the capital, right over the downtown square, and all the time the dragon had been complaining about how parched and empty the ground below appeared. Seagryn's heart had pounded throughout the flight—just because the dragon couldn't see a tower didn't mean it couldn't knock one down if it flew into one—but he'd managed to steer the beast through the maze without mishap.

None of this prevented the populace of Lamath from seeing the dragon—and being terrorized by the sight. And all who saw it also reported that a man wearing priestly green rode on one of the dragon's heads. Within days the whole of the nation would know who he was—and not Lamath only, for early in the week Seagryn often directed the dragon over the sparsely settled Marwand. But he knew his native countryside better and carried in his head memories of maps he had studied while in school; during the last two days he'd tried to keep them over Lamath. Most of southern Lamath was covered by the Telera Desert, and fewer habitations meant he had less work to do. His own energy was fading, for he was himself growing hungry; he'd had food packed in his satchel, but not enough for a week. He'd eaten the last of it days ago.

"I am starving!" Vicia-Heinox roared savagely, and Seagryn roared back.

"I am, too!" As he'd become better acquainted with the dragon, he'd also grown less intimidated by it. Since the heads bickered with one another constantly, his own griping tone of voice seemed to fit right in. "We flew over a herd of moosers early this morning! Why don't we go back and eat *them*!"

"Why is it you want me to eat moosers?" the dragon whined. "I don't like to eat moosers!"

"You haven't tried moosers!" Seagryn scolded. He knew he sounded exactly like a parent urging a child to eat her peas. In fact, he felt like a disgruntled parent at the moment.

"I do not eat moosers!" Vicia-Heinox proclaimed emphatically. "I eat persons!"

Seagryn sighed heavily. "All right, then. I guess we'll just have to keep looking." They didn't find any. Seagryn made certain of that.

Late that afternoon Seagryn decided to take a chance. He'd

wanted to try it for days but hadn't dared. He found it remarkable that the dragon continued to allow itself to be guided by him, but since it did, he steered their flight over the Rivers Region. They sailed high above a beautiful tree-lined lane, at the end of which sat a mansion—a tiny thing from this height. Vicia-Heinox never saw it since Seagryn wouldn't allow them to fly close enough to put Elaryl in danger, but there it was—there *she* was. So near, he thought to himself. Overwhelmed by grief, Seagryn sat forward and shouted in Heinox' ear, "Turn to the left—there's *got* to be a city south of us somewhere!"

The dragon banked away, and for the last few hours of sunlight they flew above the empty expanse of the Marwilds forest, passing over only an occasional cabin or wayside inn . . .

Nebalath stood in a corner of the tiny back room and listened carefully to the proceedings. No one saw him, for he had cloaked his presence in order to listen in. This was a secret meeting of a society of assassins, sworn to murder the maker of the dragon. They supposedly possessed information about the dragon's habits that Nebalath wanted to know. The more he listened, though, the more convinced he became that they knew no more than anyone else.

He controlled his frustration. The quest to find Seagryn had grown larger than he'd anticipated. While he was still anxious to find help for Dark, he'd now become fascinated by Seagryn's involvement with this twi-beast creature. The trouble was, no one seemed to know anything with certainty. He'd never heard so much misinformation in his life, especially concerning power-shapers. He'd even heard his own name evoked once or twice among the lists of most hated villains in the world—and he'd not done anything at all! But the strongest vulgarities were all reserved for Seagryn. Nebalath remembered how the man had been caroled with praises on the night of his victory in the Rangsfield Sluice—public opinion certainly changed quickly. Of course, that had been down in Haranamous, and this was Lamath, but Nebalath had no question that Seagryn would be hated just as much there, once this Vicia-Heinox began consuming Haranian peasants, too. But where was the dragon? From the people he'd talked to, it was everywhere. And everywhere the dragon went, the man was sure to go . . .

Nebalath's initial meeting with Elaryl had been a surprise for both of them. Naturally, she'd been startled by his sudden appearance in her bedroom, but no more than he. Nebalath had hastily explained how he came to be there—how he had been in the House of Talarath once before, and hadn't this spot been a courtyard then? If people kept changing their houses, how were wizards to know where to appear? She had graciously forgiven him. Nebalath found himself surprised by her combination of beauty and good sense and lowered his opinion of Seagryn. It baffled the old wizard that Seagryn would be fool enough to leave such a woman for any reason! He was also impressed by her loyalty. She appeared to be the only person who believed that what Seagryn was doing with the dragon was designed to help humanity, not hurt it.

That squared with what Nebalath remembered of the man. Seagryn was intensely moral—to the point of being obnoxious about it. And while Nebalath had heard dozens of accounts from people who'd seen the dragon overhead with Seagryn aboard, no one said they'd actually seen anything burned or anybody eaten.

Until this man, that is—Yammerlid—who was being sworn into a secret society.

"You actually know Seagryn the dragonmaker?" asked the apparent leader of this covert band.

"I've known the stinking mudgecurdle all my life," Yammerlid answered savagely, and Nebalath winced at the epithet for personal reasons. "We grew up together, and he was always the same as he is now—a slime, a false friend, ingratiating himself with those in authority, but caring only for himself!

"I recognized that in him—others didn't. My best friend, a brilliant boy we all looked to for leadership, seemed to lean particularly on Seagryn for advice, even though I warned him regularly of Seagryn's duplicity. Eventually Seagryn conspired to cut me out of the group, and no matter what I did from that point on, people would always believe him over me. I recognized at a young age," Yammerlid growled dramatically, "that I had made a powerful enemy."

Since Nebalath didn't believe him, he wasn't surprised that others hadn't believed Yammerlid either. But he could tell this man had convinced himself of the truth of his own story, and it did provide an interesting glimpse into Seagryn's early life. He leaned forward to listen.

"There was a girl," Yammerlid continued bitterly. "We all loved her—all of us—but she loved our leader. Seagryn pretended not to care, pretended that his long conversations with her were only those of a friend and not a lover, but I knew better. He was after her for himself. One day I caught him with her on the far side of the greensward. He had thrown her onto her back and was forcing himself on her, so I leaped upon him. Suddenly he turned himself into a monster every bit as repulsive as this dragon he's now made, and charged after me! He had his huge head lowered and his horn aimed right at my—right for me, and naturally I turned and ran, but my friend heard us coming. As I raced past him, I shouted the truth—that Seagryn was in fact a magic user and that he was out to kill us all! My friend tried to save me from the monster's charge—but only skewered himself upon that vicious horn.''

Yammerlid paused for dramatic effect—he certainly had the attention of his audience, Nebalath noted, whether his story was true or not.

''Naturally, I gave the alarm throughout the whole town—but Seagryn disappeared that very night. I told my story, but the girl refused to back me up. It wasn't until last year that anyone really paid attention to old Yammerlid—when word that Seagryn truly was a magic user began to seep back into our district. I tried to warn them! I told them he'd eventually return to take his vengeance and that we needed to prepare—but they wouldn't listen to me. Oh no!

''And now he's come, bringing his dragon with him! He burned our village—his own village!—and allowed this horrible twi-beast to swallow some of our finest citizens. I determined then and there that I would do everything in my power to stop him.'' Yammerlid leaned forward toward the rapt faces of his listeners. ''I know, for a fact, that Seagryn is the key member of the Conspiracy!''

The leader of the secret organization suddenly laughed, and Yammerlid jerked his head around to glare at him. ''What are *you* laughing at?'' he demanded.

''There's no such thing as a Conspiracy.'' The man chortled. Then he turned suddenly very serious. ''There are only this Seagryn and this dragon. And our responsibility concerning both is quite clear. We must destroy them!''

Nebalath shook his head in surprise. There *was* a Conspiracy, and he'd been a member of it. He knew most of these secret assassination squads had first been organized in reaction to rumors of the Conspiracy's existence, but he also knew that Paumer's spies had infiltrated most of them. He took a long look at the leader . . .

Yes. He'd seen him before. While he didn't know his name, Nebalath knew the face well, for this was an employee of the House of Paumer. The merchant liked to boast that he had his finger in every secret organization throughout the six Fragments. If so, this man was certainly one of Paumer's chief "fingers." Nebalath remembered hearing the man report such doings to Paumer immediately before meetings of the Grand Council. And he wondered: How far was this little tavern on the edge of the Marwilds from Paumer's nearest palace? Uda had said the Conspiracy was to meet somewhere in the Marwand during this week . . .

The leader was speaking somberly, and Nebalath leaned forward to listen. "Do you, Yammerlid, swear to sacrifice yourself in pursuit of the dragon and his hated maker, to pour your life out as a poison potion, a bitter drop for the dragon and his hated pet to drink? You are to answer 'I so swear.' "

"I so swear," Yammerlid said fervently, and Nebalath dismissed the man from his mind. Yammerlid was of that fanatical type so convinced of the truth of their own obsessions they become one-dimensional bores. Nebalath was far more interested now in this leader. It made sense that he would report this meeting to Paumer immediately—perhaps before the Conspiracy met?

The spy left the tavern secretively, as befitted his purpose for being there, and trekked south through the woods, completely unaware of the cloaked wizard who trailed him. Nebalath had determined he would follow wherever the fellow led.

Seagryn awoke disoriented and hungry. While he remembered clearly that he'd been riding a dragon's head for a week, he couldn't recall coming back down to earth the night before nor the last time he'd eaten a good meal. He lay on his back with his eyes shut, feeling too miserable to open them and face yet another day. Nevertheless, he knew he had to; the sun was shining down on his face, and duty called.

He opened his eyes. Then he sat up in shock and looked around, feeling suddenly very unprotected. He'd grown accustomed to sleeping within the pen made by the twi-beast's two necks, but the dragon was gone. He jumped to his feet, wanting to run but not knowing in which direction. He realized that his knees were wobbly. "Probably from the hunger and the strain," he told himself quickly as he staggered around in a full circle, searching the sky for the dragon.

Sharp mountain peaks rose to either side. He appeared to be in a valley—a high valley, judging from the thinness of the air. The sun had just topped another towering mountain to the east, and he held his hand up to block the light and studied the landscape for some clue to his whereabouts.

There! Halfway up a cliff was a huge structure of some sort, one he didn't recognize but felt somehow that he should know. It seemed to hang upon the mountainside as if it had been stuck there with some sort of glue. The floor of it hovered at least thirty feet in the air, while the top of the structure rose a hundred feet above that and was topped by battlements. It had white columns below and a line of shuttered windows above, and it looked deserted—its white paint was chipped and peeling. What was it? Where was he? More worrisome, where was the dragon?

He heard a screech in the air behind him and whirled around to see the beast dropping toward him out of the sky. A tremor of fear rippled through his empty stomach. Was this his last moment? Had the dragon grown weary of the game at last, and was he about to be eaten? He decided once again that there was no point in revealing his terror. Instead, he scolded, "Where have you been? Do you have any idea how disconcerting it is to wake up in the middle of no place and find yourself all alone?"

"No," Heinox answered honestly as the flapping of gigantic, leathery wings stirred plumes of dust up into Seagryn's face. "I can't recall ever experiencing that emotion."

"I certainly can't," Vicia agreed, burping contentedly. Seagryn frowned.

"Of course, I can't remember very much at all," Heinox admitted, philosophically rolling his eyes skyward.

"Then again, who needs to?" Vicia smiled and burped again. He stretched his long neck to its fullest extension and rolled his head about on the end of it in a gesture of preening relaxation that worried Seagryn considerably. Every previous morning the twibeast had awakened in a terrible mood, horribly hungry and ready to leap immediately into the sky to search for something to devour. This morning it looked—full. "By the way," Vicia added, tipping sideways to aim one eye down at Seagryn from high above him. "We're not in the middle of no place. We're in the middle of every place." Heinox nodded in agreement.

"How do you know?" Seagryn asked. He had a very bad feeling about this.

"A trading captain just told me," Vicia said, licking his lips and adding, "He was delicious!"

"I thought the screaming woman was quite tasty," the thoughtful Heinox offered.

"You—you ate a woman?"

"Several, really. When I told her she was next, this particular woman seemed to take it rather hard."

"Screamed, cried, carried on," Vicia explained disapprovingly. "Very embarrassing."

"So I ate her."

"Which shut her up most effectively!" Vicia cackled.

"It really did." Heinox nodded, then once again gazed reflectively up at the sky. "I especially like eating women. I wonder why?"

Seagryn fought the reflex to gag. "Where—where did you—eat these people?"

"I asked that," Vicia said, obviously proud of himself. "The captain person called this place the Central Gate."

The Central Gate! This was the only true trade route between the southern cities and Lamath, as well as the easiest road into the Marwand! Astride this pass had once sat the glorious capital city of the old One Land— Seagryn whirled around to look up again at the peeling structure clinging to the side of the cliff and realized now what it was. They were on the front porch of the Remnant!

Seagryn had been inside the Remnant before, but he and Dark hadn't come in this way. He had opened an unauthorized hole into a tunnel on the back side of this mountain, which had caused Garney, the Keeper of the Outer Portal, to expel the whole Conspiracy from the underground realm. This was the Outer Portal Garney so diligently kept!

"He said there would be another caravan along any minute—"

"—I think he was trying to get me to wait and eat *it*—"

"So I thanked him and told him I would have it for lunch—"

"—then finished my breakfast. Delicious! What a wonderful place you have brought me to, Seagryn person! Why fly about looking for food, when I can take up residence here and have fresh meat delivered daily?"

Residence? Here? Seagryn's head reeled. Much of the traffic through the Central Gate was directed to and from the Remnant. Since it could grow nothing for itself, it received all of its food from the outside. The House of Paumer had the monopoly on trade into the Remnant, if he remembered rightly, but the trading captains could hardly deliver the groceries if they were regularly being made into groceries themselves . . . He had to get the dragon to leave this place. But how? From the viewpoint of Vicia-Heinox, it was a perfect location!

"I hope that caravan comes soon," Vicia murmured, salivating. "I'm still hungry." Why did he look at Seagryn so meaningfully?

Of course! Now that he had provided the dragon with the promised supply of food, Seagryn was no longer needed! He had to get away, and quickly. He could cloak himself and slip off, he realized, but that would probably make the dragon angry and cause it to sniff around this pass until it actually noticed the structure hanging up on the side of the cliff. He decided to try a different approach. "I am, too," he announced, and he started to walk briskly away. A dragon head suddenly appeared before him.

"Where are you going?"

"I'm going to get something to eat."

"You can't leave," Heinox said flatly. "Who would I talk to?"

"Your—lunch?" Seagryn offered.

"Of course I'll talk to them, but it's difficult to form a personal relationship with someone you're about to consume . . ."

"I can see where that would be a problem."

"You, on the other hand, are more of a . . . a . . ."

"Pet." Vicia supplied the word from his own experience. Somewhere back in his dim, predragon existence, it seemed he had been that to someone . . .

The dragon's pet. It was an apt description, and it made Seagryn want to retch. Had he known Nebalath's trick of casting oneself great distances he would have made an abrupt appearance on the rooftop of Talarath's mansion, taken his wife in his arms, and tried his best to put all of this behind him. But the fact remained that he was the only person who seemed to have any influence over this beast. If the Remnant was to be saved, he would need to do the saving. But how? He needed time to think, he needed to warn those people inside the mountain—he needed to *eat*!

"Did you consume *all* of that caravan this morning?"

"Of course not." Vicia-Heinox sniffed. "You know I don't eat horses."

"Fine. Could you go get *me* one?"

Surprised, the dragon looked itself in the eyes, then Vicia looked back at Seagryn with something approaching disdain. Heinox took up for him. "Everyone has to eat *something*, I guess." Then the dragon furled its wings and flew away.

While Seagryn was hungry enough to eat a horse, his purpose at the moment was to distract the beast long enough to slip into the Remnant. But how was he going to get up to it? He knew

Garney wouldn't open it for just anybody—and probably especially not for him . . .

As soon as Vicia-Heinox was out of sight, Seagryn cloaked himself and started walking toward the peeling structure. A moment later he sprinted instead. The Outer Portal was opening!

Chapter Five

❈❈❈❈

LOST INSIDE

"I҉t's gone," Wilker said as he turned to Garney. "Open up the Portal."

"How do you know it's gone?" Garney demanded. "How do you know it won't turn right around and come back? How do you know it's not flying right here to us?"

"Garney." The handsome Wilker smiled patronizingly. "Trust me. This dragon was made by our own ad hoc advisory committee for Provincial Concerns!"

"The Conspiracy," Garney grunted.

"Exactly! Sheth made it at our direct order, and he and Paumer promised to train the thing to do exactly as we requested. Now, please! If you're not coming yourself, at least don't delay me any longer. Open the Outer Portal!"

"I don't like it," Garney growled between clenched teeth, but he gave the order to lower the stairs, and the aged structure filled with the creaks and clanks that always accompanied that procedure. "It takes several minutes to get the gate down and back up again. What if the monster returns?"

"Then simply tell it to go away." Wilker shrugged. "This dragon was made from two very obedient beasts. I'm certain it will." A rectangle of light opened before them as the forty-foot-wide staircase made the thirty-foot descent to the floor of the pass. Wilker picked up the reins of his horse and guided it toward the pitch-coated ramp.

Garney followed him, saying, "I don't see why you have to

run every time that merchant calls. These are outer peasants, Wilker! What business do we have conspiring with them?''

"That's my job, remember? I *am* Undersecretary for Provincial Affairs.'' Wilker winked in a manner Garney knew would cause every lady in the One Land to swoon. Wilker was the most handsome man Inside—next to the king, of course.

But Garney was convinced he was also the stupidest. "Just don't underestimate their capacity for disloyalty!'' the little man warned. "Remember, Wilker—these people don't care a fig for our values! It doesn't matter to them whether the King of the One Land lives or dies!'' The Outer Portal was now fully extended. The bottom of the staircase rested on the ground.

"You misjudge them, Garney!'' Wilker smiled back over his shoulder as he led his horse down. "They're each as committed in his own way to the Reunification of the One Land as you or me. I do wish you would go with me—they'll be expecting us to send two representatives—''

"I am not going to listen to outer peasants talk about us and our king as if it is they who control our destiny!'' Garney exploded. "I am not going to sit and listen as they refer to the One Land as a—a Remnant! If you must go, go on. But be careful! Those people out there have no conception of what's truly important!''

Wilker was off the ramp now and onto the canyon floor. He turned to wave back at Garney. "I'll be back in a few days. Watch for me!'' He then mounted his horse and rode off.

"Idiot,'' Garney grunted to himself. Then a disembodied voice spoke from right behind him—

"Crank your staircase back up. The dragon will be returning any minute!''

"Augh!'' Garney shouted, almost tumbling down the staircase after Wilker. When he caught his balance, he whirled around to face the speaker. He couldn't. There was no one there. "Who are you? *Where* are you?''

"Right here,'' Seagryn puffed, for he was considerably winded from his run. He revealed himself and waited for the explosion he knew would follow.

"YOU!'' Garney raged. "You would dare set foot again within this realm? You would dare return, after destroying half of our backside galleries in the worst breach of security in the history of the One Land? How dare you return, you—you outsider! Get out! Get out now, or you'll spend the rest of your life in a dungeon so deep you'll *never* see the light of one of your precious outsider days again!''

Seagryn knew Garney was excitable, and this response didn't surprise him. It did worry him, however. How was he going to get the little man to believe him? "Did you see the dragon?"

"I said get out!"

"Did you see the dragon?" Seagryn repeated with more urgency, taking a step toward the little man. Garney backed up against the wall and pointed a finger at him, and Seagryn heard a sharp rustling sound. He glanced around and realized there were at least a dozen drawn arrows targeted on his back.

"I'd suggest," Garney said deliberately, "that you withdraw down the staircase while you still have the opportunity."

Seagryn sighed. He didn't want to, but he supposed it was necessary. Instantly a dozen warriors cried out in pain, and as many bows and arrows clattered to the wooden floor as the injured guards suddenly sucked upon their burning fingers. Garney frowned. "Did you do that?" the little man asked.

"Please listen to me," said Seagryn. "It's really for the good of the Remn—the One Land."

The Keeper of the Outer Portal didn't see that he had much choice. He had a wizard Inside—but he'd had wizards Inside before. And there *was* something distinctly unhealthy about leaving the staircase down while a dragon roamed about nearby. He gave the order to close it, then turned to fix Seagryn with his coldest stare. "Very well then. Talk."

Seagryn glanced around at the wide-eyed guards who stared at him in shock, their mouths stuffed full of burning fingers. "Perhaps there's a private room?"

Garney sighed with exasperation, then lifted a lamp down from a shelf carved into the granite wall. "In here." The little man gestured crossly. He led Seagryn into a small, windowless cell carved into the mountain just off the main tunnel. He set the lamp on a table, offered Seagryn a chair, closed the door with an efficient click, then turned and sat down across from Seagryn, his ever-present frown highlighted by the single flame. "Now," he demanded. "Tell me why there is a dragon outside our door?"

Seagryn proceeded to do just that. It took a while, given Garney's tendency to interrupt with violent recriminations, but eventually the intense gatekeeper's good sense and suspicion of all outsiders won out over his personal animosity towards Seagryn, and he was convinced. He sat silent at last, his face pale with fear. Or was it just from the total lack of exposure to sunlight? "You understand now?" Seagryn prodded.

"Understand?" Garney said incredulously. "I've never understood the behavior of you outer peasants! You tell me you and this other wizard have made an indestructible weapon and planted it here, outside our door!"

"That part was an accident—"

"It was planned from the beginning!" the Keeper of the Outer Portal whispered knowingly. "Or are you too much of a fool to recognize that?"

"I guess I must be . . ."

"This whole Conspiracy has always been a trick!" Garney shouted.

"I could probably agree with that . . ."

"If there was any real interest in reuniting the One Land, the so-called 'kings' of these so-called 'Fragments' would simply make the required pilgrimage here to swear loyalty to the Sovereign Over All the Earth. But do they do that?" he demanded, his dark eyes gleaming brightly. Seagryn didn't see much sense in answering, since he felt sure Garney had already prepared his proper response. He was right. "No! Instead they plot the Only King's destruction!" Garney leaned forward and whispered again. "They know, you see, that our sovereign is the greatest single obstacle to their plan of world domination!"

Seagryn disagreed, but there was no point in arguing. He'd read the history of the old One Land and knew that those who'd retreated into the Remnant had a myopic view of their own importance. But he could forgive that, for after all—didn't everybody? "The fact remains that there's a dragon outside. What are we going to do about it?"

"We?" Garney said archly, and he leaned back in his chair. "I think *you* would do best to get out of the way and allow those of us who are trained in crisis management to deal with this."

Seagryn looked at him. "You're trained to deal with dragons?"

"The question of a dragon is neither here nor there—"

"I beg your pardon, but it is! The dragon is here! He's right outside your precious Outer Portal!"

"Please lower your voice."

"Garney, if you would just—"

"My proper form of address is 'Keeper.' "

"Fine. Listen, Keeper, if you would just let me talk to the king I'm sure he would—"

"Absolutely not!" Garney was on his feet and doing his very

best to look down on Seagryn menacingly. "You will not address the Only High Sovereign directly on this or any other subject! I will report this nuisance through the proper channels, and we shall care for the problem ourselves. You shall do nothing! Is that understood?"

Seagryn looked up into the Keeper's features, so twisted by rage, and wished for a second time today that he could do what Nebalath did. Why did he bother? The emptiness in his stomach was causing him acute discomfort. He gave up and gave in. "Do it your way, Garney. I'll be available if you need me."

"I assure you—we won't."

"Fine. Then could you please find me something to eat? I'm starving, and I'd like to get at least one good meal into my belly while you people still believe you have it to spare."

Garney eyed him with intense suspicion. "There's one act you must perform before I can arrange that."

"Fine. What?"

Garney's gaze didn't waver. "The halls to the Inside all lead through the throne room. You must greet the One and Only King."

Seagryn shrugged. "I'm ready."

"You must promise to say nothing during the audience! I will introduce you and do all the talking for you. Is that understood?"

Seagryn agreed to remain silent—which is how he came to be introduced to the King of the old One Land as a touring magician. "He's been invited Inside to do tricks for the Children's Club," Garney explained, ignoring Seagryn's wide-eyed surprise. "I'll be taking him there myself."

"Magic!" the king said excitedly, and he sat up and leaned over to look down into Seagryn's face. This was not easy for him to do, since his jeweled throne stood upon a circular dais raised thirty feet high. Seagryn had to crane his own neck to see the king, for the concentric circles that formed the marble platform ascended at a very sharp angle. He wondered how the man got up there without falling—

"Show me something!" the king commanded, and Seagryn shot a sidelong glance at Garney to see the little man nodding nervously. Seagryn shrugged and tossed a purple ball of fire up above the sovereign's head. This was only partly in response to the king's command—Seagryn was curious about this place, and the torches that guttered along its walls failed to illuminate the room fully.

It was enormous—or perhaps it just seemed so, since he knew it had been carved from live rock. The walls of the circular room were the same pink marble as the slabs that made up the dais, and rose to a height of forty feet. Above them loomed the domed ceiling, painted black, Seagryn assumed, to exaggerate the throne room's size. The place was grand—or had been. Opulently decorated with gemstones and mosaic tiles, it nevertheless seemed a bit run-down. There were bare spots on the floor where tiles had come up and hadn't been replaced. The torches that ringed the walls seemed a size too small for the brackets that held them. So this is the heart of my heritage, Seagryn thought to himself. But if he was not impressed, the king was even less so. "A ball of fire." He sighed wearily, barely tipping his head back far enough to see it. "And I suppose you can change its color at will."

Seagryn couldn't, actually—or at least, he'd never tried. He would have attempted it now if the king had not sniffed and waved him off. "Don't bother. I don't suppose that's your big finish, is it?"

"I could change into a—"

"It's a children's show, my Everything!" Garney interrupted anxiously, tossing Seagryn a scowl of warning. "They won't have seen all the tricks that you have!"

"Well, I'd thought about coming," the king answered, slumping sideways on his throne. It appeared to be a most uncomfortable seat.

"I—doubt you would find it all that interesting," Garney said, apparently a bit relieved. Seagryn waited for the little man to get to the real purpose of his visit. He was shocked when he realized that the audience was over. "Until later, Your Imperial Highness," the Keeper of the Outer Portal said. As he bowed, he looked sideways at Seagryn to prompt him to follow suit.

"Aren't you going to—?"

"In my own time!" Garney whispered fiercely. He then rose to his feet, beamed up at his disinterested ruler, and plucked Seagryn by the sleeve to lead him around the throne. Three great arches opened onto three corridors, each large enough to be termed avenues. Garney pulled Seagryn swiftly down one of these, waiting until they were well out of earshot of the king and his guards to mutter, "I told you to let me do all the speaking!"

"I was answering a questi—"

"It is imperative that you not address the king directly! You might—upset him."

So that was it, Seagryn realized. Garney didn't intend to tell the king about the dragon at all.

In his days as a student, Seagryn had read extensively about the history of the One Land. In that ancient time, the royal palace—by all accounts the largest building ever constructed and never completely finished—had eventually stretched from the center of the pass to this mountain and then had backed up against it. Long before the breakup into the Fragments, the advisors to the royal family had commissioned the excavation of a system of tunnels. These had been intended to remain a secret, but a project of such magnitude could not be concealed from a curious populace forever, and tales of a vast underground land began to circulate. It was a fairyland, some returning workmen reported—a utopia under the mountain where only the ruler and a certain number of his chosen would be permitted to dwell. The rumors became so pervasive that, to save the royal family embarrassment, the king's advisors had attempted to match them with reality. Large sums of the national treasury were devoted to that end, while growing needs on the outer edges of the One Land were ignored.

Still, there never seemed to be quite enough money to do all that the royal engineers suggested was really necessary to do the job right. More funds were required, so taxes were raised, and while people in the far north prayed for divine intervention, merchants in the south founded a thriving black market and fomented rebellion. When the royal advisors began to realize the seriousness of the discontent, the excavation project became even more important. The king's military strategists pointed out the difficulty of defending the capital city from attack, since the site had been selected centuries before precisely for its accessibility. The palace was too soft and sprawling to be protected from attack and, besides, it was almost deserted. The royal family preferred to spend its time Inside. To the fascination of the whole world, an enormous drape was stitched, a huge patchwork quilt that took the seamstresses of the capital decades to stitch together. The resulting shortages of textile materials launched the fortunes of a great many trading houses, and the difficulty of finding a qualified tailor stimulated the growth of several southern cities, the current Haranamous among them.

At last the patchwork was finished, and at enormous cost in both wealth and lives it was draped across the side of the mountain and over that part of the palace that adjoined it. For half a century the rumors only continued to grow, until a great storm swept through the Middle Mountains and tore the well-weathered veil away, revealing the demolition of a huge chunk of the palace and, in its place, the Outer Portal. The people were shocked. They'd expected much more for their sacrifice—all that expense and all that secrecy just to build this? Their disappointment with the royal family exploded into warfare against one another. The differences of opinion that had already fragmented the society internally now found expression through armies committed to ompeting ideals. The One Land broke apart. But since the king was Inside, he never noticed that it had happened. None of his advisors bothered to tell him. They'd never told his offspring either . . .

"You don't intend to tell him at all, do you?"

"That's none of your concern," Garney told Seagryn as they reached an intersection and turned left. The arched ceilings of each of these avenues had been lined with shiny, yellow ceramic tile, so they were far better lit and much more cheerful than the throne room had been. They wouldn't remain cheerful for long . . .

"There's a dragon outside his door, but if he looked out to see it he might notice that his kingdom is gone. Is that it?"

Garney halted abruptly and spun around to face him. "It is not your affair!"

"It *is* my affair! If that dragon remains in the Central Gate for very long, it'll starve everyone in these caves to death, myself included!"

"These are not caves," Garney corrected firmly. "This is the Court of the One Land, and you are a guest in it. I cannot emphasize this point strongly enough—we are in control."

"Oh, really?" Seagryn mocked.

"I'm on my way to a meeting of the crisis management team, where together we will prepare some response to the beast's presence. Or did you think that we knew nothing about it until your intrusion? We called the meeting this morning at the first sight of the dragon!"

"Why didn't you say so?" Seagryn said, encouraged at last. "I can quickly fill you in on where the beast has been and the way it—"

"You can? You will not be there. You will be here—" Garney swung open a door to a well-furnished—if windowless—apartment. "—eating, and then resting."

"Eating?" Seagryn said, more pleading in his voice than he would have liked. Garney pushed him inside, and he found there was indeed a table, already spread with a delicious-looking feast.

"You'll see," Garney explained with a touch of unexpected patience, "that we have far more provisions stored Inside than you might expect. We have always been prepared for a siege—

always. And you may rest assured that we know far better than you do how to manage our internal affairs. Please eat until you're satisfied, then rest. Your performance is not scheduled until this evening.''

"My performance?"

"Your magic act," Garney said. "For the Children's Club."

"But I'm no—"

"You'll think of something. But do not, please, turn yourself into that awful-smelling animal! This is an enclosed space, and we find offensive odors very difficult to dispel!"

Seagryn eyed the food hungrily, but something concerned him. He glanced at the door and realized that it could only be locked from the outside. "Am I a prisoner?" he asked flatly.

Garney pinched the bridge of his nose and snorted in frustration. He then raised his hands in a gesture that seemed to plead for understanding. "How are we to make a prisoner of a wizard? I've just asked you not to become that stinking beast! Why would I then encourage you to do exactly that by foolishly attempting to lock you in?" Garney sighed, then stepped to the doorway. "You're free to wander where you choose, but I warn you—don't get lost. And if you think that would be difficult, think again. I was born Inside, and yet that is my deepest fear . . ." Garney's gaze seemed to focus elsewhere. Seagryn guessed he was either remembering nightmares or scolding himself for being so self-revealing. Suddenly his eyes snapped back into this room and to Seagryn's face. "Until later," he said, then he left, closing the door behind him.

Seagryn stepped to it and listened but didn't hear the lock turn. Instead he heard the little man's heels clicking officiously as he stalked away. Seagryn wasted no more time getting to the table.

Much later—and much fuller—he arose and stumbled gratefully toward the large bed in the next room. He'd not slept in a bed since he'd left his home. As he tumbled across this one, home was where his thoughts turned. How was Elaryl? Had she forgiven him? What was she thinking about right now?

Suddenly it seemed he stood beside her, within her father's house. She sat on a sun-porch surrounded by beautiful flowering plants. But while Seagryn was entranced by their glory, Elaryl didn't seem to be aware of them at all. Her jaw was set, her brow creased with worry, and her mind was obviously miles away. Searching for his?

"Elaryl," he said, and she gasped and sat up. She stared right at him, but her startled expression didn't fade. Instead it seemed to deepen toward genuine fear. "Elaryl, it's me."

"It's—it's you? Seagryn, are you—you look so—thin—"

He smiled. "I'm afraid I've not been eating well lately—"

"No, I mean—like thin air! Like—a ghost!" The blood drained from her face, which made him sad. "You're not dead—are you?" She asked this with both hope and resignation, as if the two feelings had been warring inside her for many days.

"I'm not dead."

"Where are you?" she gasped, standing up and trying to reach out for him. He reached for her, too, but his hands passed right through her.

"I'm—I'm not there, obviously. I'm Inside—"

"Inside the dragon!" she gasped.

"No! No." He chuckled. "Inside what we've always called the Remnant. The dragon is out in the Central Gate. I've been flying around on it for the last week."

"I know," she said quietly, her eyes lidding protectively. "I watched you fly over."

"You did?" he asked brightly, but she didn't brighten in response.

"When are you coming home?" she asked flatly.

"When—when it's—all done."

Elaryl nodded, and he saw in her eyes that hope had just surrendered, and resignation had conquered at last. "Very well."

"But I'll be back!"

She nodded again but looked away. He watched her, grateful that this was only a dream. After a moment she murmured, "Father left today. Naturally, he wouldn't tell me where he was going, but I know it was to one of those secret meetings." She looked at him. "Is it being held there, where you are? Is he going to run into the dragon on the way?"

Seagryn struggled to make sense of her question. He was so tired! Then he remembered the conversation he'd overheard between Garney and Wilker. "No. No, the Conspiracy is meeting elsewhere. I don't know where, exactly, but it's not here. And he should be safe—from the dragon, at least. I expect Vicia-Heinox to linger in the Central Gate until something is done to drive it away."

"He's safe," she murmured. "But you're not." She looked back at him, then squinted her eyes. "You're fading."

"I am?" Seagryn looked at his hands—and realized he had no

hands. When he glanced back up, Elaryl's eyes had left his and settled absently on a yellow fern.

"I've talked to the Power, Seagryn, ever since you left. I think—" Her voice caught, and her eyes clouded over before she could finish. "I think I may be the only one who is. Everyone hates you, my father included, and I—I don't know—what to think." She looked back at him and sniffed. "I don't trust you, Seagryn. I'm sorry, but I don't." As the sadness filled him again, she looked back down at the table and folded her hands across her lap. "But I trust that One Whose Name Once Went Unspoken. If anything good can come from this insanity, the Power will bring it about."

"Elaryl," he said, but she didn't look at him, and then it seemed as if she slipped away from him, or, rather, he from her. It seemed as if he slid backward down an endless hallway, and it grew dark around him as she receded into a single point of light . . .

Then he awoke. He sat up and blinked his eyes, then rubbed them, and fell backward across the bed again. A dream. A very real and lifelike dream. Wishful thinking—he'd wanted so much to see her. "But then," he muttered, sitting back up again, "all of my shaping is wishful thinking . . ."

He'd slept enough. And somewhere in this sunless land a meeting was taking place, a meeting he ought to be a party to. Seagryn jumped off the bed and a moment later was out into the bright yellow corridor. Having no idea which way he needed to go, he picked a direction and started walking. Before long, he had passed through two intersecting avenues and approached a widening of the corridor. A moment later he stood on the edge of a far larger cavern than the throne room, filled to its distant, dark ceiling with structures—roofed structures, which probably hadn't needed reroofing since the day they were built. This, incredibly, was a village. He stepped into the first shop.

A moment later Seagryn stumbled back out of it, his face bright red. He'd walked into a spa of some kind, a huge room filled with mineral baths and nude bathers. In his youth, he'd been told of the terrible decadence of the Remnant. Whether this was decadent or not, Seagryn had to admit that he was unaccustomed to such a level of sophistication.

He walked more cautiously through another door and discovered an expensive-looking clothing shop, staffed—to his great relief—by fully dressed clerks. He was at first surprised to note they wore the blue and red colors of the House of Paumer, then realized he shouldn't be. Paumer's colors showed up everywhere in the old One Land, underscoring the merchant's worldwide influence. He approached a clerk, who smiled at him brightly. "Pardon me, but could you direct me to the center of government?"

"The what?" The young lady frowned.

"Where are the offices of the Remnant—where government meetings take place?"

She still frowned. "I don't understand."

Seagryn tried again. "Where would I find the primary advisors to the king?"

The young woman chewed on her lip and gazed reflectively over his head. A moment later she looked back down at him, her face expressing clearly her own puzzlement. "You could try the library . . ."

"The library?"

"I've never actually been inside it myself, but maybe they could help you. It's right down there by the—" and she swept into a series of directions that sounded like the solution to a maze, with left turns, right turns, stairways, ramps, and cautions that left him thoroughly confused. All this was accompanied by much smiling and gesturing, and ended with, "Have you got it?"

"I think so," Seagryn lied with a smile. He stepped slowly out of the shop with a new appreciation of Garney's warning not to get lost. He started retracing his steps, fearful now that he might not be able to find his way back to his assigned apartment. The yellow corridors all looked the same to him, and he couldn't recall, now, how many intersections he'd passed through to arrive at this cavern. Fear suddenly clutched at his stomach—with no sun to point the way, how could he ever find his bearings if he *did* prove to be lost? Was there a map room somewhere?

He wandered anxiously down the hall, carefully examining the walls on either side for some familiar distinguishing mark. He found none, and his anxiety grew. Once he was missed, would Garney send out a search party to find him? He felt no better when he arrived at what he thought was his own corridor, turned down it, and discovered that it opened onto another high-ceilinged cavern containing an even larger cluster of roofed dwellings, most of these three and four stories tall. There was no question about it. He was lost. He stepped into a shop and looked at a young male clerk, who eyed him curiously. "I'm a visiting magician from the outside. Could you get me to the Children's Club?"

Chapter Six

✖✖✖✖

SOVEREIGN'S SOLUTION

WHEN Seagryn beheld the Children's Club for the first time, he at last had some idea why those who lived within the Remnant could not conceive of life anywhere else. The largest cavern he had visited so far contained enough amusements to keep a child— or an adult, for that matter—entertained for weeks. The dark ceiling high overhead reminded him of a moonless summer evening, lit from below by a lively little city. A small lake filled the center of the cavern. Lights from the far shore sparkled across its surface as sailboats glided along on top of it, evidently propelled by drafts blowing from the many arching corridors that opened onto all sides of the cave. A sandy beach circled the lake, and everywhere he looked lovers strolled hand in hand. Row upon row of lamplit avenues climbed away from the lake, with the highest ring of shops backing up to the cavern wall. Children of all ages ran in and out of these shops and fun houses, shouting and laughing so gleefully that, for a moment, Seagryn disapproved. What time of the day was it? Why weren't these children in school? Then he caught himself and wondered if he was jealous. His own upbringing had been harsh—textured by the dust of the farmlands and the hard faces of the Western District peasants. Sunlight there had sharply divided day from night, and a child could only wring free time from the demanding schedule by working faster or by shirking responsibilities. In this timeless place there were no fields to be plowed nor herds to be tended. What were children to do apart from amusing themselves?

What was the king to do? Seagryn thought he could understand, now, why the man had looked so bored this afternoon. Or had it been morning? Was it evening now? Who could tell? He wondered without enthusiasm when his magic act was scheduled, but more important now was where this was to take place. He asked his helpful guide, and the young clerk pointed to a series of larger buildings on the far side of the lake, surrounded by torchlit, columned walkways. "You see the one with the dome? That's the library. The performance center is the building to its left."

The library! The girl in the dress shop had suggested he might find the answers to his questions there. The youth smiled expectantly and turned his palm up. Seagryn grabbed it and shook it vigorously. He then walked briskly away, fully understanding the young man's look of disgust but making a point of ignoring it. In Lamath, you helped people for free. Besides, he had no idea what they used for money in this place.

He struck off quickly around the lake, pleased that he'd found the library after all and pleased to be experiencing this beautiful cavern. It would be a shame for all of this to be destroyed—the builders of the Remnant had created the perfect illusion of a summer's evening. He longed to have Elaryl walking beside him.

The library dome loomed high above him long before he reached it, and he saw it was much bigger than it had appeared from the far side of the lake. He was finding it difficult to get a proper perspective on things Inside. The closer he got, the more crowded the avenue became, and he expected to have to struggle against the press, once he got within the library's halls. Instead, he found the place deserted, except for one surprised old gentleman who turned to meet him as he walked through the door. "Why are you here?" the old man demanded.

Taken aback, Seagryn answered, "Why am I here? This is the library, isn't it?"

"It certainly is," the white-haired old man countered, sizing up Seagryn's build as if he were considering a physical attack. "Are you authorized to enter it?"

Seagryn stared. "This isn't a public library?"

"Doesn't it say so on the building? We're only here to serve the public." The librarian sniffed. "Of course, no member of the public ever comes in here."

"Why is that?"

"They don't care," the librarian said firmly, and he shook his head in dismay and repeated to himself, "They don't care." Then his eyes stabbed back at Seagryn. "The only people who ever come in here are spies!" His eyes narrowed. "Now what is it you're after?"

"Ah . . . I . . . just wanted some information—"

"There. I knew it." The librarian scowled triumphantly. "Didn't I know it? You're a spy, aren't you?"

"I . . . no . . . I'm . . ." It had worked before. Seagryn tried it again. "I'm a magician from the outside. I've come to do a magic show for the Children's Club."

"Then why aren't you doing it?"

"I . . . just thought I . . ."

"You just thought you'd pop into the library for a little—*information*." The librarian made this word drip with sinister intent. "And what sort of information would a magician from the outside be interested in? Do you mind telling me that?"

Seagryn stared at the old man, then turned his gaze to examine the row upon row of books and shelves that climbed up the walls of this dome, just as the streets and shops outside climbed the circumference of the cavern. And he guessed, in a way, he *was* a spy. "I'm looking for Garney, Keeper of the Outer Portal. He was meeting with others of your leaders to talk about a national problem you have sitting on your front porch. A dragon."

"So." The librarian grinned broadly. "You are a spy."

"Not by my intention."

"I knew it." The old gentleman smiled, obviously pleased with himself.

"Do you know where Garney is, and where this meeting might be taking place?" Seagryn asked.

"Of course. I'm the Keeper of the Annals—I know everything that goes on within the Royal Advisory Board."

"Then you could direct me to him?"

"I could." The Keeper of the Annals nodded. "But the information wouldn't do you any good, since you'll be in the company of the light bearers."

"The light bearers?" Seagryn frowned.

"Yes. I sent for them as soon as you came in. I knew you were a spy."

"What are the light bearers?" It sounded to Seagryn like the name for some religious cult.

The Keeper of the Annals gave him a superior smile. "Since you're from the outside, I trust you would know them as the police."

The front door of the library burst open, and a group of uniformed warriors carrying torches suddenly filled the room, forming a ring around Seagryn. He remembered the cut of the uniforms now. It had been a group of guards dressed just like these who had expelled him and the other members of the Conspiracy through the hole he'd made into the mountain over a year ago. Seagryn wondered if he could find that room again and reopen the hole for a quick exit. He was growing weary of the attempt to warn these people of their danger. The very idea that only spies used the library! "Forget it," he snarled as he pushed through the circle of light bearers and stalked out the door. No one tried to stop him, not even the librarian, for Seagryn had just invented a new spell, and it was working quite effectively. "I think I'll call that a memory block," he mumbled to himself as he turned up the lamplit street and started walking back around the lake. "I'll have to tell Nebalath about it the next time I see him."

Back in the library, the light bearers were asking the librarian what they were doing there, and he was responding to them with equal confusion. But the answer to every such incursion came to him easily. "Spies!" he was shouting at them. "You're all spies!"

Seagryn left the gigantic cavern quickly, intent on somehow finding his way back to the throne room and out of this place. The yellow corridor he had chosen made a long, sweeping curve to the left, so he heard the oncoming soldiers before he saw them. These had to be more light bearers. This time he simply cloaked himself from view and stepped back against the cool surface of the tiled wall. Sure enough, a column of torch-bearing warriors trotted into view, led by none other than Garney himself. Seagryn started to reveal himself to the little man but decided against it. He assumed they were coming from the Outer Portal; if so, he was heading in the right direction.

Of course, I could be wrong, he thought to himself a moment later when this corridor came to a dead end. He wasn't blocked entirely—while the main corridor came to a dead end at a wall of raw stone, a small rampway curled down to his left. As he stood contemplating his options, he heard the tramping feet of soldiers jogging back up the corridor. The light bearers had turned around and were returning.

"Spread out across the corridor!" he heard Garney shout. "Link arms so that we don't run past him if he's cloaking himself!"

Seagryn frowned and ran down the spiraling rampway. After one full turn, he had a choice. The ramp opened onto a lower level, and he could either go that way or continue on down the curve. Where, he wondered, was that outside room where the Conspiracy had met? If he could find the outer wall he could break through to the mountain, but it seemed as if that would be up and not down—

The tramping on the ramp above him grew faster. He decided to go on down.

This is ridiculous, he told himself silently. Why am I running? As a powershaper, there were dozens of other ways he could deal with the warriors who pursued him. Yet he continued to run while he thought. When the ramp opened again onto a still-lower level, he realized at least part of the reason he fled instead of standing to fight: The more he saw of the Remnant, the more intimidated he became. How big was this place? What a monumental task it must have been to carve these passageways from the rock! How long had it taken, and who had done the digging? Of course, the megasin could have carved these galleries easily . . .

He stumbled to a stop and listened. Fewer feet pounded along above him, so Garney was evidently breaking up the detail to follow different avenues. Seagryn continued down the ramp, descending still deeper into this impressive maze. After two more full spirals, the rampway ended, opening onto a passageway that looked more like a cave than a corridor. As in the galleries above, torches guttered in brackets spaced evenly along the wall. But these walls were raw—they'd not yet been tiled over with those civilizing yellow ceramic squares. Seagryn felt relieved to find that this enormous underground nation did have its limitations. And while he felt both a responsibility to see the people of this place warned of their danger and frustration with the Remnant's leadership's attempts to prevent him from doing so, he also felt a keen curiosity to explore further the secrets of the maze. He walked swiftly up the curving tunnel—and stopped. A cavern opened before him. A pitch-black cavern.

His curiosity wavered. Enough light spilled around him from the torches behind to illuminate a few yards into the cavern, but this discouraged him more than it urged him to go forward. He didn't fear the dark, exactly, but it reminded him of a fearful time: days—or perhaps even weeks—spent as a captive in just such a black tomb. Only a miracle had allowed his escape—a miracle and a promise to the megasin who'd imprisoned him that he would introduce her someday to a more permanent companion. Where was the megasin these days? Could she be somewhere out there in that inky blackness, watching him?

The sounds of soldiers on the ramp above pushed him into the darkness at last. He could have shaped a ball of fire above his head—that same trick that had bored the king—but that would certainly have pinpointed his location for the pursuing torch bearers. Instead—and this felt odd to him, even as he did it—he cloaked himself, as if his best protection in a place where he was blind was to make others blind to his presence. He walked forward.

He'd been in several large caverns already this—morning? Evening? Whether because of the lack of light or because of his fear or both, this cave seemed to dwarf them all. The pool of light that spilled from the tunnel behind him shrank smaller and smaller, while at the same time he became aware of a vast emptiness opening above him. Was this a natural cave, or had it been carved by the Remnant's engineers? He recalled now how regular had been the shape of the grotto that contained the lake and the library—like a soup bowl inverted over a platter. It seemed this space might share that shape, for he judged himself to be dipping down every twenty yards from one level to another, still-lower level. He felt a great surge of confidence as his mental prediction of when the next dip would occur proved correct. It evaporated the next moment when he stumbled over something and went sprawling forward in the darkness.

He landed with a clank upon a pile of coiled chain. He could tell that much by feel. Frustrated at himself for not watching where he was going, he was about to form a ball of light when he heard voices behind him in the brightly illuminated tunnel. He rolled quietly to his feet beside the chain and turned back to watch as a group of torch-bearing warriors stopped at the cavern's edge and quietly discussed whether they should continue on or not.

"Why would he go in there?"

"He's a wizard—he's liable to go anyplace."

"Just as likely to be above us somewhere, then, as to try to make his way through the dark."

"Besides—if he's in there, the little ones probably have him already. Let's go back up." The torch bearers appeared to be weary of tramping purposefully about. They shuffled back up the ramp, murmuring quietly among themselves, and Seagryn was left to wonder who, or what, were the "little ones"? Then he heard the whispers around him.

"They're gone."

"Who were they looking for?"

"I *told* you! There was a figure in the tunnel! I saw it—then I didn't."

"Too much light, Merkle! How could you see anything in that

glare?'' These two voices came from between him and the light.
The next came from either side of him.

"Nothing over here."

"Nor here."

"I tell you I heard someone clanking over the chain! And you
heard them talking! He's a wizard, they say, and you know how
wizards are!"

"I know absolutely nothing about wizards, Merkle. Let's go."

"You're not going to convince me I didn't hear what I heard.
The sound came from right—Unnfh! Help! Someone's got me!
The wizard's got me!"

Seagryn had acted on reflex, not thought. When a figure the
size of a child bumped into him hard, Seagryn had stooped to
catch him. He was trying to prevent Merkle from falling, not to
capture him. He immediately put the struggling little man down
and stepped a few paces away. Unfortunately he stumbled over
another tiny figure, tripped, and fell himself.

"Right here! I've got him right here!" This little person
grabbed his legs and held them fast. The fellow had a powerful
grip. Feet scuttled toward them in the darkness and Seagryn
thought of insects and shuddered. "He's trembling!"

Light blossomed like a brilliant orange flower above them, and
Seagryn got his first good look at the little ones. They were all
around him—twenty or more figures the height of four-year-old
children but with arms as big around as his own. He thought at
first they had no eyes, but realized quickly that they were all just
squinting their eyes shut. Several reeled backward, hiding their
faces from that brilliant ball of flame, but those who had hold of
him—there were several now—did not release their grip.

"Oww!" the one called Merkle groaned, and he gripped Seagryn's legs more tightly. "Put that out, would you? I can't see!"

"But I can't see without it—" Seagryn explained.

" 'Course not! You're a light-lover. Put it out!"

"You let go of my legs first!" Seagryn demanded.

"If I let go of your legs you'll run away!"

"If you *don't* let go of my legs I'll light this place up like the
Capital Cathedral!" Naturally that image held no meaning for the
little man, but Seagryn knew exactly what it meant, and when
the grip on his legs and several other portions of his anatomy
grew even tighter, he remembered how the high holy place of
City Lamath had looked on celebration days and imagined
that same amount of candlelight in here. The cavern burst into

illumination, and the little ones around him shrieked with pain. Merkle let go. Quickly.

"Put it out! Put it out! Put it out!" Merkle pleaded, and Seagryn did—eventually. First, however, he took a good look at his surroundings, as well as at the tiny little persons who rolled around in pain upon this evenly shaved rock platform. He had been right— this cavern *was* bigger than the lake room above them. And he had found new reason to be grateful to the Power: the circumstances that had prevented him from going any further into the darkness had kept him from tumbling into a basin carved in the cavern's center. Evidently designed to hold an even larger lake, it would have been a thirty-foot drop. He gasped in relief, then doused the lights. Equally relieved sighs greeted his action. It took only a moment for the band of little people to recover and reassert themselves.

"Who are you?" a voice—not Merkle's—demanded.

"You're a wizard, obviously. Why?"

"Why what?" Seagryn asked. He heard several inquiring grunts. "You want to know why I am a wizard? Or why I'm down here?"

"I'd like to know both, myself."

Seagryn recognized the voice. "To tell you the truth, Merkle, I would, too." His answer caused a sensation.

"He knows Merkle!"

"Merkle knows him!"

"How does this wizard know Merkle?"

And from Merkle himself, "How do you know my name? Was it by—magic?"

"The megasin told me, Merkle," Seagryn answered. "She says she knows you well."

Perhaps it was the intensity of these little people that had piqued his dormant playfulness and caused him to answer thus. They did, after all, take themselves quite seriously, and Seagryn found it difficult to keep from smiling broadly at that. Or maybe it was talking into the darkness that summoned again those chilling memories of days spent underground. In either case, Seagryn couldn't anticipate the reaction his words received.

First there was silence. Then, in almost-holy tones, a voice said, "You know the megasin?"

"Why? Do *you* all know her?" He heard tiny feet quietly shuffling away from him. "Wait! I was teasing. . . !"

"The megasin knows *me*?" Merkle muttered, obviously horrified. At least he wasn't leaving.

"No, Merkle, she doesn't know you. I picked up your name from the others'. comments to you. Why does my mention of the megasin terrify you so much?"

Merkle paused a moment before answering. Seagryn heard only silence and guessed that the others had left them alone together. "It's just that—" The little man hesitated. "—no light-lover has ever spoken of her before—that I know about. I thought she was just a legend we use to frighten children into good behavior . . ."

"Oh, no," Seagryn said quickly, and he was immediately sorry. He hadn't realize until just now how horrible this affirmation might be to a darkness-dweller. "Well, I mean I have met her, and she is real, but she's a long way from this place, I can assure you."

"How can you assure me of that when the megasin swims through rock? She does, doesn't she?"

"Ah—" He'd never thought of it that way, but it was a perfect image. "Yes, I suppose she does."

"And she could be swimming right at us this very moment—"

"Perhaps, but why—"

"And she eats digger children for breakfast, and adults for dinner and supper—"

"No," Seagryn said firmly. "On that point let me reassure you. The megasin eats dreams. She eats peoples' feelings, not the people themselves. If she did, I wouldn't be standing here."

"I said she eats diggers, not light-lovers," Merkle grumbled quietly.

"You little people are these 'diggers'?"

"Of course."

They stood there in the silence a moment, each thinking his own thoughts. Seagryn was angry at himself. Here he was, destroying the security of a tiny man in a black cavern under the earth, while outside this cave a dragon he'd set free destroyed the well-being of the nations on the surface. What a troublemaker! Wherever he went he brought grief!

"Are you hungry?" Merkle asked, and Seagryn was surprised.

"Why—yes. Yes, I am." He'd had a good meal earlier, but he'd done a lot of walking since then. Besides, he'd not eaten regularly for days.

"Fine. Let's go eat." Merkle started away, but Seagryn didn't move. "You coming?" the little man called.

"I—can't see you. Would you rather I made a light—"

"No!"

"I mean just a little light, or would you rather take my hand and—" He stopped, for Merkle had grabbed his hand and was leading him, as nearly as he could tell, in a wide circle around the perimeter of the pit. Seagryn had a new thought. What did these little people—diggers—eat?

"You'll have to duck your head," Merkle advised him after they had been walking for several minutes.

"Where are we?"

"At the door of the double row," Merkle replied. "But you light-lovers are too tall—"

"Oww—" Seagryn grunted, for despite ducking low he evidently hadn't stooped quite low enough, and he skinned his forehead.

"You see what I mean?"

"No," Seagryn grumbled. "I told you, I can't see *anything*. How far are we from where we're going?"

Merkle had a ready answer. "Four bisfults." Long before Seagryn fully understood what bisfults were and how they related to aboveground measurements, Merkle whistled musically and Seagryn heard a door open in response.

"Who's this, then?" a tiny female voice demanded.

"He's an outlaw wizard from above we found stumbling about in the new shell," Merkle told her. "He's hungry, and I am, too."

"Get in then." Her response was muffled, for the woman was now moving away from them.

"My wife Mickle," Merkle explained. "You'll have to stoop still lower." Seagryn obeyed and followed Merkle inside.

He would have loved to have shined a little light into this home, just to see if it looked the way it felt. He sat at a low table in a chair designed for a child, aware that Merkle had sat down across the table from him and that other, still smaller diggers scuttled about in the darkness, watching him and commenting to one another. "You have children?"

"You're surrounded by them."

"How many?"

Rather than count them, Merkle called the roll. "There's Mackle and Muckle, Micheal and Meekel, Muskel and Markle and Minicle and—others." Someone—Mickle, Seagryn supposed—set dishes in front of them.

"Eat," she said. With some trepidation, Seagryn ate.

The food proved to be the same as that found in any Lamathian market—although some of it Lamathians preferred to eat cooked. He'd seen no sign of the use of fire among these people, which made sense; flames would have hurt their terribly sensitive eyes, besides filling an enclosed area with smoke. There was no meat—mostly fruit and nuts, as well as dried beans that hurt Seagryn's teeth. But how did they come to have these things if they had no contact with the light-loving villages in the shafts above? "Where does your food come from?"

"Up there," Merkle grunted, still crunching.

"They give it to you?"

"We trade for it."

"Trade what?"

"Jewels. Water."

"Water?" Seagryn asked.

"There's water running all through this rock. We know how and where to tap it to take it to where they want it to flow. We're their plumbers."

Seagryn nodded. "And I remember all the jewels in the throne room—"

"We find a lot of those. Can't understand what they want them for, since they're just rocks. But they're always asking for more."

"They give off a beautiful sparkle!" Seagryn explained, adding a bit lamely, "In the light, of course."

"Can't understand the attraction," Merkle said frankly, "but they send us a lot of food for those particular rocks, and we're careful to keep all we find."

"How do you tell that you have one?" Seagryn asked. "I mean—you can't see it, can you?"

Merkle chuckled. "When you work with the rock all the time you come to understand it. We can see it, much better than you can, but we can also feel it, and all rock has a different feel. These gemstones the light-lovers care so much for tend to be very hard. They're easy to find."

Mickle was trying to feed the children, but they evidently found the large stranger in their dining room too fascinating to concern themselves with eating. "You'd better eat," she scolded, "because if you don't, that wall over there will open and the—"

"Don't even say it!" Merkle called to her.

"What?" the woman asked, confused. "Why not?"

"Because I know things about the megasin I never knew before. This man has talked to her!"

Seagryn heard gasps all around. A moment later he had to smile, because he could now hear the earnest crunching of a number of childish mouths.

"How long have your people been down here?" he asked, but

he realized it was a foolish question before he even got it out of his mouth. Any answer he could understand would be based on cycles of a sun these people had never seen and hoped never *to* see. Even so, Merkle tried to answer.

"This is where we live—where we've always lived. We've worked with you light-lovers ever since you came into the rock, and I've been told it's been good. Better for our people than it was before, anyway. My mother's mother's mother's father once told me what he'd been told: That we've traded gemstones for food forever. Now, of course, our biggest work is cutting the new shells. The one we found you in is almost finished—they'll come down to take it over soon, and we'll move on to start another."

Seagryn doubted that. The food he ate came ultimately from the outside, borne here on the backs of Paumer House packhorses. Now that Vicia-Heinox sat in the Central Gate, how long would it be before the food stopped coming down to the diggers? "Can you get me to the outside?" Seagryn asked suddenly. "I mean, tunnel up to near the surface of the mountain and let me break on through it?"

"Why would you want to do that?"

Seagryn never had the chance to explain. A whistle beyond the door caused Merkle to rise and go to open it. When he did, light flooded into the tiny home. The children shouted in pain, and Merkle quickly closed it, but in that brief flash Seagryn had a glimpse of this place he would never forget—a simple, homey dwelling decorated not much differently from homes above, except that the emphasis here seemed to be on coordinating a variety of textures rather than colors. He would remember those tiny, childish faces that sat surrounding him—faces of children who would die, he feared, if he didn't help the Remnant resolve the dragon problem. But how was he to do that if they wouldn't listen? And how was he to do that while under arrest, for those outside were obviously torch bearers who had tracked him to this place. Merkle now negotiated with his neighbors through the door.

"But the man is a guest!"

"They have lights out here, Merkle! And they're not going to go up without him."

"He hasn't finished eating!" Merkle pleaded.

"So let them feed him up there!"

Merkle shifted to a whisper. "He knows the megasin!"

That drew silence from the diggers on the other side of the door—a pause that aggravated the warriors' impatience. Someone began pounding and shouting for Seagryn to come out. There really seemed to be no choice. He liked this little man and his not-so-little family, and he didn't wish to cause them any further trouble with the authorities. "I'm coming!" he shouted back, and the pounding stopped. Then he turned in what he thought was Merkle's direction and thanked him for his hospitality and help.

"Come back, Wizard," Merkle invited. "Tell us more about the megasin."

Light from the torches beyond drew an outline of the door, and Seagryn followed it out. As he held his hands up against the glare, he expected to be grabbed and wrestled toward the rampway; but instead, the torch bearers seemed to step back from him in respect. He guessed his reputation as a powershaper had preceeded him.

"I told you not to get lost," Garney said, and Seagryn struggled to focus his eyes on the little man. From the sound of his voice, he was smiling.

"I was being chased."

"Only because we have need of you in the throne room."

Seagryn could see more clearly now, and he gazed at Garney hopefully. "Really? Are you ready to listen?" Now he could tell; that wasn't a smile on Garney's face—it was a grimace.

"When a dragon is burning your Outer Portal, you must do *something*," Garney said, trembling. "Come!" The column of torch bearers left the little people to their darkness and their dinner.

"Is the fire out?" the king demanded as soon as Garney led Seagryn back into the throne room. Garney immediately fell to his knees and answered.

"My Only King, as I told you before—we have managed to put out the fire, but not without cost. We lost three good men to the blaze—plus, of course, the warrior the dragon ate."

"Did the warrior talk to the beast?" Seagryn asked Garney quietly.

"Yes! Hush!" Garney hissed.

"Big mistake," Seagryn muttered, and Garney shushed him again. "What did the dragon say?"

"He was looking for you!" Garney whispered fiercely. "Now will you shut your mouth and let me deal with my sovereign?"

"Who is that man with you?" the king demanded. This came as a surprise to Seagryn. Hadn't it been only hours ago that he had been formally introduced in this very room?

"As I've told you, my Gracious One, this is Seagryn, a magician from the outer provinces who has had some dealings with the dragon before—''

"Wilker should be handling this," the enraged king roared. "But where is Wilker? Garney, where is he? I've assigned the two of you full responsibility for what takes place among the outer peasants, and yet here we are, faced with this nuisance of a dragon, and Wilker's not even Inside!''

"My Everything," Garney pleaded, "it's obvious that Wilker has foreseen this difficulty and is out among the peasants even now, trying to find a resolution for this problem from amongst their ranks—''

"Ridiculous. The outer peasants cause problems, they don't resolve them. Where's the Keeper of the Annals?"

"Right here, King Over All that Is and Has Been." The gray-haired old gentleman from the library stepped forward, making a point of not looking in Seagryn's direction.

"Isn't that true? Haven't all problems been resolved from Inside?"

"Of course it's true," the Keeper of the Annals snapped. "I taught you that myself, years ago.''

If there was any rebuke in the words, the king missed it. "So then, Garney, can you explain why it is that Wilker would choose this day, of all days, to absent himself?"

"My Gracious King," Garney began with heartfelt respect. "You are absolutely right in every regard. Wilker chose a poor day for it, departing against my personal advice. But neither of us could have known that such a catastrophe would pick this day to occur. As I told you before, we did have some indication from this visiting magician that trouble was afoot—evidently this beast has been a growing problem out in the provinces. So I've enlisted the magician's aid—not to try to solve the problem for us, which would be foolish—but to make suggestions. After all, Seagryn the magician has built up quite a reputation in the world outside.''

That much is true, Seagryn thought to himself. Quite a reputation.

The king was not impressed. "He hasn't shown *me* anything."

"Nevertheless, he has had conversations with this dragon and perhaps could share insights that would—''

"He's a spy." The Keeper of the Annals sniffed.

"A spy!" The king gasped, sitting up on his throne. "For whom?"

"Oh, you know," the old man muttered. "Negative elements. The riffraff. The occasional collection of criminals who band themselves together out there, thinking that they might somehow gain our attention. Naturally, the first place they come is the library, to see if we've made any reference to their existence. He's just a spy.''

"Hmm," the king said thoughtfully.

"We had another spy Inside several months ago," the librarian continued. "Claimed to be a relative of that peasant we often trade with—what's his name, Garney?''

"The boy?" Garney asked.

"No, the father.''

"Oh," Garney said, nodding. "Paumer.''

"Yes, Paumer." The Keeper of the Annals remembered. Then he continued to the king. "The lad claimed to be Paumer's son and spent several days rooting around in the book stacks before we found him. He was a spy, like this one. We expelled him, of course—just as we should do with this so-called 'magician'!''

"Yes, expel me!" Seagryn called up to the king. "Let me go talk to the dragon for you!''

An embarrassed gasp greeted his outburst. "Didn't I tell you," the mortified Garney whispered, "that you may not address the king directly?''

The King of the One Land looked down his handsome nose at this impertinent magic-maker from the outside and sniffed with annoyance. "Let a spy speak for the One Land? How ridiculous." Then he glanced around. "Where are the other members of the Royal Advisory Board?''

"There was some announcement of a magic show to be performed shortly," a rather tall man to Seagryn's left announced. Seagryn wanted to ask what he was Keeper of but thought better of it.

Garney had evidently gathered his shattered wits about him, for he now spoke up again. "Might I make a suggestion, my King?''

"Why do you think I employ you, Garney?" the king grumbled. "Speak up!''

"I realize he is not qualified to represent us, and certainly he is as rude as any country bumpkin who ever set foot inside this august court. But there may be merit in letting this Seagryn address the dragon.''

"What?" The king frowned.

"He has spoken to the dragon before, which is apparently a rather dangerous task, as one unfortunate member of my staff has already demonstrated. Rather than risk the lives of any more of our people, let us send him out to request of the beast that he go elsewhere.''

"Ridiculous." The Keeper of the Annals snorted. ''Send an outer peasant to parlay for us? It's never been done before. Never.''

"We've never before had a dragon at our gate!" Garney exploded. The little man had finally lost his temper.

An argument ensued between the Keeper of the Outer Portal and the Keeper of the Annals, but neither the king nor Seagryn listened to it. The king appeared to be thinking; from the pained look on his face, this was evidently something he didn't often do. Suddenly he stood up and shouted, "Silence!" The argument ceased. All eyes in the room turned to the top of the dais to see what the king would say.

"I have the solution," he announced. "We'll neither send this peasant out to speak to the dragon for us, nor will we risk any more of our warriors in conversation with the beast. Instead, we will mobilize the army of the One Land to do battle with it and destroy this beast forever.''

There was a long pause before anyone ventured to speak. It was Garney who was at last brave enough to break the silence. "And—how shall we do that, my King?''

"How shall we do what?''

"Pardon," Garney pleaded, dropping again to his knees, "but I am asking what is to be our plan of battle?''

"Oh," the king murmured thoughtfully. "Well, we'll—we'll all just charge the thing!''

After another moment's pause, the throne room burst into activity. The king had spoken. The One Land was going to war.

Chapter Seven

※※※※

CONSPIRING MINDS

Nᴇʙᴀʟᴀᴛʜ's decision to follow Paumer's spy paid off immediately. The journey through the Marwilds took most of a day, but they finally came out of the forest and onto fields Nebalath thought looked familiar. They soon were within sight of a small mansion the wizard thought he'd visited before. This was a Paumer palace—he was certain of it. He followed the man to the gate, slipping inside easily when it was opened for the spy. Yes, it was a Paumer palace without question. Red and blue garments everywhere. The house steward listened to the man's whispers with a reassuring nod, then ushered the fellow up the stairs into a large, well-furnished library. Yes—Nebalath remembered being in this place before. The "bush house," Paumer called it. This room had been fitted out much like this for a meeting of what Paumer persisted in calling the Grand Council for Reunification of the One Land. What luck! Nebalath thought. He'd stumbled onto the meeting of the Conspiracy Uda had mentioned several days before! Circling a highly polished table were a dozen chairs, the back of each draped ceremonially in the colors of one of the six Fragments.

That was a bit surprising. When Nebalath had served on the "Grand Council" only five Fragments had been recognized. Paumer had refused to acknowledge the Marwand, despite the fact that young Dark kept showing up and claiming to be its representative. The lad had never been invited to a Conspiracy meeting, but his knowledge of the future was so thorough that he always

81

knew in advance where the Council would meet and invited himself. Paumer had tried everything to dodge the boy; Nebalath smiled his invisible smile at the memory. Of course, Dark wouldn't be present today, nor would young Uda. Nebalath was curious to see who actually did attend Conspiracy meetings nowadays.

This had once been a truly "grand" council, a world cabinet with integrity and purpose and real power. But Paumer's greed had ruined it. When an exceptionally fine old member from Pleclypsa had suddenly taken sick and died, Paumer had installed his ill-mannered son as a member. But Uda had mentioned some sort of feud within the family. Would that boy be present?

"To another subject," Paumer was saying to his agent, who apparently had finished his report of the secret society meeting. "Have you heard anything about Ognadzu?"

Ognadzu—that had been the boy's name. Nebalath leaned forward to listen carefully to the conversation.

The messenger hung his head. "Sir, I've talked to people all over Lamath, but, apart from those rumors that he was seen months ago in the far north, I've heard nothing new."

Paumer sighed and ran his fingers through his silver hair. "Where is that boy? No one can just disappear like that!" Nebalath raised an unseen eyebrow and thought to himself, Wizards can. As if he'd heard the thought, Paumer continued, "Unless he's become a wizard!"

Now, that was a truly frightful thought. From what Nebalath remembered, young Ognadzu possessed all the charm and tact of Sheth himself. What a terrible thought, to have two such powershapers in the world!

"And yet I've heard nothing from any source about a new shaper," Paumer muttered as he paced around the table, more to himself than to his servant. Suddenly he wheeled on the man and shouted at him. "Your agents are positioned in every part of each of the Fragments! My mercantile empire stretches from those frozen wastes beyond northern Lamath to south of the spice islands in the southern sea! Between us, we know everything there is to know about everybody! You tell me how my son could just vanish." The spy shook his head and shrugged his shoulders, obviously embarrassed at his own failure. Paumer continued to pace around the table; at one point, Nebalath had to lean well back into the corner to prevent the merchant from bumping against him. He might be invisible, but he was still as solid as ever. "Could it be," Paumer mused aloud, his finger to his lips, "that rather than disappearing from my organization, Ognadzu has somehow hidden himself within my organization? Is it possible—'' Here he stopped and looked at the spy piercingly. ''—that certain agents of the House of Paumer are now working for Ognadzu?''

The messenger looked astonished. ''Milord Paumer, are you implying that I or some other of my—''

''I don't know what I imply,'' Paumer snarled, turning his back on the man. Nebalath watched the fellow's face for some little tic or smirk that might betray duplicity, but the man remained impassive as Paumer continued, ''I just had a very strange experience when I arrived here yesterday. It's the first time I've been here since—oh, sometime last fall. The lesser servants tend not to recognize me when I show up, since I rarely think to warn anyone that I'm coming, but the core of the staff has been the same for years. Yet yesterday I found none of that core staff present!''

Paumer leaned across the table toward the man, his fists planted on its polished surface. ''Stranger still, instead of wearing the blue and red livery I've made famous throughout the old One Land, these strangers were all clothed in blue and—lime green!'' The agent frowned at Paumer, listening with evident concern. The merchant took a deep breath and shook his head. ''I was so astonished I couldn't think of anything to say, but none of them stopped me as I walked straight to my apartments to bathe and change clothes. Imagine my dismay to find my bed stripped of linens and my closet empty!''

Once again Paumer was pacing, his eyes trailing along the uppermost rows of the many volumes that lined the room. ''The staff later assured me this was due only to summer cleaning. They rushed me fresh clothing and were very apologetic as they drew my bath. By the time I was dressed, every servant in the place wore the blue and red you see today. But I wonder . . . Ognadzu was the member of my family who most enjoyed this bush house. In fact, it was from this mansion that he fled. Could it be he's hiding here somewhere? Had he been watching when I arrived, and did he instruct the servants—his servants, now—to change their livery and pretend to be in service still to me?''

The spy wore an expression of convincing astonishment at this suggestion. Nebalath assumed his own face, if visible, would look the same. But at that moment the new steward knocked on the library door and announced that the expected guests were arriving, so there was no more time to think about it now. Paumer quickly scuttled to a spot on the far wall and pulled out a book, and a section of the shelves opened up to reveal a secret passageway. The agent hurried inside and Paumer replaced the book to make the passageway close. Then he stepped to the door, took a deep breath, donned his bright, false smile, and said, "Please tell them to come in!"

As quietly as he could, Nebalath slipped around the perimeter of the room and read the title of that book. He was a wizard, true, and could pop about at will, but one never knew when a secret passageway might come in handy, even to a powershaper.

"Jarnel!" Paumer gushed to the gaunt, weary-eyed soldier who stepped through the library doors. "You were able to get away! And how is the Prince of the Army of Arl?"

"I don't know," Jarnel responded flatly, "since I no longer bear that title." The former leader of all Arlian armies had fallen into disfavor with his king and had spent the winter in a tent in the Marwilds on a fruitless search for Sheth. He assumed Paumer was mocking him. "You know that I lost my command."

"I know that you did," Paumer replied ebulliently. "But I also apparently know more than you do about the internal affairs of the Arlian High Command. Haven't you heard? You've been re-instated!" That was news to Nebalath, too, but he wasn't surprised by anything the paranoid King of Arl might do. As to Paumer knowing about it—his agents were placed in every part of every Fragment.

The wizard understood Jarnel's answering frown. Nothing would please the old warrior more than to assume again that office he had filled for years. At the same time, he hated hearing the news from Paumer. "That makes no sense." Jarnel grunted. "Why would the king dismiss Arkabet? The man hasn't had time even to fight a battle yet, much less lose one."

Paumer shrugged. "Nevertheless, that's the word from the Arlian court. Please don't feel badly that you haven't heard," he added, for Paumer was a careful student of people, and he'd understood immediately Jarnel's reaction. "You've been deep in the wilds for so long I'm certain the news just hasn't had time to reach you."

"Your message did," the stoic warrior pointed out.

"Your crazy king won't even let you reveal your identity to your own staff!" Paumer argued with a smile. "He probably doesn't even know where you are himself. I, on the other hand, knew exactly where to find you. You arrested me at the beginning of the winter—remember?"

Jarnel nodded stiffly and looked away. Paumer seemed to bring out the worst in the old general. Nebalath wondered what Jarnel was thinking.

"Is this where we meet?" a voice from the door asked, and Paumer and Jarnel both turned to see Ranoth, Ruling Elder of City Lamath, stepping into the library.

"Ranoth!" Paumer beamed, his tone of voice identical to that with which he'd greeted Jarnel. "How wonderful that you could come! Is Talarath with you?"

The question was answered even as he asked it, for Seagryn's father-in-law followed Ranoth into the room. They were quite a contrast. Talarath was tall and thin, with such a severe manner that smiles directed to him tended to die upon the lips. Ranoth was much shorter and usually had a merry twinkle in his eyes that suggested he knew far more about life than priests were supposed to know. Nebalath had known Ranoth a long time—a very long time—and they had, in fact, learned some of those things together. But Ranoth had been a person born to rule, and he'd been willing to compromise his own attitudes in any way necessary in order to rise to a position of authority. It was a pity in some ways, Nebalath thought, but not for the people of Lamath. They'd benefited from having a Ruling Elder who could be tolerant.

At the moment, however, Ranoth's gaze wasn't tolerant at all. Paumer noticed. "Is something wrong?" the merchant asked.

"With your network of spies you certainly know that we left Lamath in flames," Ranoth answered accusingly. "I would consider that something wrong—would you not?"

"Ahh," Paumer nodded, fingering the turquoise bunting that draped the back of his chair, representative of Pleclypsa. "The dragon."

"Your dragon, Paumer," Talarath proclaimed.

"My dragon." Paumer nodded, pretending puzzlement. "Wasn't a certain member of your family seen riding that dragon around Lamath?"

"I'll not claim him." Talarath snorted, but the comment had obviously embarrassed him and Paumer had regained the upper hand.

"I don't know what we're to do with—Chaom!" Paumer sang, turning again to the door and summoning once more that cloying smile that made Nebalath want to gag. "Welcome!"

A big, beefy man nodded to the others as he stepped around the table to sit in a chair draped in purple. He saved his last greeting for Jarnel, whom he'd often faced on the field of battle.

General Chaom was Jarnel's counterpart in the land of Haran, and their armies had clashed regularly over the recent years. Chaom's small features seemed lost in his big, round face, much as his quiet voice seemed to lose itself in this book-lined room when he asked, "Why do we need to do anything with Chaom?"

"I wasn't speaking of you, friend, I was talking about Seagryn. Have you seen him?"

Chaom glanced around at the others suspiciously. "Why? Should I have seen him?"

Paumer smiled patiently. "He's been sighted in Lamath riding on the dragon, and I wondered if perhaps you've heard similar reports from places around Haranamous?"

Chaom's eyes did another quick circuit of the room. "No."

Paumer waited for further elaboration, but Chaom offered none. Nebalath smiled at this. He'd worked with Chaom for many years and knew the man would say nothing he didn't feel was absolutely necessary. When the silence became embarrassing, Paumer cleared his throat, pulled out his own chair, and sat down. "Shall we begin?" The others followed his lead.

The pitifully low attendance was immediately apparent. More than half the chairs were empty. "Is this us?" Chaom asked. "Where's Dark?"

"My soon-to-be son-in-law is making preparations for his wedding," Paumer lied brightly, "as is, of course, my daughter. They won't be joining us."

An ironic smile turned up the corners of Chaom's small mouth. "And your son?"

"Indisposed, I fear," Paumer lied again, but this time with a hint of warning to Chaom to drop the subject. "To be honest, I rather appreciate this opportunity for us older members of the Grand Council to converse in private."

"I thought it was you who wanted new blood?" Jarnel said.

"Yes, well, perhaps I was in error," Paumer answered briskly, still unwilling to yield entirely his smile.

"Where are Wilker and Garney?" Chaom asked, still casually taking roll. "And where's Sheth? Does he plan to grace us with his presence today?"

"You know Sheth, Chaom." Jarnel sneered. "He's probably standing cloaked in a corner of the room at this moment, waiting to make his grand appearance after everyone else has arrived."

Nebalath hadn't thought about that, but it was true. It was a wonder they hadn't bumped into each other already.

"Sheth promised he would be here," Paumer announced. "As

to the representatives from the Remnant, Garney felt he could not leave his post at the Outer Portal. Wilker arrived last night, and I'm wondering where he is . . .'' The merchant stood, went to the door, and spoke quietly to a servant posted right outside. ''I'm sure he'll be here soon,'' he added as he returned to his chair.

Nebalath sneered. Wilker was probably downstairs in his apartments, gazing into a mirror to make sure he looked as dashing as possible. Nobody said it, but Nebalath knew they all were thinking the same. Wilker was a vain, self-serving fop whose only contribution to the Grand Council rested in the fact that he would actually leave the Remnant to attend meetings. He was one of the few citizens of that underground civilization that had ever seen the light of day.

''Shall we begin?'' Paumer asked again, and this time no one interrupted. ''First, to report the obvious, Sheth successfully completed the forging—as he terms it—of the dragon. Unfortunately Seagryn took it upon himself to interrupt the process before the beast was trained and allowed it to escape. So you see, we have a problem.''

''What problem?'' Jarnel asked. ''I thought the plan was to make a beast that would cause such terror that the Fragments would all be forced to unite to stop it. Isn't that what's happened?''

''We had hoped to be able to control the destruction to some degree—to direct the dragon, if you will, in what to destroy and what not to.''

Chaom chuckled bitterly. ''In which case a Paumer mansion would certainly never be burned, while all remaining free traders naturally would be.''

Paumer looked at him. ''That was not the plan.''

''Come now, Paumer,'' Chaom continued. ''Who was supposed to manage this destruction? You and Sheth planned to do it between you, and all of us knew from the beginning that you would eventually use the beast to advance your own interests over ours! I feel appreciative toward Seagryn, myself. At least the beast is free to create havoc at random, and that, as Jarnel said, really was the original intention.''

Ranoth spoke up quickly. ''Perhaps, if the dragon were burning your Fragment rather than ours, you'd feel less charitable toward Seagryn.''

''Apparently Seagryn is controlling it!'' Talarath added. ''The rumor in Lamath is that it was Seagryn who made the beast in the first place!''

"I made it," Sheth said flatly, suddenly appearing in the middle of the table. That's why they hadn't bumped into one another, Nebalath thought to himself—because Sheth preferred to watch invisibly from the center of the action, never from the edge.

There were few gasps at the wizard's sudden appearance. These men had all seen the trick before. "Oh, there you are," Paumer muttered. "How long have you been here?"

Sheth ignored him. "I made it, and now it's trying to unmake me." He glanced around the table until he was certain he had everyone's eyes, then went on, "It has tried to kill me repeatedly since Seagryn loosed it. Burned out my home. Chased me out of the Marwilds. That's why it's burning in Lamath now, make no mistake. It thinks I'm there."

"Then perhaps," Ranoth said, "you could hop down off the table and tell us how to convince it you're here, instead?"

Sheth turned his dazzling smile on the old priest. A certain female jester in the court of Haran had often tried to convince Nebalath that the combination of Sheth's appearance and his awesome magical abilities rendered him the most attractive man in the old One Land. While Nebalath wouldn't go that far, he did have to admit that Sheth's dimples, perfect teeth, and mysterious mustache made the wizard a handsome man. "You would love that, wouldn't you, old man," Sheth sneered.

"I would love to be rid of the dragon, yes. It is burning my villages and eating my people. I came to this meeting hoping to find a way to destroy it. Do you have any suggestions?"

Sheth shrugged elaborately and slid off the table. "The plan was to let the governments of the Fragments find a solution, not us." He slumped into the black-draped chair set aside for the second representative from Arl.

"We are the government of one of the Fragments!" Ranoth snapped, adding with a glance at Talarath, "or most of it, anyway. If you made the beast, help us to discover the means to kill it!"

"I did make it," Sheth replied firmly. He then closed his eyes. "Killing it is not my problem."

Chaom leaned forward to direct his comments to Ranoth. "If indeed Seagryn can control the dragon, it seems to me that we ought to be seeking Seagryn's assistance, not Sheth's."

Sheth opened his eyes and sat back up at that, his handsome face suddenly fierce. "Seagryn can't control it! No one can control it! I've made the most powerful monster in history, and there's not any one person who can do anything about it." His pride in his horrible creation was unmistakable.

"How do you know, Sheth?" Jarnel asked.

Sheth frowned at the general. They had battled side by side for Arl for many years, but neither made any secret of their mutual disgust. "What?"

"How do you know it can't be controlled? If this is indeed the first such beast, perhaps Seagryn has found a weakness you're too blind to see."

"Look," Sheth snarled, turning around to face Jarnel directly. "Perhaps you don't recall this, but I made a small twi-beast out of a pair of mice before I ever designed Vicia-Heinox. I tried every way I could think of to control my little mouse-dragon, but without success. It's far more powerful than I—and it's only this big!" He spread his hands in front of him to indicate the size of a large bird. He smiled over his shoulder to the others. "It takes particular pleasure in consuming cats, of all things. Can you imagine?" Then he frowned back at Jarnel. "I'm Sheth, remember? If I can't control a mouse-dragon no bigger than a tree-munk, how is *anyone* to control Vicia-Heinox?"

Ranoth raised his eyebrows. "It appears, then, that all the hatred and loathing directed at Seagryn really ought to be aimed at you."

"Seagryn's reputation is my doing, actually," Paumer confessed. "In the wake of the dragon's destruction, is was clear that someone needed to serve as the focal point for the world's revulsion. Since Seagryn released the beast, he seemed the logical choice. Apparently he's accepted the role, since we hear now that he's traveling with the dragon."

"None of which gets us any closer to a solution of the problem you and Sheth have created for us," Ranoth murmured, and his words brought Sheth out of his chair. The wizard crouched over the table, bestowing his glare on the whole group.

"Look at you all! You're supposedly the most powerful people of this age, and all you can do is sit around this table and hate Sheth! You listen to me! I did nothing but what you asked me to do! You wanted a worldwide problem that would force the Fragments to work together for a solution, and I caused one for you! Why don't you people do your part now? Why don't you get your precious governments together and solve it?"

Nebalath knew Sheth was about to disappear—it was too dramatic a speech not to use for an exit line—but Ranoth called out to him before he could go. "And what about you? Will you help us?"

Sheth pulled himself up to his full height. "Help you? I have a dragon hunting for me! It's going to be all I can do to survive!'' Then Sheth disappeared. Nebalath nodded to himself. It had been a classic appearance by his longtime rival, and he'd learned a lot from it. But not what he wanted to know. Where was Seagryn? Still on one of the heads of the dragon, apparently. Then where was the dragon? If indeed Sheth was right and this Vicia-Heinox creature was hunting him down, perhaps in a meeting with Sheth was not the safest place to be. But surely the wizard had overstated the danger. If indeed it would take a Fragmentwide effort to stop the beast, and Sheth's personal survival depended upon it, then Sheth would ultimately be willing to help find the solution. Nebalath would wager on it.

Paumer assumed the meaningful expression of the statesman about to challenge his colleagues to sacrificial service. ''Well, gentlemen. Shall we do as he suggests?''

Jarnel laughed so rarely it was a real shock when he did so now. ''What? What are you talking about?''

The merchant looked at him. ''Why, bring this up before our governments, of course.''

''Pleclypsa doesn't have a government!'' Jarnel argued. ''You have a trade board and a cultural council, both of which you control!''

''Actually,'' Paumer countered, ''my wife heads the cultural council. I certainly don't control her.''

''But you do direct the trade board, and that's the closest thing to a government your little city has. Haranamous has a king! Arl has a king! If Chaom or myself tried to suggest to our respective sovereigns that we needed to work together on anything, we'd each be convicted, finally, of being members of the Conspiracy, and would be executed. Or I would, anyway,'' he added, glancing over at Chaom.

''I likely would be, too,'' Chaom agreed.

Jarnel turned back to Paumer and demanded, ''Exactly what are you asking us to do?''

They heard an insistent knock on the library door, and Paumer seemed relieved by the interruption. ''Yes!'' he shouted.

''Milord Paumer,'' the steward called out. ''Lord Wilker has departed for his home.''

''He what?'' the merchant shouted, jumping up and running to the door to throw it open.

''He said to tell you that he's received word that the two-headed dragon has occupied the Central Gate, and that the Remnant is marching to war against it.''

That was what Nebalath needed to know. He couldn't take off for the Central Gate without first removing his cloaking spell, of course, so he suddenly appeared in the corner of the room, and both Jarnel and Chaom spotted him and gasped. ''Enjoyed the meeting,'' he told them, ''but I really must fly.'' Then he disappeared.

It wasn't really flying, of course. It was better.

Chapter Eight

❈❈❈❈

REMNANT'S RUIN

"You can't do this," Seagryn told Garney.

He'd already said it many times, and the little man was tired of hearing it. Garney whirled to face him. "Listen, Seagryn. We are the One Land. We can do anything we choose. If you truly wish to help us then think of a way you can fit into the king's strategy. If you cannot, please get out of the way."

"What strategy?" Seagryn argued. " 'We'll all just charge the thing?' That's a strategy?"

Garney sighed with exasperation and looked away, but Seagryn couldn't tell whether the little man was more frustrated with him or with the king. "You don't understand . . ."

"I think I do. If you try to tell the king the truth about the dragon, you may be forced to tell him other truths as well—like the truth about the world outside—the truth about this being only a Remnant of the once-great One Land. Is that it?" Garney sighed again and shook his head. Seagryn plunged on. "No? Well, let me tell you what I do understand. I understand about Vicia-Heinox. If you let your king march this army out to charge the dragon you can be certain it will never march back Inside again. You must know that, Garney—surely you do."

The Keeper of the Outer Portal turned to Seagryn, his expression a mixture of anger and grief. "Yes, I know that. Stay here for a moment. I'll be right back." He then started across the throne room to talk with the large cluster of men that Seagryn had come to recognize composed the Royal Advisory Board. He had to push his way through, for the room was filling up with warriors.

The army of the Remnant *looked* splendid. The Royal Advisors had fetched the ancient blue and gold armor from its storage cavern somewhere in this subterranean maze, and Seagryn could tell at a glance that whichever of these men served as "Keeper of the Arms" had been extremely efficient. The helmets shone in the torchlight. The blue tunics all matched, as if all had been dipped recently in the same dye. Obviously the Remnant had made a commitment to looking good on the battlefield.

"As if that will matter to the dragon," Seagryn mumbled to himself. Still, he felt hopeful. He peered through the crowd at Garney as the little man spoke to the others with obvious passion, occasionally gesturing in Seagryn's direction, and finally winning nods of agreement all around. Relief flooded through him as he saw Garney turn and nod at him before plunging back through the crush toward him.

"It's agreed," Garney said when he reached Seagryn again. "Follow me." He led Seagryn back around behind the raised dais to a smaller door in the rear of the throne room. Was this the way to the king's chambers? The door closed behind them, and Seagryn was suddenly aware of how noisy the throne room had been. Garney smiled back over his shoulder and said, "Quieter, isn't it?" Then he gestured for Seagryn to proceed him through a doorway to the left.

Seagryn did and had only a moment to wonder why this room was so small before that door clanged shut behind him and the key was turned. "Garney!" he shouted, spinning around to throw his weight against it, but this door was solid metal and exceedingly thick. "Garney!" he shouted again, more in shock than in anger. "I thought you said you knew you couldn't lock me up!"

"It's a special cell, Seagryn, designed and dug by the little people in the hours since you've been Inside." Seagryn could barely hear him, so thick was the metal of the door. "I didn't want to do this," Garney continued, "but you simply would not cooperate!"

"Garney!" Seagryn shouted, "you're going to die! You and all the Remnant are going to die!"

"That may be so!" the little gatekeeper called back, "but some things are worth dying for!"

"What?" Seagryn cried. "The lie? Are you dying to protect the lie?" But Garney didn't answer. He'd already returned to join his fellow Keepers as they planned the mass suicide of the Remnant.

Seagryn slumped to the floor, feeling breathless. Then he noticed that the torch in the wall bracket behind him was flickering and realized the reason. There was no air in this cell—or only the tiny amount that came from the thin slit at the bottom of the door—enough to slow his death but not prevent it.

This is no problem, he thought. He'd just take his tugolith shape—and be crushed to death! The cell was too small to contain a tugolith, and, since it had been carved out of rock, its walls would certainly not burst outward. Even if he could somehow wedge his altershape into this tiny space, he would not be able to move to force open the door. Garney's special design appeared to be most effective. Seagryn was trapped.

He reached up to grab the torch and snuffed its flame against the wall—no need to let it burn his precious air when he could make light at will. Then he leaned back against the cool rock and fought the panic rising inside of him. It had been a long time since Seagryn last felt powerless—when, exactly?

When he'd been bound by Sheth's spell in the Dragonforge, he guessed, forced to listen as that sorcerer had tortured Vicia-Heinox into the creature that now periled the world. And that time he had not freed himself but had relied instead on—

"Oh, yes," Seagryn said aloud to himself. "The Power."

His capacity for forgetting his own limitations never ceased to amaze him. How was it that he could go for days—weeks—pretending to both invincibility and immortality, never once thinking seriously about how truly powerless and mortal he really was? Elaryl had tried to remind him. Elaryl had been talking to the Power for him. Did he dare hope for yet another miracle, on her account, if not upon his own?

He leaned his head back and closed his eyes against the blackness, trying as he had before to see his way through the distance to her. He might at least be permitted to say good-bye before he died. Then it registered with him—if he had truly visited with Elaryl in some ghostly form, could he not visit someone closer? Could he get help from within this underground nation, from Merkle, perhaps? Would that little man respond to a plea from his vaporous presence and come unlock the door? Seagryn didn't disregard the Power entirely—he was willing to give that One credit for the idea—but neither did he waste any time in plunging his mind out through the rock and down, mentally searching for that uncompleted cavern he'd stood in just hours before. He couldn't explain why he knew how to do it, nor did he make the mistake of trying and thus distracting himself so much that he no longer could. Instead he traced his way through the yellow-tile corridors and down the curving ramps, racing far more swiftly than he'd been able to move on foot, down into the unfinished cavern and across it to the entrance of what Merkle had called the double row, a small tunnel with tiny homes carved from the rock on either side. He moved effortlessly through Merkle's door. He needed no light—his mind furnished all the illumination necessary—and quickly saw the table where he'd sat and the uneaten food still spread upon it. But a great uneasiness seized him as he searched, for the place was empty. The little people were gone.

"Surely the king didn't—"

Like a boulder blown out of the bowels of the earth by gushing magma, Seagryn's focused attention shot up out of the dwellings of the little people through the upper levels of the Remnant and out, into the sunlight that washed over the Central Gate, in time to see the blackened Outer Portal crank open. "No!" his insubstantial body called aloud as the military procession began, led, of course, by the King of the One Land, surrounded by the various Keepers. "No!" Seagryn shouted at them again, but the drums and horns of a blue-and-gold clad band filled the pass with stirring music, and no one seemed to heed him.

Toward the head of the column marched Garney, and Seagryn flew now to him—for that's what it felt like, this ability to throw his incorporeal presence from place to place. But Garney wouldn't look his way, even when he shouted in the little Keeper's ear. "Garney!" he pleaded. "Garney! You must turn back!" He put himself in the little man's path to block him, but the column marched through him as if he weren't there—as, indeed, he wasn't.

It seemed likely to him now that neither Garney nor any of the others were able to see him. Elaryl had told him he looked thin—shadowy. But these people, most of whom had never seen the sunlight in their lives, were fighting the brilliance to see anything at all. They moved resolutely forward, following in the footsteps of the person before them, each with one hand holding a weapon and the other shielding light-blinded eyes.

And the column was huge. Did it include everyone in the Remnant? Seagryn moved back to gaze at the line in dismay as it continued to spill down that wide, fire-scorched stairway. Women and children marched alongside the men, carrying banners and pennants and singing some hymn of praise to their king and their nation. Were the little people still inside?

The wisp of Seagryn's projected thoughts shot back into the throne room. It was still as crowded as it had been before but now appeared to be only an exaggerated corridor through which an oddly jubilant army tramped. He glanced at the throne itself. He was peripherally aware that behind it was a small door and, beyond that a cell in which his body waited, but he refused to give his focus there for fear the bonds of time and space might reclaim him. Instead his attention glided down the column of faces, a score abreast—had there actually been this many people inside the Remnant? Were they *all* actually marching out to attack the dragon? He looked for the little people among the big and found them at last. Walking in a line of their own, Merkle and his mates made their way along the wall, each carrying a metal ax more suitable for digging than for battle. They walked in lockstep, one hand on the shoulder in front of them, all of them squinting their eyes against the brilliance of the torchlight around them. Seagryn wanted to curse the Royal Advisors for including them in this parade—they were blind here in the light of the throne room! What value would they be to the king outside in the sunshine? Seagryn fell into step beside Merkle—or did he float beside him?—and addressed him earnestly.

"Merkle! Merkle, can you hear me?" he asked. But the little man made no response. He marched stoically forward, digging tool in one hand, his other hand on the shoulder in front of him, marching off to war. "Merkle!" Seagryn tried one last time, but in the stamping and shuffling of thousands of feet the little man couldn't—or wouldn't—hear him. A line of children raced through him, laughing and giggling as if on their way to a picnic. And Seagryn greatly feared it would be exactly that—for someone. Unless he could talk the beast out of it—

A moment later his transparent form floated above the head named Heinox, and for the first time today someone actually seemed to notice him.

"Seagryn person!" Vicia said brightly. "You're back!" Then that head frowned and asked in a scolding tone, "Where have you been?"

The Heinox head had rolled back to peer directly up at him, and also frowned—more out of concern than reproach. "You look very pale. Have you been eating properly?"

"I'm about to eat well!" Vicia cackled, smacking his great lips and drooling over the approaching army. He then appeared to think of something and cocked himself to one side and looked at Seagryn admiringly. "Did you arrange this feast for me?"

"In a way, perhaps," Seagryn murmured. More than he wanted to admit. Then he spoke forcefully. "Vicia-Heinox, listen. You cannot do this."

"I cannot do what?" said Heinox.

"He can't be talking to me," Vicia explained to his other head. "I can do whatever I like."

Heinox appeared less certain. "Are you talking to me?"

"I'm talking to both of you!" Seagryn pleaded. "I know you think you can do whatever you like—indeed, you have the power to do just that. But having the power to do something doesn't mean we always need to do it! Some things are right to do, while others are morally wrong. You may not see it now, but to consume this entire nation would be utterly reprehensible behavior—even for a dragon!" The two heads both stared at him in openmouthed wonder. He apparently had caught the beast's attention! Was it possible that he'd managed to make an impact on this—

"Both of us?" Vicia asked, enormously puzzled. "What does that mean?"

"Are you talking to me?" Heinox asked again.

"Ahem!" This came from below them, and they all looked down to realize that the King of the One Land had been repeatedly clearing his throat to get their attention. Several servants held a portable canopy over the king's head, shielding him somewhat from the direct rays of the sun. Seagryn credited the king's relative blindness for his utterly fearless demeanor. Certainly no one—not even a king who had never in his life been allowed to feel threatened—could gaze up into two such horrible faces and not experience at least a little anxiety. When their silence assured him that he had both heads' attention, the king called out, "Dragon, I wonder if I might have a word with you?"

The smile that spread across Vicia's ever-hungry features gave Seagryn a sick feeling in the pit of his insubstantial stomach. "You want to talk to me?" Vicia cackled. Then he glided down to hover at eye level with the king. "Nothing could give me more pleasure!" The beast's jaws gaped wide—

"So, here you are! You can't imagine the trouble I've had finding you. What are you doing in the dark?"

The voice seemed to come from behind him. Seagryn whirled around to face the speaker—and fell flat on his back on the floor of his cell, his head spinning. A small light burned in the room—not of his own making. When his eyes focused, he saw someone vaguely recognizable standing over him, looking down at him curiously. "What's wrong?" the dimly lit figure asked. "Did I catch you in the midst of a sending?"

"A . . . a what?" He recognized those features now. It was Nebalath!

"Honestly, Seagryn," the old wizard grumbled, "I do wish you'd at least learn the names of some of these tricks you perform. Of course, I realize that you've not had anyone knowledgeable to help you. Perhaps I should write that book after all . . ."

"N-Nebelath?"

"You remember me. That's encouraging. I wasn't certain you would. Why is it so stuffy in here?" Nebalath asked as his ball of light sputtered out.

"It's a new cell. Garney wasn't particularly concerned whether I could breathe or not, so long as I couldn't get out."

"Oh," Nebalath said with some concern. "Then you'd better stop flinging your *spirit* from place to place and get your body out of here." Another ball of light blossomed overhead.

"I'd be happy to do that," Seagryn growled, making the effort to sit up. "Unfortunately, I don't know how."

"Oh, you know," Nebalath chided. "You just haven't thought of it yet. One moment."

Nebalath disappeared with a sharp crack, as did his light. For a moment Seagryn was left blinking into the darkness again. Then he heard a metallic scrape coming from the door, and the tumblers of a lock dropping into line. Nebalath opened the door, and Seagryn rushed for it, thrusting his face out into the corridor beyond and gasping deep draughts of air.

"Convenient of them to leave the key in the lock," Nebalath murmured. Then he looked at the gasping Seagryn. "And a good thing for you I happened to find you when I did."

Seagryn nodded, then sighed deeply, cleared his throat, and announced, "The Power sent you."

Nebalath made a sour face. "I hardly think that's the case."

"It's true," Seagryn avowed, still breathing deeply. "I've been talking to the Power, and Elaryl has—"

"But I haven't." Nebalath snorted. "Nor do I intend to any time soon! When I was growing up I had enough of that 'One Who Must Remain Nameless' business to last me a lifetime. I just happened to need your services and I've been hunting you. It appears I showed up at a fortunate moment for both of us."

Seagryn peered up at the older powershaper. "You don't think that's a miracle?"

"The thought never entered my mind." Nebalath sniffed, then

he turned his gaze back into the cell. "Why did they lock you in here?"

"I was trying to save them."

"Ah." The old wizard nodded knowingly. "Typical Remnantic behavior, especially from those idiotic Keepers of one thing and another. I'll bet you tried to tell the king something they didn't want him to know?"

"Yes, like the fact that if he talked to the dragon he would end up being—" Seagryn suddenly stared up at Nebalath. "There may be time yet!" He bolted up the short hallway to the door into the throne room and threw it open. He then raced around the dais and into the corridor that led to the Outer Portal. The ramp was still down, and Seagryn clattered halfway down the stairs, taking them three at a time until he could see out from under the arching overhang across the pass to where he'd left the dragon and the army. Then he stopped.

The canyon floor was covered with literally thousands of brilliant gold helmets and breastplates. But the bodies that had been in them were—gone.

"It couldn't have eaten them that fast. It couldn't!" Seagryn shouted at himself, but even as he spoke, he realized the truth. Within the system of caves Sheth called his Dragonforge, that evil sorcerer had shown Seagryn his tiny prototype dragon made of two rodents. Seagryn had been obliged to watch as the mouse-dragon had incinerated a squirrel. The little monster had not thrown flames: It had just gazed at the squirrel with both heads at once and somehow created fire within the squirrel itself. Within moments only ashes had remained. Now, as he gazed at what had briefly been a battlefield, Seagryn knew with certainty that under each of those fallen helmets he would find a similar pile of ash. The Remnant was lost. And far across the pass sat the creature responsible. The two heads of the dragon appeared to be engrossed in conversation with themselves.

Seagryn screamed, venting both his grief and his rage. Quick as a thought, he took his tugolith shape and charged forward. He actually tumbled to the bottom of the stairs—they certainly were not wide enough to offer footing to such enormous feet—but his armor-plated body didn't notice the fall. He immediately scrambled to his feet and launched himself horn first across the pass toward the dragon. He would ram his horn through the thing if it was the last thing he—

CRASH!

A bone-jarring blow knocked him back on his haunches and

threatened to tear his horn loose from his forehead. It left him stunned, yet he'd never seen what had hit him. Or rather, what he'd hit—

Nebalath appeared beside him, a smug smile on his face. "Just in case I never get around to writing that book—that's called a 'barrier.' "

"My head hurts," Seagryn groaned. He took his human form and began to massage the throbbing spot right above the bridge of his nose.

"I had to do something." The older wizard shrugged. "What were you trying to do? Did you think you could just charge the thing?"

Just charge the thing. He had heard that strategy before . . . Seagryn heard a distant squawk and looked up to see the dragon take to the air. "He's coming after us instead," he muttered bitterly.

"I doubt it." Nebalath sniffed. He clasped his hands behind his back as he watched the beast rise into the air. "I've taken the precaution of cloaking us. Might I say that while you have great talent, Seagryn, you're an inconsistent powershaper? You don't think."

"Who made you my teacher?" Seagryn grumbled as he staggered to his feet.

"As someone who expects to work closely with you in the future, I consider it in my best interest to see you mature as a wizard as quickly as possible. After all, I may need you to save me someday. Shall we go?"

"Go?" Seagryn asked wearily. "Go where?"

"To Pleclypsa. Dark is in a bad way, and I hoped you might do something to help him. I've been looking for you for some time, Seagryn. It's critical that we get to him as soon as possible." Nebalath turned and started to walk toward the south.

Seagryn craned his neck to look back at the Outer Portal. It yawned wide, an open invitation to anyone to come plunder its secrets. Seagryn suddenly realized what it most resembled. "It's nothing but a giant mausoleum," he murmured. Then another thought occurred, and he added, "And that's really all it has been for two hundred years—the tomb of the old One Land."

"I say!" Nebalath called back at him. "Would you please hurry up? If it were just me, I'd cast myself back down there this instant, but since you say you lack that particular gift, we have several days of hard riding before us, if we can buy some horses from the Paumer house just inside Haranamous. On the other hand," the powershaper added, more to himself than to Seagryn, "I'm not certain if I'd want to pop back down to Kerily's palace after all. No telling *what* the woman has torn out by this time."

Seagryn pondered. What else was there to do? He could go back to Elaryl, he guessed. And yet—"What's wrong with Dark?" he asked.

"That's the point," Nebalath said. "I don't know and I was hoping you might. Shall we go see?"

They walked southward. Seagryn was grateful that, while their route took them past the battle site, it didn't lead them through it. He didn't think he could stand to see a tiny pile of ashes next to a digging tool . . .

"By the way," Nebalath said. "You do need to be careful, you know. *Everyone* in the world wants to kill you."

The two walkers were well out of the pass long before the horse came thundering up the incline from the west. Wilker had ridden it hard and the beast was exhausted, but his terrified anticipation of what he might find would not permit the Undersecretary for Provincial Affairs to rest until he got home. While still miles away, he saw that the Outer Portal was open. Chilled by the sight, he drove his mount onward. Then he saw the army of scattered helmets, without people to fill them, and he knew with certainty that his worst fears had come to pass.

He denied it as long as there was any hope. He rode to the foot of the staircase and jumped from the horse to race up the steps. He plunged down the corridor and into the throne room, then veered off down one of the yellow corridors, calling all the names he could think of at the top of his lungs.

Evening had fallen outside when he finally wandered dazedly back down the staircase and out. He peered across the pass through the purple twilight and thought he saw the form of a two-headed dragon in silhouette against the far cliffs. Something twisted inside him, and suddenly he was running, running as fast as he could toward the dragon, his arms open in an embrace of death. And he shouted as he ran, "Eat me, too! Eat me, too! Eat me, too!"

Alas, it wasn't to be. The dragon was gone. Wilker sat on a helmet and wept.

Chapter Nine

✻✻✻✻✻

DARK DREAMS

LATE the next afternoon Seagryn sat on horseback under the shade of a tree, stoically holding on to the reins of another mount. They had purchased the horses from the Paumer house located at the foot of the Central Gate's southern mouth, but Nebalath seemed unable to remain on his for very long at a time. He'd just disappeared for the third time today, and Seagryn's patience was fast wearing thin.

At the older wizard's insistence, he had tried to perform Nebalath's trick himself, but so far he just didn't seem able to do it. The other spells he knew had come naturally to him at the instant Seagryn had needed them. He guessed that he wouldn't learn this one until it became truly necessary.

"Or maybe I just don't have the confidence to do anything anymore," Seagryn murmured to himself, adding bitterly, "And why should I?" He had done everything in his power to save the Remnant, but it hadn't been enough. He knew he wasn't responsible. That rested upon the Keepers of the kingdom, who had sacrificed an entire people to protect a falsehood! Even so, he couldn't think of that tragedy without feeling horrible guilt. He mourned those Inside whom he'd come to know—especially little Merkle. More and more he caught himself directing accusations at the Power, such as, "How could you have let it happen?" Thus far he'd received no reply.

Now they were bound for Pleclypsa—or would be, whenever Nebalath returned. Would it be any different there? His shaper abilities had caused nothing but trouble for himself and everyone around him. Why should he expect to be of any help to Dark? Seagryn turned his gaze back to a particular spot in the roadway and sank deeper into despair. Where was Nebalath? What if a band of assassins were to pass by this spot? Was he just to sit and wait?

Suddenly the wait was over, for Nebalath reappeared suspended five feet up over thin air. The wizard only had time for a surprised gasp before he landed on his backside in the dust. He immediately bounded to his feet and raced toward Seagryn, screaming furiously, "Why did you move my horse? I *told* you to hold my horse and to stay right there!"

Seagryn gazed at the charging powershaper impassively. "And I told you that I'm weary of your popping in and out all the time, without telling me where you're going or how long you'll be gone."

"You know good and well where I'm going!" Nebalath snapped as he finally reached his horse and struggled to climb onto its broad back. "I'm preparing people along the way to receive us!"

"How much warning do they need?" Seagryn grumbled.

"Enough to be ready to make us comfortable! *You* may be accustomed to riding around on the backs of these smelly beasts, but I am not. I've just made sure that we'll each have a scented bath drawn at the Imperial House by the time we arrive."

"When will that be?"

"By nightfall," Nebalath answered gruffly, "if you'll quit talking and start riding!"

Seagryn shrugged. "It isn't me who keeps stopping in the middle of the road."

"Why did you move my horse?" Nebalath demanded again. "I asked you to remain there so I could reappear directly on his back! Instead you hang me out in midair, like some washerwoman's drying laundry!"

"You came down quickly enough," Seagryn said. After the older wizard finished cursing him, he calmly went on to explain, "If you'll take the time to look, you'll notice this spot is shady. Where you disappeared—and landed—is out in the hot sun. Should you decide to cast yourself elsewhere any time soon, consider leaving us in the shade." Seagryn looked around at Nebalath and gently spurred the flanks of his steed. "Are you planning to pop off again in the near future?"

"How should I know?" Nebalath grumbled as he awkwardly

urged his mount back up onto the road. "Riding horses is so boring. How do people stand it?"

"It's not so bad," Seagryn said, patting his horse's neck affectionately. He would have preferred riding Kerl, but this horse had a mature attitude, and the ride had been reasonably relaxed.

Nebalath wasn't finished complaining. "If you'd just learn to cast yourself we could *be* there by now."

"But I've never been to Pleclypsa," Seagryn answered evenly. "I thought you said you never cast yourself to a spot you've never visited, for fear you might wind up in the middle of a wall."

Nebalath snarled in frustration. "You'd be surprised how things change in *spite* of knowing where you're going. People move your horse," he said, throwing Seagryn a pointed glare. "Or they tear down whole towers . . ."

Seagryn had heard all this before, but he saw no point in interrupting. He watched the passing scenery as Nebalath waved his arms and shouted.

"That Kerily woman! Every time I go to Pleclypsa, she's changed her mind again! She's had a new dome built, you see, and when I appeared there this morning she was harassing some poor artist who was trying to paint a fresco on the ceiling. Just you watch! By the time we arrive she'll have decided to tear the whole building down and start over!"

That was still two days away, Seagryn thought to himself. They planned to spend tonight in the Imperial House and the next night on the road. As Nebalath rambled on, he turned his thoughts to Haranamous and wondered what kind of reception he would receive there. He'd left the city a conquering hero, having saved it from the Armada of Arl. The thought brightened his mood, for after all—wasn't that an example of some good he had done as a powershaper? Perhaps old King Haran would welcome him back with a fanfare of trumpets and a gala party . . . Excited by the possibility, Seagryn spurred his mount to a gallop, forcing Nebalath to shut up and ride. By the time they topped a small rise and saw the Golden City spread out below them, Seagryn was beginning to feel good about himself again.

Nebalath reined in beside him and looked down at the city. "No doubt those streets are teeming with assassins by this time. We can't take the chance of letting you be recognized. I'll disguise us as a pair of merchants."

Seagryn sighed. With that single statement the older wizard had destroyed his buoyant mood. "Will all of this ever be over?" he wondered aloud.

"Do I look like Dark?" Nebalath said peevishly. "I'm a shaper, not a seer. But it stands to reason none of this will end until we kill that dreaded dragon, and we're not likely to learn how to do that without Dark's special knowledge. We need to get the lad some help."

Suddenly Seagryn had a thought that sent a shiver of fear down his spine. "These assassination squads—they wouldn't hurt *Elaryl*, would they?" Nebalath's frown didn't help to ease his fears, but then the old wizard's face brightened.

"As I told you, I've met your wife. She seemed highly capable of handling herself in any situation. But just in case, would you like for me to cast myself up to Lamath and see how she's getting on?"

"Right now?" Seagryn frowned.

"Oh no," Nebalath chuckled, shaking his gray head. "At the moment I'm far too interested in dinner and a bath. But after we've settled in for the night, I'll pay her a visit and set your mind at ease. Shall we go?"

Seagryn felt greatly comforted by this suggestion, and it deepened his appreciation for his fellow powershaper. As they rode through the gates of Haranamous, he was already looking forward to hearing Nebalath's report.

They passed through the streets of the city without incident. Soon the battlements of the Imperial House loomed above them, and Seagryn peered up at them doubtfully. The castle hadn't seemed to like him much the last time he'd visited. He wondered how it would regard him now.

He had his answer immediately, for the Imperial House addressed them while they were still a good distance up the street. Rather, it spoke to Nebalath, and Seagryn overheard.

—So, you've brought the novice powershaper back with you, the Imperial House said condescendingly.

Nebalath rose to Seagryn's defense, sitting up in his saddle and pointing up at the walls as he called, "You just remember, House. Were it not for the help of this 'novice' wizard, you'd be flying the black flags of the Army of Arl!"

—Would that have been so bad? the House wondered.

"I don't know." Nebalath smiled. "I do know that the Arlian king is crazy. He might have thoroughly rearranged your innards. What do you think of that?"

—From all it can gather, this House would have far more to fear should it fall into the hands of Kerily, wife of Paumer. Incidentally, your bath has been drawn.

"Good, good!" Nebalath crowed. Seagryn had not seen him this enthusiastic all day long. Nebalath twisted around to Seagryn and began to report the conversation. "The House says they have everything ready for us—"

"I heard what it said," Seagryn murmured. "As well as how it said it."

"That's right, you *can* hear it, can't you? Seagryn . . . Try not to let its comments disturb you." He leaned toward Seagryn's ear and spoke softly. "You know how bad tempered older people can become? Just remember. This House is really, *really* old." He sat up straight in his saddle, smiled broadly, and called, "Open your gates, palace! We're riding in!"

—This House will try to restrain its joy, the Imperial House said sarcastically, and Nebalath cackled in appreciation. He was home, and Seagryn felt glad for him. He wondered when—or if—he would ever feel the same . . .

Fed, bathed, and dressed in wonderfully clean garments, Seagryn sat in his apartments, waiting anxiously for Nebalath's return. The older wizard had departed several hours ago. Why was it taking so long?

—Someone is coming to see you, the Imperial House suddenly announced, causing Seagryn to jump in surprise. The castle hadn't spoken since Nebalath departed—were these words intended for him?

"Are you talking to me?" he asked the ceiling.

—Why would this House talk to those who cannot understand it? It is you she's coming to see.

"Who—who's coming to see me?" Seagryn stammered, climbing up onto his bed and looking from one wall to another. Talking to this castle was unnerving. How could he look it in the eyes?

—The lady's name is Fylynn. She is a close friend of Nebalath—and highly regarded by this House as well.

"Why is she coming to talk to me?" Seagryn asked.

—You have a mutual acquaintance, if this House understands rightly. She's at the door. You *could* greet her there, the House suggested.

The Imperial House of Haranamous had watched the interactions of people for centuries and had strong feelings about the value of good manners. Seagryn didn't argue. He walked to the door and opened it before she knocked.

"Well!" the surprised woman said. She then smiled brightly

and asked, "Do you read minds? Or do you, too, have a personal relationship with the walls?"

"I—the House told me you were coming, yes," Seagryn murmured. She smiled again, then pointed into the room and raised her eyebrows. "I'm sorry," Seagryn apologized, finally getting the message. "Do come in."

Fylynn stepped past him, and Seagryn closed the door and turned around to face her. She was a big-boned woman with a jolly face whose features nevertheless seemed to argue with one another. Her mouth seemed too large to match her small-set gray eyes. Yet upon that big mouth Fylynn wore a winning smile, and those eyes sparkled with a mischief Seagryn saw instantly could be contagious. He couldn't mistake her occupation, for she wore the traditional motley of the court jester—varicolored patches of fabric stitched together into a beautifully colored yet somewhat ragged costume. It called immediate attention to her figure, which also seemed somehow mismatched. While Fylynn had a small upper body, her hips suggested she might be overfond of sweets. At the same time, her oddly matched face radiated its own kind of sweetness. More than that, it boldly proclaimed her quick wit. As she watched Seagryn's eyes forming his first impression of her, she grabbed one of the three tails of her jester's cap and held it out in front of her. "Look!" she cried. "A horn!" She struck a pose, her left hand out to her side and her left foot cocked up into the air. "Think I'd make a good tugolith?" she asked.

Seagryn's eyes widened, and his head jerked back as if he'd been struck. "A—what?"

Fylynn grinned—not with malice, but not with much respect, either. "Aren't you Seagryn the horny? Ah—that is, Seagryn the great horned beast?"

"I . . ."

"You . . ." she mocked as he struggled for words.

"I'm Seagryn, yes," he said flatly.

"And I," she grinned impishly, "am Fylynn the fat!" She let her "horn" fall into her face and bowed theatrically. Then she straightened back up and smiled at him more honestly. "But you needn't call me by my title. In fact, I'd rather prefer you didn't—" She brushed girlish light-brown bangs out of her eyes and glanced around his room. "So," she said. "Nebalath told me you were coming."

Seagryn nodded. "Was there some particular thing you wished to see me about?" Fylynn looked back over her shoulder at him, and he thought she might have blushed a bit. Then she shrugged rather shyly, as if she were finding it difficult to tell him exactly why she'd come. So—beneath her brash front there was a certain vulnerability. Seagryn found that appealing.

"Well . . ." she said, drawing out the word. Then she looked at him directly. "I might as well plunge on, right? What can you tell me about Sheth?"

Seagryn blinked. "About Sheth?"

"Oh, yes," she sighed, and there was no mistaking the love-struck look in her eyes—no mistaking it, yet Seagryn found it near impossible to believe. This was no giddy teenager. Fylynn was in her late twenties at least. She noted his surprise and smiled ruefully. "Am I foolish, do you think?"

"Foolish?"

"I mean, I know Sheth is an evil, cannibalistic monster who takes perverse pleasure in corrupting every positive notion that ever crosses his mind, that he's the archenemy of Haranamous, and that he treats me like *dirt*, and yet—those dimples!" She half lidded her eyes and sighed lustily. "That man is so pretty . . ."

Sheth, pretty? Seagryn thought incredulously. Then came the strange realization that he agreed. It shocked him to admit it, but he thought he understood the attraction Fylynn felt for the dragonmaker. He'd even mentioned it once to Elaryl, during the time they'd been forced to spend with Sheth in the Dragonforge. She'd laughed at him and assured him that Sheth held no attraction for her. But Seagryn wondered if she'd told him the truth . . . The man had a sinister power about him, an air of compelling confidence as enthralling as it was repellant. But Seagryn didn't feel at all comfortable admitting that to this stranger. "I don't know what you mean," he murmured.

Fylynn opened her eyes and smiled at him like a satisfied cat. "Doesn't matter. *I* know. And I understand you've been with him lately?"

"Not lately," Seagryn said, shaking his head. "Months ago."

"That's lately enough for me! How was he?"

Seagryn frowned. He could understand the woman's attraction for Sheth, but he found her willingness to reveal it most improper. Lamathian women didn't act this way! Or, at least, not in the presence of a cleric . . . He stiffened and answered her questions with exaggerated politeness. "I really cannot tell you much. He was quite angry with me when we parted."

Fylynn raised her eyebrows. "Really? Why?"

"He had been torturing a monster and apparently wasn't finished. I set the beast free."

"Then the tale is true," the woman said—and she sounded now like a woman and less like an overgrown girl. "Sheth made the dragon, and you released it on the world."

"That's essentially correct, yes—although I've heard it rumored that I'm the beast's maker, not he."

"I'm sure that infuriates him." She smiled knowingly. This woman obviously knew Sheth well. "But I've heard you described as less the dragon's maker and more the dragon's—pet?"

Seagryn's ears burned with embarrassment, but he still managed to shrug and say, "The world apparently is calling me many things these days."

"Oh yes." Fylynn grinned ruefully. "Such colorful names!" She let her smile die slowly. "But then, the world calls Sheth many things as well . . . some of them just as unfair." She saw Seagryn's lip curl disdainfully at Sheth's name and shrugged almost helplessly. "I know. It's difficult to see how someone could love the unlovely. But you may have noticed, Seagryn, that I am not all that lovely myself. I have known him—and loved him—for a very long time. He's a complex man; despite his great power, he is—in ways—quite weak . . ." She paused as if waiting for some response.

Seagryn nodded in curt agreement. He'd seen Sheth's weaknesses—his fears, his insecurities, and his self-doubts—and had imagined how he might exploit these the next time he and Sheth battled. He had no doubt they would again, eventually. Still, Seagryn had been a cleric far longer than he'd been a shaper. His empathy for others had forced him to try to see things from Sheth's perspective, and he readily understood how Sheth's enormous magical talent had bent the man's personality. After all, Seagryn constantly battled within himself that same warping power. If this woman truly understood Sheth, did she also understand him?

Fylynn tilted her head and looked at him compassionately. "Shapers," she murmured quietly, "are a very small, misunderstood fraternity. People hate you because they fear your power. How many of them guess that you fear it, too?"

So, she did understand. And now Seagryn understood why Nebalath—and the walls—regarded Fylynn so warmly. "Yes."

Fylynn smiled sweetly and leaned back away from him. "As for me, I guess I'm just a fan of wizards." Her eyes narrowed as she added seriously, "Perhaps because I see you as our only hope." Then, as if she had suddenly caught herself being pretentious, she clapped her hands and said, "Besides! You're all so cute!"

Seagryn had nothing to say to that. He was greatly relieved when Nebalath appeared in the room a moment later, blinking and glancing around. "Hello, Fylynn." He smiled, then turned and nodded at Seagryn. "Your lady is safe," he said reassuringly. "Said she talked to you the other day—or dreamed she did. If you can send your shadow, Seagryn, I don't see why you can't throw the rest of your body—"

"Did you warn her about assassins? Is she taking any precautions? Has anyone attacked her?"

Nebalath's frown indicated his impatience at being interrupted. "I told you, she's *safe*. Be reasonable, Seagryn. Your father-in-law is an Elder of Lamath! The house is well protected. Besides, it's widely known that you've left her and are traveling with the dragon. It's you they want to kill, not your wife. She's a formidable woman, and quite intelligent—even if she is absolutely convinced that the Power is going to care for her." Nebalath allowed himself a contemptuous chuckle as he mentioned the Power. "It's you she's worried about. Evidently she doesn't believe this so-called 'Power' is quite so able—or willing—to protect you. What's the matter, Seagryn—haven't you been acting spiritual enough?"

It was a mocking question and not worth a reply. But Seagryn thought he understood Elaryl's concern. No, he hadn't been particularly in touch with that One Who Shapes the Future recently. If Elaryl had been trying to send him a message about the value of faith, she'd succeeded. Despite the weariness of the road, he found it difficult to sleep . . .

The next morning he was surprised and pleased to learn that Fylynn was traveling with them. It seemed Pleclypsa was her home, and certainly her combination of warmth and wit made the two-day journey easier. It gave him someone to talk to when Nebalath disappeared.

The old wizard had thoroughly forewarned Kerily of their arrival, and they were welcomed to the House of Paumer with great ceremony. Uda's mother reserved her most sparkling smiles for Seagryn. "We are *so* glad you have agreed to come," she said breathlessly, batting her eyelashes at him. Just as he'd immediately appreciated Fylynn's frankness, Seagryn was instantly put off by Kerily's artificial smile. The woman wasted no time in cutting him out of the group and ushering him toward the staircase. She seemed almost annoyed when they met her daughter coming toward them. Seagryn had not seen Uda since the day he'd freed the dragon, but Kerily permitted them only a quick exchange of greetings before leading him up the stairs and into the room where Dark had spent the past few months. The woman obviously viewed Seagryn as someone come to perform a task, and she wanted the job done now.

While Seagryn was excited about seeing Dark again, he was also worried about him. He'd seen the effects of the boy's mental despair before. "How is he?" he asked Uda.

Kerily didn't seem to feel Uda was capable of responding for herself and answered for her. "He sleeps all the time, that's how he is. Didn't Nebalath tell you?"

Seagryn saw exasperation in Uda's eyes. He'd always felt sorry for the girl, knowing her father as he did. Suddenly his feelings of sympathy doubled. "Yes, Nebalath told me that," he said, "but it didn't make much sense." Seagryn walked alone into Dark's blue-walled room and looked down at the lad. "I remember that he often had difficulty sleeping."

"I'm not asleep," the lad growled, not turning around. "How I wish I could sleep!"

Uda looked suddenly at Seagryn, her eyes wide. He gave her a knowing nod, then addressed Dark's back. "Hello, my friend."

"Hello, Seagryn."

"I suppose you knew I'd be here today."

"Certainly."

Seagryn sat on the bed and patted the boy's shoulder. "Kerily says you sleep all the time—"

"I pretend to sleep whenever she comes around. Wouldn't you, if you were me?"

Seagryn stifled a smile and got right to the heart of the matter. "What is it, Dark? What have you seen?"

"Do you really want to know?"

It was the young prophet's constant inquiry, always delivered with the same flat, expressionless intonation, and always intended as a warning. Dark both saw everything that was to happen and knew at the same time that he was powerless to change it. He considered himself to live in bondage to the future—and tried as much as possible to spare others from the same fate.

"How would I know if I wanted to or not?" Seagryn answered. "You know why I'm here and probably knew it weeks ago. You know what you'll say, what I'll say, and whether any good can come from your telling me what you've seen—or if it's better that I not know. And of course, you knew I'd say this."

"Every word."

"So let's just skip on to living through the moment, shall we?" Seagryn loved Dark. And yet it seemed that each time they talked about the future he found himself angry with the boy. He didn't know why. Perhaps it was the frustration at being made to feel so predictable.

"We are, Seagryn," Dark murmured as he finally released his knees and rolled over to look at them. "This is the moment we're living through. Knowing what we'll talk about in an hour won't speed that hour to us—in fact, for me, it makes the time pass even slower. None of you can really understand me, despite how hard you try. I dread certain upcoming events, true, but I look forward with eagerness to others. In either case, though, I must endure the tedium of waiting for the rest of you to catch up. By the time you do, I'm already days ahead . . ." Dark let out a loud sigh and stared hopelessly at the ceiling. "And I can't sleep—not really. When I sleep, I dream of the future, and it's just like being awake . . ."

"Is there anything I can do to help?" Seagryn asked gently.

Dark rolled back to the wall. "You can go do whatever you choose to do, and not talk to me about it."

"But what do I—"

"At all." After a moment of silence Dark looked back over his shoulder and added, "Please?"

Seagryn gazed at him for a moment, then nodded once and walked out of the room. Uda and her mother pursued him down the stairs. "What was that all about?" Kerily demanded. "What happened?" she said again as Seagryn appeared to ignore her.

Nebalath and Fylynn waited at the bottom of the staircase. Their serious expressions reflected back his own. "Well?" Nebalath asked, his gray eyebrows raised.

Seagryn shrugged helplessly. "He's seen his own future—and doubtless ours, as well. It's filled him full of dread—yet none of us can do anything to prevent it." He lowered his head and said nothing more.

"You mean that's it?" Kerily exploded after a moment of silence. "That's all you're going to do, just walk up there and exchange two sentences with him and turn away?"

"What else do you expect us to do?"

"I don't know!" he snapped, her eyes wide. "I'm not the wizard. You are! I should have taken Ognadzu's advice days ago!" Uda, who'd been listening to all of this with embarrassment, suddenly looked at her mother and frowned.

"Ognadzu?" Uda said. "You've talked to Ognadzu?"

Kerily realized she'd said too much, for now her mouth sealed shut. She seemed to be searching about inside herself for that same enigmatic smile with which she'd greeted them.

"Mother?" Uda demanded. "Has Ognadzu been here?"

Kerily found it at last, and it blossomed upon her face: the Paumer House smile, an exact replica of that of her husband. "Where are my manners?" she said brightly. "You must be famished after all your travels!"

Fylynn had watched all of this with quiet amusement, and Seagryn knew her private commentary later would be hilarious. He glanced at her to catch her reaction and saw her gazing up the staircase in surprise. "Look!" she commanded, and they all did.

Dark stood on the landing behind them, weaving unsteadily upon his little-used legs. "Dark!" Uda cried. "You're up!"

"Of course I'm up," he mumbled, smiling slightly and clinging to the handrail. "I wouldn't miss this for the world."

"Miss what?" Nebalath asked. "This discussion?"

"Not the discussion. This!" Dark said, pointing above their heads—and then they saw it.

They stood under the same trellis from which Nebalath had rescued Kerily's green kitten. Though it had only been in place a few weeks it already looked as if it had stood there forever. In an attempt to make it look old, her gardeners had transplanted long tendrils of ivy from some ancient tower and had carefully woven them through every slat. There were a few places, however, where the sunbeams pierced the green canopy to throw patterns of light on the courtyard's tiled floor, and it was to one of these openings Dark pointed. All eyes were watching the precise spot when a tiny, two-headed creature suddenly shot down through it and glided in lazy circles above their heads on leathery, batlike wings. The watchers gasped in unison, like a choir. It was Seagryn who announced to all what it was. "The mouse-dragon! That's Sheth's mouse-dragon!"

Sheth had experimented upon rodents before transforming a pair of tugoliths into Vicia-Heinox. This had been his prototype— a tiny dragon formed of two mice. It had two mouselike heads stretching upward from a rat's body upon long, scaly necks. It also had a rat's bald, pink tail. But the creature's wings, ridged back, and glistening teeth were a tiny replica of those features on Vicia-Heinox. Although small, the mouse-dragon could terrify, and it did that just now as it hovered above them with its long necks weaving its heads about. It appeared to be looking for something. When it spotted its target, it dived.

"Mee-YOWL!" Seagryn heard some animal screech, then he

saw a green blur dart out of its hiding place and flash across the
floor. The dragon came after it in hot pursuit, and Seagryn watched
in astonishment as a cat the green of an emerald suddenly froze
in place and rose up on its hind legs to bat the pursuing mouse-
dragon from the air with a wicked right paw. As the dragon
bounced off the tiles and back into flight, the cat raced on, making
a wide circle around the courtyard in search of a place to exit. But
the dragon proved to be faster: it trapped its prey against the base
of the trellis. The kitten took the only escape open to it, shooting
up the latticework. As the dragon swooped upward after it, Kerily
screamed in horror, ''My kitten! That monster is after my kitten!''

It was indeed. While Seagryn was amazed both by the young
cat's intelligence and speed, he didn't give it a prayer of escaping.
He'd seen this mouse-dragon roast a squirrel with a single look.
Once this green kitten froze in place, the dragon would roast it to
cinders.

Not cinders, exactly, but a mass of smoking hair and lifeless
meat tumbled onto the courtyard floor a moment later. The kitten
had indeed hesitated, and the mouse-dragon had fixed upon it all
four of its eyes. As the once-cuddly kitten hit the tiles, so did
Kerily, passed out in a dead faint. The mouse-dragon had no
interest in its remains. Instead it shot back through the trellis and
up into the clouds, in quest of more felines to fry. This all had
happened with amazing speed.

Seagryn turned his head back up to look at Dark. He was smiling down at the woman who was passed out upon the mosaic
floor, surrounded by a circle of fanning servants. Dark's eyes met
Seagryn's. Then the boy winked.

''OHH!'' Kerily wailed as she regained consciousness, whether
in shock or grief, Seagryn couldn't tell. What a pretty little kitten
it had been, he thought to himself as he walked over to inspect
the smoking carcass. He could understand Kerily's attachment to
it. He gazed down into the little cat's lifeless eyes and grieved
with her.

''My snuff!'' Kerily cried, and a pair of servants scrambled
away to fetch whatever it was she was calling for. Seagryn had no
idea what a snuff was, and he walked over to the circle of servants
to investigate.

''So. That was the mouse-dragon.'' Nebalath breathed quietly
when Seagryn stepped up beside him. The old man seemed
shaken.

"What a lovely visit!" Fylynn said, perfectly imitating Kerily's false smile. "I'm so glad we came, aren't you?"

Seagryn looked at her soberly. "Your beloved Sheth made that creature," he murmured. "What do you think of that?"

She met his gaze evenly, her own expression turning as serious as his. "I think he's enormously talented." She then glanced past his head and muttered, "What are they giving her?"

One of the servants raced to Kerily with a vial of something in his hand. She jerked it from his grasp, opened it, and sprinkled some powdery green substance into her palm. As she carefully closed the vial and handed it back to the servant, Seagryn leaned forward to take a better look at this mysterious substance. Its color matched precisely the darker stripes of the dead kitten's furry coat. Kerily buried her nose in the powder and once again passed out. This time, however, a peaceful smile spread across her face, and she didn't wake up.

The servant who held the vial cupped it protectively in his hands and stepped away as others scooped up Kerily's utterly relaxed body and carried her past Dark and on up the stairs. Seagryn reached out and plucked at the servant's sleeve. "What is that substance?" he asked the man, who looked frightened by the question.

"What? What substance?"

"That snuff you hold in your hand," Nebalath said as he approached the servant from the other side.

Nervousness gripped the servant's features, and he cringed away from both of them as he sought to answer without revealing anything. "It's—she calls it—her—snuff. That's all I know, honestly! Just that!"

"But what does it *do*?"

"It kills dreams," Dark announced loudly from above them. His words silenced animated conversations all over the courtyard and drew all eyes to himself. He looked meaningfully first at Seagryn, then at Nebalath. Then he turned and began climbing the stairs back to his room.

Chapter Ten

※※※※※

SEASICK GREEN

I⊤ fell to Seagryn to bury the green kitten. He didn't have to, certainly. He could have left the mess for the servants to clean up. But when he overheard them discussing how best to skin the carcass in order to sell the beautifully striped pelt, Seagryn grew violently nauseated and decided Kerily's house staff ought to be just as sickened by the idea as he was. At his magical prompting, they all suddenly became so, their faces turning as green as the creature they'd planned to skin. They all fled the courtyard, clutching their stomachs and retching violently. Thus abandoned, Seagryn tenderly lifted the already stiffening remains and carried them out to the palace garden.

He didn't know why he cared, exactly—although he had noticed that he just seemed to care more about all living things these days. At least he felt no guilt this time. He'd had nothing to do with the making of the mouse-dragon. Yet he wondered—could it be he was trying, in this small way, to atone for all the unburied host of the Remnant he'd left back in the Central Gate? He found a spade and dug a hole near a grape arbor. Then, after he quietly pronounced over it the ritual words a Lamathian priest always spoke at graveside, Seagryn buried the little kitten.

By the time he returned to the house, Fylynn was coming down the stairway from Kerily's apartments. "Is she still asleep?" he asked.

"Like a baby. You should see her—sleep makes Kerily look

almost innocent." Fylynn smiled. "Think that green powder could do something for me?"

"I think it possibly could do something for Dark," Seagryn answered seriously.

"Hmm." Fylynn nodded. "That's just what Nebalath said before he disappeared."

"He's gone again?" Seagryn blurted out.

"He said he'd be back by nightfall." Fylynn shrugged and added, "Do you think we could get something to eat around here?"

True to his word, the old wizard reappeared in the courtyard before sundown, holding a few grains of the green powder in his hand. He plunged into his explanation without preamble. "This substance is so rare that not even the Imperial House seemed to know much about it. That's almost unheard of, you realize—that castle hears everything. It was able to tell me that the powder is extraordinarily expensive. The House of Paumer controls the existing supply, but his people contend there is simply no more available anywhere. What does exist has been parceled out in tiny packets like the one Kerily had. Each pack provides only enough of the substance for three or four good sleeps."

Seagryn frowned. "So we don't know where it comes from . . ."

Nebalath smiled victoriously. "Oh, yes, we do! I found references to both the powder and to its source in one of the most arcane works in my library!"

"You call those junky piles of books you're always sitting on a *library*?" Fylynn scoffed. "I thought you were just too lazy to send for furniture!"

"And what did it say?" Seagryn demanded.

"The powder originates on the most westerly of the spice islands!" Nebalath crowed with excitement. "Tomorrow we'll go down to Telimas and find a ship to take us there!"

"Tomorrow?" Fylynn said. "But I just got here! I'd like to spend a few days with my family."

Nebalath frowned. "You weren't invited, my dear. Seagryn and I are powershapers. We'll go alone."

"The spice islands," Seagryn muttered doubtfully. He'd been prepared to travel anywhere in the One Land to find help for Dark's problem, but to cross the sea? "Nebalath—I understand it takes weeks to sail to the spice islands. Months sometimes! And what with storms, and pirates, and sea monsters—"

"Why are people from Lamath always so negative?" Nebalath asked Fylynn.

"But Dark hasn't even told us he needs this powder!" Seagryn argued.

"He doesn't need to tell us," Nebalath said with certainty. "We already know."

"Oh?" Seagryn asked. "Are *we* prophets now, too?"

"No," the old wizard said, shaking his head. "But we wizards are excellent students of human nature. Think about it, Seagryn. Anything we believe can help us, we immediately begin to want. Whether the substance will do him any good or not, Dark thinks he needs it, and doubtless has thought so ever since he's known of its powerful properties. Who knows how long that's been? My guess is that this is what put the lad to bed: his foreknowledge of what the powder can do combined with his own imaginings of how much better it might help him feel. He's just a boy, remember, and he's not going to be of any use to us until we find him some of this green powder and let him get a few good nights of dreamless sleep."

"But why can't he use some of Kerily's?" Seagryn asked.

Nebalath raised a gray eyebrow. "You've met the woman. Do you think she'd willingly part with anything she possesses for the possible good of someone else? Especially her soon-to-be son-in-law, whom she views with such obvious scorn? Seagryn, we're right here at the coast. We're wizards, for goodness sake! What do we have to fear from a few pirates? True, we do have to sail over there because we don't know where exactly we're going. But once we've got it, if we get into any trouble we can just cast ourselves back to this courtyard!"

"You can, you mean."

Nebalath sighed. "If you must insist on your powerlessness, very well. I still contend you can do it, too. And when you need to, Seagryn, you *will*."

Despite the opulence of the room Kerily had provided, Seagryn slept poorly. Thoughts of perils on the sea kept him tossing and turning, and he eventually began wishing for a dose of the green powder himself.

Nebalath shook him awake far too early. "I've booked us passage on a ship out of Telimas that leaves at noon," the older wizard murmured. "We must be on our way."

Too sleepy to debate the issue, Seagryn rose and packed. Before he fully awoke, they were mounted again and riding south through the predawn gloom. They'd been on the road for several minutes before he realized that Fylynn rode beside him. "I thought you weren't going with us."

"I just couldn't stand to send you two off to a strange land alone," she explained. "Someone needs to take care of you. Besides, the more I thought about it—the sea air, the sunshine, a nice tan . . ."

"She thinks she's going on holiday," Nebalath growled.

Fylynn sniffed at that comment, as if she considered it unworthy of a reply; but when she didn't correct the old wizard, Seagryn guessed Nebalath had hit the truth. But why was he going? He didn't want to—he hadn't planned to—and what would he tell Elaryl? For several miles he pondered turning his horse around and riding back to Pleclypsa, but the longer he thought, the further south they rode, and turning back grew ever more difficult. Dawn was breaking, and he noted with curiosity the high-peaked houses of southern Pleclypsa. They were like none he'd ever seen, and they piqued his sense of adventure. Soon he would be seeing the South Coast and the fabled blue-green clarity of the southern sea— he could always turn back once he got there, and send Nebalath on without him. But to be this close and not even take a look? Besides—why should he want to return immediately to the burden of being Seagryn the Dragonspet?

"I need to stop here," Fylynn announced as she reined in her horse by a tiny shop and dropped from the saddle. "The owner is my cousin," she explained. "I need to send word to my parents not to expect me."

As Fylynn ducked inside, Nebalath scowled over at Seagryn. "Why did you tell her she could come?"

"Me?" Seagryn blurted. "I didn't tell her anyth—"

Seagryn stopped in midsentence, for Nebalath had suddenly shot him a look of warning and held up his hand for silence. A group of walkers passed by them, also heading southward to the sea. Seagryn would have glanced at them without really noticing anything about them had Nebalath not studied them so cautiously. They were walking too quietly . . .

All at once one of the men laughed aloud and turned to pass along to those behind him the joke he'd just been told. They laughed heartily, and several of them nodded at Nebalath before the group walked on out of sight.

Seagryn looked back at Nebalath curiously. "Did you recognize them?"

"No," the old wizard murmured, "but knowing how many

people would like to kill you, we cannot be too careful. Where is that woman? Fylynn!''

Seagryn sighed. The burden of being Seagryn the Dragonspet was something he wouldn't miss for a few weeks. He finally felt fully committed to the trip.

The two powershapers eventually had to go into the shop and drag Fylynn out in order to get back on the road. The sun was well up by the time they reached a high wall and Nebalath complained that they were behind schedule. Seagryn didn't listen. He was gazing up at the enormous wall that rose before them. "Is that the wall around Pleclypsa?" he asked. "I hadn't remembered the northern wall being so high."

"It's not," Fylynn answered. "This is the beginning of the Telimas Corridor."

"The what?"

When she saw his puzzled look, Fylynn cocked her head and looked at him with disbelief. "Haven't you ever heard of the famous double wall of Pleclypsa?" she asked. "Where have you been?"

"Lamathians are notoriously provincial." Nebalath shrugged.

Fylynn pointed forward. "You see ahead of the break in the wall? There appears to be a gate down to the south . . ."

"Yes . . ." Seagryn said, shielding his eyes to peer directly down the road. "But—it looks as if the walls continue on either side of the roadway . . ."

"They do. Come on, I'll show you." Soon they passed out the city gate, and Seagryn craned his neck to look up at the walls on either side. They each stood at least forty feet tall and formed a long, slender corridor toward the south as far as his eyes could see.

"What are they for?" Seagryn asked.

Fylynn answered with a touch of civic pride. "When the city fathers of Pleclypsa realized that the One Land was falling apart, they agreed that something needed to be done to protect our city's livelihood. This happened years ago, of course," Fylynn added as an aside. "I may have wrinkles but I'm not that old. Since the city's wealth was based on the sea trade, they knew Pleclypsa would always need to keep a route open to the ocean—but as you'll see from the ride this morning, we're really some distance from the port of Telimas."

"I'd just begun to notice that." Seagryn nodded.

"So, the city fathers decreed we would build walls on both sides of this road all the way to Telimas—a double wall all the way to the sea. There it is." She gestured upward.

Seagryn shook his head in amazement. "It's magnificent!"

Fylynn shrugged. "Yes—for another few miles. Then it just . . . stops."

"Stops? Why?"

"Why else?" Fylynn laughed. "The city ran out of money!"

Regularly spaced towers allowed access to the battlements on either side of them. From atop the walls warriors could defend the road from any attack—if there were any defenders. "I see no guards . . ." Seagryn said.

"It's not defended anymore." Fylynn shrugged.

"Never was," Nebalath corrected.

"But then why—"

By this time they had caught up with that band of travelers that had seemed too quiet, but they were all so lost in the conversation about the corridor that neither Seagryn nor Nebalath had noticed. Following the unspoken rules of the road, the footmen parted to let the riders pass. Seagryn thanked them without thinking—that was simply good manners. But at the sound of his voice one of the hooded walkers still before them whirled around and threw off his cloak. Seagryn looked back—and gasped. "Yammerlid? Is that you?"

"Thought you'd burned me up, didn't you, Seagryn Dragonspet? Thought you were rid of old Yammerlid! Here's news, magic user! You'll never be rid of Yammerlid! Not until the day you die!" As Yammerlid pulled a sword from behind his back and charged, the other walkers threw aside their disguises. A trap! They had ridden into an ambush, here between these walls!

Seagryn was too stunned to take any action. Fortunately he wasn't the only powershaper in the party. "Oh, dear," Nebalath mumbled, instantly cloaking the three of them from the attackers' view. It was the simplest of defenses and far too overused, he realized. Yet it was effective. Nebalath rubbed his invisible chin and pondered what to do next.

Yammerlid's cohorts reacted to the cloaking in differing ways. Some had never been in a magic battle, and this sudden disappearance so frightened them that they ran from the vanished wizards. Since there were really only two ways to run within this narrow corridor, the roadway quickly became very congested. The more daring comrades thus had time to rally their fellows before they ran away by shouting, "He's trapped! We have the wizard trapped!"

That quickly became obvious. The empty space in the middle of the mêlée was difficult to miss. Their courage returned, most of the attackers began flailing their weapons before them. They could hear the terrified snorting of the three riders' horses and clearly heard Fylynn shriek, "You two are supposed to be powershapers! Do something!" The assassins cheered with excitement and closed the circle tighter. Suddenly they heard the unseen horses whinny in surprise and wheel around. Startled anew, the band of assassins fell back, retreating still further as the cloaked animals bolted back toward Pleclypsa. A dozen attackers went down beneath invisible hooves as the horses broke through their ring and charged northward. The horses abruptly became visible, and those assassins still standing immediately gave chase. They all could see that the mounts now appeared to be riderless, but that only meant the riders continued to use their magic to hide themselves as they rode back toward the city. "Back to Pleclypsa!" someone shouted.

"After them!" Yammerlid called. None of the assassins who'd been ridden down appeared to be seriously hurt, but as the band of zealots chased a trio of horses up the Telimas Corridor, some were obviously moving much more slowly than others.

Nebalath paused halfway up the ladder inside the nearest tower to watch their flight through an arrow slit and murmured a heartfelt, "Good riddance!" He then snorted downward at Seagryn. "You might have used your abilities, too! Am I going to have to do all the work on this journey?"

"Would you move your bony little body?" Fylynn grumbled. She was between the two of them on the ladder and could neither go up nor down unless one of them budged. Since Seagryn was obviously too bemused to think straight, she'd directed her comment upward.

Seagryn was shaking his head in self-deprecation. "I don't know why I didn't! It's just, I . . . I don't think . . ."

"No, you certainly don't," Nebalath agreed as he pulled himself over the top rung and stepped out onto the battlements. He was relieved to see that the road below them was now clear. "It would help my feelings enormously if you would start."

Seagryn still stammered his explanation. "It was just—the shock of seeing Yammerlid . . ."

"Shocked me, too," Nebalath murmured, squinting his eyes against the morning sun as he watched the dust cloud churned up by their attackers rise further off toward the north. "He's the one I watched swear an oath to kill you. You remember me telling you about that?" he asked as Fylynn and Seagryn both joined him. "He's certainly come a long way in a short space of time,"

Nebalath mused. "It's as if he knew you were coming here." He looked at Seagryn meaningfully. "Makes me wonder who told him."

This thought took Seagryn completely by surprise. "But—who? Who knew we were coming?"

Nebalath's eyes didn't leave Seagryn's as he murmured, "Think about it." Then his gaze dropped away, back toward the road, and then toward that receding cloud of dust to the north. "We've fooled them this time, in any case. But what a nuisance! *The Norck Stork* is due to sail at midday! Without horses we won't get there until sundown!"

"The Norck Stork?" Fylynn said doubtfully.

Nebalath glanced back at her. "The name fits. You'll see when we get there." Nebalath winced in frustration and continued. "Which won't be by noon. I guess I'd better appear on the docks and try to delay the man—"

"Don't go!" Seagryn shouted, grabbing Nebalath by the shoulder. "I can get us all there *before* noon."

Nebalath rolled his eyes, then nodded his grudging agreement while Fylynn frowned. "How?" she asked.

"By tugolith," Seagryn answered, and he stepped back into the tower and descended the ladder. By the time that Fylynn reached the ground he had already taken his altershape and stood waiting in the middle of the road. "Get on," he rumbled in a deep bass voice.

"Oh!" the woman said first, gushing at the novelty of it. Then "Oh!" she said again, this time with less excitement and both hands clutching her nose. "What a smell!"

"You call this a smell?" Nebalath snapped in an oddly defensive way. Then his tone softened. "Believe me, child—it could be much worse. Climb on." The woman pulled herself up onto Seagryn's forehead by means of his scales and soon was seated behind his horn. Nebalath climbed up behind her, then leaned over to call into one of Seagryn's huge ears, "We're ready!"

"You don't have to shout," Seagryn grumbled. "My tugolith eyesight may be poor, but there's nothing wrong with my hearing. Shouldn't you cloak us?"

"It's already done," Nebalath replied, shifting his bottom to try to find a more comfortable perch. Then they were off—one horned monster with two riders, whom nobody on the road would now see. Seagryn did indeed get them to Telimas before midday.

The Norck Stork was a free trader, a vessel owned and operated by a certain Captain Norck. Seagryn had wondered how the man had avoided being incorporated into one of the giant trading houses. After one look at the *Stork*'s spindly masts and the awkward profile of its hull, he knew. It did look like an ungainly seabird. Nevertheless, Captain Norck was fiercely proud of it. As they cleared Telimas harbor and moved out into the open sea, he gestured up at its billowing green and orange sails. "You see those colors? They're registered in Pleclypsa! The House of Norck. I've hoisted those colors all over the southerly sea, and I can assure you they're highly regarded in foreign ports!"

"Which foreign ports?" Nebalath asked.

Norck looked at him, suddenly suspicious. "All foreign ports!" he answered firmly. "Why?"

"You've been to Emerau, then?"

"Emerau?" Captain Norck replied, his tone vague. "Emerau. No, I must have missed *that* one—"

"But you've certainly been to Looulam," Nebalath said.

"Why—of course!" Norck responded with a false smile.

"East or west port?"

"East or west . . ."

Nebalath watched the captain carefully. "Ports. On Looulam."

"Ah—yes! Both. Many times."

Norck was obviously lying, but Nebalath didn't challenge him. "Very good. We want to sail past Looulam's western port and southwest from there to the isle of Emerau."

"Ah." The captain nodded. "And—you have the charts?"

"Charts?" Nebalath frowned.

"Charts. Maps, if you will."

"Maps of the spice islands?" Nebalath frowned.

"Of the seas surrounding them, yes. I need charts to sail into those waters, my friend. Without them . . ." Captain Norck gave a doubtful shake of his head.

"Hmm," Nebalath mused. "I suppose I could find some . . ."

"And how would you be doing that when we're under sail?" Captain Norck smiled condescendingly. "Allow me to make a suggestion. We set a course due south to Mazeur on the northern tip of Faghar, and perhaps you can find your charts there. Or else another ship's captain who knows this island . . . what was it?"

Nebalath mulled this over. Suddenly he smiled pleasantly. "I think I may have the charts you need after all. Excuse me while I go look."

As the old wizard disappeared into the cabin, the captain gave

Seagryn a puzzled look. "What is he going to look through? You've brought nothing aboard!"

This was true. All of their possessions had been carried back toward Pleclypsa on the backs of their fleeing horses. Seagryn looked at Fylynn, who looked back at the captain and smiled pleasantly. "Rather a mystery, isn't it!"

"Here they are," Nebalath called from inside the cabin as he stalked back up the stairs to rejoin them on the deck. When Norck saw the charts, he looked astonished.

"Where did you get—"

"Doubtless he's been to Haranamous to fetch them." Fylynn shrugged. She then patted the bewildered seaman on the shoulder. "He's a most unusual travel companion. You'll get used to him."

Nebalath unrolled the map and pointed to a particular spot. "We want to go here."

"But how did you—" Norck spluttered as he took the charts and looked them over. Suddenly the captain began trembling like a sail come loose in a storm. "*There?* But that would take us right past Ushlar and near the tip of Main!"

"So it would appear." Nebalath nodded, craning his neck to try to read the chart upside down.

"But those are pirate waters!" Norck croaked.

Nebalath absently scratched his chin. "Pirates?"

"Pirates and more pirates! I cannot take you to Emerau," Norck announced as he rolled the chart back up.

Nebalath frowned, but the captain appeared to have his mind made up. The wizard didn't argue. He just said, "Very well. You're in charge." But as Nebalath walked back to sit in the stern of the ship Seagryn saw a determined look on the old wizard's face. He wasn't at all surprised, then, when the captain had a most difficult day. As Norck did his best to direct his vessel to the south, he found with every check of the compass that they had moved further to the west instead.

Late in the afternoon Seagryn came to sit beside Nebalath. "How are you doing this?" he asked.

"Doing what?" Nebalath said, feigning innocence.

"You know what I mean. Blowing us off course."

"As far as I can tell, we're very much *on* course." Nebalath chuckled.

"Then you are doing it."

"And how could I cause such a thing?" the older wizard protested.

"By changing the wind—"

"The wind!" Nebalath laughed. "Can you direct the winds?"

Seagryn frowned. "Well—no, but—"

"I've never met a wizard who could shape the winds! Nor any other natural force of the weather or of the earth," Nebalath said. "Oh, fire we can shape, surely. But not the rain that puts it out or the wind that spreads it. And fire is—well it's right there in the air, all the time. People, Seagryn—we have an impact on people, through what they believe they feel and see. I'm doing nothing, actually. It's the captain who is sailing us to Emerau—though he believes he is doing his best to avoid that very thing. And—yes. I am helping that along." Nebalath glanced down the length of the deck. "Where's Fylynn?"

"She's gone below. I'm afraid she's a bit seasick—"

"You may want to help her, then. I need to concentrate my attention on bending us toward the west—"

Fylynn sat on a bunk inside the cabin, a bucket between her knees. As Seagryn came down the steps, she gave him a weak smile. "Do you think green is my color?" she asked, pointing to her face. "I'm not certain it goes with my hair—"

"Can I get you anything?" he asked.

"Some dry land might be nice . . ." she joked, then she swallowed and stared straight ahead for a few moments as she listened to what was taking place inside her stomach. When the tide of her nausea ebbed, she looked at Seagryn again. "You don't seem to be—affected," she said, choking on the last word.

"I suppose I've grown accustomed to motion sickness. I've—spent a lot of time up in the air recently." There were pillows scattered about on the bunks, and he propped several of these behind her back. "Better?"

"A little. I'm certainly glad I came along to take care of you two—"

Seagryn smiled. "I'm sure you're here for a purpose."

"What purpose?" she asked. It was an honest question that caught him off guard.

"I—don't know. Yet."

"But why would you even think in such terms?" she asked, swallowing several times to maintain the momentary balance in her stomach. "I certainly don't."

"You don't?"

"Of course not. I don't have any purpose. I just—live." She frowned. It startled Seagryn, for Fylynn rarely allowed that expression onto her face. "And as I do, I stumble into situations in which I don't belong, and thereby cause those around me grief."

"You're not causing me grief," Seagryn said kindly.

Fylynn grinned at him. "Just wait until I fill this bucket and you have to empty it. *Then* you'll know grief! Ohh . . ." she added, for the ship suddenly seemed to shudder in the water, then abruptly floated upward. This was accompanied by much shouting on the deck above them. Fylynn looked up at him, her eyes lidded wearily and her body weaving on the bunk. "You're a priest, aren't you? You think prayer would do me any good?" He couldn't tell if she was joking this time.

"Pirates!" someone shouted, and Seagryn jumped to his feet in alarm.

"Send them down here," Fylynn murmured, pointing at her bucket. "I'll give them something to remember me by—"

Seagryn bolted up the stairs and searched the western horizon for a sail.

"Dead ahead," a voice above him called, and he turned to see Captain Norck standing on top of the cabin and pointing over the bow. "A bloodred sail—that's their sign. Makes it easier on Paumer's crews—all they need do is pull down their blue!"

"You think the pirates serve Paumer?" Seagryn shouted up over the noise of battle preparations.

"Of course they're Paumer's!" Norck called back bitterly. "How else could *his* fleet sail these waters unhindered, while any free trader that strays to the southwest is immediately boarded and scuttled! Tighten that line!" he shouted at one of his sailors. Then he jumped down off the cabin and ran forward, shouting instructions Seagryn didn't understand.

The shaper glanced around for Nebalath—and found him still seated quietly in the stern of the ship, in the place where he'd spent the whole day. Seagryn went to join him. "Looks like you've gotten us into some trouble."

"I told you before, Seagryn. I'm not afraid of a few pirates. But I *would* prefer not to reveal our abilities to these sailors. They're notoriously superstitious. Suppose we just handle this between ourselves?"

"Sounds fine to me," Seagryn agreed.

"But please don't take your enormous altershape while we're aboard this ship! Your weight would break it in two."

"I know." Seagryn nodded. "I've sunk ships before." He peered at the oncoming sail. He could see it clearly now, and it did resemble the shade of red used by the House of Paumer. "Norck believes these are Paumer's ships in pirate disguise."

"Could be." Nebalath nodded. "Or his son's."

"Ognadzu?" Seagryn smiled. "But he's just a boy!"

"So is Dark," Nebalath muttered seriously, his gaze focused upon that red sail. "I'd rather not cloak the ship. They've already sighted us, and if we disappear they'll know there are wizards aboard. That might make them pursue us more vigorously, and I'd rather not have them follow us to Emerau."

"We could set fire to them—"

"And how would we do that without revealing ourselves?" Nebalath asked wryly. "Shall we stand in the bow and toss fireballs, you and I? Use your imagination. Think of something subtle . . ."

"Prepare to be boarded!" Captain Norck shouted as he raced around the cabin from the bow of the ship, wildly waving a sword in each hand. When he came in view of the two wizards he stopped, pulled himself up into his most dignified posture, and walked toward them, offering the weapons to them. "Gentlemen, I very much fear we shall be taken, but I'd prefer not to go without a fight. Prepare to defend yourselves."

"How are we to do that?" Nebalath answered for both of them. "We're merchants, not swordsmen."

"Necessity makes sometime warriors of us all. Take these swords," he ordered as he thrust them both into Seagryn's hands. "I have other weapons in the cabin below. I'm on my way down to arm the lady—though I doubt she'll be able to prevent her own ravishment unless she turns the knife upon herself—"

"Ravishment?" Fylynn asked from the cabin doorway behind him. She stood supporting herself against the doorjamb with one hand while still holding her queasy stomach with the other. "That's the best news I've heard all day . . ."

Captain Norck entirely missed her humor. "Alas, my lady, I fear it is to be," he mourned as he pushed his way past her and down the steps. "Come—I'll arm us both."

"Don't I have a better chance if I just wait around up here?" she called down after him, then turned her head and winked at the two powershapers.

The red-sailed ship quickly closed on them. It was twice the size of their vessel and a sleek, speedy design. They would never outrun it. Seagryn looked at Nebalath. "Any ideas?"

"It'll come to me," the old man said. A look of alarm suddenly passed across his face, and he pointed at Fylynn. "What's she doing?"

Seagryn whirled to look. The woman's eyes were wide and round, and she was gulping like a fish. She suddenly raced for the gunwale and draped herself over it, and her whole body jerked. Seagryn crouched at her side. "Can I help you?"

"No need," she answered brightly. "I seem to be doing it quite well all by myself!" When she proved this again, Seagryn stepped back out of the way—and had a thought.

The *Stork* was tacking to starboard to avoid the onrushing pirate, but the larger ship had veered to meet her. Norck scrambled out of the hold and climbed again on top of the cabin. He waved his sword and danced about, shouting meaningful threats across the water.

"Good view from here, isn't it." Fylynn gulped, then her head bobbed downward again. It was indeed. Seagryn could clearly see the pirate captain—a fierce-looking man with bulging forearms and an ugly grin. Then he imagined what that captain might see if . . .

The man's grin disappeared, and his face blanched. It was quite apparent—as were the expressions on the faces of the pirate crew who lined the opposing vessel's side, grappling hooks in hand. They were horror-struck. Norck, too, saw this abrupt change in their demeanor and stopped shouting. For a moment, poor Fylynn was the only person making any sound . . .

Then the pirate crewmen burst into action, adding sail and steering hard away from *The Norck Stork*. The larger vessel had three oars on either side for navigating through reefs, and these now shot out and started cutting into the water. Norck watched them flee, his jaw sagging open in shock. Then he was shouting again—this time in triumph.

Fylynn bobbed her head back up. Between swallowing and spitting she managed to gasp, "Are they leaving?"

"They're leaving."

"I guess this means I don't get ravished . . ."

Seagryn patted her on the back. "You sound genuinely disappointed."

"What did you do?" she asked, climbing unsteadily to her feet and sighing with deep relief.

"Oh—never mind." He smiled, turning to watch Norck's victory dance around the ship. The captain raced from sailor to sailor, shaking each one's hand and congratulating them on their glorious victory. Seagryn glanced back at Fylynn. "Do *you* feel better?"

"Oh, much. For the moment, anyway." She let him help her to the nearest freshwater barrel and dip her a drink with the ladle hanging on its rim. Then he helped her stagger back to the stern where Nebalath still sat like a king enthroned. The old wizard wore a smug look.

"I played my part." He chuckled. "Did *you* do anything?"

"Of course," Seagryn snapped, a bit miffed by Nebalath's accusing tone. "Fylynn gave me the idea. I created—for pirate eyes only—the illusion that every soul upon our ship was throwing up into the sea. I'm certain they thought the plague was upon us, and that's why they fled in terror. What?" he asked, for he'd noticed Nebalath's eyes growing larger.

The old man laughed out loud. "Why, I created the image of a crew of corpses!" Then he glanced away, a puzzled look upon his face. "I wonder what they actually saw? Seasick skeletons?"

Whatever the vision, it proved horrible enough to cause that particular pirate vessel to put great distance between them. They saw no other ships over the next week and a half. Buoyed by his bloodless victory, now Captain Norck sailed fearlessly to the southeast, following Nebalath's ancient charts to a shore he'd never before seen—Emerau.

Chapter Eleven

❈❈❈

VICTORY'S SCENT

"I would come ashore with you, of course—" Captain Norck protested earnestly, his eyes fixed upon the silent green coastline.

"Of course." Seagryn nodded, trying to make it easy for the man.

"—but then who would stay here to watch the vessel?"

"I understand. You've got to stay with your ship."

"I mean," the captain continued, turning to scan the horizon from which they'd come, "there could easily be more pirates in this area!"

"There could be." Seagryn nodded again. He paid no heed to Nebalath, who stood behind Norck and rolled his eyes derisively. "But you will stay at anchor here and wait for our return?"

"Naturally," the captain agreed. Then a second thought obviously raced through his mind, for Seagryn saw it dance across Norck's features. "Ah—how long will you be?"

Seagryn looked at Nebalath, who shrugged and answered, "A few days, a week, two weeks—what does it matter? Wait for us and we'll make you rich. Leave us—" Nebalath pulled from within his tunic the weathered pages he'd fetched from his rooms in Haranamous. "—and you lose your charts."

The argument obviously wasn't lost upon the captain. Norck raised his eyebrows, then smiled warmly. "I'll have someone row you to shore."

Emerau had a long, gentle shoreline. The waves began breaking well off the beach, and it took several minutes for each to wash up onto the snow-white sand. The rowboat bounced around considerably as they made the trip; thus it was no surprise to Seagryn that as soon as they scraped bottom Fylynn hopped out of the craft and splashed up onto the land. She fell headlong into the sand, first shouting in thanksgiving and then in moaning with the frustrating realization that, despite this firm foundation, her stomach continued to churn as if still at sea. "When will it end?" she pleaded with the two wizards as they sloshed up onto the beach behind her, after helping the oarsman turn the rowboat around and shove it back out toward the anchored *Stork*.

"Give it a few minutes," Seagryn encouraged. "You'll get your legs back." He jumped up and down twice. "My own feel a little rubbery."

"Why is it so quiet?" Nebalath asked as he eyed the tree line suspiciously.

"I don't know," Seagryn answered, immediately suspicious himself.

Fylynn stood up and shook the powdery sand from her clothing. "Perhaps the trees don't find much to say to one another. You can hardly blame them. I imagine they don't get around much." The two wizards frowned at her, and she shrugged. "Are we going?"

Stepping from the beach into the forest felt like plunging through a green curtain into an entirely different world. None of them had ever seen foliage this flat and wide, in this many shades of green, nor such competition among plants for all of the available growing room. So thick was the jungle that within a few paces the sea had disappeared completely. The only way they could tell its direction was the noise of the waves constantly lapping at the shoreline. A few paces more and even that sense was denied them, for the thickness of the greenery and of the humid air itself seemed to suppress all sound, crushing it to the root-tangled ground. They stumbled forward, glancing at one another for encouragement but finding little of that available. As if on cue, they all stopped walking together—and the silence engulfed them.

"Where are we?" Seagryn whispered to Nebalath. It seemed disrespectful—even dangerous—to speak normally in such a place.

"I don't know," Nebalath whispered back.

"You're on the verge of Mora," a voice only an arm's length away explained, and the three voyagers all gasped in surprise and grabbed one another for support. It was Fylynn who recovered first.

"Oh, that's a relief. I'd thought we were in the middle of no-where."

."No," the voice said, and the speaker stepped into view. "Just on the verge of it."

He was very tall, dressed in a shining material that looked like high quality fish-satin. The garment was wound round and round his body like a Lamathian funeral shroud. What most startled them was his skin color: He was purple. Not that they could be certain that this was a he—the speaker's darker-purple hair hung to the shoulders of his shroud wrap, but his voice sounded deep and resonant. He didn't seem to be joking.

"We're on the *edge* of nowhere then," Fylynn corrected her-self when it became apparent that her two male fellow travelers were still dumbstruck.

"Very much so. We've come at some hardship to fetch you."

"We?" Fylynn asked. As if in answer, about a dozen similarly shrouded figures stepped out of the green curtain and surrounded them. Their faces weren't at all menacing, but still Seagryn's heart pounded. They were all so tall—and so purple.

"And—how did you know where to come?" Nebalath had finally found his voice.

The speaker seemed puzzled by the question at first, then ap-parently made some mental connection and nodded. "We've been expecting you. Join us, won't you?" Then he stepped to one side and gestured for them to precede him.

Fylynn looked at Nebalath. "Aren't you going to do some-thing?"

The old wizard's forehead creased with concern. "I tried," he said—obviously very uncomfortable with the idea.

"Yes," the purple speaker nodded. "You tried to make us believe you three were invisible. Why is that?"

Nebalath shrugged. "Oh—no reason."

The speaker paused, looking down. Then he looked back up at Nebalath. "No, you tried to make us believe this because you wished to escape. Why would you wish to escape from us?"

"It—seemed a good idea at the time." Nebalath obviously felt humiliated; when his eyes met Seagryn's inquiring gaze, he snarled, "Why don't *you* try something then?"

"I didn't know if I needed to—and now, I don't know whether it would do any good." He looked at the purple speaker, who watched with apparent patience. "I had understood that you—people who live in the spice islands spoke a different tongue from that of the old One Land. How do you know our language?"

"Oh, we don't. Our masters do—and they tell us."

"Umm." He nodded. "And are your masters from the old One Land?"

The speaker paused, eyebrows knitted, his eyes focused above their heads. Then he answered, "No."

"Ahh," Seagryn said, nodding again and trying to think of another question that would help him make sense of the purple speaker's flawlessly pronounced words.

"You want to know how our masters know your speech," the speaker supplied, smiling slightly, and Seagryn, surprised, could only nod. "They understand your thoughts—the thoughts of all three of you. Our thoughts as well. They place answers to your questions in my mind, and I speak them to you. It's really quite a simple system, really. Shall we go?"

Fylynn and Seagryn started forward obediently, but Nebalath was not yet convinced. "If they can place these thoughts in your minds, why can they not place them in ours directly?"

"Oh, they could," the speaker explained with a magnanimous smile, "but you're not yet domesticated. Please," he added with a warm smile, "come with us. You've been traveling far, and certainly you'll want to get out of these uncomfortable garments and put on something more compatible with the climate. Oh, and one of you is hungry, as well!" he added.

Fylynn looked back and forth at the two wizards, then sucked in her stomach and snapped, "Why not? I haven't kept a meal down in days!" She stalked past the speaker, then turned her head to call back over her shoulder, "Although, looking at him, I'm not certain I'm going to want what they serve . . ."

"You'll find it delicious!" The speaker smiled, falling in to walk behind her and letting the wizards trail them both. "Already our masters have picked from your mind your favorite foods and are giving instructions as to their preparation. You'll find it a delightful meal!"

Seagryn glanced at the placid purple faces that ringed them, and shuffled forward. Nebalath stepped right in behind him and leaned forward to whisper, "What are you thinking about?"

"Elaryl, actually," Seagryn replied with a sigh.

"Good. Keep thinking of her."

He got Nebalath's meaning but disregarded it as having come much too late. He'd already made the assumption that they might be in danger if these "masters" learned of their mission and opposed it. But since the masters obviously could read thoughts, they doubtless knew already why these voyagers had arrived upon their shores. And if he and Nebalath couldn't shape the local powers, then their situation looked very nearly hopeless. All of this had led his thoughts back to Elaryl—why hadn't he turned around and returned to her when he had the chance?

All these thoughts tumbled over one another in his mind as they stumbled deeper into the jungle. With each vine they struggled under, each huge leaf they dodged, it seemed the air grew both hotter and wetter, until he could imagine they were walking under a stifling green ocean rather than a canopy of trees, and he began wondering if it was possible that he could drown. He almost stepped on the heels of the speaker, for the man paused, then looked back over his shoulder at Seagryn. He shook his long, purple locks and answered, "No." Then he turned and plunged on.

"Nebalath," Seagryn murmured wearily without looking back, "why won't our magic work here?"

"I thought you were thinking of Elaryl!"

"But now I'm thinking of magic. If ours won't work here, why should these creatures be concerned if we talk about it?"

"Isn't it obvious?" the old man snarled. His normally sour disposition was not being helped by this humid march. "I've told you before, wizardry hinges upon our imaginations! If they can read our thoughts, then they'll recognize our illusions for what they are! Thus—we're in trouble."

Seagryn pondered that. "Is it that they read your thoughts and knew they were imagined, or did you somehow *reveal* to them that you didn't believe the illusion yourself?"

Nebalath sighed heavily. "What do you mean by that?" he moaned.

"Only that—perhaps—this particular circumstance might require faith."

The old wizard grunted. "Meaning that if you believe it, they'll be fooled into believing it, too?"

"I don't consider that being fooled, Nebalath. I *do* believe it, remember?"

"Let me put it this way," Nebalath said gruffly. "If faith in some Power or other can extricate us from this situation, then I'll have to leave our rescue up to you. Though I was born and raised in Lamath, I never had a thimbleful of faith. Not even a grain of it."

Again the speaker stopped and turned around. "The masters want you to reflect more upon this Power." Just that—then he was off and walking again. He was a voice and nothing more.

"Now I see it!" Nebalath cackled, and Seagryn frowned back at him in some confusion until he explained. "What better way to confuse them than to get them thinking about theology! Your faith may get us out of this after all!"

Feeling rather naked, Seagryn nevertheless did as he'd been instructed—and, he reminded himself, as he himself chose; he thought about the Power. The speaker did not turn around again, and before much longer Seagryn noticed that the jungle was thinning out—or, rather, becoming more orderly. It was soon quite clear that somewhere they had crossed over out of the bush and into a tropical garden. The air seemed less dense here. Despite his worry, Seagryn couldn't help but enjoy the beauty that now surrounded them. Waxy magenta flowers grew from dangling vines, and multicolored birds swooped and darted around the trees that now seemed to arch together much higher over their heads. The green of this garden seemed less yellow-green and more the richer, cooler blue-green of the forests of home. Then they began to encounter dwellings—large, rectangular buildings faced with a glistening white stone. Seagryn was finding it difficult not to be impressed with these purple-tinted people—and, by extension, with their masters.

As the stone houses became more frequent, the garden yielded to them, and certain purple members of their party left the column and went off to—apparently—their homes. Nebalath called Seagryn's attention to this with a touch on the shoulder and a gesture. He did so again when the last man behind him abruptly dropped out of line and angled toward a house where violet children played. "Why are they leaving us?" he whispered.

"You think they couldn't immediately swarm back out and surround us if we took it in our minds to flee?" Seagryn asked. He noticed that the speaker had reached out to pull Fylynn back even with him, and now he gestured to the two wizards to join them. The warmth of the gesture was unmistakable. They walked four abreast into the heart of the city. They each glanced to the speaker to gauge their direction and soon saw they were headed for a long, low building some distance away, which appeared to be somewhat larger than the houses they'd passed. When finally they reached the door, Seagryn took a deep breath and plunged inside. He was prepared to meet the masters.

"Oh, they're not here," the speaker told him. "No," he went on, "I really doubt if they'll reveal themselves to you. But look! Here's a table, and a feast spread upon it!" The words were almost an understatement. The table before them struggled to stand beneath a load that would surely have challenged the tables of the King of the old One Land . . . "When there was such," Seagryn mumbled sadly to himself, remembering little Merkle.

"Such a small person," their host marveled. "And white as a house, too . . ."

"If the masters aren't here, where are they?" Nebalath demanded, stepping to the table and picking up what appeared to be the leg of some roasted bird—some large roasted bird.

"That's—not for me to say," their purple guide responded.

"You can't say? Or you don't know?"

"Oh, I know, certainly—we all know. But—we don't speak of such things."

"Or even think about them?" Seagryn prodded, and the man's purple curls bounced as he nodded vigorously.

"Exactly. It isn't done."

Seagryn looked at Nebalath, shrugged, and plunged ahead. "What about a powdery green substance that puts the mind to sleep? Do you talk about that?" Their host froze in obvious horror. "Or—even think about it?" Seagryn added a moment later. When the man's silence continued, Seagryn murmured to Nebalath, "The masters are obviously instructing him what to say next."

"I wish someone would instruct me what to *do* next," Nebalath said back. "Did you have some plan of action behind this frontal assault? Or did the idea just pop into your head?"

"The masters would like you to sleep here tonight—or for as long as you choose to stay. This is your home. You'll find bathing facilities and clothing provided in the anteroom beyond. As to what you choose to do next, or where you choose to go—that's entirely up to you. If you wish a guide, just ask the masters, and they shall provide you one." As abruptly as he'd appeared to them that morning near the beach, the tall island dweller turned to go.

"Wait!" Seagryn called, and the man stopped immediately and looked back. "What would they do to you if you thought about such things—the masters, I mean?"

The man smiled broadly. "Are you teasing me?"

"Not at all! What would they do?"

The man's disbelieving smile didn't fade. "They'd eat us, of course." Then he was out the door and gone, on his way home, Seagryn assumed, to rejoin his family and put his day with these odd visitors out of his mind.

"He didn't lie. It's delicious." Fylynn had made several circuits of the table by this time and was looking rather overstuffed.

"Too delicious," she added, her hand on her stomach. "Since you gentlemen have yet to eat, I'll just go bathe and find some clothes. These," she said, looking meaningfully down the front of her garments, "smell as if they've been worn by a fish." She disappeared through an archway on the far side of the hall, and they soon heard her splashing. Nebalath continued to gnaw his bird leg, while Seagryn surveyed the table and made his own selections.

"What do you think?" he finally asked.

"I'm still trying *not* to think," Nebalath answered. "There doesn't seem to be much future in it." He tossed aside the bone and settled down into a chair, which was obviously built for a much taller frame. Since his feet didn't reach the floor, Nebalath pulled them up into the chair with him. "Still, I suppose we must do some planning. I suggest we get a good night's sleep and get up before dawn."

Seagryn groaned. "Why is it your plans always seem to start so much earlier in the day than mine?"

"We need to find something that these purple people are forbidden even to think about. We can't cloak ourselves here, thus we must move under cover of darkness. We're all dead tired after our jungle trek. Early morning seems the most obvious answer."

"And what do you think these masters will be doing? Dreaming? We may become somebody's breakfast."

"We've not yet seen these masters, nor heard from them directly. I have a feeling about them."

"And that is?"

"I think they're powers of some kind. These games they appear to be playing in our minds are a type of shaping. And who knows? A good night's sleep, and we might be shaping *them*."

"Help!" Fylynn cried from the other room, and both of them jerked with surprise. A moment later they raced through the arch to find her struggling, wrapped in the coils of—a garment of some kind?

The clothes laid out for them by their hosts were naturally of the same wraparound design the purple people wore themselves. On them, the wraps had looked neat and even. Fylynn appeared rather more like a poorly bandaged warrior. In some places the yellowish cloth wound around her too tightly, cutting into her and restricting her movement. In other places it sagged open, exposing more of Fylynn's flesh than she wished to show or they wished to see. "Can either one of you figure out how this goes on?" she pleaded.

Neither one could, with the result that well before dawn the next morning they rose and donned the same old clothes they'd worn from Pleclypsa, still moist from being washed out the night before.

"What difference does it make?" Fylynn whispered when Nebalath grumbled about this. "They'd be dripping wet again by midday anyway . . ."

The people of Emerau were not early risers. No one challenged them as they slipped out of the large guest house into the predawn mist. Not knowing which way they needed to go, they'd agreed previously to head toward the center of the island. Silently they turned toward the south and soon slipped past the last white-stone house. As far as they could tell, no one inside stirred. Once the dwelling was out of sight, both Seagryn and Nebalath held hands out before them and made the attempt—and both created balls of fire to light their way before and behind. This was a cheering portent. "So. We can shape here," Nebalath whispered. He sounded much relieved.

The garden narrowed on either side of them but did not immediately close before them. Indeed, it seemed to funnel them forward, as if they walked a carefully tended pathway through the jungle. This made the walking itself easy but made them feel distinctly uneasy, as if they wandered into a trap or something watched them from beyond the bushes. As Seagryn let his mind run through lengthy speculations about the nature and appearance of the masters, he wondered if anyone was listening to him. 'Yes,' said a voice right behind him, and he stopped abruptly.

"What is it?" Nebalath whispered.

"You didn't hear that?"

"Hear what?"

"A—voice. Inside my head, I guess." He started moving forward again, his head down in thought. "I believe one of the masters just spoke to me."

"You mean they haven't spoken to you before?" Fylynn asked, and both wizards looked at her. "They've been chattering at me all morning. At least, I guess it's them."

"Why didn't you say something about it?"

Fylynn shrugged. "I suppose I just assumed they were already speaking to you as well. Didn't you dream about them?"

"No," Seagryn said, vaguely disappointed. He couldn't explain why it bothered him, but he somehow felt rejected because they'd not spoken to him before. Nebalath's next question revealed they'd not been talking with him, either.

"What are they saying?" the old wizard asked.

"Oh, things like 'turn back,' 'depart the island immediately,' 'you're in grave danger,' 'don't trust these two wizards'—that sort of thing."

"And you've not answered back?" Seagryn asked, amazed.

"Of course—to them directly. In my head."

Nebalath and Seagryn exchanged a look of deepest concern. "What do you make of it all?" Nebalath finally asked her.

Fylynn raised her eyebrows. "I just figure we must be going in the right direction."

'Why were you such a fool?' the voice in Seagryn's head said. 'This morning you will die.'

"They just spoke to me again," Seagryn murmured.

"And to me," Fylynn said.

"And to me," Nebalath whispered, his head rolling backward and his eyes rising toward the sky. Suddenly those eyes focused. "Look!" he said, and pointed.

A majestic structure loomed above the tops of the trees before them—a tall, slender cone. It appeared to be shaped of the same glistening white stone the people of Emerau used for their houses. In the dawn's light, it glowed a rich violet-pink. "That's where we're going," Fylynn said quietly. "I expect someone will be waiting there for us—"

As if in answer to her words there came a deafening roar. The sound emanated from all around them, and while none of them had ever heard its like they each could tell the roar was a chorus of many living voices—frightful voices. Even Nebalath trembled. "What was that?" he managed to whisper at last.

"The collected anger of the masters," someone nearby answered them, and they all turned that way to see their purple host from the day before. His face looked gaunt, hollowed out by grief. His ready smile had disappeared. His hair tangled around his shoulders in matted knots, as if he'd not had time to groom it. He spoke somberly, the way Seagryn had been taught to address mourners at a funeral. "I told you—this place is forbidden."

"Who are these masters?" Nebalath demanded. "What are they!"

"They're huge green cats," Fylynn supplied, and both Nebalath and Seagryn looked at her in surprise. "I told you," she explained, "I dreamed of them all night."

"Green cats?" Seagryn said. "Like the one Kerily had in—"

"That was a kitten. These are full grown."

"And very angry," their guide added with great resignation in his voice. Then he turned toward the lustrous cone. "Shall we go?"

"It's forbidden, yet they'll let you lead us there?" Nebalath asked.

"The masters permit no encroachment on their sleeping chamber. They'll kill us all. I simply thought you might wish to look more closely at the place that you've come so far to die for. Then again, perhaps it is that *I* want to see it myself, to try to understand the why of my own fate."

"Why did you come if it will cost you your life, too?" Seagryn asked, feeling the tickle in the back of his mind of that grinding guilt that constantly plagued him. The man's answer sent it pumping through him like blood.

"I had no choice. The masters summoned me to greet you here and explain their temple to you. I know things about it now I've never known, nor had any wish to learn. Since I do—I die with you. Shall we go?" He turned back toward the shining monument and started walking. They followed him, unwilling to look at one another.

After only a few minutes of walking they stepped out of the garden and into a grassy meadow. The cone rose high above them here, and they could see now how massive it was. Seagryn tried to peer inside one of the three openings in its base visible from this side, but the interior of the cone appeared to be black. As they walked closer to the structure they could see that its face was not as smooth and featureless as it had appeared from a distance. They could see the cracks where the gigantic sheets of stone had been fitted together. Seagryn started to walk up to it but froze when a menacing green form slipped suddenly out of that shadowy interior and stopped to stare at him. Then it roared.

Seagryn had seen teeth much bigger than those the huge cat showed him. He had, after all, gazed into the drooling jaws of Vicia-Heinox. But he'd never seen eyes the likes of these on any beast. They were not human eyes—they were more. A deep, rich violet in color, they gazed at him that moment in his thoughts. At the same time Seagryn felt the beast—the being?—did not understand him at all. Not because it lacked the capacity; rather, it did not choose to be understanding. It chose to be enraged.

'You are a fool,' it thought to him, and he heard the thought expressed clearly. 'All people are fools.'

Seagryn could not take his eyes off this threatening creature, so he felt rather than witnessed the other green cats that slipped out of the cone or the forest to encircle them. He heard the guide speaking behind him, intoning in a flat, listless voice words the man obviously was being required to repeat.

"These are the masters—the true Emeraudes. We are their pets—and their responsibilities. They rule us not by choice, but because they must—they hear the thoughts of each of us, and hear them constantly, their minds ever filling with the ridiculous prattle of the world of men. They had no respite until they found the spores which, when inhaled, allow them to sleep in silence. Many years ago they guided the strongest men of the land to erect this structure, to give the green spores a place to grow and flourish. They then devoured the builders to erase the knowledge of this tower from the memory of my people. The green powder you came seeking fills all the cracks of this palace of sleep, this temple of peace and quiet. Your coming has disturbed their rest—again. As a result we all must die."

"Perhaps not all of us." Nebalath smiled grimly, and he angled toward the face of the cone, his eyes watching the Emeraude that was nearest to him. Fylynn followed him, sticking close, and Seagryn and their guide moved too, watching the slowly closing circle, not the way they were going. Thus the little group moved as a clump, and the ring of cats tightened around them, pinning them to the wall.

'You think to grab a handful of the powder and disappear?' one of the Emeraudes thought toward Nebalath, but Seagryn heard the thought, too, and he looked at the older wizard accusingly.

"It was just a thought." Nebalath shrugged, glancing at Seagryn. His gaze shot immediately back to the nearest Emeraude, who seemed to be preparing to pounce. For the first time since he'd known the man, Seagryn had seen true terror in the old powershaper's face.

Fylynn put her back to the cone, her own face tense. "If I'd not come the two of you *could* just grab some of the stuff and disappear—couldn't you?"

Seagryn backed up to the glossy surface beside her. "As I've tried to tell Nebalath, I've not yet discovered how to perform that little feat."

'But you are too noble to try, in any case,' the Emeraude who stared him down supplied. 'Your foolish loyalty condemns you. You think to stay and die rather than to abandon this corpulent woman to our vengeance.'

"Corpulent!" Fylynn gasped, her back stiffening and her jaw jutting forward. Then she glared at Seagryn. "Was that *your* descriptive thought or that of this foul feline?'' Seagryn did not reply but watched as she slung a water bottle down off her shoulder and uncapped it.

"What are you doing?" he whispered.

"I'm going to throw water on them," Fylynn huffed, scowling into the nearest pair of violet eyes. "You cats hate water, don't you? Well, have some!" She grabbed the container tightly with both hands and pitched it forward, throwing an arc of water out toward that face. The huge cat nimbly danced aside, and Fylynn looked at Seagryn. "Makes you wish we'd brought along that little rat-dragon, doesn't it?"

A powerful roar shook them all again, as they simultaneously heard the thought, 'What are you doing?'

Fylynn glanced to the side to see that Nebalath had turned his back to the threatening Emeraudes and was facing the cone itself. He had tied a scarf over his nose and opened an empty leather bag looped around his neck, and was now scooping handfuls of green powder out of a crack.

"You have plenty of the stuff," his muffled reply came. "I have a friend in Pleclypsa who needs some."

All the Emeraudes roared at that, and the entire jungle around them trembled at the sound. Effortlessly one cat leaped toward Nebalath's back, jaws gaping wide and claws extending forward. The old wizard was doomed.

Or would have been. The cat never made it. Instead it found itself spitted in midair upon a huge, pointed horn, then tossed backward over its fellows to land wounded and bleeding on the edge of the jungle beyond. The ring of cats dodged outward but did not flee, as Seagryn in his tugolith form stepped out before his human companions and looked balefully into many pairs of violet eyes. "Fylynn!" he rumbled in the deep bass voice of his altershape, "take the purple guide and duck inside the cone! They can't read your thoughts in there—they'll fall fast asleep. It's your only chance of escape! Nebalath—you go, too. I'll hold these creatures off as long as I can!"

"I really hate to do this," Nebalath grumbled behind him.

"Go!" Seagryn roared, his head lowered and his point shifting from cat to cat to cat. The Emeraudes had taken his measure now and closed around him. In another moment they would be on him, their claws ripping through his scaly hide and their teeth tearing at his flesh. He knew he was dead, but he would take some of these ferocious Emeraudes with him. He promised himself, how-

ever, one last brief glimpse of Elaryl in the moment before all his
senses fled.

"I suppose you've gathered that I never wanted to reveal my
altershape," Nebalath confessed.

"Go! Run! Now!" Seagryn rumbled, but Nebalath seemed
amazingly nonchalant in this moment of doom.

"There's been reason for that, of course. It's a shame, it really
is, but I very much fear I shall have to take it now—"

An Emeraude leaped. Seagryn speared it and tossed it aside so
quickly that the tip of his wicked horn looked like a blur. It was
ready to pierce and discard the second leaper, and the third, but
he knew he'd not withstand all of them. He stepped back, planting
his huge rump against the wall of the cone and hunching his neck
in preparation for the next charge.

It never came. Instead he heard the most horrible mewling,
moaning, screeching howl he'd ever heard in his life, and the cats
melted before him into the forest. Before he could ask himself the
reason, he inhaled it. The *stench*!

It was a smell unlike any his olfactory sense had ever been
required to endure. In the past, Seagryn had stood in the midst of
a vast host of tugoliths, and the aroma of that gathering had so
benumbed his nostrils that he'd felt a little dizzy. Yet there was
no comparison. The memory of that stink, great as it had been,
seemed in this moment but a brief, distasteful whiff upon the
breeze. The billowing odor that now rolled up and around this
cone would doubtless taint this place for eons. A monumental
stench, a mythical stench, a stench of almost mystical proportions
bore witness to the fact that old Nebalath's altershape was none
other than that most insidious of furry forest creatures—a mudgecurdle.

Mudgecurdles looked like bunny rabbits. Exactly like bunny
rabbits, with long, floppy ears and wriggling noses and cute little
powder-puff tails. But blessings upon any poor creature within
sight of a mudgecurdle when it fluffed its cute little puff. So horrible was the aroma of the mudgecurdle that it had made all bun-
nies suspect. Rabbits proliferated in areas where mudgecurdles
had been spotted—or rather, scented—with the result that they
were a terrible nuisance to grain farmers. But what was a peasant
to do? The risk of chasing a bunny from one's barn was simply
too high. "You mudgecurdle!" had become the foulest of epi-
thets, meaning as it did both traitor and stinker in one thought.
Seagryn immediately took his human form again for one compelling reason: as a tugolith he couldn't hold his nose.

The clearing around the cone remained empty of Emeraudes. The purple guide, Seagryn was told later, had fled screaming. Fylynn had taken refuge within the temple of peace and quiet and could be heard clearly, gagging and retching, while Nebalath—human again—leaned against the wall of the cone and studied his fingernails self-consciously. He refused to meet Seagryn's eyes as he quietly murmured, "Shall we go?"

Chapter Twelve

✳✳✳✳

ELARYL'S STAND

"If there's anything to you at all, why don't you *do* something?" Elaryl shouted as she shook her fist at the sky.

Weeks had passed since she'd been visited by the strange old wizard who called himself Seagryn's friend. In the days since his last appearance she'd waited in vain for some new message from Nebalath concerning Seagryn's safety and whereabouts. Her patience—with both Seagryn and the Power—was growing thin indeed. And since Seagryn was unavailable, Elaryl blasted the Power daily with her frustrations. The rooftop of the new Talarath mansion made an excellent place to ventilate these feelings. She didn't know whether the Power was up, down, inside her or all around her, but wherever the Power *was*, on the rooftop she could at least shout.

"My father taught me you were the most powerful agency in the cosmos! I believed it, Seagryn believed it—all Lamath believes it still! So what are you *doing* about my husband?"

"My Lady," a tiny voice called hesitantly, and Elaryl whirled to face her maid.

"What is it?" she demanded. "Can't you see I'm talking to someone out here?"

Her maid—a slender brunette named Jocelath—trembled at these words but shook her head. She stood inside the dome that roofed the stairway down into the house. Elaryl knew that on no account would Jocelath come outside. She also knew why, and it greatly irritated her. She turned her back on her maid and continued her conversation with the Power silently. As she knew it would, the maid's plea came again—more urgently. "My Lady!"

Elaryl spun around again. "What?"

"My Lady, the dragon has been seen about, and . . . Please—my Lady. Won't you please come inside?"

Elaryl again turned her back on the curly-haired girl and walked decisively to the battlements. "Why should I?" she demanded, peering at the western horizon of Lamath. It had been in that direction that Seagryn had departed. Though she knew in her head he'd traveled all about the world since that time, emotionally she couldn't help but watch the west for his return.

"It will do no one any good if your husband returns to find you've been eaten—"

"Maybe I want to be eaten, Jocelath! Have you thought about that?"

"My Lady, don't even joke about—"

Elaryl ignored the girl's protests, continuing, "Maybe I consider that the shortest route to the Power's presence! I hear certain idiots are thinking such these days . . ."

Jocelath anxiously scanned that portion of the sky she could see through the doorway. "My Lady, *please*! You know that the dragon has recently been sighted very near this region, and if you care at all about your personal safety you'll—"

"Who's that?" Elaryl snapped, for in pacing around the low wall she'd noticed a cloud of dust on the road to the north. That usually meant riders from the capital city, which in turn usually meant news. Before Jocelath could finish her plea, Elaryl had bolted past her on her way down the stairs to investigate.

"Father!" she shouted as she hustled down the hallway past Talarath's apartments. "Riders from the north." She hurried down to the next landing.

"Riders?" Talarath responded, popping his dour head out the door and calling down after her. "I wasn't expecting any—any riders . . ."

She didn't pause as she continued down to the first floor, but she did feel troubled. It seemed to Elaryl that her father's tone of voice had changed markedly in recent weeks. He seemed so much more uncertain about things than she'd ever heard him sound before. What had so shaken his confidence that he hesitated now before he spoke? "Nothing," she grunted to herself as she marched down the entryway and opened the door. "It's my imagination." Or was it that Talarath was getting old? She had a difficult time permitting herself that thought—especially with Seagryn off so far away . . .

It was several minutes before the source of the cloud of dust turned up the long, tree-lined lane that led up to the house. By that time she'd been joined by her father and several of the servants, including Jocelath. Once she'd identified the oncoming carriage as that of Ranoth, she glanced aside at her timorous maidservant, and the girl smiled back at her, happy that her mistress would not be eaten today, at least. Jocelath was certainly loyal; she couldn't fault the girl for that. "Run up to my apartments and lay out the light-blue velvet with the high waist. Now what is it?" she sighed, further annoyed by the girl's quick frown.

"My Lady, it's still summer—"

"It's not that hot! Go do it!" She turned back to look out the door in time to catch Talarath hiding a frown of his own. There it was again. He never used to hide his displeasure!

"It's early to be dressing for dinner," he murmured. The implication was clear, and Elaryl responded to it immediately.

"I am going to meet with Ranoth this time, Father. There's no use in your trying to prevent me from it!"

"I think that's a decision that should be left up to the—"

"I said I am," Elaryl said with finality, not expecting for a moment that it would actually be the last word. To her surprise, it was, or very nearly so.

"I see." Talarath nodded stiffly. Was he trembling slightly? "If you insist. Cheragon," he continued, turning to the steward of the house, "they've been here so frequently, I'm sure Ranoth and his party know precisely where they'll be staying. See that they're made comfortable. I'm going to dress myself."

Elaryl watched him carefully as he climbed the stairs, certain that he moved a step or two more slowly now than she'd remembered. And did his head droop forward more? Was he sick? As she climbed the stairs after him, she realized she was drooping some herself . . .

"My Lady," Jocelath began doubtfully, but this time Elaryl cut her off. It was the third time her maid had protested the choice of this dress since lacing her into it, and Elaryl grew weary of the issue.

"It feels *fine*. It's an excellent fit, the weather is cooling, and it promises to be a pleasant evening, perhaps a nice night for a walk—"

"You're not going outside?" Jocelath asked, a fretful finger to her lips.

"I don't know!" Elaryl groaned as she walked quickly toward the door, Jocelath trailing her anxiously. "I might. And what difference does it make? The dragon doesn't fly at night, does he?"

"I don't think anyone knows . . ." the maid said, still worried.

"Except perhaps my husband," Elaryl grumbled.

"But just in case . . ."

Elaryl stepped out on the balcony and looked back at her curly-topped servant. At times like this, she wondered who was working for whom. "Very well. If it will make you feel any better, I give you my word I will not go outside this evening." Jocelath smiled and let out a relieved sigh. "I don't know why I put up with you," Elaryl scolded softly, but she didn't dent her maidservant's grin. "I don't know whether you're my maid, or my best friend, or my mother!"

Jocelath shrugged. "I like that second one, myself. I still say you're going to be hot in that thing," she added.

"Then I'll be hot!" Elaryl snapped, and she trotted down the stairs. By the time she reached the door of the library she could already feel the perspiration trickling down her ribs . . .

"Elaryl!" Ranoth exclaimed grandly as she pressed on through the doors, and he threw open his arms to embrace her. He had greeted her thus all her life—the only difference now being that the little man had to reach up to her instead of down. "And how is the golden flower of the Rivers Region?"

"Not all that well," she answered with polite firmness. "I would certainly be much improved if you've brought some good news." It was the most direct statement she'd ever made to the chief Elder of her land, and she could imagine the frown it caused to chase across her father's face. She didn't see it, however, for her gaze stayed fixed on Ranoth, gauging his reactions. His slow, sad smile told her all she needed to know. "There is none, is there?"

"Elaryl, you overstep—" Talarath began with some of the old fire, but Ranoth stopped him with an upraised hand.

"No," he murmured. Then he took a deep breath and regarded this young lady's face as if he'd never truly looked at it before. "I remember after your mother died and we'd laid her body away in the crypt of Elders in the capital, you came to stand before me with just that same expression upon your face and demanded to know why. You were ten. Do you remember that?"

Mention of her mother's death brought too many memories to

Elaryl's mind for her to single out the incident Ranoth was recalling. She shook her head, and he nodded.

"Just that same expression. And I told you I didn't know why,
because I didn't—I never do, with death. And you nodded—much
like you are right now—and seemed satisfied that I had at least
told you the truth. Somehow . . . somehow I have the same feeling today I had back then—"

"Is Seagryn dead?" she demanded, her jaws clenched to ab-
sorb the shock of the blow, but her cheeks coloring in bright
testimony to her terror at its coming.

"No. Not Seagryn."

Her clenched muscles suddenly went slack, so much so she
thought she might topple over. She caught her balance and sighed
in relief: If it wasn't Seagryn and it wasn't Talarath, then she could
stand the news, no matter how grim. "Then who?" she asked,
her mouth dry.

Ranoth looked at Talarath, who looked back at him noncom-
mittally. Finally he shrugged. "Rather a what, an idea, a way of
life."

"What is it you mean?" she asked, troubled by his hopeless
tone. Did this have something to do with her father's recent mood?

"What's dying is the Land of Lamath as we have known it.
And we?" He looked wearily at Talarath. "We are coconspirators
in its murder."

Elaryl fully understood the meaning of the Elder's words, and
she couldn't mistake the despair in the faces of these two men she
had honored all her life. She just couldn't make sense of how it
all related to the world she knew. "How can you possibly say
such a thing? You two are the chief among the Ruling Elders—"

"And likely soon the only survivors among the Ruling Elders!" Ranoth interrupted, with a savagery that surprised her.
His anger wasn't directed at her; she knew that. But it *was* very
much in evidence.

"The others are—"

"Dead. *Devoured*, if you will, by the dragon your husband had
a hand in making."

Once again Elaryl reeled. This time her feet wouldn't hold her,
and she had to reach behind her to find her way into a chair. "But
how— Is he . . ."

"Seagryn has nothing to do with it," Talarath snapped, sitting
himself. Ranoth remained standing. He evidently needed to pace.

"Your father's right. Seagryn's not a cause of any of this. Nor is he being of very much help, either, but that's quite beside the point. Did you know that the Remnant is no more?''

"The Remnant?"

"It's been utterly consumed. Swallowed up by the dragon." He waited for some response, but Elaryl was too shocked to make any. She'd never been inside the Remnant, but she'd heard her father tell tales of a magic place under the mountain . . .

Ranoth continued his explanation. "Since that took place, a certain party has learned how to manipulate the dragon and direct it to kill whomever he chooses. This party has made threats upon all of the Elders, and has already, apparently, succeeded in having the beast eat two. He makes no secret of his purpose in all this. He has, in fact, demanded a meeting with myself and your father."

"With—" Talarath grunted in surprise.

"With the two of us, yes. He wanted to meet in the Heartland, but I refused—too dense a population there, Talarath. You understand."

"Then he's coming—"

"Here. Yes. In fact, I had anticipated he might arrive before me—"

At that moment someone outside the door shouted, "Tugolith! Tugolith upon the road!"

"A tugolith!" Elaryl cried as she bounded to her feet with joy and rushed out of the library. In the hall she was struck with a dilemma—the rooftop to witness his arrival? Or the doorway, to be ready to greet him? She decided on the doorway and raced down the steps for what seemed the hundredth time today, joyfully calling, "Tugolith! Tugolith! Tugolith!" with absolute assurance that her husband had finally come home.

She was not the first to the doorway this time, but she crowded through the servants clustered around it so that she stood in front on the porch, smiling and waving wildly at the beast who rumbled up the lane. Then her hand froze above her head. This wasn't Seagryn at all. It was something else entirely.

There was not one tugolith rumbling up the lane, but a half dozen. They were harnessed together in pairs with links of chain she'd only seen previously in seaports, anchoring huge ships to the docks. Each huge link had to be the size of her own head. The roadway was large enough for two wagons to pass one another easily, yet the lead pair spanned the whole of it and beyond, from the line of trees on one side to the line of trees on the other. Elaryl could tell at a glance that these trees would never be the same after this visit, for what the team of tugoliths pulled behind them dwarfed their own great bulk.

It was a gigantic armored wagon of metal-sheathed wood, although it looked less like a wagon than the siege engines of which she'd seen drawings in books. It had battlements lined with arrow slits and a central tower, and seemed to bristle with armed men bearing spears and swords and arrows. This grand conveyance suggested nothing less than a castle on wheels—four wheels on a side, she counted now, and each twice her own height in diameter. With its scales of metal sheeting and its ungainly profile, the wagon had a hideous, almost reptilian appearance that made her shudder. At the same time, she immediately wanted to see inside it, curious as to how its interior might be decorated.

The immense carriage made slow progress up the lane, despite the power of the six tugoliths pulling it. Grand old tree limbs groaned as they bent before its insistent pressure, and not a few of them finally snapped and crashed to the ground in the battle-wagon's wake. It occurred to her that if this was the nemesis of Lamath arriving, his rolling fortress was at this very moment most vulnerable—unable to turn from side to side and not really capable of making quick progress. She watched hopefully for some sudden surprise attack by green-clad Lamathian guardsmen—but none came. And when they finally shouldered past the two lines of trees onto the large lawn that graced the front of her rebuilt home, the tugoliths moved with an agility that surprised her as they turned the great wagon around. It was only as she watched a wide door open in its rear and a stairway being lowered to the ground out of it that Elaryl realized her father and Ranoth now flanked her on either side, watching the mobile castle's arrival with identically grim expressions. Warriors dressed in a livery she didn't recognize clattered down the stairway to form two protective columns. A moment later their leader walked down these same steps with much greater leisure, and Elaryl struggled to place the young man. He, too, wore these lime-green and navy-blue colors that meant nothing to her. She leaned over to Ranoth and whispered, "Who is he?"

Ranoth didn't take his eyes off the man as he answered, "That, my dear, is Ognadzu, chief heir to the House of Paumer. Or perhaps I should call him the head of the House of Ognadzu, for it appears that in the last few months he's wrested control of much of the family empire from his father's hands. And yes, as you've already guessed—this is the man who threatens us."

"But—he's a boy!" she couldn't keep herself from observing.

"Yes. A very angry, very powerful boy. Shall we greet him?"
Ranoth stepped forward and assumed his ceremonial voice as he
called out, "Lord Ognadzu! On behalf of the people of the five
regions I welcome you to the Fragment of Lamath! I'll allow our
host to welcome you to this house. Talarath?"

Elaryl watched the mocking arrogance with which Ognadzu
received this greeting, and decided immediately she didn't like
him. Her father cleared his throat. "My—ah—Lord Ognadzu,
you are—most welcome. I—had no prior knowledge of your coming or we would have prepared a feast. I—I'm not certain how
many rooms will be needed to house you, but if you'll give me
some number, I'll inform the steward and he'll begin immediately
to—"

"Save yourself the trouble, Talarath," the boy flippantly replied. "I did know I was coming, and there's a feast already
prepared for you inside my home. Would you join me, please?"
This was not an invitation. It was, rather, a command, launched
with calculated arrogance and designed to indicate to all those
listening Ognadzu's relative strength in this encounter. Elaryl
didn't just dislike this boy—she found she immediately despised
him.

She wondered if she'd somehow reflected this realization on
her face, for suddenly Ognadzu's eyes focused on her, and his
gloating smile hardened into a grimace of dangerous self-doubt.
Ognadzu didn't smile easily—his guile was not yet as practiced
as that of his father. She saw him struggling to recover as he
asked, "And who is this woman? The blonde?"

Ranoth opened his mouth to reply, but Elaryl broke in to answer for herself. "I am Elaryl, wife to Seagryn," she proclaimed
proudly.

"Oh, ho. So, you are the famous Elaryl," Ognadzu said,
"cherished spouse of the man who helped my father and Sheth
to construct the dragon." The boy was mocking her.

"Yes."

"That almost makes you a part of the family! By all means
you, too, must join us for dinner."

Elaryl wondered for only a moment what the lad would do if
she declined the invitation . . . But, of course, she wouldn't de-
cline. The events this childish boor had come to discuss involved
her far too deeply. Besides, she couldn't pass up the opportunity
to see the inside of this fascinating vehicle. "If you insist."

"My Lady!" Jocelath whispered anxiously from behind her.

Elaryl didn't look back, deciding instead to see if she could charm this adolescent merchant into providing her some information.

"That's my maid," she explained to Ognadzu with a slight smile that again threw him off guard. "She's afraid if I step outside the house the dragon will swoop down and swallow me."

Her words had more impact than she'd intended. Both Ranoth and Talarath winced and looked away, while Ognadzu swelled up to his full height, the arrogance in his smile fully replenished.

"You may inform the girl she has nothing to fear. The dragon eats no one unless I command it!" He stepped to one side and gestured toward the doorway of his massive carriage. "Shall we dine?"

Could it be true? Elaryl asked herself as she glided by him and gracefully ascended the staircase. Could he actually summon the beast to do his bidding? If so—what had he done to Seagryn? Her heart pounded as she walked down a narrow wooden hallway, flanked on either side by closely set doors. The hall was dark, but she could see another stairway ahead of her, illuminated by light from above. Her feet sank an inch into the red carpet that covered the stairs as she climbed expectantly to a large, open room. Obviously the main room of the carriage, this appeared to be a small replica of the great hall in a castle. Tables for Ognadzu's warriors lined each of the walls, while at the rear of the room on a raised dais sat the head table. Windows ran the length of the carriage on either side, covered with varnished shutters and draped with lime and blue curtains. These clashed violently with the rich scarlet carpeting, and Elaryl gave a slight shudder when she beheld them together. She'd not realized Ognadzu was right behind her until she heard his chuckle.

"My mother thinks it's garish, but as I told her—if I like it, then it's art."

"It's—bright," she breathed at last.

"That's what I like about it. The rooms below are only barracks for my retainers—my bedroom is in the tower above us, and it's even brighter." He leered at her. "Perhaps you'd like to see it?"

She found his puerile attempt at seduction laughable but managed to keep a straight face. "Did you say dinner was already prepared? I'm starving."

"Certainly," he answered with an exaggerated suavity that only made him appear more of a buffoon than ever. He clapped his hands twice, then took Elaryl by the elbow and led her to the head table as servants began to hurry from doorways, bearing steaming golden salvers toward the head table. By the time Ognadzu had seated Elaryl to his right, Talarath and Ranoth had made the climb into the dining room, followed by hosts of lime-and-blue–clad guards. Neither looked very pleased at having to be here, and Ognadzu's attentions to Elaryl appeared to please them even less. The thought hadn't occurred to her until that moment—what if Ognadzu simply decided to pull in his staircase and order his tugoliths to carry them all off? It was a bit late to be sorry about such now, she decided. Besides, the two of them would have been trapped inside here whether she was or not. Elaryl chose to sit back in her plush-lined chair and enjoy the meal—if that was possible.

She found very quickly that it was. Ognadzu may have been a poor decorator, but he seemed to be something of a gourmet, and they feasted on exotic dishes that thrilled her palate. The boy took great pleasure in her enjoyment of them, explaining at length the contents of each and the trouble he'd had to go to in order to provide it. Elaryl was happy to eat and let him talk—she was learning more about him with every sentence.

It was obvious that Ognadzu was a talented merchant—perhaps even an organizational genius. It was also apparent that his hatreds ran deep, and those included in his grudges were anyone he'd ever perceived to have insulted him. From bits of comments he dropped, she gathered that Seagryn was among these, and that made Elaryl shiver. But nothing he said suggested he had talked with Seagryn recently or had done her husband any specific hurt. Not that he didn't wish to—his fawning all over her, she soon understood, was really an insult directed at Seagryn. But his strongest words he reserved for his father, Paumer, and the wizard who had designed and made the twi-beast. Evidently he had found a powerful ally in his quest to be avenged on those two unfortunates.

"The dragon listens to me," he boasted to her when the dinner wine began taking its toll on his young body. "Oh, not me directly—" He chuckled. "—but to one of my tugoliths. He was made out of a tugolith you know—oh, but, of course, you know that." He giggled, pointing at Elaryl. "You were there!"

Elaryl had been present at the dragon's making. But how did Ognadzu know? She didn't reply, waiting for him to continue.

"Anyway, he—he? Is the dragon a he? Who knows. Whatever the thing is, it listens to tugoliths. And I have in my employ a tugolith who's not afraid of the dragon—not afraid at all. I give it instructions, and it goes right into the Central Gate and tells the dragon where to go and whom to swallow. Pretty good assassin, wouldn't you say?'' Ognadzu cackled, winking at Elaryl and taking another sip of wine. ''Pretty effective?''

Elaryl waited for a pause in his self-congratulatory giggling, then asked, ''Why does the dragon do this for you? Out of friendship?''

''Friendship? You think the dragon is my friend?'' This set off another fit of giggles, and Ognadzu wobbled unsteadily in his chair as he struggled to contain himself. Elaryl took the moment to glance at Ranoth and Talarath. Neither man had entered much into the conversation. She couldn't tell from their closed expressions whether they appreciated her efforts to pry information out of this tipsy teen or not, but she'd chosen to pursue the topic and wouldn't back away from it now.

''If not out of friendship for you, or for the tugolith, then why does the dragon do as you ask?''

''Simple,'' Ognadzu growled, and suddenly his face was fierce and the effects of the alcohol were no longer apparent. ''I tell the twi-beast where Sheth may be found, and the dragon goes and burns that place.'' He turned his head to look at the two Elders of Lamath seated on the other side of him and announced, ''That's why the Hall of the Elders will burn in Lamath, Ranoth.'' He snarled maliciously, then locked eyes with Talarath and added, ''And it's why this brand new mansion of yours will soon go up in smoke, Talarath. That is, if the two of you prove to be as foolish as your counterparts in the Western and Upper regions. You knew they burned, I assume?''

''You sent me word yourself,'' Ranoth answered crisply.

''Ah, yes. But you verified it from sources you *trust*, did you not?'' Ognadzu prodded, and Ranoth answered with a troubled nod. ''Good. Good. Then perhaps the two of you will be more responsive to my invitation.'' Ognadzu smiled, and he turned to grin back in Elaryl's direction. She found the expression hideous.

''And that invitation is?'' Ranoth asked.

''Why, to rule Lamath with me.'' Ognadzu met the eyes of the two Elders frankly. ''You *did* realize that I will rule Lamath, didn't you?''

''Lamath chooses its own rulers,'' Ranoth said carefully, ''from the ranks of its spiritual leaders . . .''

''Oh, and I need not apply, since I'm obviously not spiritual? From all I can gather, Ranoth—neither are you,'' Ognadzu snarled. ''Neither is Talarath there, nor any man who's sat in an Elder's chair in years. Elaryl,'' he asked, turning suddenly her way, ''did you realize that Lamath has been ruled by a cadre of spiritual pragmatists for years? I've studied your history, both in your own libraries in Lamath and in the once-great library in the Remnant. It's a dead faith, your religion of Lamath. A dead faith waiting for renewal . . .''

He seemed to hang upon that last word, as if expecting some response from his audience. Elaryl looked at her father and the Ruling Elder. Both of them seemed to understand what the boy was saying, but she didn't. She decided to ask. ''What do you mean by renewal of the faith?''

He turned to face her. ''You don't know? Quite simple, actually. Lamathians are very simpleminded people. You may not know that, living as you do in the house of a priestly leader, but it's true. They want a religion they can understand, a religion they can prove is true. And some have begun to discover the truth of the dragon.'' Ognadzu smiled at her chillingly. ''They're calling it the scourge of the Power . . .''

''The what?''

''The scourge of the Power!'' Ognadzu said with a sweeping gesture of his hand, imitating the flight of the dragon over his plate and goblet. ''The dragon is the Power's personal avenger, swooping to swallow all those who *pretend* to lead in faith, but hunger only after power. Persons like . . .'' He turned back to the two Elders. ''. . . the two of you.'' Ranoth and Talarath watched him grimly. ''How else do they explain the precision with which the beast makes its attacks, unless it is being directed by your precious Power to rid the Land of Lamath of impure leadership? I think you must certainly understand my meaning, Ranoth.''

''I do,'' the little man murmured.

''*I* don't,'' Elaryl snapped, and for the first time Ognadzu frowned at her. ''What is it you want from Lamath? You have everything your daddy's money can buy!'' It was the wrong thing to say, but Elaryl had known that before she said it. Ognadzu's grand expression withered in humiliation, then flowered back full in rage, as he pointed his finger and shouted at her.

''You, woman, will burn *first*!''

''No!'' Talarath shouted, coming out of his chair and around Ranoth's to grab the boy up by the lapels and lift him into the air. Ognadzu looked at the much bigger man, his eyes wide with shock. Immediately the roomful of warriors jumped to their feet, and just as quickly Talarath set the boy back on his feet and released him. But Elaryl's father wasn't finished—he'd just chosen a different tack. ''She's not one of the leaders of Lamath; she's merely protecting her father. Ranoth and I understand you. Tell us what you want us to do.''

From the moment he'd burst from his seat in her defense, Elaryl's pride in her father had been swelling. Here, at last, was the father she remembered, the man of rigid principles who would face down an army for the faith. But with these last words the illusion exploded—for it was an illusion, had been an illusion, she realized, for a long, long time. The boy had spoken the truth—much as she hated to admit it to herself. The people of Lamath were simple folk, who wanted a simple faith. But ever since watching her beloved Seagryn be made a pawn in the Elders' political maneuvers, she'd realized that the leadership of the faith no longer subscribed to it themselves. There was no dependence upon the Power in her own household—Talarath depended instead on strength, timely action, and closely guarding all information. Elaryl understood in that moment that there was no essential difference between the power politics of her father and those of this slimy young merchant. And she wondered—were Seagryn's motives any different?

''Yes,'' she said aloud to no one who happened to be present. ''Yes, they are.''

''What?'' the boy snarled at her, certain, now that she'd insulted him, that anything she said must be another barb aimed to further hurt him.

''I'm not talking to you,'' she said flatly, for she wasn't. She realized Ognadzu took this as more humiliation, for she saw him coloring out of the corner of her eye. But her gaze was reserved for her father—and it was full of the same stern righteousness he'd projected at congregations throughout her lifetime.

''Father, what do you think you're doing? Are you about to negotiate some agreement with this—boy? What are you thinking about? Ranoth!'' she shouted across the livid young merchant's head. ''What do the two of you think you're doing? I thought you were the leaders of Lamath, not its betrayers! I thought you had true faith in the Power!''

''Daughter,'' Talarath warned, but it was a weak warning, motivated only by terror, void of moral character. She ignored it.

''I simply won't believe it of you. Neither of you! If there truly is anything to this Power you've taught me about all my life—if there is truly anything to believe in—then I will not see an adolescent merchant rob my nation of its faith!'' She spun around, marched off the dais, and started down the aisle toward the stairway.

"Stop that woman!" Ognadzu shouted, and a half-dozen warriors stepped out to do just that.

"Yes, stop her!" Ranoth called after them, then looked at Ognadzu. "For we're going with her. Oh, you can have your guards kill us, if you choose, but I have my own warriors ringed around this place, and I daresay—tugoliths or no—you'd have a difficult time leaving the region without seeing that it is this precious mobile mansion of yours that goes up in flames, not our homes. You overstep yourself, young Ognadzu. You're much like your father in that way." He turned to Talarath. "Your daughter's right. Let's leave this fool to his wine." Ranoth stepped down off the dais and walked swiftly between the tables to join Elaryl. Talarath quickly followed, but the guards who blocked Elaryl didn't budge until Ognadzu spoke.

"Let them go," he announced finally, sitting heavily into his chair. Then he picked up his goblet and saluted them with it. "You may all prepare for martyrdom. The scourge of the Power is upon you!"

"Why don't you just kill us now, Ognadzu?" Ranoth challenged. "You haven't the courage to act directly, do you? That's like your father, also."

"Insults!" Ognadzu cackled, taking a drink. "Listen to them heaping up insults! Oh, no no no, Ranoth. I'm not fool enough to kill you here. Much more effective to let the dragon do it. More impressive. Burns itself into the minds and memories of the peasantry. Have a pleasant evening . . ." he added, raising his goblet again, and the guards stepped aside. Elaryl shot down the stairway as quickly as possible, hearing the heavy tread of Ranoth and her father behind her. Once outside, she saw by torchlight that the massive carriage was indeed ringed with Lamathian warriors who had not been in evidence until now. But what difference did it make now? she realized. Ognadzu would be true to his word. The dragon would be upon them as quickly as the boy could send word to it. She, however, would not be here.

"Daughter," Talarath began when they got inside the mansion, but she didn't pause to talk to him. "Elaryl!" he called up to her, and she stopped on the stairs to look down.

"Yes?"

His old face, craning to look up at her, seemed twisted by a dozen emotions he'd never taken the time to learn how to express. She loved him, she knew—but she hadn't the time now for him to try to learn how to talk to her. "I—" he began, then stopped.

"Father, I'd suggest you and Ranoth get out of this place as quickly as possible. Store the things you want to preserve from this house somewhere in the village, and hide yourselves among the warriors.'' She glanced around at the mansion, still smelling so new. ''We really didn't live here long enough to build many memories into the walls. I, for one, won't miss it.'' She started up the stairs again.

''But where will you be?'' he called, strangling on the words and their implication.

''Me?'' she said, leaning over the bannister. ''I'm going to find my husband. From the looks of things, he's the only one left who can do this nation any good. I love you. Good-bye—'' Then she was off again, once more racing up the stairway as she had been all day.

She found Jocelath curled up in a corner of the room, trembling in terror. ''What's the matter with you? Get up!''

''My Lady!'' her maid shouted, bounding to her feet and rushing to embrace her. ''I thought you were surely kidnapped or dead!''

''I'm neither one yet,'' Elaryl muttered, dashing to her closet and throwing it open, ''but I wouldn't give either one of us much chance of living into tomorrow unless you get busy and help me pack.''

''Pack?'' Jocelath gasped, her face draining to a pasty white.

''Yes, pack. Here,'' she grunted, throwing a wad of clothes in her maid's direction.

''But—where are you going?''

''We are going—wherever. Would you hurry?''

''But—'' the woman said again, her eyes wide with terror. ''Where will we sleep?''

Elaryl hadn't thought of that, and she paused to consider it. ''Outside, I guess.'' She returned to stuffing clothing into a bag.

''Outside?'' Jocelath murmured, swallowing with difficulty. ''With the dragon?'' Elaryl noticed her maid suddenly doing something strange with her hands, but she didn't stop to look more closely. She was trying to make some plans. Where was Seagryn now? Where would he be in the next few days, so that she could go meet him there?

''You know,'' she told Jocelath as she tied the neck of her tote bag and tossed it over her shoulder, ''for the first time I can remember, I really miss Dark the prophet.''

Chapter Thirteen

✻✻✻✻

CRYPTIC ANSWERS

"IT smells funny," Dark complained as he sniffed at the pile
of powder in his palm.

Nebalath turned red and snarled some reply, but Seagryn didn't
hear it. He was preoccupied with the same thoughts that had
plagued him for days.

"Works, though . . ." the young prophet murmured after in-
haling the green spores. He drifted toward the pleasant oblivion
of a dreamless sleep.

Seagryn watched the boy's brown eyes roll backward and realized he'd missed an opportunity. "I wish he'd let me ask him
some questions first," he told Nebalath. Dark heard this comment
and managed to focus his gaze on Seagryn for just a moment.

"Has Sheth talked to you?" Dark asked, his speech slurring.

"Sheth?" Seagryn frowned. "No . . ."

"Tha's righ'." The boy nodded weakly, drowsing off. "We
talk abou' tha' later . . . When I wake u . . ."

Seagryn stooped over Dark and shook him once, gently, then
again a little more firmly. "Too late." He looked up at Nebalath.
"Again."

"Too late" had been a frequent refrain between them in the
days since their encounter with the Emeraudes. After scooping
sacks full of the foul-smelling green spores from the cracks of the
cone, they'd arrived back at the coast too late to prevent *The Norck
Stork* from being attacked. A larger vessel, sailing under lime and
dark-blue colors that neither of them recognized, had sighted the

161

Stork and was pursuing it. While they'd managed together to cloak the ship, allowing it to slip away, they'd been forced to wait a week in the steamy jungle until Captain Norck had made a full circuit of the island and come back for them.

Fylynn suggested repeatedly that it was probably for the best. "Norck would have fled at the first scent of us anyway!" she'd said. "Now we can burn our clothes and bathe every day in the sea until he returns." She'd made the most of the time herself— sunning on the beach, hunting for seashells, and dancing through the surf—but Seagryn had taken the delay hard.

He'd been unable to relax. Although the green cats had given them a wide berth, he was always aware that they were prowling the perimeters of the shoreline campsite, effectively preventing any further contact with the purple inhabitants of the isle. And with Fylynn playing down by the beach, he'd spent most of the week alone. Nebalath had disappeared for longer intervals each day, and while he always returned with things they needed—fresh clothing the first day, food every day, towels, soap, books, some much-needed cologne—the old wizard had seemed less and less willing to talk. Nebalath had permitted himself only one comment on the day they'd finally boarded the *Stork*. "I hope we're not too late," he'd mumbled.

"For what?" Seagryn had asked—but the old man never had answered.

That day they'd been caught in a storm. "It's too late in the year to be sailing in these waters," Captain Norck had explained as the winds blew them westward. The storm had lasted for days, and they'd spent two weeks returning to their original course.

To add to his frustration, throughout this period Seagryn had been unable to contact Elaryl. He'd tried. He'd spent whole days laying in his bunk, working without success to dream his way back to her. Nor did Nebalath seem inclined to help him as he had before, and Seagryn couldn't understand why. Hadn't he done everything the old man had requested? Why, then, wouldn't Nebalath go and visit Elaryl for him and bring him back a report? When asked, the thin-faced wizard had brushed the request aside as if it were beneath him. Then Seagryn began to wonder—had Nebalath attempted to visit Elaryl already and found her condition so wretched he couldn't bring himself to share the truth with Seagryn? Did his "too late" apply to Elaryl? Toward the end of the journey, Seagryn had started sampling Dark's green powder himself. It took his mind off his troubles, at least.

They'd arrived this evening, all three of them feeling battered by the journey and much relieved to find a safe haven at last. Fylynn had gone right to bed, while Seagryn and Nebalath had rushed the treasured medicine to Dark's bedside. Now Seagryn looked down at the prophet lad's peaceful expression and battled against his own envy. He wished he could sleep so blissfully, for, despite his weariness, his mind had not allowed him to rest for days. Having missed this opportunity to hear a hopeful word from Dark, he'd doomed himself to yet another sleepless night. Unless—he glanced over at the sack of green spores . . .

"No," he grunted, and Nebalath looked up at him in surprise. "No what? What are you talking about?" the old wizard asked.

"Nothing," Seagryn snarled. "I'm going for a walk."

"Be careful," Nebalath said, craning his neck to look around him suspiciously. "This house goes on forever. It's easy to get lost inside it."

Seagryn didn't reply. He stalked out of the room and trotted down the stairs, almost running over Uda, who was on her way up.

"Is he all right?" the girl asked. "Is he sleeping?"

"Like the dead," Seagryn snarled, and Uda's blue eyes flew wide open. "He's not, of course," Seagryn quickly added, angry at himself for frightening her so. She'd grown so much since he'd first met her, and not just in height. The troubles of the last year had forced her to mature quickly. Seagryn welcomed the change. "He looks as if he's sleeping comfortably. Perhaps he'll wake up a new man."

"I do appreciate your trying to help him," the girl replied earnestly, and Seagryn was touched. This was the first time he could remember anyone thanking him for any of his efforts. Then Uda frowned, and added, "But I wonder if it's good for him."

Seagryn sighed. "I don't know what's good anymore, Uda. I used to think I did. When I was a cleric, good and evil seemed so sharply defined. Now it seems every evil thing wears a mask of propriety, while every good thing seems to have some counterbalancing evil price to pay. Do you understand what I mean?"

The girl's blue eyes studied him thoughtfully as she ran a hand through her waist-length black hair. "No," she said at last. "I'm sorry, but I don't."

She had grown, true—but she hadn't grown that much. Seagryn mumbled some meaningless response and trotted on down the steps, wishing he could find someone to talk to who could understand—someone like Elaryl. Lost in such thoughts, he wandered the eccentric halls of Kerily's museumlike mansion without really seeing anything. Thus he reacted with great surprise when he realized he'd walked out onto the stage of a large, open-roofed amphitheater—Kerily's own in-house performance hall. He turned in a slow circle, first gazing up at the sharply sloped seats, then around behind him at the set. It looked like a garden scene, with live shrubs and trees and a fountain that sparkled in the moonlight. "What is this?" he murmured to himself.

"What does it look like?" a disembodied voice nearby said, and Seagryn whirled about, trying to find its source. "I'm right here," the voice said again, and Sheth appeared before him— or, rather, a wavy, vaporous image of Sheth appeared. As always, the mustached wizard appeared to be smirking.

He'd not seen Sheth in months, but he hadn't missed him, either. "What do you want?" Seagryn asked flatly, squaring his broad shoulders around to face his dimpled nemesis.

"You look as if you're ready to fight." Sheth chuckled.

"That's what we were doing when we parted ways," Seagryn reminded his rival. "Or had you forgotten?"

Sheth's smile hardened, and his voice took on a keen edge. For some reason, Seagryn felt comforted by this. "Forgotten? You think I could forget how you spoiled my creation and sent it thundering through the roof of my home?"

"What you were doing was evil," Seagryn muttered quietly.

"And what you did was not?" Sheth snapped back. "You wrecked my Dragonforge! You released a monster on the world before he was fully trained! That's not evil?"

"It didn't seem so at the time," Seagryn countered.

"And how does it seem *now*, Seagryn? Now that the dragon has devoured the Remnant, as well as most of your country's Ruling Council!"

"The Ruling Council?" Seagryn frowned. Elaryl! he thought. What about Elaryl?

"What's the matter? Did Nebalath not tell you about that?" Sheth's smirk had returned, making Seagryn want to flatten that nose with a blow of his balled-up fist. But as the full impact of Sheth's news spread through his mind, all he could do was gasp for breath. "It's true," Sheth continued. "At the prompting of the sniveling son of Paumer, the dragon has consumed most or all of the Ruling Council, including your beloved father-in-law! I can't believe Nebalath hasn't told you all this. He's known it for days."

"He hasn't told me anything," Seagryn said. He thought he now understood why.

"So then, Seagryn Dragonspet! What are you going to *do* about it?"

Seagryn swallowed hard, fighting the urge to cry out in anguish. "What *can* I do?" he finally managed to choke out.

Sheth's cleft jaw jutted out in an obvious challenge. "You can come to the Marwilds and help me destroy the thing!"

Seagryn stared at him. "You know a way to destroy Vicia-Heinox?" he asked.

"I made Vicia-Heinox!" Sheth answered arrogantly. "You think I would make such a beast without also planning some means to dispose of it as well?"

"Yes," Seagryn replied quickly, causing Sheth to fill the amphitheater with curses. Seagryn waited until the other wizard had vented his rage, then went on calmly. "If you know how, why haven't you already done it? And why would you seek my help?"

"I've always known how!" Sheth roared. "But the process takes time, and materials, and cooperation! Don't you remember anything about the Conspiracy's design? This is exactly what we'd planned to have happen!"

"The destruction of the Remnant?" Seagryn countered angrily. "The consumption of the Ruling Council of Lamath? If that indeed has happened as you claim, I certainly doubt Ranoth planned it! No, Sheth. Something's gone terribly wrong with your plan, or you wouldn't be requesting my help. And I know too much about you and that slimy Paumer to spend any more of my energy aiding you! I'll find a way to stop this dragon myself, but I'll not do it in partnership with you. I've tried that before—remember?"

Sheth's blue eyes bored into him, but Seagryn didn't care if this man hated him. He turned and started back the way he'd come, barely listening as the wizard shouted, "You'd better come help me, if you ever expect to see your pretty wife again."

Seagryn stopped and whirled around. "What?" he demanded.

"Your wife." Sheth grinned. "I've got her. And she is a pretty little thing. She'll be really hurt when she hears you didn't even ask about her—"

With the swiftness of the thought itself, Seagryn's mind formed a ball of blue-white fire and flung it at Sheth's head. It flew through the shimmering outline of the wizard and flamed out against the amphitheater's stone wall.

Sheth stared at him incredulously. "I'm not actually there with you, Seagryn—surely you're not so dense as to believe I am. . . ?"

"No," Seagryn muttered, struggling to keep his feet beneath him. "That was—reflex. You . . . have Elaryl?"

"I would think that news would please you," Sheth mocked him. "Especially in light of the word about her father."

"Why . . . is she . . . with you?"

"Why with me? I would think that would be obvious." Sheth brushed invisible fluff from his vaporous garment, preening himself like one of the exotically plumed birds from the jungles of Emeraude.

"I'm afraid it is not obvious to me."

"I've decided very little is obvious to you, Seagryn," Sheth said. "You're quite talented, but you're also dense. I think it has something to do with your religious heritage—you often fail to think for yourself."

Seagryn struggled to remain calm. "Why is my wife with you, Sheth?"

"Simple." The dimpled wizard smiled. "Because I need you to come help me, and that was the easiest way of getting you here."

"You're lying," Seagryn rumbled low in his throat, and Sheth laughed. "If she's there with you, show her to me!" Seagryn roared, his temper finally loosed. "Prove to me you have her!"

Sheth laughed again—insulting laughter—then said, "You're a powershaper yourself, Seagryn! You've learned many of the tricks of the trade, so you tell me just how I could go about doing that!"

"I don't care how you do it, but I don't believe you!"

"Then why don't you go ask Nebalath?" Sheth shouted. "He knows. Ask Dark if the dragon didn't burn your new house in the Rivers Region! Better yet, why don't you just throw yourself up there into the ashes where it once stood! If you were half the wizard you think you are, you could do it! In the meantime," he continued, "I'll be waiting here in the Marwilds—along with your wife—for you to come to your senses. Don't make me wait too long, Seagryn. The next time Ognadzu sends the dragon to find me, I might need to use her for dragon bait."

Seagryn roared in rage and leaped at the other powershaper, reaching out to throttle Sheth with his bare hands. He grabbed nothing but empty space and fell heavily to the floor of the stage, banging his knees and elbows. When he bounced up to his feet, Sheth was gone—disappeared. He screamed in frustration and heard his voice amplified powerfully all the way up to the top row of seats. Kerily wouldn't build an amphitheater without perfect acoustics.

Despite the fact that he ran all the way, it still took him several minutes to race back to Dark's bedside. The boy still slept as Uda sat quietly beside him, watching him. She glanced up in surprise as Seagryn puffed into the room. "What is it?"

"Where's Nebalath?" Seagryn demanded, his head flying from side to side as he searched.

"He . . . said he wanted to sleep in his own bed tonight—in Haranamous. He said Dark would sleep until morning, and to tell you that he would be back then. Is—everything all right?"

"No," Seagryn grunted. "Everything is not all right." He looked at her. "But I'm going to go do the only thing I can think of that might help right now."

"And what is that?" Uda frowned, not comprehending any of this.

"What Elaryl would do. I'm going to go talk to the Power."

His room was located down the hall from Dark's. He walked swiftly to it, closed its door, and threw himself facedown on the bed. "Elaryl," he murmured, summoning from memory an image of her face and gazing into her knowing eyes. She was the truest believer he knew, and remembering her seemed to help him focus on the Power more easily. "Elaryl, I'm coming home . . ."

And then he was. Whether by nightmare or through terrible vision he couldn't know until later, but he was there in Lamath in the Rivers Region, on the site of the house of Talarath. And as he had in his visit to the village of Gammel, he stood in ashes.

"Seagryn . . ."

It was Uda's voice, and it confused him. He woke up and looked at her.

"It's morning," she told him. "Nebalath's back and Dark is calling for you."

Seagryn jumped off the bed and dashed down the hallway. Dark and Nebalath faced the door, and by their expressions apparently anticipated his anger. Of course—Dark would have warned the old wizard already . . .

Seagryn glowered at Nebalath accusingly. "Did the dragon burn my house?"

Nebalath shrugged. "Apparently so. I wasn't there at the time."

"But you *did* go there—sometime during our return."

Nebalath sighed deeply and nodded. "I did, yes."

"Why didn't you tell me?" Seagryn thundered. "I was desperate for news and you knew it!"

"You were desperate for *good* news, Seagryn, not bad,"

Nebalath said. "I had none to give you. I kept searching for some, but . . ."

"What information did you seek?" Seagryn demanded, his jaws tight.

"I wanted to tell you something about the location and safety of your wife . . ."

"She's with Sheth!" Seagryn roared. "He told me last night that he had her! And you knew *that*!" he went on, turning to Dark.

"I knew what, exactly?" Dark asked.

"You told me Sheth would talk to me, but you were too eager to go off to megasin-sleep even to warn me what it was about!" Seagryn wished he didn't feel so betrayed by these two friends, but he couldn't feel otherwise.

"What's megasin-sleep?" Nebalath asked Dark.

The boy brushed off the question with a quick "You'll learn later" and returned his attention to Seagryn. "I told you we'd talk about Sheth's visit after I woke up—"

"Why bother, now? It's already happened! I already know my wife survived the dragonburn, but that Sheth has somehow taken her captive! Nebalath and I need to ask questions about what's still to come, and we've gone to great trouble to get you healthy enough to answer them. Is your gift still intact?"

Dark nodded curtly. "My gift is very much present."

Seagryn looked at Nebalath and explained harshly, "The megasin robbed him of his prophetic ability by stealing his memories. I'd wondered if the green powder might do the same."

"What is this megasin?" Nebalath asked again, his curiosity growing.

Dark raised both his hands to draw their eyes back to him, and asked, "Before I answer your questions, is it all right if I say something?"

Seagryn chuckled unkindly. "Surely you already know if you say it or not—"

"Listen to me, both of you," Dark interrupted. "I want to say that I'm fully aware of the danger you encountered in fetching the dream-killing substance for me. And I can tell you already, it helps. Thank you."

Seagryn's anger cooled. He sat in the chair Uda had occupied through the night. "You're feeling better, then?"

Dark brushed his brown hair out of his eyes. It had grown too long over these months, and his normally tan face had thinned and paled to the point that he might have been unrecognizable even to his mother. But his brown eyes had a little of the old sparkle as he smiled slightly and replied, "I am feeling better." He pointed to the bag of green powder and went on, "At least now I have the promise of some relief from my own foreknowledge. I mourn tragic events well in advance of their happening, you know. I wish my personality allowed me to celebrate the happy ones the same way."

"Are there happy events in our future?" Seagryn asked, unable to contain his anxiety any longer. Dark's face fell, and Seagryn was immediately sorry. "Please forgive me, Dark. I don't mean to plunge you so quickly back into the very thing that troubles you so—"

"You can't help it," Dark muttered, raising his feet and rolling them off the edge of the bed and toward the floor. "None of you can help it." He sat up, took a deep breath, and stood. Both Nebalath and Seagryn stepped forward to support him if he fell. "I'm all right," he protested, waving off their aid. He walked unsteadily to the window on the far side of the room and pulled the blue velvet drapes aside. "Humph," he grunted as he looked down on the gardens below. "Kerily certainly has changed things since the last time I looked out this window." Then he turned around, sat on the sill, and gazed at them with that expression Seagryn knew so well: He was about to ask, "How much of this do you want to know?" But Dark surprised him.

"You say you have questions for me. Ask them."

This was a different approach to telling the future than the boy had ever taken with either of them, and Seagryn and Nebalath glanced at one another in recognition of the fact. "Why don't you just tell us what we need to know?" Nebalath asked.

"Because I don't know what you need to know," the young prophet said with a confident assurance neither Seagryn nor Nebalath recognized. "You give me too much credit, friends— and too much responsibility as well. I've decided to bear it no longer. You ask your questions and I'll answer them as best I can. But I'll not ask them for you, nor tolerate your anger at me later if you fail to ask the right ones."

Now Seagryn understood. Dark had never felt comfortable suggesting possible courses of action. How could he, when he knew only one would be taken and what its results would be? Nor did he feel free to make value judgments for others, despite their demands that he tell them what they should or shouldn't do. He had evidently chosen to absolve himself of such responsibilities in the future, and Seagryn could understand why. Still, it troubled him. "You'll not even hint to us which questions we should ask?"

Dark's veiled expression didn't change. "How would I know?"

Nebalath chuckled at that, and Dark smiled. But Seagryn still felt uncomfortable with this declaration, and he thought he knew why. "I can appreciate what you're trying to do, Dark, but I have a problem. You see, *you* involved me in all this. If it hadn't been for you I'd never have joined the Conspiracy, never have been involved in making the dragon, and would not *now* be feeling such a responsibility to set things right again."

Dark was naturally unsurprised by Seagryn's comments and nodded throughout them. But neither did his attitude change. "How do you know that, Seagryn? I don't know it, myself. You might have taken a different course into the Conspiracy, and then again you might not have. Who knows? But if my mother is to be believed—and *I* always believe her—the Power has purposes for us that surpass all our human understanding."

Nebalath hooted derisively, and Dark looked at him.

"Even you, Nebalath," the dark-haired lad continued. "Whether you believe it or not."

"I don't," the old wizard grunted.

Dark looked back at Seagryn. "But you do." When Seagryn didn't respond, Dark stood up and walked toward him. "Come now, Seagryn! Surely you know there's always been far more at stake here than who rules which Fragment and what merchant house dominates the old One Land's markets!"

"What is at stake?"

"Ah." Dark nodded, his eyes alive. "A real question. To which I answer—everything."

Seagryn blinked. Nebalath stepped around to see Dark's face, his old eyes wide with curiosity. "Everything?"

"Yes."

Seagryn's lips had suddenly gone dry. He licked them and asked, "Do you mean such things as—good and evil? The Power and those things that oppose the Power?"

"Exactly." Dark nodded, studying Seagryn's face earnestly.

For the first time in his relationship to this lad, Seagryn felt like he was being tested. It seemed of critical importance that he ask the right questions . . . "The Power is behind all this, then."

Dark frowned. "Is that a question?"

Seagryn understood and rephrased it. "Is the Power behind all this?"

"All of what?" the lad demanded, unyielding in his demand for specific questions.

"The making of the dragon?"

"That's already passed. I tell the future. You can analyze past events as well or better than I."

"All right then," Seagryn snapped, "is the Power behind Sheth's plan for the dragon's destruction?"

Dark's eyes glowed with intense excitement. "Yes," he murmured, hissing the end of the word dramatically.

Seagryn was stunned. Sheth, working in concert with the Power? "Then—I should go help him?"

Dark rolled his eyes. "Whether you should or not is up to you, Seagryn. I can only tell you that you will."

"Right." Seagryn nodded, working his mind for the proper question to ask next. "And this plan . . . Will it work?"

"To do what?" Dark asked, his eyes slightly lidded.

"To destroy the dragon!"

Dark looked at Seagryn thoughtfully. Sadly? He couldn't tell. Finally, the lad spoke. "Yes. Sheth's plan will destroy the dragon . . ."

Seagryn felt as if the boy drew his words out to summon from him some further question—but what?

"And am I to work on this plan as well?" Nebalath asked.

Dark turned to face the older wizard, his expression impenetrable. "No."

Seagryn felt tremendous pressure to ask exactly the right question and to secure precisely the right information. His understanding and appreciation of Dark's dilemma grew rapidly, for he realized now how difficult it must have been for the boy to bear that same responsibility for all the adults around him. "Do we go directly from this place to where Sheth is?" he asked.

"No," Dark said flatly, shaking his head.

"Then where do we go?" Nebalath demanded.

"And do we go together?" Seagryn put in.

Dark still shook his head. "You don't go together, but you both go to Haranamous."

"But why?" Seagryn frowned.

The more questions he answered, the less expression Dark put into his voice. He seemed to realize that his words alone were provocative enough without his adding any emphasis to them. "Because of something you learn from me."

"What?" Nebalath demanded, sensing danger behind Dark's flat tone. "What do we learn? Is there danger to the city?"

"There is danger to the city." Dark nodded, apparently relieved to have been asked.

"What is the danger?" Nebalath shouted.

"Ognadzu will inform the dragon that Sheth is in Haranamous and give the twi-beast instructions how to get there. You race from this place together to defend the city against the dragon."

"When?" Nebalath hounded the boy, grabbing him by the shirt and shaking him.

Dark didn't look at either of them now. He fixed his gaze someplace on the floor, even as Nebalath shook him from side to side. "The battle takes place tomorrow . . ."

Nebalath disappeared. The normal crack of the air rushing to fill the place he'd stood seemed exceptionally loud this time, and Seagryn jumped, shocked by it. Dark, of course, was not.

Seagryn waited a moment, but Dark didn't look up at him. "He didn't ask if we win," he finally murmured.

"No," Dark told the floor, "he certainly didn't."

Despite the young prophet's attempt to cull all expression from his words, this reply sounded ominous. Seagryn hesitated before going ahead to ask the obvious follow-up question. Still, he reasoned, if Sheth's plan to rid the world of the dragon was going to succeed, and Sheth himself said he needed Seagryn's help to enact it, then that would certainly guarantee his survival, so . . . "Do we win?" he finally asked.

When Dark's eyes finally rose to meet his, they were utterly empty, like a stranger's eyes. It was as if the boy had made himself someone else. "Who do you mean by 'we'? And what do you mean by 'win'?"

Seagryn understood. "It's not going to be that simple, is it?"

"It is not," Dark soberly agreed.

"Do we—Nebalath and I—drive the dragon from the city of Haranamous?"

"You do," Dark answered. He offered no elaboration.

"If this battle takes place tomorrow, and I'm to be there, I guess I'd better take my tugolith shape and begin running northward now. Am I right?"

"Only you would know how long it takes you to get from place to place in that form. But that is what you choose to do, so—yes."

Seagryn nodded and sighed deeply. Not even a full day's rest . . . "I'll be off then. But before I go—will I see my Elaryl safe again?" He asked the question plaintively, pleading for a favorable answer but suggesting he expected the worst.

"You will." Dark nodded—and he smiled.

Enormously relieved, Seagryn bolted for the door but grabbed the doorjamb to stop himself and peered back inside at his friend. "You can't imagine how much better that makes me feel. Thank you, Dark!" As he rushed down the stairs, he barely heard the boy prophet calling after him.

"Never thank me until you've lived through what I predict!"

It didn't matter what else he predicted, Seagryn thought to himself. For if he was to survive a battle with the dragon tomorrow, and if Sheth's plan was to result in the destruction of the dragon, and if Elaryl was to be safely returned to him, then all was right with the world. Seagryn even had appreciative thoughts for the Power who had apparently arranged all this. Buoyed by good news, he could run all night to Haranamous if need be.

"There you are!" Kerily said, standing in the entryway to the mansion amid a large group of people, including her daughter. He rushed toward them as the woman continued, "Uda here told me you'd arrived last night, but I apparently missed you at breakfast. It seems that in deference to Dark's faith, my daughter wants a cleric to officiate at this wedding. That goes quite against my better judgment, but if she wishes—I can manage. Where are you going?!" she scolded, for Seagryn had as politely as possible pushed his way through the group, and he headed now for the door.

"Sorry," he mumbled. "I must be off."

"But you will officiate, won't you? I said you will . . ." But Seagryn could not reply. He was out the door and gone. Kerily whirled around to face Uda, who waited expectantly for her mother's inevitable explosion. "That's what I despise about these Lamathian clerics!" Kerily shouted. "They never have time to help people in need!"

Chapter Fourteen

❈❈❈❈❈

BURNING WIZARD

Seagryn lumbered northward along the road to Haranamous,
and the traffic scattered to let him pass. Not many of those who
scrambled aside actually knew what to call him, but anyone with
eyes could see he was a huge, sharp-horned monster who was
moving very quickly. Only a few lacked the good sense to get out
of his way. These were mostly wagon drivers who seemed to
believe they owned the road. He did his best to be polite, but
when one driver of an eight-horse team became particularly bel-
ligerent, Seagryn speared the side of the man's wagon and tossed
it into a ditch. It wasn't that he was trying to be nasty; he just had
a date to fight a dragon and he couldn't afford to be late.

When he wasn't dodging to avoid stepping on pedestrians, Seagryn thought about that upcoming battle. They would win, Dark
had said. Or rather, they would drive the beast from Haranamous.
What did that mean, exactly?

Seagryn made a mental list of the magical abilities he knew
how to use. He wondered why he and Nebalath could not simply
combine to cloak the city from view. After all, he'd managed in
that way to keep Vicia-Heinox from consuming the capital of
Lamath. Why couldn't Haranamous be hidden as well? Was it
because of the directions provided to the dragon by this upstart
son of Paumer? Seagryn struggled to remember the boy's name
but could call to mind only his snarling face. What had King
Haran done to cause the surly lad to send the dragonburn down
upon his land? More to the point, what could Seagryn and

Nebalath do to stop it? After the battle with the Emeraudes, he'd been forced to face the fact that he possessed only a limited collection of magical weapons. He too often failed to use his imagination. Would he remember to use it tomorrow?

Twilight drove most travelers from the road, but Seagryn couldn't stop. As he trotted by a cozy roadside inn, he cast a longing glance at the warm light streaming from its windows and wondered about the people bedded down there for the night. Were they on their way north to Haranamous? Would they arrive in the capital city in time to become victims of the impending disaster? He thought momentarily of stopping to warn the inn's occupants but decided against it. He was in a hurry, after all. Besides—why should they believe him? Better to spend his energies helping Nebalath avert the crisis. His resolve renewed, Seagryn sprinted ahead more quickly.

Hours later, running headlong into the pitch-blackness, Seagryn happened upon a group of highwaymen who'd apparently barricaded the road. He'd learned long ago that tugoliths suffered from night blindness, but in this instance the robbers suffered rather more. His forequarters splintered the barricade before he saw the thing, and the half-dozen rogues who manned it fled the scene screaming. He'd been feeling rather hungry from his day-long race, and he realized with horror that the tugolith in him wanted to chase one of these thieves down for a midnight snack. He resisted the urge by promising himself a large breakfast at the tables of the Imperial House and struggled to run even faster.

Not long after dawn's first rosy glow, he spotted the battlements of that castle on the horizon. The rest of the journey seemed to pass much more quickly. He terrified a few early rising townsfolk before taking his human form again at the palace entrance. He cloaked himself to prevent his being stopped and questioned by the Imperial guards, but once inside immediately removed the cloak in the face of a fusillade of protest from the castle itself.

—That *hurts*! the Imperial House of Haranamous informed him before launching into a series of uncomplimentary statements regarding his parentage. Seagryn ignored the diatribe.

"Where's Nebalath?" he demanded quietly of the wall in the hallway.

—Upon the roof. The castle sniffed. Which is the only place where magic can be practiced without giving this House intense pain! Truly *sensitive* powershapers have always understood that fact and adjusted their actions accordingly! Only the uncouth have been gauche enough totally to disregard the feelings of this House—

"I'll certainly try to do better," Seagryn mumbled as he hurried past the great hall. The aromas that issued from its doorway caused him to pause—he remembered promising himself breakfast—but that would have to wait until he'd talked to the older wizard. He dashed up the steps of the main staircase.

He found Nebalath standing atop a turret on the northwestern corner of the Imperial House. The man studied the northern horizon intently as he grumbled, "So. You finally made it."

"It was a long run," Seagryn said. "I started right after you left."

"I know." Nebalath nodded. "I've been back there twice since you left. I'm to tell you that Fylynn is very angry that you just left her there without saying good-bye—"

"She was still in bed—"

"And that Kerily has forgiven you as long as you'll agree to perform the wedding. By the way," he added, finally looking Seagryn in the face, "she's decided that you're to wear red."

"I'm to what?"

"In the wedding." Nebalath smiled grimly, turning his eyes back to the north. "I can visualize that. Seagryn in red."

"And when is this wedding to be, finally?" Seagryn asked, shielding his face from the morning sunlight and peering northward himself.

"If Dark knows, he isn't saying," Nebalath said wearily.

Seagryn had the strong impression that what Dark had said to Nebalath had not been cheerfully received. He hesitated before asking, "What *does* Dark know? Any further information about today's battle?"

"Not much." Nebalath shrugged.

Seagryn frowned. "What are you not telling me?"

Nebalath finally looked at him, and the old wizard's eyes were hard. "Things you don't need to know." His gaze drifted back across the battlements to the mountains from whence the dragon would come; then softly he added, "Things I didn't need to know."

Seagryn thought he understood the older man's feelings. He'd often reacted with the same depression to Dark's revelations. "The lad went too far again, did he?"

"No," Nebalath said, raising his eyebrows. "I did."

Seagryn waited, but the old powershaper didn't elaborate. Seagryn knew better than to push. He leaned across the battlement and looked down at the dark river swirling around the base of the palace. "Very well. If there's anything you feel I *do* need to know, I'll rely on you to tell me. Until then, perhaps we should spend our time together talking about strategy?" He looked at Nebalath, and the older man shrugged his shoulders in acquiescence. Seagryn plunged ahead. "I've been thinking about how best to deal with this beast. I probably know Vicia-Heinox as well as anyone, and I wonder if we might exploit the difference between the two heads."

"I don't know what you mean," Nebalath said flatly.

"I mean simply this: we've discussed at length how the beast was made. You know the two heads don't always agree, or even always get along—"

"So you've said."

"I've seen them fight one another for control of their body!" Seagryn argued. "So I wonder. What if you take one head and I take the other?"

Nebalath considered this proposal without much apparent enthusiasm. "A kind of divide-and-conquer tactic?" he finally murmured.

"Right," Seagryn said, with forced optimism. "Since you have far more battle experience than I, as the dragon approaches us, you take the head on the right. That's Vicia, the more mean-spirited of the pair. I have a special relationship with Heinox, the head that will be to our left—"

"She's an old girlfriend, right?"

"Something like that." Seagryn nodded, wincing. "In any case, Heinox has always seemed more willing to listen to reason, so—"

"So you're going to try to talk one head out of attacking us while I do shaper-battle with the other head. Is that it?" Nebalath's tone of voice made the plan sound grossly unfair.

"Have you a better idea?" Seagryn asked, trying hard not to take offense at Nebalath's attitude.

"Yes," the older man said, and he turned to look Seagryn squarely in the face. "Let's go eat breakfast." Then he turned on his heel and trotted down the staircase.

Seagryn pursued him. "Was breakfast your better idea?" Seagryn asked. "Or do you intend to explain your plan when we get there?"

Nebalath seemed intent on avoiding the subject altogether. "The Imperial House has stopped talking to me," he said. "I did a little shaping in my room and it took offense."

"This House has never had much use for me," Seagryn muttered, looking up at the chandelier that hung high above the spiral staircase. He wondered if the castle could make it fall on someone if it chose.

"That's only because it doesn't know you. Unfortunately, it appears now that it won't ever get the chance. After you," Nebalath added, gesturing for Seagryn to proceed him into the great hall.

"What do you mean by that?" Seagryn asked, blinking in surprise.

"Why don't we eat?" Nebalath said brightly. "Dark knows how long it might be before we get the chance again . . ." The older wizard smiled mysteriously and waited for Seagryn to move.

"Yes, he probably does," Seagryn murmured. He hesitated in the doorway, deeply concerned by Nebalath's apparent state of mind. What had Dark told the man? But once again, he sniffed the enticing aromas wafting from the Imperial kitchens, and he could resist them no longer. "Let's do eat . . ." he muttered, and went in.

They found a quiet corner of the great hall and made it quieter by their presence. The population knew Nebalath well and avoided him as much as they could. Many also knew Seagryn by sight, and those who didn't were soon informed of his identity in hushed whispers. Common people didn't go near powershapers if they didn't have to—one never knew what a wizard might do next. Two wizards together could signal only one thing—trouble. So while they ate in the company of hundreds, Seagryn and Nebalath enjoyed absolute privacy.

Or rather, almost absolute privacy.

—This House is waiting for an apology, the Imperial House stated flatly through a sweating of its walls.

"From whom?" Nebalath grumbled. "Him or me?"

—Both of you have exercised injurious abilities within these walls! While this House has little means of comparing its condition to those of you who must live within a sack of flesh, some in times past have suggested that the feeling is similar to that of a human ulcer.

"I've never had an ulcer," Nebalath mumbled, savoring a strip of bacon.

—It *hurts*, the walls said emphatically. Or so this House has been informed.

"We've both practiced shaping within you because we're both interested in preserving your life," Nebalath told the House as he spread a still-warm loaf of bread with butter. "What's left of it," he added. Seagryn had been about to bite into a piece of fruit, but now he frowned instead. The castle's unexpected response sharpened his concern.

—Is this House alive? it asked. Or merely conscious? For the periods of consciousness are slipping away. There are times now when this House sleeps as it did before Nobalog's first spell awakened it.

Nebalath saw Seagryn's expression and nodded. "Have you noticed it?"

"Noticed what?"

"That the powers are withdrawing," Nebalath said. "Don't you recall how our shaper powers seemed restricted on the island of the Emeraudes?"

"Of course." Seagryn nodded. "But I thought we attributed that to the mental abilities of the green cats themselves."

"We did," the older wizard agreed. "But now I wonder. While you were waiting for a boat ride home, I toured about the old One Land, and became more than a little puzzled by the seeming inconsistency of my own abilities. There are places in the northern Marwilds where I can now do things I could never do before. In other places—here in Haranamous, for example—my own shaper powers seem limited indeed. And the Imperial House is right. There are times, now, when it seems to be in a daze."

Seagryn expected some sharp retort from the House, but none came. Instead, it listened quietly to their conversation, rather like a patient waiting for a pair of healers to agree on a treatment. "Do you have any explanation?" he asked the older wizard.

Nebalath chewed reflectively, his eyes focused somewhere over Seagryn's head. Then he swallowed and shrugged. "I thought it had something to do with the dragon," he began, and Seagryn nodded. "But now . . ." Nebalath's voice trailed off, and the wrinkles that circled his eyes seemed more pronounced now than Seagryn had ever before noticed. Suddenly the aged powershaper hunched forward across the table, his gaze intent on Seagryn. "You know I was born in Lamath, don't you?" he asked.

Seagryn stopped eating in surprise. "I—I knew you had a Lamathian-sounding name, and that you seemed to know the land well—"

"Upper Region," Nebalath grunted. "A coastal town called Pourelia. You've probably never heard of it."

"I studied maps," Seagryn countered evenly. "I know exactly where Pourelia is."

"But you've never been there . . ."

"No."

Nebalath sighed. "If you ever had, you'd know why I got out. A pious fishing village—too pious. I could never buy the idea of the presence of a caring Power. I lost too many friends to the sea. Death seems to polarize faith; it makes those who already believe more believing, while those who doubt just get angrier. I got too angry to stay and jumped a merchant trader bound for the south. This was a long time ago . . ." Nebalath's mind seemed to wander for just a moment, but he quickly returned to his point. "I still can't believe in any benevolent Power. Too much I've lived through argues against it. But have you sensed, as I have, the pervasive spreading of an evil presence through the world? Am I just getting older, Seagryn? Or are things really getting worse?"

—You're getting older and things are getting worse, the Imperial House offered.

"I'm talking to Seagryn here," Nebalath growled at the ceiling, then his eyes returned to search the face of his younger friend. "What do you think?"

This string of questions took Seagryn by surprise. It wasn't because he hadn't considered them. The relationship of the Power to good and evil had been a constant topic for debate in the schools he'd attended. He'd just not had much time to think about it in the days since. His experience as a cleric had convinced him that evil expressed itself through people. Evil in the abstract had been replaced by clear and present evils that needed to be battled daily. It was a foregone conclusion among Lamathians that the powers associated with shaping were evil—that's why he'd been expelled when his own talent for wizardry had revealed itself. He'd come to terms with his own ability to shape the powers, and questioned now whether they were inherently evil. But was there some evil presence behind the lesser powers, perhaps linking them all together in opposition to the One Whose Name is Beyond Speaking? Could there be one among a group of powers who, like evil persons Seagryn had known, somehow managed to influence lesser powers to perform evil deeds, and who linked these deeds together to enact evil on a grand scale? If so, how could the Power deal with such a being? He knew that the Power, too, expressed itself through people . . .

Seagryn never got the chance to answer, for the Imperial House quietly announced—The dragon is here.

Nebalath disappeared with a snap that directed all eyes in the great room to the wizards' table. Seagryn leaped to his feet and sprinted for the door. The entire room was silent for a moment, then suddenly erupted in a frenzy of excited speculation. What had happened? Where were the shapers going? Had they quarreled? And breakfast in the court of Haranamous continued at its leisurely pace.

"Where's the dragon now?" Seagryn demanded as he raced back up that winding staircase. It seemed he'd done nothing these past two days but run . . .

—Circling the city, the Imperial House replied.

There was no energy, no passion in the castle's response. The Imperial House sounded drugged. Apparently the powers were receding from this place, as Nebalath had suggested. But if that were the case—what tools did they have for opposing the dragon? He reached the top of the stairwell and bolted outside onto the rooftop.

He spotted Nebalath at once. The old wizard stood on the peaked pinnacle of one of the castle's corner towers, bracing his feet on the shingled roof and clutching a flagpole with one hand while he raised his other arm above his head. Seagryn had never seen the man looking more like the image of a wizard: The wind billowed his long robes out around him, and his hair blew wildly around his face. He squinted up at the beautiful morning sky, his jaw set in an expression of fearless resolve, his lip curled back in a defiant sneer. He seemed to be challenging the twi-beast to come and do its worst—and that worried Seagryn greatly. He'd witnessed the dragon's worst on more than one occasion, and it was terrible indeed. Seagryn craned his neck, shielding his eyes against the morning glare as he searched for that familiar two-headed form—

"Where is it now—" he began, but before he finished the question he had the answer to it. The dragon had circled below the roofline of the palace. Suddenly it swooped up and across the roof toward him, and Seagryn saw Vicia's jaws gaping wide and diving directly at him. He flattened himself upon the rooftop tiles and felt the rush of wind as the beast flew over.

—Very brave, the House commented, but without its usual rancor. Seagryn didn't have time to talk. He leaped to his feet and looked back up at the tower.

Nebalath still stood braced atop it, but he'd turned all the way around now and shook his fist at the receding dragon. Seagryn whirled to watch as the great green beast turned in a lazy loop and glided back toward them. His imagination raced . . .

On this pass the head named Vicia angled toward Nebalath.

Those jaws again gaped wide, and the eyes glittered with cruel delight. Seagryn glanced back at Heinox and raised his hand confidently. "You know me, Heinox!" he shouted, and it appeared at that moment that the better head recognized him and pulled up to pass above him. Seagryn hadn't the time to look back toward Nebalath, but he didn't really need to. He visualized in his mind the illusion he wanted Vicia to perceive: Nebalath, still, but now standing on a pinnacle that was ten feet shorter. Vicia adjusted his aim by dropping down lower—and ran headlong into the side of the tower. The whole castle shook at the impact—

For such a last-minute thought, this spell had remarkably far-reaching consequences. The enormous dragon body seemed to pause in midflight, then continued on at a much-altered course. Rather than flying on in a straight line, the twi-beast appeared to be spinning helplessly out of control. Seagryn looked sideways in time to glimpse the perplexed expression on Vicia's face, and he couldn't help smiling. Vicia's huge eyes crossed and his tongue lolled out to the side. As the rest of his green body flipped over the battlements that lined this rooftop like great teeth, Vicia just seemed to hang upon the tower by his nose. Then his long neck abruptly jerked him away, and he, too, disappeared over the edge. A moment later Seagryn heard a loud—and very satisfying—splash.

His satisfaction was tempered, though, by great concern. The initial blow had weakened the masonry of the pinnacle and set it wobbling. The pressure of the dragon's neck snaking around its base now tore it loose from its foundation altogether. The weight of the tower was up in its tip, and Seagryn watched in horror as this collapsed inward toward the center of the rooftop—and through it. He was in no danger himself, but as the rock work tumbled through the floors below—

"Why'd you do that?" Nebalath demanded, and Seagryn was relieved to see the older wizard standing beside him.

"Why? To save your life! Vicia was about to swallow you!"

"I realize that, and don't think I'm not grateful. But look at that!" Nebalath pointed to the huge hole that now gaped in the center of the Imperial House. "How many people do you think you've killed below us?"

Once again Seagryn felt inundated with guilt. It wasn't his fault—not really. He was here, after all, to do battle with a dragon, and if he'd failed to act, then Nebalath would certainly not be standing beside him. Yet the statement was true—his actions had killed again. And a brief thought flitted through his consciousness: How might this situation have been resolved if he'd endeavored to let the Power shape him, instead of acting to shape the powers?

Nebalath was on his knees beside him, shouting at the Imperial House. "House! House, are you all right?"

—This House appears to have lost one of its towers . . .

"Are you all right, though? Do you hurt anywhere?"

—There is no pain. In fact, considering the circumstances, this House seems to have weathered the shock rather well. Not that it will be capable of weathering a rainstorm any time soon, what with this huge tear in its ceiling. If anything, this House is feeling rather drafty at the moment . . .

"What of the people inside you?" Seagryn asked quietly. "Are many . . . dead?"

—It would appear so. There are bodies littering every floor—some of them moving, but many of them not. The great hall has collapsed inward. Incidentally—one of those not moving is King Haran.

Seagryn and Nebalath exchanged a look of quiet despair, but they had no time to speak. A gurgling roar rose behind them, and they looked toward the northern wall in time to see the dragon soar, screaming, into the sky above the castle. Its fluttering wings shed gallons of water at every flap, and its slick green scales glistened threateningly in the sunlight. Vicia-Heinox was very angry, and the target of its anger stood watching in horror on the rooftop below. The dragon hung in midstroke and focused all of its eyes on that one spot—

"Cloak!" Seagryn shouted as he pushed Nebalath in one direction and dived off in another. Intense heat exploded into flame in the spot they'd occupied, heat created by the focused animosity of the dragon. The fire quickly consumed the paint that coated the rooftop tiles, then burned itself out. By that time Seagryn had rolled across the open space to lodge against the battlement, cloaking himself all the way. Safely hidden, he glanced around to see if he might spot Nebalath.

—This House feels constrained to warn you that you are not very popular among the people below. They appear to be clamoring for your arrest.

"One thing at a time, House," Seagryn murmured. "Where's Nebalath?"

—It appears he's taken it into his head that he's to die falling from one of the spires of this house. He's currently standing atop the most southerly tower.

"Nebalath!" Seagryn shouted in dismay as he looked in that direction, for the older wizard was indeed standing on that pinnacle and in plain sight. "Nebalath!" he shouted again. "Cloak yourself!" But Nebalath couldn't have heard him, for the dragon was screaming with renewed rage at the sight of the wizard on the tower, and those two heads were focusing upon it with dreadful purpose.

A moment later a brilliant light suddenly flashed between Nebalath and Vicia-Heinox, and all four of the dragon's eyes blinked. The twi-beast howled in frustration and flapped furiously to maintain its place in the sky as it shook its heads, trying to clear its sight. In the relative quiet, the dragon heard a powerful voice booming these words skyward.

"Vicia-Heinox, we need to talk!"

Seagryn was a practiced speaker. He'd learned to project his voice in the large, featureless halls where the faithful of Lamath met to worship. He'd been able to make himself heard when he'd addressed the assembled wheels of the tugoliths at the Great Wheel far to the north. The very shape of this castle roof amplified the sounds and carried them upward, so it was easy for the dragon to hear. It was easy, too, for much of Haranamous to listen in, for the shoreline of the two rivers that met at the castle's base was lined with spectators. And what they heard did not enhance Seagryn's reputation among them.

"Who is that?" Vicia snarled down angrily. "I can't see you!"

"And neither can I!" Heinox added, equally incensed.

"I'm Seagryn, whom you know quite well!"

"Seagryn?" Heinox said eagerly. "Where are you?"

"And where did you go?" Vicia added, obviously still vexed.

"I'm here on the castle rooftop. Whom is it that you seek?"

"I seek Sheth, the fiend who tortured me!" Heinox screamed. "I'm going to rend him into tiny little pieces, then swallow him bit by bit!"

"And I'm also going to fry yonder fellow who just made me bump my head!" Vicia added.

"I made you bump your head, Vicia, not he," Seagryn shouted upward. "And I'm here to tell you that you've been deceived. Sheth is not here at all!"

Both of the dragon's faces frowned. "He *is* here. A tugolith told me!"

"That tugolith was either mistaken or he lied! I've been all through this palace and I can assure you—Sheth is not here!"

"Where is he, then?" Heinox demanded, not yet mollified.

Seagryn answered with unfeigned passion, "If I knew that, believe me, I'd find him and wring his neck myself! He's not here. Now I want you to go away!"

"What?" Vicia screeched.

"I *said*, go away!"

"Why should I?" Vicia mumbled, sounding more like a petulant child than a dragon.

Seagryn found himself responding in character. "Because I said so!"

"And what if I won't?"

The pattern had been established. Seagryn had no choice but to threaten. "If you don't, I'll—I'll ram your head into another tower!"

—Please don't, the Imperial House asked with remarkable restraint.

The dragon had begun to circle the castle again, flying low over the city. "But I'm hungry," Vicia protested. Many of the spectators below suddenly decided they'd heard enough and sought shelter indoors.

"Then why don't you eat that tugolith the next time he comes and lies to you!" Seagryn shouted. Still hidden within his cloak, Seagryn stood away from the wall and followed the twi-beast's circular flight with his eyes. When the dragon did not reply after several circuits, Seagryn shouted again, "I told you, *go away!*"

"Very well, Seagryn. For you, I'll go away."

Seagryn breathed a sigh of relief, then clenched both his fists and his eyes in a silent shout of victory. He missed seeing those four eyes lock once again onto the tower where Nebalath still stood watching. "But first—" Vicia said, and Seagryn's eyes flew open in time to see the shingles on that pinnacle burst into flame as the fiery figure of his friend and companion plummeted from it to disappear beyond the far wall.

"Nebalath!" Seagryn shouted, and started to race across after him but found his path blocked by the enormous gash in the rooftop.

—Too late, the Imperial House informed him quietly. You could do nothing in any case. The boy prophet had informed him he would go that way. He was trying to get it over with quickly.

Standing grief stricken on the lip of the hole, Seagryn was only marginally aware of the dragon's departure from the sky over Haranamous and of the subsequent arrival on the rooftop of a contingent of armed guards. These were led by Chaom, the tall, beefy general who had sat at the table with Seagryn when both had first heard the plans for the making of this horrible dragon. Seagryn could understand, then, the hesitancy in the man's eyes as Chaom loudly announced, "Seagryn Dragonspet, by agreement of the surviving court of King Haran, I hereby place you under arrest."

"On what charge?" Seagryn asked, gazing at him, and Chaom had to look away.

"On the charges of vandalism of the Imperial House of Haranamous, creating and fraternizing with a lethal creature, and premeditated regicide."

"They think I planned the death of your king?" Seagryn asked, incredulous.

"There was some conversation in the court last night between the king and Nebalath. It seems the wizard revealed the certainty of King Haran's death, as well as his own."

"Dark again." Seagryn sighed.

"You can certainly see why they might conclude you had a part in planning this catastrophe," Chaom said quietly. "Especially in light of your conversation with the dragon moments ago."

"Yes." Seagryn nodded, then he looked at Chaom directly, recalling their shared reactions to the dragon plan at that picnic luncheon at Paumer's house. "I suppose it could be said that we both did, months ago."

Chaom shrugged, obviously hoping the guards who were with him wouldn't ask too many questions when they returned to the barracks. "Come along, Seagryn. By the time we get back downstairs I'm sure they'll have added a charge of contributing to the murder of a wizard."

Seagryn's hands were manacled behind him, and he was ushered toward the stairway and down. Stairs—he felt that he'd been on these stairs for days. And this time he descended much farther into the bowels of this castle than he'd ever gone before, down deep into a dungeon he thought surely must be below the level of the river. They marched him through a maze of unlit passageways until they arrived at the door of a cell, into which Seagryn was unceremoniously shoved. The door slammed behind him, the key turned in the lock, and a moment later he was alone. Fortunately, he had the House to keep him company.

"I wonder what else could happen today," he murmured to the walls of rock.

—This House is not Dark the prophet. It sees and hears what does take place, not what is about to take place.

"That was a rhetorical question," Seagryn said. But it did

bring an idea to mind. "You could tell me what they plan to do to me . . ."

—Isn't it obvious? They'll execute you.

"Oh."

—This House will not see it, of course.

"Why not? Will the execution take place somewhere out in the city?"

—No. They're currently digging a stake pit in the center of the stables.

"A stake pit?"

—This House could explain more specifically, but would suggest that you really do not wish to know. It does, however, involve a deep hole, sharpened stakes, and horse manure.

"Thank you for not telling me," Seagryn said sardonically. "But if this is happening in your stables, why won't you witness it?"

—Oh, by that time this House will be asleep. Dark informed Nebalath of that as well.

"Dark has a big mouth," Seagryn mumbled to himself as a new wave of grief swept through him. First Nebalath, and now the Imperial House, too? Why? Seagryn pictured in his mind the face of the son of Paumer, the wretched lad who had caused all this, and plotted all manner of retribution against him. Then his thoughts returned to that breakfast-table conversation about the nature of evil. Was there some single, malevolent power binding together the horrible influences of all the other powers and holding a vast majority of the world's persons in thrall? If so, Seagryn hated it.

He hated it much worse when, sometime later during this timeless night, the Imperial House dropped off . . .

Chapter Fifteen

※※※

TRAITOR'S EXECUTION

Seagryn couldn't make fire.

He'd not always been able to make fire, of course. In fact, only within the last year had he learned he could create small balls of multicolored flame to light his way through the darkness. Still, once he'd mastered the trick he'd used it often. Realizing he could no longer do it came as a shock.

He had awakened to find his circumstances unchanged. He was still in a pitch-black dungeon, his wife was still missing and—he presumed—kidnapped by Sheth, a dragon he'd helped make that still burned the world, and the Imperial House of Haranamous slept on. He spent a few moments pondering the fate of Nebalath. The old wizard couldn't be dead, surely—didn't he have the ability to disappear instantly to any spot he chose? Seagryn had seen him burning, true, but certainly sometime before he hit the water on the far side of the castle, Nebalath had departed—hadn't he?

Or had he? After all, Nebalath had reported that the powers were leaving this region and had complained of his own diminished shaper ability during yesterday's battle. Was that why the old wizard had fought so ineffectively—because even as they struggled to drive the dragon from the skies over the city, the very powers they shaped were departing? That would mean Seagryn could no longer perform many of the feats he'd become accustomed to doing—like turning into a tugolith at will. Obviously the magic that had brought this House to life had gone, or the walls would still be talking . . .

188

Seagryn tried again to make a flame—and again he failed. He pictured himself as a tugolith in an attempt to take his altershape. He failed in that, too.

Now he shivered, and not because this dungeon was all that cold. Seagryn had just fully realized that he was in serious trouble.

He got to his feet and stepped tentatively forward, holding his hands out before him. He found the wall with his fingertips, then walked sideways, tracing its outlines first into one corner, then to a second, then to a third, then past the door into a fourth. The cell was small and windowless, and just knowing that made him feel stifled. Until this point he'd not been afraid. Why should he be? He was a wizard! But a powershaper without powers to shape was as helpless as any other prisoner in this dungeon. And the castle's last few words had assured him of his own doom.

With some desperation Seagryn thought of Dark. Hadn't the young prophet told him that the plan to destroy the dragon would be successful? Yes, but the boy had also said they would drive the twi-beast from the city without detailing the cost to Nebalath. Seagryn now understood the old wizard's mood as they'd prepared for battle. What had Dark not told them about the ultimate success of Sheth's plan? Hadn't he said specifically that Seagryn would seek Sheth out? And hadn't he promised that Seagryn would see Elaryl safe again? Yes—yes, he had!

But for the present, Seagryn stood in an utterly dark dungeon with no means of escape, at the mercy of the powers that be. Then it struck him: Hadn't he always been so? Had there ever been a time when he controlled events, rather than being controlled by them?

"No," he told the surrounding black. And he remembered in that moment something he had himself often said to congregations in Lamath in his days as a rising cleric. "The One beyond powers is power to the helpless."

"That's the trouble with magic," Seagryn told himself aloud. "It makes you self-dependent, and that robs you of all peace . . ."

By feeling the dungeon floor, Seagryn found his way back to the pile of straw where he'd slept and lay down again. He had no control, but he did have hope. Somewhere between the two themes of impotence and promise, he discovered a place of peace, and he settled down into that spot and relaxed. He might as well. He had no other choice.

He woke again when the door slammed open and the room

filled with torchlight. "The stake pit is ready for you!" someone announced cheerfully as Seagryn was dragged to his feet.

"Better not torment him," another voice warned. "He's a wizard, you know."

"If he's such a fine shaper, how come he's still here in this dungeon?" the first voice demanded as the group of guards hustled him through the door and down the corridor. "He's no shaper!" the fellow answered himself in a derisive tone. "He's nothing but a traitor who's gotten himself in good with the dragon!"

"He won us the battle of Rangsfield Sluice," the guard on Seagryn's left argued. "I was there."

"Nobody's ever proved he had anything to do with that victory! For myself, I think it was old Nebalath in disguise who won us that battle! This mudgecurdle just served him as a useful dodge! Come along, you," the guard on Seagryn's right growled, jerking on his shoulder and twisting it painfully.

"I think you're wrong," the other guard muttered. "I think everyone's wrong about him, including the king."

"Yeah? Well, you'd better keep your mouth shut about it or you might get tossed into that pit right after him!"

This was evidently sufficient threat to silence the other man's protests. There was no more conversation until Seagryn was thrust out of a tunnel into the sunlight of the stables. So, he thought to himself. They plan to execute me at high noon.

The small enclosure off to one side of the castle's entryway was surrounded by cut-rock walls four stories high, so the sun could only shine into the stables around midday. Its light hurt his eyes, and its heat immediately stuck his shirt to his back. The smell of the animals, the buzzing of flies, the humid air—what an unpleasant way to end his life, Seagryn thought to himself. He clung to Dark's promise that he would see his Elaryl again, hoping he'd not once more misinterpreted his friend's words. But as they marched him to the edge of the hole and he got his first glimpse of the sharpened stakes thrusting up out of the rich, black earth, Seagryn doubted.

A dozen purple-clad warriors surrounded him. "Pitch him in," one of them ordered, as if he were so much garbage to be disposed of, and Seagryn responded by trying again to take his tugolith form. Nothing—and now he was slung between four Haranian guardsmen, each holding one of his limbs. This couldn't be happening! Fear and disbelief tingled through him, causing his body to quake. "He's shaking now," someone snickered—what did it matter who?

"One," they all said in unison. "Two."

"Stop."

Chaom! He recognized the voice. General Chaom had come to rescue him!

There'd been not a hint of emotion in the command. Nevertheless, it was instantly effective. They stopped swinging him, and those holding his arms immediately let him go. He might have wished it had been the pair holding his legs instead, but as his head hit the soil it was his sense of relief he paid attention to, not the pain. The two who held his legs followed suit, and he had the chance to draw a deep sigh before they once more dragged him to his feet and turned him around to face Chaom. Then Seagryn grunted in surprise. The burly general wore the gold and purple robes of royalty! Seagryn smiled in recognition of the fact, but the new king did not smile back.

"Take him to the rooftop," Chaom grunted. It took a moment for Seagryn to register the fact that the former general—now the king—was not going to address him directly. "Too many people want to witness this execution," King Chaom announced, "and I'm not about to deprive them of that joy in my first act as ruler." The big man never even looked at Seagryn as he turned his back and left the stables.

"Come on," a voice behind him growled as Seagryn once more was wrenched into motion. Chaom had betrayed him!

The guards pushed him inside and down the main hallway. Seagryn had not taken much notice of this corridor since his first visit to the Imperial House—usually right along here he'd been engaged in conversation with the walls. But they were silent now—as dead as he was soon to be. He couldn't remember ever feeling more lonely.

They passed the wreckage of what had been the great hall. Rubble was still piled at least a story and a half high in the middle of it, brightly illuminated by the sunlight streaming down through the hole in the roof above. Seagryn was allowed one long look, then he was propelled up the winding stairway to the site of his most recent—triumph?

The half of the roof that remained was crowded with dignitaries. That seemed rather foolish to Seagryn, since he doubted the remaining structure could stand the added stress, but at this moment he didn't have a high degree of concern for Haranians anyway. They'd all obviously gathered here to celebrate his death, for as soon as he appeared they hushed their chatter and began whispering to one another gleefully. For these people he'd risked his life at the Rangsfield Sluice? For these grinning ghouls he'd battled a dragon?

Like the prow of a ship parting the waters to either side, Chaom led the contingent through the crowd to the battlements and climbed up onto the charred wall. There he ceremoniously turned around, and pointing his finger directly at Seagryn, he trumpeted loudly, "Seagryn Dragonspet, your heinous crimes against the nation of Haranamous are well known to all of us assembled! You are charged with conspiring against this state! You are charged with—"

Seagryn could take no more of this. "What about you, Chaom!" he snarled back. "What about your own participation in the—" He got no further. A gag was suddenly looped over his face and wound around his head, and before he could reach up to jerk it off another pair of hands were binding his hands behind him.

Chaom never paused. He just shouted more loudly. "You are further charged with making, loosing, and consorting with a beast so monstrous as to rival the very worst of human nightmares. This entire city has witnessed your familiar conversation with the beast, here upon this very spot!"

Seagryn tried to answer this charge, too, through the gag. It did no good. At the moment he wished that very dragon would reappear in the sky and fly off with him in one of its mouths. He really felt less fear than he felt anger at Chaom for so callously betraying him.

"You are further charged with causing the death of the former king," Chaom continued, "a man greatly admired and respected for decades."

And one whom you conspired to undercut, Seagryn thought to himself, glowering in rage. He recalled how at one time he'd thought highly of Chaom, considering him one of the more responsible members of the Conspiracy. Now he wished the man nothing but evil. Loyalty was one of Seagryn's foremost values, and Chaom was demonstrating none at all.

"Still further, you are charged with causing the death of the covering shaper of Haranamous, the wizard Nebalath, who tumbled to his death yesterday at about this time. It is altogether fitting that you die upon this same spot, and that I, in my first act as king, should be the one to slit your throat and push you off these walls!'' On these words Chaom drew from his belt a large, curved dagger and flourished it above his head.

The crowd greeted his announcement with a great cheer. Seagryn was hustled forward and forced onto the battlement beside the king. He wondered if he might be able to throw his weight into the man and at least take the mudgecurdle with him, but Chaom was much bigger than Seagryn, and had been a warrior far longer than he'd been a king. He immediately had the bound wizard in a choke hold and was turning him to face the river. As the noise of the throng swelled behind them, Seagryn saw the dagger flash before his eyes and felt its cool blade press against his neck.

''Take a deep breath before you hit the water,'' Chaom growled in his ear. Then the big man cut through Seagryn's gag and pushed him forward.

Seagryn wanted to ask, ''What?'' as he plummeted toward the surface of the river, but he had the good sense not to do so. Instead he inhaled deeply—

Cold! Deep! Drowning! Seagryn struggled in vain to get his hands untied, but they were bound together too tightly. Then suddenly he felt something grab him! A huge fish or some kind of water monster had seized him around the neck and now wrestled him down deeper into the murky dark! He would have screamed in terror, but if this was to be his last breath, he could hold it just a few moments longer. He tried again in desperation to take his tugolith shape, to fight this monster with another—

But now he felt himself being pulled back up! As his head broke the water's surface, he gasped in a giant breath, then looked around wildly for the thing that held him in its grasp—but it was dark! Where were they? Under the castle? They had to be, for they'd not been below the water long enough to get far from its base. Was this Nebalath? Surely it must be Nebalath who had him! Nebalath had saved him! He tried to roll around and look at his rescuer but couldn't turn his body, for whoever this was still held him around the neck. Were they heading for some kind of subterranean dock? Since Seagryn's hands were still bound, he couldn't help—but then neither could he hinder. He gave thanks to the Power that his rescuer was a powerful swimmer. But could Nebalath swim like this? Could anyone he knew?

Seagryn felt them bump against something solid and tried to throw his body onto it, but he was forced to wait until the one who'd saved him from the river pulled him out. Then he lay shivering on the wet rock shelf, gasping for breath. Safe! Of course, he'd known all along he wouldn't die, hadn't he? After all, Dark had promised! He laughed at himself in relief . . .

"What's so funny?" the woman who lay beside him asked, gasping for breath herself.

"Fylynn?" he said, almost choking.

"It's me," she gasped back.

"How did you—"

"Later!" she grunted, and he heard her rolling onto her back. A sensible suggestion, he realized, and he filled his lungs with fresh air while letting his heart calm. Finally they were both rested enough to talk, and Fylynn began.

"It was Chaom's idea, but I knew already he would have it before he made the suggestion, because—"

"Dark had told you he would," Seagryn finished for her when she had to stop for a breath. "I had no idea you were such a strong swimmer!"

"After all those days on the beach at Emeraude Island? What did you think I was doing, getting an allover tan?"

"You did some of that," Seagryn recalled.

"You're a Lamathian cleric!" she scolded. "You weren't supposed to be looking."

"But why did we have to go through all that?" Seagryn puffed. "Why couldn't Chaom just release me and say I escaped?"

"The people had too much interest in seeing you dead, and Chaom has wanted to be king too long to jeopardize his new standing. If you were said to have escaped, he would have to mount a search, and if he failed to recapture you, he would appear to be incompetent. This way they all think you're dead. They can celebrate your demise in the streets tonight while we slip off to meet Sheth."

"Sheth," Seagryn grunted. "Have you seen him?"

"He visited me in Pleclypsa!" Fylynn said, thrilled. Seagryn remembered then that she was enamored of him. "He's so beautiful!" she gushed.

Seagryn recalled Sheth's dimpled sneer and the way his mustache turned up in a snide smile—and kept his opinion to himself. After all, Fylynn had just saved his life. "Do you mind untying my hands?" he asked, and she turned immediately to the task.

"The knot's wet," she murmured. "I have a dagger in my bags. Let me go search them . . ."

As she crawled away into the darkness, Seagryn tried to piece together where they were. "What is this place?"

"A boat slip under the palace," Fylynn called back. "There's a boat over here . . . somewhere . . ." Even as she spoke he could hear the sounds of a small rowboat bumping against a dock and of someone climbing into it. "Here it is. We'll use it tonight, after the sun sets."

"Is Sheth somewhere in the city?"

"No way," Fylynn called back to him, her voice echoing around the chamber. "He said his power was diminishing in Haranamous, and that he wouldn't be back. Of course," she added with a lusty chuckle, "I diminished his power a little further before I would let him go!"

Seagryn didn't want to talk about Sheth or his power; he wanted to know about his own lady. "Did he mention my Elaryl?"

There was a moment's pause, then Fylynn answered sharply, "Why should he?"

Seagryn recognized a jealous edge in the woman's voice and decided against pursuing it. If they were going to Sheth, he would learn more soon enough. "She's supposedly somewhere in the Marwilds," he explained. "From something Nebalath told me I just assumed that Sheth would be there, too. Do you know?"

"I think that's where he is," Fylynn replied, placated. By now she'd returned with her dagger and, by working together, they soon had his hands free.

"You're not certain?" Seagryn asked. "How are we supposed to find him?"

"You'll see. Here—dry clothes," she said, thrusting some garments into his hands. "Change into these, then let's eat. After that you'd better try to get as much sleep as you can. We'll be traveling all night long."

They both changed clothes in the darkness, then sat down to eat. Fylynn was well prepared—but then, she'd evidently had the aid of the new king. They lay down then, and Seagryn tried to follow her suggestion and rest—but he found he couldn't sleep. Elaryl! He would see her in just a few days! He could hardly wait for the daylight to pass so they could slip away into the night . . .

"Is it dark yet?" he asked, much later.

"How many times have you asked me that?" the lady jester complained, but this time he could hear her standing up. "Wait here and I'll check . . ." He heard her slipping out of her clothes again and diving into the water. It seemed a long time before she returned, but she finally did. "It's night. Help me out." He reached blindly toward her voice and helped pull her from the water. Within moments, she was dressed and they were both in the boat. "There's a small door at the end of this tunnel," she explained quietly. "Chaom says it's disguised as a rock on the outside, and that it's so low we'll have to lie flat in the boat to get out of it . . ."

They soon bumped against the door and, knowing what to expect, were able to maneuver themselves out onto the river without problem. Moments later they were gliding across its calm surface, an unnoticed skiff in the night traffic of a great waterway.

The city of Haranamous was alive tonight. Many fires burned in the streets, and lamplight flickered in open windows. As they floated past dark quays and closed warehouses, Seagryn felt a surge of excitement. No more waiting. They were on their way! He silently congratulated Chaom for his wisdom in resolving the problem this way. But soon his mind moved on to wonder how exactly they were to know where they were going? At the moment they were traveling east, not west, downriver rather than up toward Arl and the Marwilds. Were they to meet with a ship and go north by way of the coast and then inland? He didn't ask. He'd traveled with Fylynn long enough to trust her, and she'd showed more abilities today than he'd given her credit for. Then again, she'd not been called on to demonstrate much of her talent; she'd been a nonshaper in the presence of two wizards and had been content to rely on them. Now, in the absence of the powers, she proved herself to be quite capable.

As they came in sight of the city's eastern river gate, Seagryn became concerned, wondering if they would be stopped. But for years there'd been little danger of attack from the east, so they found the gate unguarded. The number of docks dropped off quickly, and soon they were passing fields and stands of trees. When they reached a forested area, Fylynn slipped out the oars and rowed for shore. Seagryn peered under the trees but could see nothing. It was not until they'd dragged the boat out of the water and unloaded it that he heard the sounds of horses whinnying in the woods behind them.

"What is all this?" he mumbled as he struggled to shoulder two heavily loaded saddlebags.

"Provisions," Fylynn answered—a little too brusquely, he thought. "Come on."

A moment later, he thought no more about it as he heard an unmistakable voice call out, "I'm over here."

"Dark!"

"Yes," the boy admitted stiffly as Seagryn dropped the bags beside the horses and embraced him. When they broke apart, Dark said, "You see? You did survive."

"But not Nebalath," Seagryn replied quietly. It would have been hard for anyone listening to tell if this was a statement or a question. He left it open-ended in the hope that, without being asked directly, Dark might give him some hint as to what actually had happened to the old powershaper—and perhaps some hope that he lived still. But Dark volunteered nothing, and Seagryn struggled once more against the senseless anger he felt at this boy who couldn't help knowing everything in advance. "Why did you tell him?" he demanded with a quiet intensity born of unexpressed grief. "Didn't you know it would cause him to give up?"

"Of course," Dark murmured. "But I didn't make him do it."

"But you did!" Seagryn pleaded quietly. "Don't you see that?"

"I answered his questions, that's all," the boy prophet said. "I'd do the same for you . . ." It seemed in that moment the lad was almost begging Seagryn to probe further, and he was sorely tempted to do so, for there were many things he wanted to know: How long would it take them to destroy the dragon? Would he survive the attempt? Would Elaryl? Would they ever live happily and in peace? But Nebalath's recent experience haunted him, and he recalled Dark's own terror at the possibility of one day foreseeing clearly his own death. Nebalath had been unable to live with the certainty—and Seagryn decided he would be, too. The silence between them grew longer—and deeper.

Fylynn's impatience finally broke it. "Are you two going to stare at one another until dawn, or can we get on with this?"

They loaded the bags on their horses and mounted up. But before riding north, Seagryn reached out, put his hand on Dark's, and said, "Forgive me. I've still not learned how to handle your gift."

"Don't blame yourself." Dark sighed. "I haven't either."

"There is one question I *must* ask, however," he began seriously. Fylynn was shocked to hear Dark laugh outright even before Seagryn finished it, also laughing. "What will Uda do when she discovers you missing?"

"She'll come after me, of course!" The boy cackled with relief. "So can we hurry up and go?" They all three laughed together, then wheeled their horses about and rode hard to the northeast.

"Get out of my *way*!" Uda roared, and the diminutive girl shoved the cringing guard aside and threw open her mother's door. "He's *gone*!" she shouted, and her mother shot straight up in her bed.

"What? Where? Who?" Kerily shouted, waving her arms helplessly before her. She'd blindfolded her eyes before retiring, and it took her a moment to remember where she was.

"Dark, that's who! He's run *off*!"

At last Kerily's fingers found their way up to her face, and she released her eyes with a gasp of thanksgiving. She blinked several times as she searched the room for her daughter. When she spotted Uda, she threw open her arms and said in her most motherly voice, "Come here, my baby. Tell me all about it."

Uda hopped into bed and let herself be cuddled but refused to be at all comforted by her mother's soothing words. "He left with that—that jester woman! How could he *do* that? She's fat!"

"She is that . . ."

"And ugly!"

"You're far prettier . . ."

"And old!"

"She certainly . . . Well, now I wouldn't say she's old," Kerily corrected her daughter. Age was a sensitive topic in Kerily's quarters.

"She's much too old for Dark!"

"Now that's probably true."

"Oh, Mother!" Uda cried, unplanned tears welling in her eyes. "How could he do that?" She buried her head against her mother's side and sobbed at the reality of rejection.

Uda didn't cry often, so, when she did, she usually made a real event of it. Kerily understood this and didn't try to interrupt. She just rocked her child against her, waiting for the storm to spend itself. She saw a worried maid appear at the door and waved her away, instructing her by gestures only to close the door and leave them alone. When Uda was finished crying, she sat up, and Kerily offered her a part of the silk bed sheet to wipe her face. "Now then. Tell me exactly what you know."

Uda sighed deeply twice and wrung the sheet tightly between her fists before finally controlling her frustration enough to speak. "He's left Pleclypsa, taking some of our best horses and that Fylynn woman with him. They were spotted riding toward Haranamous, but it seems no one here tried to stop them."

"Well now, consider that, child. After all, since the boy could know exactly where the guards would be at all times, he could have slipped by any of them easily, couldn't he?"

"It doesn't work that way, Mother," Uda scolded, feeling free to take out her anger on this one who brought her into the world. "What I want to know is, why?"

Kerily regarded her daughter seriously, pursing her lips in thought. "Well now, Uda, you did throw yourself at him, you know."

Suddenly Uda glared at her mother. "You arranged all this, didn't you?"

"What?" Kerily gasped.

"You helped him escape just to get him out of your sight!"

"Uda!" her mother exclaimed. "I'm hurt! How could you even suspect me of something like that!"

"I'm sorry," Uda immediately mumbled, and she truly was. "But I know you never liked him . . ."

"How could I like the boy?" Kerily protested. "He's—so odd!"

"A little eccentric, maybe," Uda defended, but Kerily overrode her.

"No, I mean definitely odd! You tell me one mother who would enjoy having for a son-in-law a person who always knows what she's going to say before she says it!"

"It's just that his gift is so overpowering . . ." Uda pleaded. She really didn't understand why she continued to defend him, since at the moment she loathed Dark passionately.

"Well, as far as *I'm* concerned, you're well rid of him! Oh, now don't start crying again," she added more softly, for once again Uda was crumbling toward her, her pretty face misshapen by grief. Kerily cradled the girl against her and changed her approach. "Now, darling, don't you worry. We'll get him back for you, you just wait . . ."

"How?" Uda demanded. "With Father's help? He doesn't like Dark, either."

"Actually, your father's been somewhat indisposed in recent days. I was thinking more of asking your brother . . ."

"Ognadzu?" Uda said, sitting up and staring at her mother in surprise. "What could he do?"

Kerily drew a deep sigh and looked away. "Your brother has grown—rather influential, of late."

Uda frowned. "How?"

"Oh." Kerily shrugged, obviously not wanting to say much more than she had already. "By . . . things he's done. Arrangements he's made. He really does have a sharp mind, you know."

Uda's frown hadn't faded. "Does Father know all this?"

Again Kerily looked away. "I . . . believe he has some knowledge of it, yes. Of course, we've not talked recently."

"Where is Father? Do you know?"

Kerily smiled at her daughter brightly. "Now that's a good question. No, I really don't. But then . . . at least he's not here!" She yawned, stretched, and said, "I'm ready for breakfast. What about you?"

Uda hopped off the bed and started toward the door. "I'm ready to go after Dark."

"Darling, wait," Kerily pleaded, and Uda's black hair swirled as she turned and looked over her shoulder.

"Let me go with you!" Kerily said. "It's been ages since I've been out of this house . . . it'll be fun!"

"Fun?" Uda asked, wrinkling her nose.

"Of course! We'll make a holiday of it! Ognadzu will help us locate him, there's no question about that. We'll just pull together a staff and some luxury tents and an entire caravan and go chase the poor lad down!"

"But Mother! That'll take days!"

Kerily slid off the bed and wrapped a lace shawl around her shoulders. "We have plenty of time. There's not a place he can go in the old One Land where we don't have our people. You know that—and since the impertinent little mudgecurdle knows everything, he knows it, too. It's inevitable that we'll find him and recover him, but since we don't know when, exactly, we might just as well travel in style. I'll get the kitchens busy planning the menus," she finished, starting past Uda toward the door. Her daughter blocked her.

"But what about the wedding?"

"Oh, that . . ." Kerily sniffed. "You know, I was getting rather bored planning all that, weren't you? And it just seemed as if things weren't coming *together*. Now Uda, darling, I've been planning productions for years, and when things tie up like that, sometimes it just means you have to back off and take a good look at the whole concept. You're my only daughter, and this is my only opportunity, so this wedding just simply must be aesthetically perfect. A trip like this is just what we need to give me a little perspective on it all!"

"But by the time we get everything together—"

"Hush now, hush!" Kerily commanded, instinctively aware that she was once more in full control of the situation. "To travel properly takes planning, and perfect plans do take time. Relax, darling, and just let me take care of everything. I feel certain we can be away from here by—oh, in two weeks, at least!"

"Two weeks!" Uda moaned as her mother dashed out the bedroom door, shouting for the steward. "Two weeks?" she asked again of the empty bedroom, and groaned dramatically. Still, Uda was satisfied. After all, her mother was right. Uda had traveled briefly with Seagryn and had learned deprivation at the hands of Sheth. Traveling in luxury was better. Besides, she knew she'd never get what she wanted unless she got all the family assistance possible. And she'd been Dark's little mother far too long. She was looking forward to being a scheming girl again!

Chapter Sixteen

✹✹✹✹✹

SUBMISSIVE SHAPER

THEY circled the northeastern wall of Haranamous and joined the northbound road, then followed it all night long. By dawn they'd reached a bridge that allowed them to cross the river, and then turned off the road and headed northeast.

"Why this way?" Seagryn wondered aloud.

"We're going to circle the Middle Mountains to the south," Fylynn explained. "It's safer than trying to pass through the Central Gate."

Seagryn grunted disapprovingly. He'd flown over the base of that range on the head of Heinox and knew the forest there was a tangled jungle. "Why not dare the pass?" he asked.

"You want to face the dragon again this soon?" she challenged him.

"The twi-beast is often not there—"

"Too risky," the woman said flatly, dismissing the idea. "Besides," she added, "you want to go where Sheth is, don't you?"

Seagryn glanced at Dark's face, softly illuminated by the pink light of dawn, but the boy was giving nothing away. Seagryn just shrugged, and they rode on.

The night's ride had been tense, for they'd all needed to concentrate on the road, and Seagryn had felt the fear of being recognized by Haranian warriors guarding the road. Now that the sun was up and they galloped through the countryside, all three found their spirits much improved. They were weary, of course, and saddle sore, but the air had a crisp, early fall scent that cheered them all, and the sky was a cloudless blue. They were all excited, after all—Fylynn was en route to see Sheth, Seagryn was on his way to find Elaryl, and Dark had been looking forward to this jaunt of freedom for months. So Fylynn joked while Dark and Seagryn laughed, and the camaraderie born of the long night's journey turned into midday silliness.

"You stole us some fine horses here, Dark," Seagryn exclaimed as they skirted a farmer's cornfield.

"These are not stolen," Dark mockingly protested. "They belong to me! Part of my dowry."

"Men have dowries where you two come from?" Fylynn frowned. "Remind me not to marry a Lamathian!"

"Anyone who marries into the house of Kerily deserves a dowry," Dark said, and it sounded as if he meant it.

"The House of Kerily?" Seagryn wondered. "Not the House of Paumer?"

"That house is definitely Kerily's," Dark said, telling his companions nothing they didn't already know well. "As for the House of Paumer . . . I'd really call it the House of Ognadzu, now. He's stolen most of it from his father."

"Really?" Seagryn said.

"An early inheritance," Fylynn explained. "The new way for the truly wealthy. After all, why wait for your father to die?"

"Ognadzu's not waiting at all," Dark said. "In fact, he's tried to hasten that along. He's sent the dragon after his father several times. Paumer's been shrewd enough to avoid the beast so far, but he's terrified."

"I think I'd want a dowry to join that family, too," Fylynn murmured with a frown.

"Where's Paumer now?" Seagryn asked, and Dark looked at him with some surprise. Seagryn realized, then, why—this was the first direct question he'd asked since inquiring about Uda's frustration.

"He's—with Sheth," Dark said carefully. "You want me to—"

"No, no," Seagryn said quickly. "I'll wait."

Dark nodded and took a deep, happy breath. Seagryn hadn't seen the boy this relaxed since before the dragon was made, and it pleased him enormously.

They reached the southernmost edge of the Marwilds by late afternoon and found a camping site in a charming meadow beside a brook. Fylynn gathered firewood and dropped it before Seagryn expectantly. "Well?" she asked.

"Well what?" he said, puzzled.

"Any of the old powers restored yet?" she explained in a tone that shouted, "You're certainly dense."

"Ah . . ." He held a hand out before him, palm up, and thought. Nothing happened.

Fylynn sighed. "I guess we rub two sticks together—" she began, but Dark snorted at her and held out a flint. "Imagine that," she murmured as she took it, then looked again at Seagryn. "I wonder how he knew?"

By dawn they were up and riding again, but the going was far slower now that they moved through the thick woods. They worked harder and joked less, and Seagryn was unsure why. It did seem to him, however, that Dark's mood had turned gloomy again. He didn't ask. He just steeled himself for the worst. They spent two more days in exactly the same conditions before it happened, but when it did Seagryn was immediately angry with the boy for not warning them.

They'd been moving through nearly impassable underbrush all morning. Seagryn had long ago grown weary of this wall of green; when it seemed he saw some blue sky ahead, he'd become very excited and encouraged the others toward it. Dark didn't call out to him nor hold back. He just drove his mount forward in pursuit of Seagryn's, and suddenly the three of them jumped a bush and found themselves right in the middle of an Arlian military compound. It was unmistakable—the Pyralu emblem was embossed on everything, and the regiment's Pyralu standard graced the top of a pole in the midst of the camp. Black-helmeted soldiers all around them turned to stare at them, while those who were more alert sprinted toward them with weapons drawn. They had the time for only one exchange before they were surrounded. "Dark!" Seagryn yelled. "Why didn't you warn us?"

"Why didn't you ask?" the boy wailed—then the three of them were being pulled off their horses and hastened toward the large pavilion in the center of the camp. Seagryn tried at each step to turn into a tugolith—nothing. The tent flap was tossed out of the way, and they were unceremoniously frog marched inside.

"My Prince!" the chief guard shouted. "Invaders!"

The Prince of the Army of Arl bounded up from his chair and whipped around to stare at them. Then he dissolved into laughter. "Seagryn! Dark! So you've come to visit me again!"

"Jarnel," Seagryn murmured. The last time he'd seen the Arlian general he'd not really seen his face. Jarnel had remained hidden throughout that interview behind a terrifying mask formed in the shape of a pyralu. That encounter had taken place far to the north in the middle of last winter, and the general had been terribly suspicious of all of them and particularly resentful of Seagryn. Today the mask was gone, and Jarnel seemed to regard them with genuine warmth. Seagryn sneaked a peek at Dark, hoping to gauge their danger by the boy's expression. As usual, the prophet's expressionless face gave him no clue.

But Jarnel seemed sincere. "And who is this with you?" he asked, taking Fylynn by the hands in a gesture more characteristic of a court charmer than the no-nonsense soldier he'd always appeared to be before.

"My name is Fylynn—my Prince," Fylynn replied, curtsying with a grace that belied her figure. She, too, had lived at court and knew how to pick up on a title and use it.

"You're welcome here, Fylynn." The general bowed. "Please don't be offended if I seem to direct my attentions to these two. We've just known each other for some time." He walked toward the chief guard, gesturing for him to leave as he said, "These are not invaders, nor spies either. They've come with information vital to the interests of Arl. Did—you arrive by horseback?" the general asked, looking at Seagryn and raising an eyebrow doubtfully. "Or by—some other beast?" Of course! Jarnel knew well Seagryn's ability to transform himself.

"Yes, on horseback." Seagryn nodded.

"Very good." Jarnel turned back to the lieutenant. "Return their goods and horses to them, and extend them every courtesy while they're in this camp. You're dismissed." As the warrior left the tent, Jarnel turned again to Seagryn and smiled. "Now. What is the purpose of your visit?"

Seagryn shook his head. "There is no purpose. We were traveling north and trying to avoid the dragon. We've stumbled into your camp by accident."

Jarnel looked at Dark. "With the whole of the Marwilds surrounding us, you've come across this compound by pure chance? And with this lad along? I'm convinced there are no accidents with Dark. Are there, boy?"

Dark didn't flinch before the Pyralu general's gaze. "If you truly want an answer to that question, General Jarnel, then yes— there are accidents with me. Accidents happen. I just know about them before they do."

"But surely—?"

"Jarnel, listen," Seagryn interrupted apologetically. "If I had known you were here, I'd certainly not have come this way. We were traveling north. That's all."

Jarnel pursed his thin lips and grunted thoughtfully. "It's difficult for me to accept such a thing as a coincidence." His thin face grew thinner as he hollowed his cheeks and looked back at Seagryn. "You can surely understand why? And it's my duty to learn your purpose, to insure that it doesn't run counter to the purposes of Arl."

Dark spoke up again. "Perhaps the purpose is hidden—even from us."

Jarnel chuckled. "And how could that be, boy, since you see everything?"

"Perhaps our meeting is in the purpose of the One Who Allows me to See?"

Jarnel's gray eyebrows shot up and the lines that streaked his high forehead furrowed. Then his face relaxed, and he smiled once again. "Oh, that's right. You two are Lamathians, after all. Are you, dear lady?" Jarnel asked Fylynn. She was so shocked by the sudden attention she could only stammer and shake her head. "But if you've been around these two believers long, you know that they regard things differently from the rest of us." He looked back at Dark. "A higher purpose, perhaps?" Dark shrugged, and Jarnel began pacing about the pavilion. "I once had a higher purpose myself. But of course, you shared it, didn't you—the Grand Conspiracy!" He shook his fist over his head, then smiled at them mockingly. "Dedicated to the higher purpose of reuniting the One Land. Of course, it cost me my command—cost me my army, too, Seagryn, for I would never have attacked Haranamous as foolishly as my ambitious subordinate did, and you would never have had the opportunity to destroy it. That purpose almost cost me my family—and it certainly cost me last winter. I'd been accustomed to wintering with my troops in Arl, and spending the time with my grandchildren. Instead I spent the season chasing Sheth through the northern woods, while he—and you—made the dragon that will ultimately consume us all." Jarnel's face had now lost all its warmth. He looked again like that stern Pyralu general Seagryn had first met in the Remnant—while there still was a Remnant. And what the man said was true.

Yet suddenly, strangely, Jarnel smiled. "But that's all past now," he went on. "The Conspiracy is dead, its members gone on to new pursuits, and the grand design of a reunited One Land is forgotten. Isn't it?" Those thin eyebrows arched expressively.

Seagryn looked at Dark. "Ah—we—I guess we're more interested in stopping the dragon now than anything else."

Jarnel's laugh was devoid of friendliness. "Stopping the dragon! But you're the very ones that started the dragon! Oh," he mused, looking away, "I guess that was the plan, wasn't it? But it's no longer necessary, is it? After all, the dragon is under control now, and, by agreement between my king and his new trading partner, the One Land will be reunited." Rich sarcasm vibrated in his voice as he added, "But I wonder what they will call it then? Greater Arl? Or Greater Ognadzu?"

"Paumer's son and the Army of Arl are in league with one another?" Seagryn asked.

"Of course." Jarnel pointed toward Dark. "I'm certain he knew that already. He didn't tell you?"

"And the two of them—guide the dragon?"

"It's simple!" Jarnel shrugged, smiling bitterly. "Our army captures whole villages and feeds them to the dragon. We took a little place called Ritaven last week, but we'll be getting around to Lamathian villages soon. In return, that hungry dragon follows the instructions provided by Ognadzu through a tugolith messenger. To be honest, Seagryn, I had thought you were involved somewhere in the whole scheme. I'm still not certain that you aren't." Jarnel looked again at Dark and smirked. "A higher purpose, I think you said?"

Dark had kept silent throughout this account. Now he raised his head, and Jarnel paused to hear him. "General Jarnel, have you heard anything about some falling out, some disagreement between your king and his ally?"

Jarnel frowned thoughtfully. "No. Is that the case?"

"It is," Dark announced. "Would you mind if I stepped outside? I'm feeling a bit closed in and need a little fresh air . . ."

"Certainly." Jarnel smiled. "Every courtesy, you remember?"

As Dark left the tent, Seagryn glanced at Fylynn. Apparently she'd known none of this either, for her face was white and her eyes wide and staring. "So, General," Seagryn asked, trying to control his own dismay, "you know all of this—and have no urge to stop it?"

"The censure in your voice is unmistakable, Seagryn," Jarnel replied evenly. "It causes me some resentment, since I know a few things about your ethical choices. But why should we bicker, hmm? After all, we're prisoners, both of us. I know you did what you did in the hope of finding some comfort and stability at home, and I understand that. I've made the same choice.''

"But whole villages—"

"It's your dragon, Seagryn, and it would eat those villages anyway!" Jarnel roared, his face suddenly red. His temper cooled quickly, for he seemed to feel a deep need to explain himself. "I would choose to do differently if I could, Seagryn. I can't. Things have changed, and we must adapt. It's wrong, but I've decided that I'd rather the town of Ritaven be consumed than to have the beast destroy my children. I'd rather that I be the Prince of the Army of Arl than have someone else fulfill the rôle! And under some control, the dragon is really a very precise weapon. Instead of burning the entire city of Haranamous, it will be instructed to burn just the palace. Isn't it better to kill Haran and Chaom, and allow their army simply to surrender to us in the field?''

"You knew the dragon was attacking Haranamous?" Seagryn asked.

"Of course. Why?" Jarnel demanded. "Has it already happened?''

"Several days ago. But Nebalath and I chased the beast away. Oh, Haran is dead, but Chaom lives still. He's now king over Haranamous.''

"Chaom is king!" Jarnel brightened, then his excitement died. "I'd not thought of that. Chaom as a king. He would have made a good one." Jarnel sighed.

"Would have?" Seagryn asked.

"You're here. The dragon is not. How protected do you think that city is without you?''

Seagryn wouldn't have known what to answer, had he been given the chance to do so. But he wasn't, for Jarnel was wrong about the whereabouts of Vicia-Heinox, and Dark had been very right about the disagreement between Ognadzu and Arl—

The shouts began on the eastern edge of the camp—indistinct at first but growing steadily louder and clearer as the warning cry rolled toward the pavilion. "Dragon! Dragon in the sky!"

Seagryn and Jarnel stared at one another in shock. Then the general raced to the tent flap and threw it aside.

The Prince of the Army of Arl had not risen to his post through intrigue or family leverage. He'd proved himself a competent warrior over many years of battle experience. He'd survived dozens of surprise assaults and appeared to Seagryn fully capable of enduring this one. But as they both watched the supply tent next door erupt upwards in a brilliant spire of flame, Jarnel's first reaction was simple human terror. He jerked the tent flap down again and scrambled backward to the far wall, knocking aside a table and field chairs on his way. When he looked again at Seagryn, his bulging eyes and shallow, raspy breaths made him appear almost fishlike. The general was afraid. Seagryn guessed he should be, too.

But he wasn't, really—or, rather, not afraid of the dragon. These moments had become commonplace to him. Every new attack now only deepened his resolve to do something about this world-plaguing monster. He glanced back at the stunned Fylynn and shouted, "Outside. Let's go." She raced past him toward the split in the canvas and knifed through it. He looked back again at the general—and saw that Jarnel now regarded him with mingled fear and fury. It was obvious that he held Seagryn responsible.

"You!" the general raged, first pointing a trembling finger at Seagryn and grasping blindly for the sword that hung at his side. "You've done this!"

"I rather think Ognadzu has done this," Seagryn muttered as he grabbed the fallen table up by its legs and held it between them as a shield.

"Traitor!" Jarnel shouted as his sword flashed towards Seagryn's face. Seagryn knocked the blow aside. "Assassin!" the general shouted again, this time stabbing forward, and the point of the blade buried itself in the wood.

Seagryn saw no sense in debating the question. Jarnel would never hear him anyway. Instead he dropped the table and dodged backward through the flap and out of the tent. He found Dark and Fylynn waiting for him, already mounted. "Get on!" Dark shouted, and Seagryn jumped into his saddle. As they dashed off, Seagryn glanced backward in time to see Jarnel fighting his way out of the pavilion, wildly swinging his sword. Then the fires around them made riding treacherous, and Seagryn was forced to give his full attention to it. "That way!" Dark directed, pointing through the smoke, and they galloped quickly for the entrance to the compound as fleeing warriors dodged out of their way.

Once his horse knew where they were bound, Seagryn threw his head back and looked up. With the grace of a blue flyer, Vicia-Heinox rode the fiery updrafts. In flight, the twi-beast appeared an almost-beautiful creature. Seagryn wondered how he could even think such a thought at a moment like this, but it was true. It wasn't the dragon itself that was hideous, but rather the evil that directed the beast to make these attacks. And how could a plan initiated by such a callous criminal as Sheth ever deal with the root of the problem?

The compound blazed behind them. Seagryn reminded himself that tents flamed quickly and could easily be replaced. He hoped that this instance of dragonburn would prove more confusing than life threatening. There'd been some warning, after all. Had that given the men of Arl enough time to dash from their tents to the shelter of the forest? He could concern himself with it no longer. He needed to find Sheth—and Elaryl—before the dragon did.

At least they now had a road to follow. The military minds that had planned the compound in the dense tangle of the southeastern Marwilds had obviously seen the need for a quick way into and out of it. The track ran northwest, and while Seagryn couldn't remember seeing it from the head of the dragon, from this vantage point it was a wide, well-marked avenue. During the brief interruption in the journey, their horses had been fed and watered, giving them energy to respond powerfully to the motivating flames and smoke they were leaving behind. They galloped a long distance before slowing to a more comfortable pace. Through the rest of the day, the three riders took turns watching behind them for Arlian search parties dispatched by the angry Jarnel. They saw none.

By late afternoon the nature of the forest had changed. They now found themselves surrounded by giant trees, their trunks spaced well apart down on the forest floor but their boughs interlocking tightly above. It was like looking up at a ceiling of leaves— green, this week, but soon they would be turning orange, yellow, and red. Seagryn wished he might have a chance to see that. He did love autumn. But he supposed he would be spending another fall buried away from the dragon's sight in a cave someplace.

"Are you all right?" Fylynn asked, peering at him.

Seagryn came up out of his reverie with a grunt. "Hmm? Oh. Yes," he answered before thinking. Then he thought about it and frowned. "I think so. Why?"

"You look—sad." She shrugged, stroking the neck of her mount. "I know you're often burdened by worry—and guilt, too, I suppose, with so many people despising you and holding you responsible for the dragon problem. I just wondered if what that Arlian general told us was weighing you down further."

"I'm trying not to let it," Seagryn said, feeling comforted by her concern. "While I'm appalled by this arrangement between Paumer's son and the King of Arl, I'm not surprised by it. I've come to expect these powers to disrespect people—'' He stopped himself abruptly, for he'd seen her smile. "Why are you—?"

"Powers. You called them powers, as if these two human leaders were themselves elementals." Fylynn's gray eyes focused on some point out ahead as she reminisced, "I remember juggling for Ognadzu at court when he was just a boy. His little sister enjoyed my performances, but nothing I tried to do ever delighted him. Oh, he watched me, of course, but as a predator watches its prey, waiting expectantly for it to make a mistake. When I would miss—and sometimes his malice seemed to force me to—then he would laugh, and clap his hands with glee." She shifted her weight in her saddle and looked back at him. "Is he a power and not a person? Is that why he values power, instead of people?"

Seagryn considered that. But for some reason he thought not of Ognadzu but of himself. He was apparently hated by much of the world. He felt certain many would regard him as an evil power, rather then as a single individual caught up in a sequence of uncontrollable events. But did he value power? Or simply try to use that which he had to protect and defend others—to help? Not always, he admitted to himself. He thought of his conversation with General Jarnel and realized that he had no right to judge that man when many of his own choices had been based more on his own comfort and security than on any ideal of care and concern for others. He thought all this and said, "I don't know who—or what—Ognadzu is. But I know that at times there are powers in me that compel me to shape events to my own best advantage. I'm certain they're in Ognadzu as well. How they come to be there—I don't know. And holding them in check seems to be beyond human ability."

"You're too kind, Seagryn," Fylynn said, her eyes hard. "You give Ognadzu too much credit. He's evil!"

"Apparently." Seagryn nodded. "But so am I."

This confession made Fylynn angry. "How can you even consider yourself in the same category with him? He's trying to rule the world! You're trying to save it!"

"Or so I tell myself," Seagryn murmured. "But then, I told myself I was trying to save the world when I helped your Sheth make the dragon that now threatens us. Wasn't that evil?"

His mention of Sheth gave her pause. "Well—"

"You love him, true, but you surely realize that many would regard Sheth as the personification of evil."

"They don't understand him," she argued, adding, "or you either!"

"Fylynn, I don't even understand myself. I know what I want to see changed, but my efforts to change things often bring more grief than comfort. If it weren't for the Power—" Again the lady jester was laughing. "Now what did I say?"

Fylynn blew a strand of hair out of her eyes and smiled. "I'm sorry. It's just this Power business. I have a hard time understanding why you Lamathians cling to such a notion."

Now it was Seagryn's turn to smile. "You can speak blithely of elemental powers and take for granted the shaping of them, yet dismiss the notion of a Power beyond them, a Power whose presence can shape us?"

Fylynn chuckled, then shrugged self-consciously and let her smile die. "We've already talked about why. I've witnessed too much evil to believe there's any real grand design to life that people haven't imposed upon it. I don't think there's any higher purpose beyond our own imaginations."

"Even when Dark speaks of such as already in motion?" Seagryn argued. "You know Dark's always right."

"I know Dark's always confusing." Fylynn smiled, and she looked behind them to see if Dark had heard and would respond. Her face froze. "Dark's gone."

"What?" Seagryn gasped, as he jerked on his reins and twisted around to look himself.

It was true. The boy prophet had been riding behind them for a long time, and they had no way of knowing when he'd left them. Had he left them? Or had he been taken? He'd been very quiet ever since their flight from the burning camp, but they'd both become so accustomed to the lad withdrawing inside himself that neither of them had given it much notice. Without giving his ability to do so conscious thought, Seagryn tried penetrating any magical cloak that might have been tossed around the boy, then opened his senses wide to apprehend the presence of shaping anywhere around them. He felt plenty of powers but no Dark. He glanced across at Fylynn and found her staring at him. "What are you doing?" she demanded. Only then did he realize he was shaping again, and for some reason that embarrassed him.

"There are—powers here," Seagryn explained. "Many of them. This must have been one of the places Nebalath spoke of— a region suddenly much richer in magical resources."

"What about Dark?" Fylynn asked, riding her anxious horse in circles.

"Nothing. No sign of his presence—nor of any other shaping nearby." Seagryn frowned back toward the way they had come.

"What do you make of that? Has he been kidnapped? Are we being watched by Marwandian raiders, or an Arlian search party—"

"Where would they be hiding?" Seagryn asked, gesturing about them. But for the huge tree trunks, the forest floor was open and empty, like a vast cathedral without pews supported only by intermittent columns. There was no underbrush in which to hide, and Seagryn had already made certain there were no wizards active in the area. They paused a moment, listening, but all they could hear was the distant thump of an ax being laid to wood.

Fylynn looked at him, her eyes wide with worry. "He would have known, of course . . ."

"Of course. But he wouldn't have told us." Seagryn licked his lips. "He must have just left us. We're not all that far from his home . . ."

"I do wish he'd warned us first," Fylynn grumbled. "Sometimes he acts like such a child!"

Which was exactly what Dark was, Seagryn reminded himself. "Maybe he needed to see his mother," he said lamely. He turned his horse around slowly, peering off deeply in every direction. Nothing moved. Leafy giants towered above them as far as his eyes could see. He was struck by how evenly they were spaced, almost as if some gardener of mythical proportions had planted them here in rows . . .

"Where do we go now?" Fylynn demanded. "How do we get to Sheth?"

"Perhaps we'll need to let Sheth find us." He craned his neck, marveling at the distance from where he sat to the start of the lowest boughs. There was enough space for the dragon to maneuver about easily, and that realization made him suddenly very anxious. "We can't stay here," he announced, and Fylynn agreed. They rode on, uncertain of where they were going but guessing it didn't make that much difference. "After all," Seagryn reasoned, "if Dark says Sheth and I are to work together on Sheth's plan to destroy the twi-beast, we have to get there eventually. I just hope you have enough food in these bags to hold out."

For some reason his mention of the bags they carried startled Fylynn, and she quickly scanned what was loaded onto her own horse, then on Seagryn's. She sighed with apparent relief. "Is there enough?" he asked, and she nodded. He made a mental note to check their contents once she slept.

While they couldn't see the sun, they could tell it was setting by the darkening green of the leaves above them. When Seagryn spotted a house off to the left, he suggested that they head toward it and see if they might find lodging there.

"But it's so tiny we'd never fit inside it!" Fylynn said. "It must be a cottage for little people, like those you met in the Remnant!"

Seagryn chose not to argue. "We'll see," he answered as they rode toward it. He knew it was a normal-sized house—perhaps even a large house. It just stood next to a tree trunk that dwarfed it.

Fylynn soon saw her mistake, but rather than correct herself she went on and on about how precious the cottage looked. Seagryn thought so, too. He liked the clean look of its white paint, and the bright blue shutters did bring cheer to this grand but changeless forest. The house backed up to the tree, hiding from their view, until they got right up to it, a storage shed that also leaned against the far side of the trunk. It was from this shed that a man walked out to meet them—a big man, as tall as Chaom but with less beef and more muscle. He carried the ax they'd been hearing, but he didn't bear it threateningly, and his smile of greeting appeared genuine. Seagryn quickly concluded he was a woodcutter. Once they were close enough to see into the shed, the stacks of wood piled all about seemed to confirm that judgment. "Welcome!" the man shouted in a voice to match his height, then he turned and shouted back to the cottage. "Thaaliana! We have guests for supper!"

A pleasant, girlish face ringed by a halo of mousy brown hair appeared in a second-floor window and looked down at them in surprise. "Guests? Here?"

The woodsman looked back at them. "You must excuse my little wife. People just don't pass through here often. I'm March, and that's my wife, Thaaliana . . ." He pointed back up to the window, but the woman had disappeared inside. "Or rather, that *was* my wife. Thaaliana?" he called, walking in the front door and waving at them to follow him, "is supper ready?"

"We have food," Fylynn protested, dropping from her saddle and leaning against her horse to stretch her legs. "Please don't let us impose—"

"Nonsense," March shouted, thrusting his head back out the door. "She can have it ready in no time at all. Come in! Come in!"

It took longer than that of course, but March had plenty to talk about as the three of them sat comfortably before his fireplace while Thaaliana scurried frantically around her kitchen. Fylynn offered to help the woman, but the woodsman wouldn't let her.

He was obviously pleased to have them as an audience, and they soon learned that it took him two weeks of solid chopping to fell one of the great giants, and that it took so long to split one up that he could only cut one tree a year—or actually two trees in three years—and that no matter how much they might *look* the same, each tree was different, requiring a great deal of thought and planning. He stroked his long chin and explained how sometimes he had to sharpen his ax twice a day, why an ax was far superior to a saw, how important the wind could be when it began whistling around these trunks just as he got almost through a bole, and on, and on, and on. His pale-blue eyes stared into the fire as he spoke, but at frequent intervals shot up to their faces to insure they were still listening to him. He never asked them why they were there, which was really just as well, as far as Seagryn was concerned. He allowed himself to be interrupted only long enough to introduce his two children as they made their way through the room toward the table in answer to their mother's summons. "You'll meet my mother tomorrow," he informed them, adding, "She's already asleep. She's old, you know, has to sleep a lot. Thaaliana, is that ready yet?"

"It's been ready," she sang back, but something had just reminded him of a point he'd meant to make about marketing his wood, and by the time he'd completed it the children had finished eating and been sent off to bed themselves. Seagryn guessed that eventually March decided he was hungry, for he finally moved them all to the table, where he continued his discussion between bites of bread and slurps of a delicious soup. Their host was certainly an amiable bore, but Seagryn did have lots of time to wonder to himself how the nervous little woman who listened quietly could put up with the man day after day. Seagryn began to worry that they'd be forced to listen to forestry tips until dawn . . .

Surprisingly, when he finished his meal, March finished his monologue as well. The big man suddenly stood up, patted a stomach that *had* to be full, given all they had watched him consume, then announced, "Big day tomorrow. Gotta chop some wood." He winked at his wife, and she smiled back at him lovingly—Seagryn guessed that this was a nightly joke between them. He could see from Fylynn's expression that she was not impressed. "I've got to get some rest. Thaaliana will show you where to sleep. I get up early, so if I don't see you at breakfast in the morning, it's been good to talk to you." That's exactly what had taken place, Seagryn thought to himself—March had talked to them. Now the man was clumping up the stout staircase and disappearing into the upper level of the house, and Seagryn and Fylynn could finally turn their attention to the diligent woman who had worked so submissively through the evening.

Her expression told them all they needed to know, but she spoke the words anyway. "Sorry. I *do* love March, but he does enjoy hearing himself talk. Did you have any trouble with the dragon today?"

"The dragon?" Fylynn asked, shocked. Seagryn almost said the same words.

Thaaliana smiled, and her obvious intelligence made her brown eyes sparkle. "Didn't think we would know anything about the dragon under here, did you?"

Fylynn snorted and said, "Unless the beast was burning his wood, I doubt your husband would notice."

"Fylynn!" Seagryn scolded her sharply, but Thaaliana laughed gaily, her small body twitching with barely restrained energy.

"Don't worry, you can't offend me. There's not anything you could say aloud that I haven't already thought. Are you ready to go?"

"I'd—thought *we* might talk before we go up to bed," Seagryn offered, but the woman shook her head curtly.

"You're not sleeping here," she said, then she laughed and added, "You'd never *get* any sleep anyway! He chops all day and saws all night!" Fylynn and Seagryn both laughed with her but looked at her inquiringly. Thaaliana threw a glance at the ceiling. "They're all asleep. Come on. We'll talk there." The woman hopped up from the table and darted toward the door. They exchanged a look behind her as they followed her out.

Neither moon nor stars could pierce the canopy above them. They might as well have stepped out into a pitch-black cave. "Shouldn't we get a torch?" Fylynn suggested, taking a step back inside.

Thaaliana didn't stop walking. "I've got light here," she called back—and a ball of yellow flame the size of March's head blossomed above them. "Hurry," she added, rubbing her shoulders. "It's chilly tonight. I've got a shawl stashed up in my bower."

Deeply astonished, Seagryn and Fylynn pursued the bouncy powershaper as she scampered away with the light bobbing along above her. They found it difficult to keep up.

Chapter Seventeen

※❂※❂※

THAALIANA'S BOWER

THEY walked briskly, changing direction several times. With only Thaaliana's ball of fire to light the way, Seagryn found it difficult to judge exactly how far. He started estimating distances by counting the regularly spaced trees of this forest and judged that they'd passed about twenty-five before Thaaliana paused beneath one and looked up. "This is it," she said, and by a wordless act of her will the incandescent ball floated upward along one massive trunk. When it passed the lowest boughs the leaves obscured it from sight.

Fylynn frowned and asked, "This is what?"

"Hmm," Thaaliana grunted. "You really can't see it from here—I'll be right back." The ball of flame suddenly snuffed out, and Fylynn and Seagryn realized just how much light it had been providing, despite being lost in the trees. The forest turned pitch-black again as they heard Thaaliana say, "Seagryn, if you're as powerful as I've been led to believe, I'm guessing you can provide some illumination of your own."

"Led by who—" Seagryn began, but Thaaliana didn't answer. Instead they heard a pattering of tiny toes clawing their way up bark. "Thaaliana?" he said, and a purplish ball of flame blossomed above his own head. It appeared just in time for them to see the fluffy tail of a squirrel as it squirted through the leafy ceiling and on up out of sight.

"She's a squirrel," Fylynn murmured, low in her throat.

"She is indeed," Seagryn replied, equally astonished.

"Watch out down there!" the woman called from high above them, and they stepped away from the trunk of the tree as they heard something falling rapidly toward them. The bottom of it hit the ground with a heavy thump before either of them realized it was a rope ladder. Fylynn grabbed hold of it and started climbing. Seagryn hung on the bottom of it to weight it for her and make her climb more stable; he sent the light up right beside her. Soon she, too, was through the leaves. "Seagryn!" she shouted down with obvious delight. "You've got to see this!"

He needed no further encouragement and started up. Penetrating that lowest level of leaves was like the reverse of slipping beneath the surface of water—much that had been hidden before was suddenly visible. As Fylynn had done before him, he paused a moment just to scan the breathtaking view, for his ball of flame had been joined by more fire dropped down by the powershaper who waited above, and the underside of the structure was now brightly illuminated.

"You see it, Seagryn?" Fylynn called down as she pulled herself up into the lowest deck. She turned around immediately to peer down at him, her round face beaming. "It's a tree-castle!"

It was indeed. Thaaliana had a castle in the trees, anchored to the boles of four of these forest giants. From this angle it appeared to be huge. He hurried on up to get a floor beneath his feet so that he could take a closer look. Once he'd joined the two women on the lowest level, he shook his head and asked Thaaliana, "Did you build this?"

"Oh no." She half laughed, glancing around as if she were seeing it for the first time herself. "I ran across it moments after I'd found my altershape. And I mean I quite literally ran across it—I was moving through these trees very quickly, following the sound of March's ax." After having listened to her husband all evening, Thaaliana seemed excited to have the chance at last to tell her own story. This was the most momentous event in her otherwise mundane life, and she related it with gleeful relish. "You see, one of my children had gotten sick in the night. I'd wanted to take her to the healer—the nearest one is in Marlest, the large village to the west of us here where March does most of his trading—but March insisted she'd get well if we'd just let her sleep, and he went off into the woods to cut. She didn't, of course—I was right—but he'd taken our only horse! I left both children with their grandmother and ran toward the sound of his chopping—you can hear that ax of his echo all over this forest when he really starts to work." Seagryn nodded and glanced at

Fylynn. They'd both heard him working for a good deal of their day's ride. "I was concentrating on my baby—didn't know what to do, had to get her to the healer, needed the horse to do that, wished I could run faster—and I glanced up into these trees and wished I could run along the branches like the squirrels. Suddenly that's exactly what I was doing! I was scratching my way up one of these trees and running along a limb as if I'd been doing it all my life, knowing precisely when to leap from one limb to the next, which branch would intersect with the next so that, while I ran a zigzag course, I was always making progress toward that sound. Suddenly I was into this thing." She gestured around her, and the light she provided suddenly swelled in intensity in response to her gesture, revealing more clearly this bottom floor. "I couldn't believe it! Of course I couldn't stop, but I resolved to come back and look it over more closely once my crisis was resolved. Moments later I ran down the far side of the tree March was chopping and suddenly appeared beside him." She interrupted herself with a girlish giggle and added, "I think it's the first time I ever saw him speechless! 'I *need* the *horse*!' I told him and, without saying anything more to him, I jumped on it and rode back home, grabbed up my daughter and got to Marlest by nightfall."

"Was she all right?" Fylynn asked earnestly.

"Oh, she was fine—just had these little red dots all over her body. The witcher-woman told me that before my baby lost hers everyone in the house would get them, and she was right. But she also gave me some lotion to put on them when they itched."

"My sister and I had that once," Fylynn began, "and the healer in Pleclypsa told my mother—"

Seagryn put his hand on Fylynn's shoulder and broke in, "So she was fine and you brought her home and then you came back here?"

Thaaliana nodded happily at her good fortune. "Not immediately, of course. It was several days before all of us cleared up, and March is a real baby when he's sick. But all the time I took care of them I was thinking to myself, 'I was a squirrel! I was a squirrel!' and wondering if I could become one again. I can't tell you the thrill I felt when I found out I could! And naturally, this was the first place I came . . ."

Again she gestured around, and Fylynn and Seagryn turned to look more closely at this castle in the treetops. "How many floors?" Seagryn asked.

"Six full floors," Thaaliana answered authoritatively, walking toward a stairway and inviting them to follow her as she added, "although towers run up the trunk of each of the anchor trees—rather like spires." She grinned back at them over her shoulder. They followed her up to the next level, where she looked around earnestly, as if she missed something. Then she shrugged and looked back at them.

"How many rooms?" Fylynn asked.

"Oh," Thaaliana murmured, "a *lot*. Enough for an army—though I'm not certain it ever held one. I found a diary left by the woman who had it built—a powershaper named Parshia. I can't tell when she lived, exactly, because—" She blushed. "—I'm no good at history. But I think it's been several generations, at least."

"I would think March could guess the age of the wood," Seagryn said, examining the beams that supported the floor above. He didn't see the woman's blush deepen.

"Oh, he probably could," Thaaliana agreed apologetically, "but—he's never seen it."

Seagryn immediately understood. After all, he'd hidden his own altershape from Elaryl for as long as he could manage. "You haven't told him you're a shaper," he said.

Thaaliana winced and nodded. "I don't know *how*," she said honestly, adding, "I'm afraid it would—ruin him . . ." Suddenly the woman looked very weary, and her bright smile drooped. "I need to get back. You can sleep wherever you like—you'll find beds and linens in several of the rooms on this floor, and there's water!" She pointed upward, and a hint of her delight in this place returned as she explained, "The whole top level is a reservoir for catching rainwater, and it runs all over the castle through tubes of some wood I've never seen anywhere else! I guess this Parshia woman must have been well traveled," she said wistfully, and Seagryn thought he saw a woman who would have liked to have traveled herself. Then a grin spread across her face. "I like to think I'm her descendent!"

"You may be." Seagryn nodded. His words seemed to please her enormously.

"Well. I guess I'd better run on. I'll see you again first thing in the morning." And run on she did, first dousing her light and then skittering off through the branches in the general direction of the house she shared with March.

Fylynn and Seagryn just looked at one another, his purple ball glowing between them. "What a day," the jester said for both of them, and they quickly found their separate ways to bed.

Seagryn woke with a start to the sound of chopping. He knew

immediately where he was, and the sound caused him to leap to his feet. Was the woodsman cutting on one of the castle's anchor trees? He rushed out the door of the room he'd chosen, down the varnished hallway, and out onto a balcony that overlooked the forest. His worry disappeared long before he got to the railing, for he could tell, now, that March was some distance away. That anxiety was replaced by astonishment as he turned around and craned his neck to look up at the tree-castle in the daylight.

Wooden spires poked up through leafy branches. Stairways and ladders connected the half-dozen wooden layers. Varnish made the entire construction glisten in the green-filtered sunlight of the morning. Seagryn grunted in awe at the effort that had been expended—how long ago?—to cut the massive logs it all rested upon and to get them up into these trees. Parshia must have controlled a small army—or else she'd been very rich.

He wondered why it had gone so long undiscovered, but decided that wasn't really surprising. Little traffic passed through this area, and what traffic did would move mostly during the summer months, when the tree-castle was shrouded from view by the leaves. He glanced up and tried to gauge how deep the leaf pack on the ground would be during the fall—the height of a man, perhaps? That would certainly discourage autumn travel. And winters in this part of the Marwilds were rumored to be horribly bitter, a further discouragement to travelers who might have sighted this construction when its supporting branches were bare. Even so, what a sight this tree-castle would make, frosted with snow and dripping with icicles! He would have to bring Elaryl to this place—

Elaryl. The thought of her absence robbed him of all joy. He turned to look off through the leafy vistas and to wonder where in the world she was. He couldn't see the forest floor, of course, nor, looking up, could he see the sky, but he could see great distances across this in-between layer. "A lot of good that does," he grumbled to himself. He decided to climb into one of the towers. He went back to his room to put his boots on first, then peeked in on Fylynn before starting to explore. She slept soundly, snuggled under a down-filled comforter, her brown hair spilling wildly across the bolster. He recognized that he felt a keen affection for her and guessed he understood what it might have been like to have grown up with a sister. He closed her door quietly so that he wouldn't wake her and started toward one of the spires, his boots clumping heavily on the plank floor.

While the sides of the tree-castle's six levels were open, the trees themselves had been enclosed. Stairs spiraled up around the circumference of the trees with a landing at each level. As he climbed the stairs he paused occasionally to glance out a window slit to see if the view improved. He saw little change and decided to climb on up into the room at the top of the spire, braced around the next great junction of branches. Suddenly he stopped. He'd heard something above him.

Seagryn waited for a moment, listening. What was in the tower room? An animal of some kind? Must be. He reasoned to himself that with the castle's open sides, this must happen often. A tree-munk, perhaps? A cuddly little plagu? It must have heard him coming, for it made no further sound. Seagryn continued up through the floor—

As Seagryn popped his head through, a figure crouched against the wall shouted, "Don't come any closer!" The man pointed a long pike at the powershaper's face, and Seagryn was startled. "What—" the man grunted, for Seagryn had suddenly disappeared. The next moment the pike was being jerked out of his hand and spun about, and now Seagryn stood over him, pointing the pike down into the face of—

"Paumer? Paumer, is that you?"

"It's me!" Paumer gasped, scrambling away from the pike's tip on his hands and his bottom. "Who are you? Where are you?"

"Right here," Seagryn said, releasing the cloak that had shielded him. "It's Seagryn. What are you doing here?"

"I'm—hiding," Paumer murmured, and Seagryn could see now that the merchant was trembling.

"From me?"

"Of course not from you. I didn't even know you were in the tree-castle. I'm hiding from my son!"

Seagryn looked at this pitiful figure in dismay. He remembered the smiling, silver-haired merchant not only from the meetings of the Conspiracy that he'd attended but also from the weeks spent together in the making of the dragon. He'd ridden with Paumer through the northern Marwilds and lived beside the man in Sheth's Dragonforge. Never before had he seen him like this—unkempt, unshaven, his hands shaking, and his clothing dirty. Seagryn shook his head. "Ognadzu has done this to you?"

"He'd do worse if he could," Paumer mumbled, his voice trembling like his hands. "He'd like to kill me. He's tried!"

"He's sent the dragon after you?" Seagryn guessed.

"Several times! So far we've managed to dodge that—"

Seagryn interrupted. "*We* have? Who's we?"

"—but even if Vicia-Heinox doesn't get me, the heartbreak eventually will. Have you any idea what it's like to raise a son who hates you? And who not only tries to kill you, but who steals your business from you as well?"

"Who is we?" Seagryn repeated, his suspicions growing. "Has Sheth been with you? Do you know where he is now?"

"It was all his inheritance anyway!" Paumer explained, his fingers twisting upward as he held out his palms in supplication of Seagryn's understanding. "I loved that boy! Isn't a father entitled to pass along his inheritance when he chooses to do so, rather than having it ripped away?"

"I agree with you," Seagryn muttered, deciding the only way to get answers from this man was by indulging him. "Do you know where Sheth is?"

"Who ever knows where Sheth is?" Paumer mumbled, adding with some of the old sharpness, "Are you listening to my story?"

"Do you know where my wife is? Elaryl? You remember her from the Dragonforge?"

"I'm sure my son could tell you," Paumer said bitterly. "His spies are everywhere. I know—they used to be my spies."

Seagryn had grown curious at last. "How did they become his, then? Were none of your people loyal to you?"

"Many of them were. Still *are*," Paumer added with emphasis. "He hasn't controlled all of my houses yet, not all of them. He's convinced Kerily of course—"

"Kerily!" Seagryn said. "But I was just in Kerily's house a week ago!"

"Kerily's house?" Paumer smiled wanly. "That used to be my house. You were surrounded by his spies, then, and his mother is foremost among them. If you told anyone there your plans, he knows them by this time. Anyone but Uda," he corrected himself quietly.

"But how did he do it?"

"Where have you been?" Paumer scolded. The merchant obviously considered his family tragedy the primary plot line currently being played out through world events. "I thought you had contact with those tugolith creatures?"

"Not much recently, no—"

"He went up there where you were and convinced them that he's their Wiser—whatever that is. I guess you would know . . ."

Seagryn did indeed know. Suddenly he tasted bile, and he felt a little dizzy. He had been the Wiser—the spiritual leader of the tugoliths. But he had left them to come back and help Sheth make the dragon. They were simple creatures, naïve and gullible. He could easily see how Ognadzu might have— "Oh, no," Seagryn murmured. The more he thought about the implications of this news, the worse he felt.

"You're beginning to understand," Paumer said, finally beginning to feel justified. "He's used them as a battle force against those of my houses that resisted his control—and they've turned. He's trained several of them to be his messenger lads to Vicia-Heinox, and has arranged somehow to provide that monster with people to eat. That's how he maintains his control over it."

"Inconceivable," Seagryn murmured.

"A very effective arrangement. The boy is shrewd," Paumer said, smiling faintly. "I'd be more proud of him if I weren't myself one of his targets." When the smile faded from his lips, Paumer looked old. He shook his head and peered earnestly into Seagryn's face. "He was a good boy, I thought. Always seemed to be. What kind of evil would make a lad turn on his father like that?" Paumer begged, his eyes tearing up. "What kind of evil has a grip on my son?"

Seagryn thought again of Nebalath's warning, and it occurred to him that, if the powers were so much stronger in this region, they must be close to the source of the evil as well. He grieved over the lost innocence of the tugoliths and wondered how much his abandonment of them at a critical time had contributed to their fall. "I don't know," Seagryn muttered. "Something horrible."

Paumer nodded, his face ashen. "Incidentally," he added, "I understand he's also convinced the tugoliths that you were a false Wiser, and that you misled them."

"Misled them!" Seagryn exploded. "I saved them!"

"Oh, yes?" Paumer nodded knowingly. "Well, they're a fickle race, then, for the simpleminded beasts are thoroughly convinced that you should be ripped limb from limb."

Seagryn was suddenly struck by the irony of listening to this man, the instigator of so much horror in the old One Land, decrying the evil plans of others. "So," he said acidly. "The tugoliths have joined themselves to the Seagryn assassination squads you yourself organized!"

Paumer looked up at him, fear of reprisal spreading slowly across his features. "You—you know about that?"

"Nebalath was an invisible witness to your last Conspiracy meeting," Seagryn snarled. "He heard your report and shared every word with me."

Paumer said nothing for a moment—just studied Seagryn's face as he sought for some effective defense. "It's all changed now, Seagryn," he said finally. "When the dragon came, everything changed so quickly . . ."

That was certainly true, Seagryn thought. He remembered the Remnant. He remembered Nebalath. He remembered the pleasant village of Ritaven—all gone now. Everything had indeed changed, and he'd come to help correct it. "Do you know where Sheth is? I've come to help him destroy the twi-beast."

Paumer arched his eyebrows, then nodded. "I'm sure he'll be very glad to hear that when he returns."

"When he returns?" Seagryn demanded. "He's been here?"

"We've both been here—waiting for you and Fylynn. Is she with you?"

The words stunned him. "Sheth has been—*here*?" Seagryn jumped forward and jerked Paumer up by the front of his robe. "Then where is my Elaryl?"

Paumer jerked his head away but didn't try to fight off Seagryn's hands. "I haven't seen her."

"Sheth said he had her with him!" Seagryn shouted in Paumer's face.

"He did?" the merchant replied, turning his head. "Then I can only guess it was a ruse to get you here. An effective one, apparently."

Larger openings ran the length of each side of this octagonal room. The impulse to throw this traitor out one of them was very strong. As he wrenched Paumer out of the corner where he'd crouched and dragged him down the length of the wall, the merchant caught on to his intentions and began shouting, "It's not my fault! It's Sheth's! I just told you the truth! Why do you want to kill me for it?"

Seagryn stopped dragging him and threw the man to the floor. "When is Sheth returning?"

"Who can say?" Paumer pleaded, holding his hands up now to protect himself. "This is Sheth we're talking about, remember? He may be hiding from the dragon's wrath, but he's still the foremost powershaper of the age! I certainly don't know his schedule!"

Seagryn felt betrayed. "Who told you to expect me here?" This was a foolish question, but he needed to ask it anyway.

"Dark, did, of course! Sheth collected some packets of the Emeraudian dreamkiller and traded it to the boy for information!"

Seagryn nodded, his cheeks burning. He wondered how much

of this old Nebalath had known during their voyage home from the spice islands. And how much had Fylynn known all along . . . ?

Seagryn pounded down the stairs, making nine full circuits of the tree before reaching the level on which he'd slept. He ran headlong down the veranda, then cut sharply up the hallway to Fylynn's door. He flung it open, shouting, "Why didn't you tell me that—" He got that far and stopped. Fylynn sat up quickly in bed, but she was not alone.

He had only a glimpse of Sheth before the man cloaked himself. He glanced immediately around the room, however, and saw a pile of garments disappear off the shiny wooden floor. Sheth obviously picked them up and was now clothing himself in them. Seagryn's eyes came back to Fylynn, who had wrapped herself in the comforter. Had he just missed seeing Sheth earlier? Had the shaper been here all night?

"Why didn't you tell me, Fylynn?" he asked, managing to sound as if he had his emotions under control.

"Tell you what?" she frowned, obviously embarrassed.

"Didn't you know that my Elaryl wasn't here?" he asked flatly.

"Of course she didn't," said Sheth, now appearing by a mirror on the wall and checking his appearance in it. The vain shaper was apparently satisfied, for he now turned and shot Seagryn a dimpled smile. "I never told her." Sheth shared his smile with Fylynn and sauntered around the end of the bed. "She's too loving a lady to carry such deceit around with her. And she cares too much for you. So absolve her of guilt, Seagryn. The fault is all mine." He spoke these words with apparent sincerity but also with that same mocking grin Seagryn had come to loathe so much.

Seagryn stared at his rival, his eyes blazing with barely contained rage. "You should have the altershape of a mudgecurdle, not Nebalath. Your stench is great enough to drive every soul from the Marwilds."

Sheth's blue eyes didn't blink in response to the insult, nor did his black mustache even twitch. All he said was, "Is *that* Nebalath's altershape? I'd always wondered! He never once used it against me in battle!"

"He's gone now," Seagryn murmured, fighting his feelings.

"So I just learned. And the Imperial House is silent. Pity—I always liked those old walls, and the House seemed to like me, too. But . . ." Sheth shrugged and sat on the bed next to Fylynn. He slipped his arm around her and began toying with her hair. She squirmed uncomfortably under Seagryn's gaze but didn't push Sheth's hand away.

"And you, Fylynn? What's your part in all this? Besides consort to the shaper, of course." He couldn't prevent the bitterness he felt from dripping from his words.

Her eyes flashed up to meet his, now snapping with anger. "That's not fair, Seagryn! You know how I love Sheth, you've known it all along!"

"Besides, she had a job to do," Sheth said, hugging her to him protectively. He looked at her. "You did bring the stones, didn't you?"

"They were loaded on our horses yesterday," she said, sitting up, and he patted her.

"Relax. Thaaliana knew you were coming, and she's surely hidden them in her house. She'll bring them with her later this morning—" Sheth craned his neck toward the open window and listened a moment. "She should be here soon. The mighty woodsman is already busy chopping."

"Thaaliana is involved in this, too?" Seagryn asked, overwhelmed by all the twists he'd not even guessed at that everyone else apparently knew.

"She is. Had to be. I learned from Dark that Nebalath wouldn't be available for this act of shaping. That's when I set out to secure the help of the little squirrel-lady." Sheth gestured at their surroundings. "I hadn't anticipated the tree-castle, though. That was an added plus. It's a wonderful advantage, for Ognadzu knows nothing about it, and, following my practice in the past, his people are seeking us in caves. Here we can make the crystal thorn in relative security—you, me, and Thaaliana. It took both of us to make the dragon, Seagryn. It's going to take all three of us to unmake him."

"So—Paumer is right? Your appearance at Kerily's, your threats to Elaryl—these were just a ruse to bring me here?"

Sheth sighed. "I tried to make it more than that. I've spent a good deal of time searching for your lady friend in hopes of having her here, waiting for you. It's in my best interests that you be happy, Seagryn, I know that. But I'm afraid I failed to find her."

"Then—you have no idea where Elaryl is?" Seagryn asked, his voice as void of any emotion as he could make it.

"Sorry, my friend. I can tell you a lot of places she's not." Sheth smiled again. Was he aware, Seagryn wondered, of the impact of those curling lips? "But listen!" Sheth said grandly. "Didn't young Dark give you a promise you'd see her safely again? Isn't that enough for the moment?"

"It is not enough!" Seagryn shouted, and he left the room,

walking swiftly toward the staircase that led down to the lowest level and the rope ladder.

"Seagryn, wait!" Sheth called, dashing out into the hall after him. "I need your help! The whole One Land needs your help!"

"I heard a similar appeal once," Seagryn called back without looking over his shoulder. "It caused me to betray an innocent tugolith, and to help make a horrible monster. At this moment I'm far more concerned about my wife than about the old One Land. Oh—hello," he added as he got to the bottom of the stairs and found Thaaliana—in human form—waiting for him.

The woman cocked her head, looking puzzled. "Are you going somewhere?"

"Don't try to stop me," Seagryn warned, pointing a finger at her and shaking it meaningfully.

Her brown eyes widened. "I wouldn't think of it." She pointed downward. "I just brought your horses—and the stones."

Seagryn wondered exactly what the stones were but thrust the thought from his mind. The rope ladder was wound up onto a beaten-metal wheel. Seagryn released it and began to crank it downward.

By this time, Sheth had chased him down the stairs, followed by Fylynn, who moved with some difficulty since she was trying to stay wrapped in the comforter. "Seagryn," Sheth said, almost pleading. "Won't you please reconsider?"

Fylynn added her plea. "We've come so far, Seagryn! Won't you please stay and help Sheth do this thing?"

Seagryn didn't respond. The ladder was fully extended, and he started climbing down it. Angry as he was, he couldn't help but notice that once he descended through the lowest layer of leaves, the forest floor seemed to open up into a cathedral of green. They'd climbed up in the night and missed this view. He took it all in on his way down, marveling at the way these majestic brown columns made his heart pound. Then he was down, and he turned to his horse.

Sheth had preceded him. There were advantages, of course, to that ability he'd shared with Nebalath to pop up here and there at will. "Are you going to try to prevent me?" Seagryn asked quietly, stepping off the ladder to face Sheth squarely.

Sheth already sat in the saddle of Fylynn's horse. "Not at all. I've decided to go help you find Elaryl."

Seagryn stared at the man. "You're going to help me?"

Sheth shrugged, then nodded affably. "Seemed the least I could do." He pointed upward. "Fylynn said she would come, too, but she's not dressed. Paumer still hasn't come down out of the tower—you really terrorized him, apparently. Thaaliana says she can't leave her children. So I guess it's just the two of us.''

"Are you—did Dark tell you that you and I would—''

"Dark told me nothing about this," Sheth interrupted. "But if finding your lady and insuring her safety is your condition for aiding us, then so be it. While you were climbing down I moved the stones up into the bower. There's breakfast in your bag, there. Shall we ride?''

Sheth wheeled his mount around and started toward the northeast. Without thought, Seagryn followed Sheth's lead. After all, his companion was the most powerful shaper in the world. Without quite realizing why, Seagryn suddenly felt honored by his company . . .

Chapter Eighteen

✳✳✳✳✳

DRAGON'S DEVOTEES

"**W**HY are we riding in this direction?" Seagryn finally asked Sheth.

The other wizard arched a black eyebrow and shot Seagryn a look of both shock and amusement. "Do I look like Dark?" Sheth asked. "I'm following *your* lead, not the other way around!"

"Oh. Have I been leading?" Seagryn replied with a smile. "I'm afraid I really hadn't noticed . . ."

They'd spent a good morning together—an enjoyable morning. By the time they'd left the giant trees behind, each had related what had happened to him since their most recent magical battle, the day Seagryn had freed Vicia-Heinox from Sheth's Dragonforge. These stories had not been devoid of rancor—they'd been archrivals for over a year, and insults and betrayals had festered into hatred on both sides. But the fact that they were talking at all so astonished Seagryn that he managed quickly to forgive his adversary. Amazingly, Sheth seemed eager to do the same. Once the bitterness was out of the way, they'd swapped experiences with that rising tide of excitement that comes when new companions realize just how much they share in common. Soon they were laughingly recounting the more ludicrous elements of their fights with one another. Seagryn decided that the summer of fleeing the dragon had mellowed and matured Sheth; for his part, Sheth seemed at last to be accepting Seagryn as an equal. What would have seemed impossible the night before now appeared to have already happened—he and Sheth were becoming friends. The speed of it made Seagryn's head swim.

Of course, to do so they'd had to lay aside all thoughts of the horrors their rivalry had unleashed on the peoples of the six Fragments. It wouldn't do for Seagryn to remember the Arlian bodies floating past the Imperial House, or the host of the dead Remnant scattered across the floor of the Central Gate. Those things were past now, anyway. He could do nothing to set them right. He *could* perhaps do something to prevent them from recurring—if indeed Sheth knew a way to end the ravages of the dragon. With peace made between them and a commitment to finding Elaryl their top priority, Seagryn's thoughts returned to this task. "How can I help you stop the dragon?" he finally asked.

"To kill it, you mean?" Sheth asked, turning to pierce Seagryn through with his blue eyes. "Because that's what it's going to take, you know—the death of the twi-beast. And I wonder if you still have protective feelings toward half of it?"

Seagryn had thought long and hard about that, and he answered with conviction. "No. None. Heinox is the better head of the pair, but it's all still one dragon. Berillitha is dead."

"Then you can cooperate with us in killing it without reservation?" Sheth probed.

"Once Elaryl is found—yes." Seagryn nodded. "How do we go about doing that?"

Sheth's gaze returned to the trackless forest ahead of them. "We're going to make a magical weapon—a crystal thorn which I, myself, shall plunge into the beast's black heart!"

This certainly sounded dramatic enough, but Seagryn frowned. "A what?"

"A thorn, formed out of precisely crafted slivers of diamond!" Sheth answered, his eyes glowing. "The stones are already cut—that's what you and Fylynn brought in those bags. They were found on an island off the North Coast—huge diamonds, bigger than your head!—by a band of Marwandian raiders I know."

"Marwandians hate you," Seagryn stated flatly.

"That's true," Sheth curtly agreed. "But they hate the dragon more. And when I promised to do away with the beast, if they would just find me these stones and convey them to Haranamous, they agreed."

"Why to Haranamous?"

"Only the craftsmen of Haranamous had the skill to cut the stones into the precise shape I required," Sheth answered. "Paumer knew exactly who to send them to—he made all the arrangements. That's why Ognadzu sent the dragon to burn the city. He somehow learned of our intentions and tried to destroy the place before Chaom could send the cut stones back to me.''

"I see. Jarnel seems to think the attack was to benefit Arl . . .''

"You've been with our friend Jarnel?'' Sheth smiled grimly. "I'm sure he does. Ognadzu is like his father. He'll say whatever's necessary to gain some advantage, then turn on you an instant later.''

Seagryn thought that a good description of Sheth himself, but they were allies now, so he didn't bring it up. "It sounds as if Ognadzu is more deserving of destruction than the dragon,'' he murmured.

"It's been tried, believe me,'' Sheth said emphatically. "I've tried. Several times. But the lad stays as much on the move as Paumer and I do, and I've not been able to catch him. If his father would just use that network of spies he's built up through the years, I could corner the boy easily and he'd be gone. But Paumer won't do it. His son keeps trying to kill him, but he won't lift a hand in his own defense.'' Sheth glanced over at Seagryn. "Hard to imagine, isn't it?''

Seagryn nodded, and Sheth appeared to be satisfied. But as he remembered that pitiful figure who'd trembled this morning in his grasp, Seagryn found it very easy to understand why Paumer would withhold such information. He was a father. He loved his son. Seagryn's thoughts returned to the carefully cut stones. "What gave you the idea of this 'crystal thorn'?''

Sheth suddenly turned evasive. "Oh, I—just thought it up.''

"You just thought it up?'' Seagryn repeated, incredulous. The other wizard had been so open all morning that he found this response bothersome.

"Like we think up all spells,'' Sheth said offhandedly. "Why should that be surprising?''

"Then you don't know it'll work.''

"It will work,'' Sheth answered with a finality that came close to being threatening.

"I see. And how are you going to get close enough to the dragon to plunge it in?'' Seagryn countered.

"I'll cloak myself,'' Sheth snarled back. "Why so many questions? Do you have a better solution?''

"No,'' Seagryn responded honestly. But he also felt less faith in Sheth's scheme than he'd been feeling throughout the morning. The thought of faith raised another possibility . . . "I wonder what the Power intends out of all this—''

"Your Power has nothing to do with it!" Sheth said with startling vehemence. "At all!" he added, then he glared back at the forest before them. Apparently he would tolerate no further conversation on the topic. Seagryn honored that, and they were still riding silently some time later when the woods opened onto a clearing, and they saw a pair of figures standing in the middle of it. Both of them reined in their horses sharply. The figures were clothed in the clerical green of Lamath—and they appeared to be waiting for them.

"Ranoth? Talarath?" Seagryn wondered aloud. "I thought they were dead!"

"Now that's a rumor I haven't heard," Sheth responded. "But what would they be doing out in the middle of the Marwilds?" He spurred his horse forward, and Seagryn followed. A few paces forward and the identities of these two were clear—to Seagryn, anyway—as well as the explanation for their presence here. "I recognize Dark," Sheth murmured as they trotted forward, "but who's the woman with him?"

"Her name is Amyryth," Seagryn answered. "She's his mother." Amyryth was a warm, free-spirited matron whom Seagryn had grown to love quickly during a brief visit in her home. "She's the one who rescued me after you left my head buried in the mud."

"I'd wondered how you got out of that."

"Dark's gift." Seagryn smiled—the same gift that permitted the prophet and his mother to stand here in the middle of nowhere, waiting. But as they rode closer, Seagryn's concern grew. The look on Amyryth's face was one he'd not seen before—harsh, distant, and stern. "Greetings, Amyryth," he said as they slowed to a stop. "Why such a grim expression?"

"These are grim times," the woman said. "Shall we go?"

"Where are we going?" Sheth asked archly.

"Lord Sheth," Amyryth said graciously, "please take no offense at my haste. I know you and Seagryn have come in search of his Lady Elaryl, and we have a long way to ride in order to save her. I will show you all the honor you deserve once we're moving." She spun around then and walked purposefully away from them toward her horse. Seagryn recognized it as the steed Dark had ridden from Haranamous. Dark didn't move.

"I can't help noticing," Sheth began in that oily tone Seagryn found so aggravating, "that you have only one mount. How, pray, shall we ride anywhere?"

Amyryth was now up onto her horse's back. Seagryn was mildly

surprised at how comfortably the older woman sat in the saddle.
"We thought perhaps that Seagryn might take his altershape, and
Dark could ride his horse?" She voiced this as a question, but it
was really a statement. Nor did Seagryn debate for even a moment
that this was the way things should be arranged. At the implied
promise that he would soon see his love, he threw himself down
from his mount. As he trotted far enough away to give his altershape room to appear, Dark mounted up. A moment later Seagryn
again wore the heavy scales of a tugolith, and his mounted friends
looked much smaller.

"Which way?" he shouted, and Dark spurred his horse forward to take the lead. They spent the remainder of the afternoon
in a mad dash that made the morning's pace seem like a casual
canter. At one point, they'd faced a wall of impenetrable tangle
that made Seagryn think Dark had lost his way. Instead, the boy
suggested he go before them, plowing a path with his great shoulders. Once again, Seagryn didn't argue; though he wouldn't have
thought so, he found his altershape well suited to this task. By the
time he'd torn through the dense brush, the sun had set, and Sheth
was making no secret of his hunger. But Amyryth was unmoved—
apparently there simply wasn't time to stop. Seagryn's excitement—and anxiety—continued to grow.

When the light faded completely, Sheth projected a ball of fire
out before them to light the way—a huge ball, and exceptionally
bright. "Is that normal for you?" he rumbled at Sheth in his
tugolith bass.

"I've made one that size before," the other wizard responded
casually, but Sheth also appeared rather impressed with himself,
and Seagryn wondered if this was not, perhaps, more indication
of the concentration of powers in this region. He'd felt his energy
growing through the long day instead of depleting. But he was
also feeling something else—something threatening. The farther
they traveled, the more certain he became that they were entering
the presence of a force of immense evil. As the bobbing light
wove its way through the woods and they followed in earnest
pursuit, he started to ask if others felt it, too.

"Hush," Amyryth whispered before he got all the words out.
"Listen," she said.

Seagryn listened—and heard an odd sound coming from directly in front of them. "Singing?" he whispered back, which
was no easy task for his tugolith voice. Amyryth chose not to
respond. Soon, Seagryn didn't need her to—the chants and songs
had become clearly audible.

"Lord Sheth," Amyryth said quietly, "would you be so good as to douse your light?"

Sheth did so without a word. Once Seagryn's eyes accustomed themselves to the sudden darkness, he realized they were moving toward the distinctive red glow of a bonfire. In the darkness, it seemed he could distinguish more clearly the words of the sing-song chant . . .

"I believe in the torch of the powers—

"I believe in the two-headed scourge—

"I believe in the traitor who freed him—

"I believe in the dragonburn's purge—"

"The what?" he managed to strangle out, but he needed no one to respond. The chilling words were repeated over and over again. "I believe in the traitor who freed him," he murmured, and his forequarters trembled in shock. "They're singing about me."

As the others reined in their horses and silently dismounted, Seagryn returned to his human form and crept through the brush toward the edge of the clearing. He crouched there in the shadows, watching the proceedings in horror.

"Strange, isn't it," Sheth whispered, and Seagryn realized now that he had kneeled down beside him. "Have you ever heard anything so weird in all your life?"

"Regularly," Seagryn murmured back. He was certain his reply had startled the other wizard, but he didn't take the time to explain. How could he convey his sense of dismay to one who had not grown up within the halls of faith—to one who had not chanted the original of the creed this midnight congregation now intoned? Seagryn had himself led such worship—but using very different words. That's what shook him so deeply. Nothing is so strange, he thought to himself, as to see and hear the familiar twisted into something perverse.

Amyryth had crouched down on the other side of him. They were at the very edge of the bonfire's perimeter, and in the dim light Seagryn saw the silhouette of Dark kneeling beyond her. "Look," she breathed, and Seagryn followed the indication of her pointing finger to the back of the worship leader. He watched intently as the man led the chorus, both his arms waving in highly stylized gestures that some in the congregation were trying to follow. But there was a line of devotees kneeling in the front who could not: their hands were bound before them. Seagryn scanned the faces, utterly certain before he spotted her that he would find Elaryl among them. And there she was . . .

Elaryl! A bound captive! Up from deep inside him gushed a violent urge to leap from behind the bush and scream out his rage. He contained it, but not before uttering a strangled gurgle. Amyryth and Sheth both grabbed his shoulders to restrain him. "Not yet!" Sheth whispered in one ear, and "Think!" Amyryth whispered in the other.

Seagryn couldn't think. He still reeled from the inner battle that had briefly stormed through him, as his tugolith self had longed to plunge forward and spear the leader on the tip of his horn. But he managed to collect his wits, the worship leader turned around—had he somehow heard them over the drone of the chant?—and Seagryn's jaw gaped wide in partial recognition. He knew this face! He'd seen the man—where? At the meetings of the Conspiracy! He was—Seagryn searched his memory for the name and found it. "Wilker," he breathed. Wilker, the lost Remnant's Undersecretary for Provincial Affairs—the man whom the dragon had left behind.

"Keep watching," Amyryth whispered, her mouth still inches from his ear. "He's not the only one you'll recognize."

Seagryn could see now that Wilker was too lost in the ceremony to hear any distractions. The man whirled about to face the congregation again, both arms extended above his head and both hands flopped over, palms down. The chanting stopped as he spoke, moving his cupped fingers in rhythm to his words. It took Seagryn a moment to catch on, and when he did so, it was with utter astonishment. Wilker moved his hands as if they were puppets—a puppet image of the dragon!

"I am Vicia!" his left hand said. "I am Heinox!" his right said. "I am the Power's scourge!" both said. "I am Vicia! I am Heinox! I bring the fire's purge!"

"No." Seagryn groaned, and again those on either side of him clutched his shoulders tightly. "No," he whispered again to Wilker's back. "You've missed it. You've missed it entirely."

The whole congregation had now taken up Wilker's words, waving their cupped hands above their heads in time with his and turning his rhyme into a song. A new fear rattled down Seagryn's spine. Had Elaryl been *entrapped* by this new heresy? Did she believe it? He twisted his head to peer around Wilker's back and found reason for both relief and new rage in her eyes. His wife stared vacantly into the bonfire, her face the picture of panic.

"I wanted to go!" Wilker suddenly shouted, and the chanting immediately hushed. "I, myself, *longed* to be eaten! 'Take me, too!' I shouted at Lord Dragon. 'Take me, too!' I cried! But it wasn't to be, and it hasn't been. Though I long for it still, that is not my calling. I have instead been appointed to enlist the willing, and to send them two by two to the Lord Dragon's mouths! Let those who long for reunion all rise!''

Seagryn had known from the first moment the purpose of Elaryl's captivity. She was obviously part of a group who were soon to be fed to the dragon. Even so, his head reeled at the eagerness with which many devotees in that front row leaped to their feet. He saw in their eyes that same crazed eagerness for self-sacrifice that Wilker had himself expressed. But Elaryl only looked terrified, as did Jocelath, whom he now noticed being jerked to her feet down the line from her mistress. Then Seagryn identified the face of the man who handled his wife's companion so roughly. It was Yammerlid—Yammerlid, his boyhood rival.

He could wait no longer. He pivoted on one knee to grab Amyryth by the wrist and turned her to face him. "Tell me the plan," he whispered fiercely.

Dark's mother looked back at him, her grim expression unchanged from the early afternoon. "There is none," she whispered back. "There is only you—and the Power." Then she pulled her hand away and motioned to Dark, and both of them backed away from the clearing's edge, leaving Seagryn and Sheth behind. Seagryn understood. They had done their part. They had gotten him here—as, he supposed, the Power had prompted them to do. He realized now why Amyryth had needed to take the lead; Dark's foreknowledge robbed him of the will to decide anything. The lad never felt the freedom to act without someone else leading. "There is only you—and the Power," she had said. Why, Seagryn wondered, had the woman not included Sheth?

"Looks like we've been abandoned," the other wizard whispered, but he didn't appear at all worried or displeased by it. In fact, Sheth seemed almost relieved, as if their departure had put him back in control of his own destiny. "No need to attempt the spectacular," Sheth murmured confidently. "We just need to get Elaryl away from them and get on back to the tree, so let's do this. You cover the two of us while I cover the clearing with a spell of self-doubt. They'll all be shaken with such overwhelming self-consciousness that none will notice when one woman disappears into our cloak. Are you ready? Then let's go—''

"It won't work," Seagryn said flatly.

Sheth had already risen from his knees to a crouch. Now he kneeled again. "What?" he whispered, obviously aggravated.

"Can't you feel it?" Seagryn asked quietly, struggling to give expression to feelings that his conscious mind did not want to face. "This is not just a meeting of madmen in the forest. There's something much greater present here—something as loathsome as it is powerful."

Sheth gazed at him, his eyes wide with fear. Then the shaper blinked away the terror he felt and scowled instead. "I'm not listening to this," he growled. "You're as much a fool as those idiots out there! If you're not up to it, I'll do this myself!" He jumped to his feet and threw his arms wide, and a dozen flaming balls went hurtling over the heads of the dragon's devotees. Seagryn saw through the bush the shocked faces of the crowd and heard the collective gasp—

Then he saw nothing, for a dense fog abruptly settled on the clearing—and not a cool, white mist, explainable in natural terms. This was a hot fog, and black, absorbing the light of the fire even as it absorbed all of Seagryn's power. Was this Sheth's spell of self-consciousness? Seagryn wondered. Had he been caught in it, too? As if in answer, he heard the other wizard thrashing about in the underbrush, saying, "What is this? Are you doing this?"

"No," Seagryn called out into the darkness—but his own voice seemed to be coming from far away. Then he felt hands grabbing him roughly and heard distant cheers.

"We've caught him! We've captured Seagryn himself!"

He was terrified. Or rather, up until that moment he had been terrified. Now, he guessed he felt more puzzled than anything else, for the coming of the black fog summoned up from within him a relaxed peace he'd not recently experienced, which always puzzled and surprised him. Something horrible enveloped Seagryn—but something far more powerful resided within him. "You can't shape me." He chuckled, amused that this power thought it could. He shrugged off the arms that clutched at him and waved away the darkness. Millions of stars filled a sky that had been only black a moment before, and a cool, fresh breeze blew through the clearing, not only dispelling the fog's wet heat but also snuffing the bonfire.

"What is this?" Sheth shouted at him again. "Seagryn! Is this you?"

"No, it's not me," he called as he heard Sheth fleeing back toward the horses. Seagryn let him go, confident that he would be safe, that he would find his way back to the tree-castle, and that they would soon be working together on that crystalline object. But Seagryn knew, now, that there would be far more to that creation than Sheth himself understood. This plan had all been initiated by the Power—perhaps years ago—and it was the Power that acted through him now. He was not shaping powers when he caused the ground in the clearing to glow with a light-blue radiance, enabling Elaryl and Jocelath to find one another. Rather, he was himself being shaped, and the One who shaped him worked this wonder through him. When he vaporized the ropes and cords that bound all unwilling captives in the clearing, Seagryn was not doing magic—he performed a miracle. What a vast difference distinguished the two! Magic took the forces available and shaped them into illusions. Miracle created the perfect solution—out of nothing. Wizardry required cunning, quickness, and bravado. Miracle-working required only faith and surrender. Powershaping gave Seagryn the feeling of personal potency. Acting as the instrument of the Power's miraculous outpouring made him feel humble. At this moment, in the face of a horrible presence far more powerful than he, Seagryn laughed aloud, elated by the Power's ability to use his weakness. He guessed his laughter might sound maniacal to the dragon's devotees, but he couldn't help that. It wasn't he who acted.

The sinister assembly broke up and scattered. People were knocked down and stepped on. Some screamed. Others fled silently, too terrified to do anything but get themselves off the glowing carpet of light at their feet. Wilker fell to his knees in the eerie glow and raised his eyes to the starlit sky. He crossed his arms above his head and moved his cupped hands in unison as he chanted out his continued faith in the dragon. Yammerlid disappeared into the night. Elaryl had recognized his laughter and now pushed through the chaotic crowd toward him, pulling Jocelath behind her. Seagryn stepped into the clearing to meet her, his arms wide open, and she ran into them and locked herself around him. Jocelath stood anxiously by, watching around her as these mad folk who had seized them rushed crazily about, until she could restrain herself no longer. "My Lady, hadn't we best depart before they grab us again?"

"They'll not grab you anymore, Jocelath." Seagryn beamed as he freed an arm and reached around her to give the maid a hug. "You're safe. But we do need to be on our way. We've got a lot of distance to cover . . ."

"More travel?" Jocelath murmured. The ground's blue radiance was fading, but her wince was still clearly visible.

"Let's go then," Elaryl said, and Seagryn put an arm around each woman's waist and guided them out of the clearing into the forest. He found Dark and Amyryth waiting for them, as he'd somehow known he would.

"You see now, Seagryn?" Amyryth said, that familiar smile he remembered finally returned to her round face. "You and the Power can be quite formidable!"

Seagryn smiled back, then glanced around. Amyryth and Dark both sat astride one horse as Dark held the reins of another. "Is Sheth gone?"

"Your fellow powershaper grabbed his horse and fled without a word," Amyryth said. "He looked terrified."

"There's reason," Seagryn responded grimly, and Amyryth agreed.

"There is indeed."

"Elaryl, you and Jocelath take this horse," Seagryn said as he cupped his hands to boost his wife aboard its back.

"Sheth took a horse?" Elaryl said as she climbed up. "Why didn't he just—snap himself away?"

"He may have been too frightened to try. We both lost our shaper powers in the face of whatever thing that was back there—"

"Something evil," Elaryl murmured.

"It is that."

"But you didn't lose your powers, my Lord Seagryn!" Jocelath boasted as she settled herself behind her mistress, and Elaryl started to agree.

"Oh, but I did," Seagryn corrected. "Those weren't my actions back there in the clearing—they were the Power's."

"Call it what you like," his wife's maid said proudly. "It came through you." Her smile was clearly visible in the starlight.

"Shall we go?" Elaryl asked.

They could, of course, but for one thing. Lacking a third horse, Seagryn would have to take his altershape again—and he found the thought distasteful. He'd now experienced working miracles! Mere shaping would never again hold the same wonder for him. Still, it did appear to be necessary at times . . . "Hold your noses," Seagryn warned, and turned tugolith.

"Follow us," Amyryth said. "Our cottage is not far from this place." She proved to be correct. In less than an hour, the weary travelers relaxed in the welcome shelter of Dark's home in the Marwilds. Amyryth quickly found food, and they ate it gratefully as Elaryl told of her encounter with Ognadzu and her decision to seek out Seagryn.

"Did the dragon burn the house?" Seagryn asked. "I've—heard rumors . . ."

"We don't know," Elaryl answered, looking at Jocelath. "We've been on the road ever since, avoiding caravans, dodging capture, trying our best to determine where we might find you."

"Did you come through the Central Gate?" Seagryn asked sharply, and Elaryl shot him a sarcastic look.

"Sure we did, and spent a pleasant afternoon with the dragon . . ."

"You *talked* to it?"

"Of course not! You think we'd have no better sense than to walk directly into the twi-beast's lair?"

"I . . . I didn't know—" Seagryn mumbled.

"We came through the Marwilds," Elaryl informed him, "following much the same path you and I took on Kerl when we left Sheth's cave!"

Jocelath leaned over to Dark. "They talk to each other like this all the time at home."

"I know," the boy said, adding with deadpan expression, "and if you ask me, the future doesn't look much different." It took Jocelath a moment to realize the boy prophet was joking. Once she did, she giggled merrily, her brown curls dancing around her face. Dark grinned. He'd not had much call for his wit lately, and he was glad she'd picked up the humor in his comment.

Seagryn and Elaryl never heard it, so locked were they in their conversation. "When were you captured?" Seagryn demanded, his jaws clenched. He was angry at his wife for putting herself in danger. Now that he knew she was safe, he could allow himself that freedom.

Elaryl shrugged. "Several days ago. We'd managed to cross the forest and found this peaceful little town, and had just settled into a room at the inn when the Army of Arl attacked us."

"Ritaven?" Seagryn asked. "You were in Ritaven?"

"I don't know what they called the place, only that we happened to be there at the wrong time. The soldiers rounded up everyone and marched us out to a camp, and the next day that crazy man who loves the dragon came and told us all how blessed we were to have the opportunity to be eaten."

"Wilker." Seagryn nodded, and Elaryl looked puzzled. "That's his name."

"You know the man?" Elaryl said. She arched one eyebrow. "That figures."

Jocelath spoke up. "At first we thought they'd arrested the

whole town because of us. That's because a man who'd pursued us all the way from Lamath was helping lead them.''

"What man?" Seagryn asked.

"I don't know his name," Jocelath said; then she shivered and added, "I wouldn't want to know."

Seagryn looked at Elaryl. "A thin man, long face, sandy-blond hair?"

"That's him." She nodded, adding dryly, "You know him, too, I suppose."

Seagryn looked back at Jocelath. "Was he holding on to you at the bonfire tonight?"

"That was the man," the maid said emphatically, and shivered again.

"It's Yammerlid," Seagryn murmured, and he looked at his wife apologetically. "He's hated me since childhood." Elaryl made no response, and they just looked at one another for a moment. Both realized there was still much between them that needed to be cleared away before they could be fully comfortable again. Still, they were together. Perhaps there would be time. "So you know nothing about your father?" Seagryn finally went on.

"Not since we left Lamath," Elaryl answered. Then, as if on cue, both of them looked at Dark.

"What?" the boy asked—though he knew in advance the question that would be coming.

"Is Elaryl's father alive and well?" Seagryn asked flatly.

"He's alive, and she will see him again," Dark answered, and Elaryl breathed a relieved sigh. "But he's not all that well. How could he be, with all of Lamath in an uproar?"

"What's happening there?"

Dark's young face took on that ageless expression that meant he spoke prophetically. "While there were captives like these two in that group tonight, did you not see those eager to be swallowed? Those were Lamathians longing for 'union,' as Wilker calls it. And many more will follow them. You see, now, how shallow the vaunted faith of Lamath has really been. One major crisis and half the believing population want to throw themselves down the gullet of a monster. And old Talarath knows: Whose fault is that, if not that of the leadership?"

Seagryn winced. He'd been part of the leadership of the faithful. And while he still felt the afterglow of the Power's presence inside him at the bonfire, he also knew how infrequently that happened within the prescribed rituals of Lamathian worship. "Then I suppose the only thing to be done is to go find Sheth and help him make the crystal object. You did say that it will destroy the dragon, didn't you? . . .''

Dark nodded, but he avoided Seagryn's eyes. ''Eventually,'' he said. Seagryn frowned.

''*How* eventually?'' he demanded, and Dark looked back at him, his brown eyes full of conviction.

''It will happen, Seagryn. It cannot happen without your help. You've understood tonight that the object Sheth is planning has far greater significance than just the death of a dragon, fearsome though that beast may be. You've recognized that the Power's presence in these activities is no recent thing, as if the Power has suddenly taken an interest in events that were previously of no concern. The Power has always been at work! I've told you from the beginning, Seagryn, that the Conspiracy, misguided though it was, still offered the best hope. And I will try yet again to say something no one seems to understand, even when I shout! While I know what will happen, it only can happen because those who play a part choose to act. It is the tapestry of freely willed actions by individuals that the Power weaves into a means of rescue. You must choose to play your part—or not to.''

Seagryn listened quietly. When Dark finished, it was Elaryl who spoke first. ''What is this thing you're to make? You're to do it with Sheth?'' Her time with Seagryn in the Dragonforge had not endeared that wizard to her. Seagryn understood how she must feel. Still . . .

Amyryth had been like a rock throughout the day. She'd stepped aside this evening to let her son speak, but Seagryn wondered what her counsel might be. ''Amyryth? Share your wisdom with us.''

''What wisdom?'' she said, smiling slightly in self-deprecation. But she put down the towel she'd been using to wipe the dishes and looked at Seagryn squarely. ''You know you faced far more than the dragon tonight. And you know that you withstood that attack not by reason, nor magic—but by faith. My counsel is that you go back to the tree and help Sheth in the making, but that you remember—the poor man has no idea what it's for. And if you were to suggest its purpose is to confront that horrible darkness that encompassed you both, he'd probably run just as swiftly as he ran this evening. We don't battle mere flesh and blood, mere bones and scales and teeth—we battle far more than that.'' As she spoke, Seagryn realized that even though dressed in the garb of a peasant, Amyryth had the bearing of a priestess.

Elaryl saw it, too. More than that, Elaryl recognized the source of the woman's strength, and that verified for her Amyryth's words. She turned to Seagryn. "Then there's no other alternative. We must go."

The peace he'd felt all evening now warmed inside him. "You want to go?" he asked quietly. "Even if it means my working again with Sheth?"

"We have to. When do we leave?"

"Tomorrow, child," Amyryth said firmly. "There'll be no more traveling tonight for any of us. And as for sleeping arrangements—" She opened a door and motioned for Seagryn and Elaryl to follow her through it into the hall. Once they could see, she gestured toward a large, quilt-covered bed that dwarfed the room in which it sat. "You take the bed I shared with my husband." Her round face wrinkled into an enormous smile as she added, "I'm certain you can find good use for it!"

Chapter Nineteen

✠✠✠✠✠

BEYOND HEARING

Seagryn awoke early and slipped from the warm covers without disturbing Elaryl. He stood beside the bed a moment, watching her breathe, feeling proud that this woman had chosen to love him. He still quietly reveled at his victory the night before—the Power's victory, he reminded himself, but he had played his rôle in it. And as he contemplated the circumstances of that event, together with Elaryl's presence and a clear purpose for the days ahead, Seagryn wondered if he'd ever felt so blessed. When he opened the front door of the cottage and got his first taste of the crisp morning air, his spirits soared even higher, up among the branches above. Autumn had come to this region of the Marwilds, and Seagryn gloried in it.

He'd not been able to see the leaves when they'd arrived the night before. They'd all been weary, and the warm glow from the cottage fireplace had drawn them immediately inside. Now, with the sun slipping up through the trees behind him, he could gaze up into the multicolored canopy and remember all the autumns past. Fall came so vividly and left so quickly that it seemed to freeze individual moments within frames of red and gold. The scent in the air—that sweet aroma of decaying foliage mingled with wood smoke—seemed to loop through this moment like a needle, knitting it to the same instant in previous years. Let others mark their calendars as they chose—for Seagryn, the beginning of every new year dated from this first whiff of autumn. And this year, he would be spending it in the treetops . . .

No one else in his party quite shared his excitement as they made the journey southward to Thaaliana's bower. Elaryl had wanted to sleep until noon and was a little grouchy that he'd not let her. As usual, Dark seemed to be elsewhere—doubtless in the future. And Jocelath had days of empty meanderings to report, which she did—at length. Tugoliths had excellent hearing, so he couldn't quite tune her out. Fortunately, it was highly directional hearing, so by aiming his enormous ears away from her, he was able to miss most of Jocelath's monologue. That is, when she wasn't riding on his back.

The journey was too long to subject the already weary pair of horses to carrying more than one rider each, so his fellow travelers each took a turn riding Seagryn. He barely noticed the weight—indeed, he could have carried all three of them easily—but as others had told him in the past, the scales that ran down his spine made his neck an uncomfortable perch. Stuffed pillows seemed to help, so they'd borrowed several from Amyryth before leaving. As for the tugolith smell—Seagryn couldn't do anything about that. He ignored it himself, concentrating his acute olfactory sense on enjoying the scent of the season. By midafternoon they had left the changing leaves behind them. That was all right, Seagryn thought to himself. The fall colors would follow them south.

They chose not to travel at night, so it took them a day and a half to reach the giant woods. Seagryn had arranged for Elaryl to be riding on him when they arrived, and he turned his ears back to listen as she *oohh*ed and *ahh*ed at the spectacular scene. A smile turned up the corners of his large, leathery lips. He couldn't wait for her to see the tree-castle and made the mistake of telling her so.

"This is *it*?" she said when they finally arrived beneath it.

"You can't really see it yet," he muttered. "Just wait until you're up in it."

"I'm not sure I *want* to be up in it . . . ," she said, her blond curls spilling down her back as she peered straight up the huge trunk.

"You'll be safe," he growled, waiting for her to climb off before turning back into a man. "Hop down."

"I don't know," she murmured doubtfully as she dropped to the ground. Jocelath and Dark had been trailing behind them, and they arrived at the tree just as Seagryn resumed his human form.

Seagryn cupped his hands around his mouth. "Sheth!" he yelled skyward. "Fylynn? This is Seagryn! Let down the ladder!"

"A ladder?" Elaryl asked. "You mean we have to climb?"

Seagryn reminded himself that she had done nothing but travel for days on end and managed a slight smile. "Did you think you'd get to ride up in a basket?"

"That's not a bad idea," she said, again looking toward the tree. At that moment the rope ladder came plummeting through the leaves, and Elaryl jumped back in surprise as the end of it popped the ground twenty yards away. Seagryn looked back at Dark and gestured toward it.

"You go," the boy suggested, his hand on Jocelath's shoulder. "We'll climb up after you."

Seagryn put Elaryl on the ladder before him and stabilized it with his weight. Up she went. Once she was ten yards off the ground he motioned for Dark to anchor the bottom rung and went up behind her, listening expectantly. Finally her voice came.

"Seagryn!" she gushed. "It's—beautiful!"

Seagryn smiled happily and followed his wife into Thaaliana's bower.

They were greeted on the bottom level by Fylynn, Sheth, and Paumer. Sheth beamed broadly, showing his white teeth as he grasped Elaryl's hand and helped her up the last few feet. "Welcome! Welcome!" he said grandly. "I see you weren't digested after all!"

"Thank you," Elaryl mumbled, making a point of not looking at him as she made a quick survey of her surroundings and waited for Seagryn to climb on in. "Hello, Paumer," she said when her eyes crossed the merchant's face. Seagryn had told her Paumer was here; otherwise she wouldn't have recognized him. He seemed to have aged ten years since the last winter. "Hello." She nodded to Fylynn, who eyed her strangely.

Seagryn pulled himself up inside and took a deep breath. "So. We made it," he announced. He put his arm around Elaryl and began the introductions. Jocelath joined them just as he finished, and he had to make the rounds again. Dark, of course, knew everyone.

"Well, then." Sheth smiled, his dimples at their deepest. "Are you ready to go to work?"

This was too quick, Seagryn thought to himself, but he recognized the reason for Sheth's haste. The wizard didn't want to talk about his flight from the bonfire—especially since it was apparent that Seagryn had prevailed without his help. "Where's Thaaliana?" Seagryn asked.

"She's with her family," Fylynn answered for Sheth. "March took them all into the village for market day."

"Who's Thaaliana?" Elaryl asked. "Who's March?"

Was it possible that, in all his discussion of the tree-castle, Seagryn had not mentioned the one who had found and occupied it? He guessed it was . . . perhaps because he'd been uncertain what Elaryl's response to a female powershaper might be. "She's—" he began, but faltered. He didn't need to answer, anyway. Fylynn already was answering, and she could provide many more details. As she explained, Seagryn glanced around this bottom level, noting stacks of boxes and barrels that hadn't been here when he'd left. By the time Fylynn finished, Elaryl was looking at him suspiciously. He ignored her gaze and gestured at the boxes. "What's all this?" he asked Sheth.

"Food," the powershaper answered, still smiling. "That's what I've been doing while you were on your way back—robbing the pantry of the King of Arl. Come on up!" he said directly to Elaryl, sweeping his hand toward the stairway to the upper levels. "See the rest of the castle!"

Elaryl smiled primly and walked past Sheth to the stairs. Seagryn caught the cool look of appraisal Fylynn gave his wife as she climbed, and understood. "I'll take her on the grand tour," he announced, stepping past Sheth to the stairs. When he looked back he saw that Fylynn wore a relieved smile. "This level is individual rooms . . ." he began when he reached the second level, but Elaryl was still climbing. He followed her up.

"This is unbelievable," she said flatly as he joined her, astonishment at her surroundings robbing her voice of all expression. "Look at this."

Seagryn did. They stood in the great hall in the center of the third level, a rustic room filled with dark, varnished columns. The large room was dark, and the open spaces on three of the four sides made him feel one with the trees.

"Why so many of these wooden beams?" she wondered, rubbing her hand along one.

"To support the water—above us there's a reservoir, a kind of giant barrel for trapping rain. Let's go look inside the towers." He led her into the tower on the opposite side from where he'd discovered the hiding Paumer, and found an open room at the top with a large bed in it.

"This is where we're sleeping," Elaryl announced, and she turned around to fall backward across the coverlet. "Good night," she said pointedly, and closed her eyes. Within moments she slept.

Seagryn walked to one of the windows and gazed out at green leaves—a broad vista of them, stretching out as far as he could see. Should he rejoin the others below? That would be the polite thing to do, he guessed. Then he looked back at his wife and mumbled to himself, "But who needs to be polite?" He leaned down the staircase and shouted, "We're sleeping in the northeast tower!" Then he kicked off his boots and joined his wife on the bed. That night, refreshed by the long nap and a dinner cooked by Fylynn and Jocelath, they lay cuddled under the covers and listened to the wind as it gently stroked the leaves outside their window . . .

The next morning Elaryl and Seagryn cooked breakfast together for the whole group, learning their way around the kitchen as they worked. The ovens were located on the eastern edge of the third level, adjoining the great hall. Each tile-lined stove had a bamboo tube suspended above it, linked to the reservoir on the upper level. Fire in this structure would cause immediate catastrophe, so this was obviously a safety measure to insure against it. The tubes were closed by ingenious spigots, but they'd not been replaced in a long time and all of them leaked, meaning the wooden floor was constantly slick. When winter came that would be a hazard, Seagryn thought to himself, for the kitchen floor would freeze. And it wouldn't be long—this was a frosty morning. But they were comfortable now—the warm oven insured that. They moved a table close to the fire and served the food upon it, even though most of the others in the tree-castle had not yet left their warm beds. And it was here—soon after they heard the rhythmic chopping of a distant ax—that Thaaliana joined them.

She scampered into the kitchen, squirrel-like, even though she was now in her human form. Once she spotted them, she froze and watched them, motionless for a moment, as if she'd suddenly confronted invaders in her nest and was fearful they might attack her. Although she knew Seagryn, she'd obviously not been expecting to find him here. She didn't know Elaryl at all and perhaps found this new woman's unkempt beauty and frank blue eyes somewhat threatening. Seagryn stood quickly to set her at ease, but his abrupt motion only caused her to jerk back a step or two. "Thaaliana, good morning!" He smiled. She didn't immediately smile back. "I'm Seagryn, remember? I take it you didn't expect to see us here."

"No," she said. He gave her a moment to elaborate, but she didn't make use of it.

"This is my wife, Elaryl. Elaryl, this is Thaaliana—the powershaper I told you about."

"The powershaper you didn't tell me about is closer to the truth," Elaryl said peevishly, and Seagryn remarked to himself how quickly his lady's mood could swing. Then Elaryl was up and moving toward Thaaliana with a friendly smile, and he relaxed. Her statement had only been an entrée to allow her to meet and greet Thaaliana herself. "You must find it disconcerting to discover people you've never met before sitting at your own breakfast table."

Seagryn looked at Thaaliana. He still wasn't certain whether she would stay or dart out the door.

She stayed. "It's . . . not really mine . . ." she murmured, gesturing around at the tree-castle. "I . . . found it." Despite her words, there was a wistfulness in her voice that seemed to suggest the opposite—that she had at one time felt ownership of this hiding place, and that each new arrival robbed her of another piece of it.

"Do you have children?" Elaryl asked—still bright and friendly. She was trying hard to establish some link.

Thaaliana seemed unwilling to see that. "Why?" She frowned slightly.

"I—Fylynn told us you'd gone to market yesterday with your family, I just wondered . . ."

"Two children. That's my husband chopping wood." Thaaliana nodded her head toward the sounds of the ax. "Do you have children?"

"None yet." Elaryl smiled at Seagryn, conveying—whether she actually felt this or not—that she wished they might have a child soon. Growing up in the home of a leader of Lamath, Elaryl had learned all the social graces early and well. She had the ability to set anyone at ease, and Seagryn felt duly impressed and proud of her.

Was it perhaps that very charm and poise that put Thaaliana on guard? For although she'd been very personable on the night of Seagryn's first meeting with her, the little squirrel-woman still had not warmed to either of them this morning. Or was something else bothering her? She quite obviously turned away from Elaryl and looked at Seagryn. "Sheth said when you arrived the three of us would begin the process. Is he ready?" Her tone was businesslike and curt.

"I'm not even certain he's up ye—" Seagryn began, but before he finished the sentence she'd left the room. He met Elaryl's eyes. They looked at him accusingly.

"Why doesn't she like me?" she asked.

"I—I don't know if she really doesn't like y—"

"She probably likes you," his wife said flatly, and sat down to finish her breakfast.

"That makes no sense—"

"It makes perfect sense. You're a powershaper, she's a powershaper. I'm not."

This was the first time Seagryn could remember Elaryl expressing some jealousy toward his gift. Then again, this was the first time either of them had met a female shaper. "If that were true, then wouldn't she like Sheth more?"

"She may." Elaryl shrugged, wiping her mouth on a napkin. "She probably does. There's an affinity between the three of you that I can't share. I don't matter."

"Of course you matter—" Seagryn began, but Elaryl cut him off again.

"Not to her." She was about to go on, but at that moment Dark bounded into the kitchen, and both of them were so shocked, they focused all their attention on the lad. For the first time in months, Dark was acting his age.

"Good morning!" he sang, and leaned across the table to grab a roll and toss it above his head. He tried to catch it in his teeth, but it bounced off his chin. He juggled it between his hands before finally trapping it against his chest, then he looked at them both and smiled. "Slept well, did you?"

"What's got into you?" Elaryl asked, lips frowning in mock concern but smiling with her eyes.

Dark cackled happily and tossed the roll up once again. "No wedding!" he crowed while it was in the air, then caught it with a flourish. "I just saw that this morning!"

"No wedding for whom?" Seagryn asked.

"For me, of course! What did you think's been causing me such depression for so long?"

"Why, I can think of many things far more depressing than that," Seagryn responded. He didn't want to chide but found that he was doing so. He had taken Dark's depression as a warning of terrible events to come. He realized it was only natural, but still it bothered him to learn that the boy who knew the future of the world was so affected by his own personal fortunes.

"I can't," Dark said. Then he turned a chair around, straddled it, and began to fill a plate. "This tastes wonderful!"

"You haven't even taken a bite yet," Elaryl pointed out, still amused by his youthful exuberance.

"I'm Dark, remember? I know already—" He took a bite and grinned at her. "See?" he said with his mouth full.

Seagryn was still back at the wedding. "Are you saying you didn't know until this morning that you weren't to be wed?"

Dark swallowed. "That we weren't going to have the wedding? Right. Not until today. I've been hiding that part of my future from myself—using the green powder you brought me. I still have a good supply, by the way," he said somewhat defensively. "I'm not misusing it, just letting it help me sleep . . ."

"But then how did you—"

"When I get within a few weeks of any event, I know. It becomes just like your recent memory—clear and present, rather than dreamy." He grinned and took another bite. "Wonderful morning!" he said as he chewed. Seagryn didn't feel so certain about that.

Paumer drifted into the kitchen, his long face still haggard. He barely greeted them, his eyes on Dark. He appeared to be wanting to ask the boy a question but needed to be encouraged to do so. Dark wouldn't look at him. Jocelath found them next, coming straight to Elaryl and kneeling by her chair, apologizing profusely for oversleeping. Seagryn had never completely understood the relationship between them, but he had observed that Jocelath had a talent for doing the wrong thing at the wrong time. She'd often been saucy when she needed to be deferential. Now she was being obsequious, to Elaryl's embarrassment. "Oh, do get up, Jocelath," he heard himself snap. "You're getting your skirt wet."

"I am?" the maid said, hopping up and looking down. Indeed, the water spilled from the bamboo tubes had soaked her hem, and this brought a new apology to her mistress.

"Would you sit down and eat?" Elaryl ordered, and her maid closed her mouth and obeyed.

"So! We're all here, then?" Sheth boomed as he marched into the kitchen from the great hall. Thaaliana followed him, looking as if she felt herself important. Behind them both came Fylynn, self-consciously clenching a dressing gown around her bulky form. She was regarding Thaaliana's back in much the same way as the squirrel-woman had looked at Elaryl a few moments earlier. Seagryn was immediately reminded of some of the unpleasant interpersonal relationships in the Dragonforge. Evidently Sheth had the same thought, for he clapped Seagryn on the back and smiled broadly. "Just like old times, right?"

"Some differences," Seagryn replied, picking up a napkin to wipe his face.

"Not many," the other powershaper argued. "Oh, Thaaliana is new, and Fylynn. Dark's little girlfriend is missing, but here's this new young lady to keep him company." Sheth gestured at Jocelath, who blushed. Dark never looked up from his plate. "So . . . shall we begin?"

"You're not hungry?" Fylynn asked him, obviously a little disturbed, if that was the case. She'd already sat down at the table and filled her plate.

"Only to make magic!" Sheth announced dramatically, and left the room. Thaaliana followed him dutifully, and Seagryn chose not to meet Elaryl's knowing glance.

A moment later he finished his own breakfast and stood up. "I guess," he murmured quietly, "that it's time to start." He joined Thaaliana and Sheth in the great hall.

The two sat together at the head table, along which was arranged six sparkling objects. Seagryn moved quickly to look at them, but Sheth warned him just as quickly, "Don't touch."

Seagryn took his place at the end of the table and examined the object closest to him. It was some kind of crystal carved into a tall, thin pyramid shape—three sided, exactly like its five neighbors. "What are they made of?"

"Diamonds," Sheth breathed, his own excitement evident.

"A diamond? This size?"

"Six diamonds this size. Incredible, aren't they?"

Seagryn nodded in agreement, his eyes lost in the depths of the gem.

"Very well," Sheth commanded. "Let's begin."

"To do what, exactly?" Seagryn asked, earning himself a frown. It was obvious Sheth felt himself to be in charge here.

"I'll tell you," Sheth answered, implying it would be in his own good time. Seagryn shrugged and waited. "When we're finished, these six stones will fit together in a cluster—thus," he said, miming with his hands how the six would be pulled together into one object. "A thorn of crystal, to stab into the dragon's heart!"

Amyryth's words dashed across Seagryn's mind—the revelation that this object was far more important than just a weapon to kill the dragon. But he remembered, too, her warning—that to tell Sheth the Power had inspired its making might frighten him away. Seagryn determined that he would be silent and follow Sheth's lead. If the Power was in on the making of this thing, then certainly they would be told its purpose eventually.

"Now," Sheth murmured, some nervousness apparent in his voice. "To begin. Concentrate your shaper ability on this pyramid. Will yourself inside it! When we meet each other there— well. We'll know then what to do next." Sheth then clasped his hands before him, took a deep breath, and closed his eyes. Thaaliana looked at Seagryn, shrugged, and did the same. Seagryn looked at the crystal and imagined himself within it, then closed his own eyes and shaped.

This was shaping, not miracle-working. That was certain, for he felt himself fully in control and experienced a kind of haughty authority over the powers that his mind molded. They bowed to his will, yielding before him, as he moved his spirit forward against the crystalline substance. It felt as if he were flattening his nose against the pyramid's cool edge and trying to push on through it. The resistance was great—the stone was hard! And yet, in a moment, his nose pushed through, then his face, and he gazed rapturously upon an empty place filled with a pale-blue mist. He glanced down at himself, but he wasn't there—it was as if his whole body were one triangular plane of this gigantic pyramidal form. He might have panicked, then, had not his shock at the sight caused him to jerk his hand forward, through the plane and into the pyramid. He was not yet fully inside. He plunged a foot forward and his leg came through—then his other arm, and finally his other leg. Then he was falling, and would have felt terrified had not his fall been slow and graceful, more like the flight of a snowflake than a raindrop. His feet touched the floor of this glassy world, and he paused there, looking about. There was nothing but a light-blue fog any way he turned. He started forward, calling, "Sheth? Thaaliana? Sheth! Thaaliana!"

It seemed he wandered there for some time before he heard Sheth calling back to him and walked toward the sound. Sheth's face suddenly loomed from the mist, wild with excitement and relief, and they embraced one another as old friends and began calling to Thaaliana in chorus.

"Quiet," Sheth said suddenly, and they both hushed. Then they heard her, crying out desperately for either one of them to find her. They shouted her name in unison, and out of the fog Thaaliana came running, her eyes wide with terror and her arms outstretched. She leaped onto both of them, hugging both necks at once, and they all squealed with the joy of three children suddenly reunited after being lost in the woods at night.

"Now what?" Seagryn asked Sheth, although he intuitively knew the answer already.

"Now we say together, 'Three shapers, three sides, and power in each.' "

Thaaliana and Seagryn repeated the chant with him. "Three shapers, three sides, and power in each!"

"And now?" Thaaliana asked, a little breathlessly.

"We go back—the way we came."

"I don't know which way I came," she murmured.

"I'm turned around, too," Seagryn said.

"It doesn't really matter," Sheth told them. "Let's just all take a direction and go." He turned around then and started off. Thaaliana and Seagryn glanced at each other, establishing their own directions, and plunged back into the fog.

At length Seagryn bumped against the slanting plane again, but he realized it was not the crystal he touched now, but the air. Leaving the crystal was easy—like popping one's head above water. As soon as he did so, his eyes flew open, and he saw that he sat at the table with the other two shapers—but in a different seat.

There was a sudden explosion of celebration around him, as Fylynn—who had been standing behind his chair—rushed to embrace Sheth, and Elaryl dodged around her to grab Seagryn and smother him with kisses of relief. It was with some consternation that he realized the sky beyond the great hall's windows had turned black . . .

"All day!" Elaryl was crying. "You've been gone all day long!"

"We have?"

"All three of you!" Fylynn said, whooping in joy that Sheth had returned to her. Seagryn glanced around the room. Dark leaned against a glistening column, smiling warmly. Jocelath rushed around doing something. He didn't see Paumer.

Then he glanced down at Sheth, whose smile of shared triumph was as genuine as any Seagryn remembered. They were comrades, now, in a new way—along with Thaaliana, of course, who sat in her new chair, amazed and elated, her eyes wide with excitement. Suddenly they filled with alarm. "My children!"

Elaryl nodded at her, understanding her concern. "Your husband has been calling for you ever since sundown—wandering around in the woods down below. I was going to go down and tell him but Paumer told me not to—said he didn't know about you.''

"I haven't told him," Thaaliana said quickly, her guilty eyes focused down on the tabletop. "Maybe I'll have to now—'' Before any of them could reply, a squirrel jumped down from the chair to the floor and skittered out of the great hall toward one of the four tree towers. With a flash of her tail, she was gone.

"Tomorrow, remember!" Sheth called after her, then he slumped back in his chair and looked at Seagryn. "I'm exhausted!" He sighed.

"Me, too," Seagryn replied, rolling his head back as Elaryl massaged his shoulders. He felt exactly as if he'd stooped over a table all day long—

"You all disappeared at the same instant, and we've been watching and waiting ever since," Fylynn explained. "Then just a few minutes ago you suddenly were back—but in different chairs!''

"Where have you been?" Elaryl leaned over Seagryn and demanded. "The thing on the table kept glowing, and we wondered if you were inside—''

"We were." Seagryn nodded, rubbing the back of his neck.

"We tried to look into it, but couldn't see you," she mumbled.

"Are you hungry?" Jocelath asked, serving full plates to each of them.

"Hungry?" Seagryn frowned. "I just finished breakfast!''

He did, however, have an appetite. And once his head hit the pillow in their room in the tower, he couldn't remember another thing.

Thaaliana did not come the next day. That was just as well, for Seagryn and Sheth both slept past noon. When they finally did get up, they sat together beside the one pyramid that now glowed, and looked wearily at the five others that still sat lifeless. They decided that they would attempt to fill another stone every other day and took the rest of the day off.

The next morning Thaaliana rejoined them, but, from the tension on her face, she'd obviously had less rest than they. "I'm a mother, too—remember?'' she'd snapped when Sheth commented on it. But they moved much faster on the second pyramid, for they all knew now what to expect. They were out by late afternoon—time enough for Thaaliana to get home to her children and mother-in-law before March quit chopping, and time enough for Seagryn to enjoy sunset from the top of the tree tower he shared with his lady.

* * *

By the time it finally was finished, the six pyramids all glowed with a blue radiance that never varied. "Tomorrow," Sheth breathed quietly when they came out for the sixth and last time, "we make them all into one."

That night Seagryn had difficulty sleeping. He rose before Elaryl and donned a heavy coat to go pace the open balconies of the tree-castle's second level. The days of pyramid filling had been fun—far different from the making of the dragon. He felt bonded to Sheth in a new way, and to Thaaliana, too—although he didn't speak of that to Elaryl. The two women had still found no common ground between them, and he thought he knew why—Elaryl envied Thaaliana her power, while Thaaliana envied Elaryl's relationship to Seagryn, and his to her. Knowing March, Seagryn could understand why.

But that wasn't the problem that caused him to pace this morning. He contemplated the larger concern of the finished object's real purpose. He had no doubt that Amyryth had told him the truth. She had a prophet for a son; but more than that, she had her own spiritual wisdom born from years of experience—wisdom surpassing that of most of the Elders of Lamath. But when would the Power reveal that purpose? And what would be Sheth's response?

He didn't have to wait long to find out. Thaaliana had sent her husband off early this morning, and Sheth was already in the great hall when Seagryn finally clumped in off the wooden portico.

"You're here," the older wizard said crisply. "Good." He was holding two pyramids, which he passed to Thaaliana with the instructions, "You hold these two." Then he picked up two more and held them out to Seagryn. "You take these." Seagryn crossed the room quickly to do so as Sheth picked up the last two. "Now—into a triangle," he said, nodding to indicate where each of them was to stand, well away from the table. Then he held out his pair before him, and they did the same, bringing the six stones together into the cluster he'd demonstrated to them that first morning. "And now, we all say together, 'And thus let the six be one.'"

Just as Seagryn had known intuitively on that first morning what words needed to be said, he knew now. And this phrase was incomplete. He glanced at Thaaliana to see if she knew, too. No. Perhaps he was wrong. He shrugged off the thought and repeated the phrase with the others. "And thus let the six be one." Nothing happened.

They tried again. Still nothing. The six fragments did not

meld . . . Six fragments! Seagryn thought to himself, and his head reeled slightly. He understood, now, what these crystals represented, and what melding them together into one would symbolize, and a chill ran up his spine as he remembered how all these events had come to pass. The Conspiracy—sworn to reunite the old One Land but hated by people in each of the Fragments—had moved inexorably upon the course that the Power had set before it. Not directly, perhaps—Seagryn doubted if the dragon had been in the Power's purpose. But who could know? And what did it matter? *This* had been the purpose of the Conspiracy all along—to make this gem cluster, not as a weapon to be plunged into a dim-witted dragon's heart, but to reunite the unbalanced Fragments of the old One Land into a single, balanced whole. But something was still missing. Seagryn knew what it was.

"Try again!" Sheth growled, and once again they repeated the formula he'd prescribed. Nothing. The older wizard cursed in frustration.

"Maybe we're not doing it right," Thaaliana suggested.

"We *are*!" Sheth snarled at her. "Try it again!" he yelled as he thrust his pyramids out before him so violently they clacked together with Seagryn's.

"Yes," Seagryn said calmly. "Let's do try again." Once more they repeated the phrase, only this time Seagryn enlarged on it. "By faith I plead that the six be one," he began. Sparks shot from their hands before he could finish, "If such be the will of the Power!"

Sheth screamed. Thaaliana did, too, and both let go of the melded object to save their burning fingertips from any more pain. Seagryn was left holding the crystal gem, but to him it felt strangely cool. He had to grab under it quickly to support its weight. As he clutched it to him, there came from it such a sweet, compelling aura of acceptance that he nearly swooned away. He barely heard Sheth's stream of invective, cursing him to every kind of misery for having brought the Power into the gem's making. Soon he couldn't hear Sheth at all. A low, powerful note sounded through the room, vibrating the flooring of the tree-castle and terrifying all but Seagryn. Lyrical higher tones followed, and the music swelled around them, sustaining the bass notes while filling the scale above. At last the sound crescendoed with a crashing blast, and the blue mist they'd found inside the pyramids suddenly enveloped the tree-castle. It was no longer a fall day in the lower Marwilds. Neither was it night. Instead, all of them—the three wizards and those who'd raced in fear to join them in the great hall—hung suspended somewhere in a mist of cool, loving blue, as One they Could Not Name formed meaning in all of their minds at once. And while they later debated the precise words used to express the ideas, the sense of the message came clear to all of them—crystal clear.

The gem cluster Sheth thought he'd designed was a gateway back to the Power for those powers who had long ago abandoned that One's presence. Once successfully opened, it would bind the One Land together again, because the powers that now divided the Fragments from one another would be once again united. It was not a tool of destruction. It was not to be used as a weapon. Most important of all—it was not yet finished. There was a high place located where faith and magic met, where the powers now were clustered and where the gate should be completed. The Marwandian raiders who'd found the jewels and transported them had poured their lifeblood into it. The jewel cutters of the south had blessed it with their expertise. Now the wizards had invested it with the power to shape. But until believers poured faith into it, the Power's gateway would not be perfected. Once that was done, the gate could be opened—an act that would require the highest cost of all.

Sheth argued with the message, and all of them heard him, not with their ears but with their spirits. "But it's my design! I made it! How can you tell me what to use it for, when I'm the one who made it!"

They all said later that each of them knew the answer before it came. The One Beyond their Hearing had first made Sheth. By his own logic, how could Sheth argue with his own designer?

Still Sheth debated. "I made the crystal thorn for a specific purpose! I know it will kill the dragon!"

Certainly the dragon would be killed, the answer rolled back within all of them at once. The dragon had been shaped by powers—it was a magical beast. When the powers all returned then all magic would cease, and the dragon would no longer live.

"All magic?" Sheth pleaded with the mist. "My powers, too? My shaper ability?"

The answer was clear. In the aftermath of the powers' passing, there would be no powers to shape—only faith to express.

"But I have no faith!" Sheth railed at the bright blue cloud, and again they each heard the answer in words they could understand.

That is a choice, not a given. Faith could be expressed by anyone, just as everyone was to some degree a powershaper. But

by its very nature, faith required the wizard to sacrifice indepen-
dence, to become no longer the shaper, but the shaped.

Sheth clapped his hands over his ears and shouted, ''I'm not
listening.'' The others all recounted later feeling grieved by
the futility of the gesture. There was no voice to silence. The
meanings still came clearly to all. Whether heard or not, the
truth remained true. The gateway was incomplete without faith.
Moreover, it could not be opened without the sacrifice of a
powershaper—

''Wait!'' Sheth bellowed, uncovering his useless ears and peering up into the sky-blue fog. ''You mean one of us has to die in
order to unleash the power in this thing?''

A ''yes'' settled like dew upon each of them, as the mist melted
away and the morning sky restored shape and dimension to the
tree-castle that surrounded them. They gulped the air and stared
at one another, like sleepers suddenly awakened, trying to distinguish between reality and a dream. But this had been a group
dream—a shared vision. And while they later debated the exact
identity of the messenger and the images used to express the ideas,
the meaning of the message had been utterly clear to each of them.
All of them looked at Sheth.

He peered around the circle of faces, his own expression growing angrier and angrier with each new pair of expectant eyes.
''Not me!'' he exploded finally. ''I'm not sacrificing anything.''
He reached across the top of the gem and pounded his finger on
Seagryn's chest. ''You're the one who brought the Power into all
this!'' he raged. ''You sacrifice yourself!'' Then he was gone—
vanished. The air rushed in to replace Sheth with a sharp snap,
blowing Seagryn's hair and chapping his cheeks.

No one said anything for several minutes. Thaaliana finally
broke the silence with a whine. ''I can't do it,'' she told Seagryn.
''I have *children* . . .''

''And we may, yet!'' Elaryl broke in, throwing herself into the
center of the circle to block the squirrel-woman's view of her
husband. ''Other people have lives, too!''

''Elaryl . . .'' Seagryn said quietly, and she whirled around to
glare at him, her face contorted by torment.

''I know what you're doing! I know the way you think! You
always think you're the one who must make the sacrifice! You
always assume there's no one else as well qualified to do it! That's
not humble surrender, Seagryn! That's nothing but your pride!''

''Elaryl,'' he said again—privately, intimately, a lover's soft plea to a loved one to spare through silence later embarrassment. She wasn't listening.

"I'll not have it!" Elaryl thundered, pounding a fist against a wooden column. "You never started any of this! You didn't plan this crystal—whatever it is! If anyone is to make some sacrifice then Sheth should do it! He's just too much of a coward to admit it!"

Fylynn swung Elaryl around to face her, her own face now livid. "Sheth's not doing anything he doesn't want to do! Sheth didn't free that dragon! Seagryn did!" Fylynn shot her onetime friend a killing stare, then stormed out of the great hall toward the rooms she'd been sharing with the now-departed power-shaper.

"Fylynn's right," Seagryn murmured, and once more his wife spun to face him.

"You see?" she pleaded, tears beginning to shimmer in her blue eyes. "You feel guilty. But you didn't start the Conspiracy, did you? You didn't make the dragon! You didn't cause the world any of this grief! Why must you feel as guilty as if you had?" She grabbed him around the neck, trying to insinuate herself between the gem cluster and her husband. "Let's go home, Seagryn! Let's leave this place today and just go!"

Seagryn's eyes rose wearily above Elaryl's head and settled on Dark's. The boy wore the expression of an old man again. Seagryn expected nothing from him except that knowing, passive gaze. But Dark surprised him. For once, he acted.

The boy reached out and took Elaryl by the shoulders, and with Seagryn's help pried her arms away from her husband's neck. "I'll take care of this," he murmured soothingly, and he managed to shift the woman's face from Seagryn's shoulder to his own and led her down the line of polished tables to the far end of the great hall. Thaaliana watched them go, then looked back at Seagryn.

"Then you'll go? You'll do it?"

Seagryn cleared a lump from his throat. "I've been prepared for this moment by my whole life—I'm the only shaper who also understands the nature of faith." He shrugged at the squirrel-woman. "I've got to go."

Thaaliana looked at Paumer and Jocelath, the only remaining faces in the circle, and scowled. For her, the project had soured. Strangers had come to occupy her private space. Her mother-in-law was angry at her constant absence, and her husband suspected her of infidelity. She'd cooperated willingly in the making of an object that would rob her of the very powers that gave her identity.

She uttered a brief, bitter, "Good." Then she departed the tree-castle. For all she knew, it was the last time she would see it, but Thaaliana never looked back.

Paumer and Jocelath both looked at Seagryn, but he had nothing left to say. His attention was elsewhere, on the quiet tête-à-tête between Dark and his wife. He was thinking about that evil thing that had opposed him at the meeting of the dragon cult. Would that being willingly return to the Power? Or would it be compelled to go, once the crystal gate was opened? One thing seemed certain—Seagryn would not be alive to know the outcome of his sacrifice. Or would he? He did have a new appreciation for miracles . . .

Dark and Elaryl were returning, arm in arm. That, too, surprised Seagryn. But so many things had surprised him this morning that this one seemed modest by comparison. And given what he knew about Elaryl's faith in the Power and realizing the persuasive force of Dark when he spoke prophetically, Seagryn was not surprised at all when Elaryl quietly announced, "I understand now. Spend the rest of today here with me. Tomorrow, you can go with my blessing."

Chapter Twenty

※※※※

TUGOLITH'S BANE

THE rest of the day disappeared in a moment, as do all last days before lovers must part. Seagryn struggled to cram forever into those few hours and failed miserably. He could not hold off the coming of night, nor the dawn of the next morning. He awoke long before daylight but only stirred from his place beside Elaryl when he heard Fylynn calling up to him from the main part of the tree-castle. He wrapped himself in a robe and went down to her.

She was dressed and packed. "I couldn't just leave without saying good-bye," she murmured, half in apology and half in defiance. "We've shared too much."

"Yes." Seagryn nodded. He didn't know how to respond. He felt somehow as if he were officiating at his own funeral.

"You'll kill him, too, you know," Fylynn murmured, her anger finally overwhelming her warmth. "He'll die without his shaper power."

"Yes," Seagryn said again. "Well, it's not my choice, you know."

"You could choose not to go," she argued. "Let the Power find another shaper, and just leave all of us out of it . . ." But Fylynn spoke with little passion. She knew it was hopeless. Seagryn's mind was made up.

"Where are you going?" he asked.

"Back to Haranamous. I'm a jester, remember?" She smiled bitterly. "I'm sure Chaom will need a laugh or two in the days to come. You look as if you could stand one yourself," she added, slapping him on the shoulder. They gazed at one another then, and words failed. He hugged her, and she squeezed back—hard. Then she sighed deeply and climbed down out of the tree-castle.

An hour later it was his own turn to go. Elaryl, Dark, and Jocelath all stood around him, and even Paumer had appeared to bid him adieu. He had words for each of them but couldn't recall them later, so immersed was his mind in his plans for the journey.

"You're where Dark spends most of his time," Elaryl murmured as he held her. "You're off in the future, instead of here with me."

"I wish I could stay here with you," he mumbled, and kissed her. Then he tore himself away and descended the rope ladder, the crystal object safely stored in a sack strapped to his back.

As he climbed down, he realized she was right. Already his thoughts had turned away from Elaryl toward what was to come, and that somehow made him feel guilty? Then again—what didn't make Seagryn feel guilty?

That was the heart of the matter. Everything did. And this morning he was off to set everything right. By the time he reached the ground, Seagryn had decided he would never again shape the powers. The gem cluster contained enough magic—what it lacked now was faith. From this point forward, he would be simply a believer. If there were miracles the Power wished to work through him, fine, but Seagryn would no longer be a wizard. Since that meant no longer taking his tugolith form, Seagryn mounted one of the four remaining horses and rode north. Although he'd never been there, he knew exactly where to find the mountain of the Power. He knew it by faith.

Seagryn felt no elation. How could a person celebrate self-sacrifice? And yet he did experience an overwhelming sense of peace and well-being. What he was doing was right—utterly right. In fact, for the first time in many months, he actually felt righteous. And by the time he reached the boundary of the giant woods, he was even beginning to feel justified as well.

The trees of this forest had already lost their battle with the fast-approaching winter. He could see the sky through their skeletal branches, while their foliage drifted in piles at his horse's feet. As he contemplated the depressing brevity of autumn, a mound of multicolored leaves loomed curiously before him. His horse stopped dead at no command of Seagryn's—Seagryn was too shocked to speak. He stared into the face of an enormous bear.

"Give me the crystal thorn," Sheth growled.

But Seagryn still could not respond. His horse stood frozen in terror.

"It's mine, Seagryn," the bear growled again. "Return it to me now."

Too easy. This had all been too easy. He should have known Sheth would not yield his creation without a fight. "It isn't yours," he answered when he finally found his voice. "You know its purpose as well as I. Step aside, bear, and let me pass."

Sheth roared. But for Seagryn's tight grip on its reins, the horse would have bolted. "Give it to me, Seagryn, or I'll bite your head off!"

"Sheth, be sensible!" Seagryn called in a commanding tone of voice. "You yourself have seen the One With Whom we Work! There's no possibility of altering that One's plan!"

"Do you have that on Dark's authority?" the bear sneered. "Or only on your own?"

"Please, for your own good," Seagryn implored, "move aside!" But his voice quavered slightly. There was something about the intelligence shining in those huge eyes that mocked the reason in his words. And when the bear uttered a series of grunting roars, and Seagryn suddenly recognized it was laughing, he trembled.

"My own good?" The great bear chuckled. "Listen to me. I'm going to eat you, Seagryn. You've eaten humans before, you know how we taste! I've not experienced the pleasure in a long time—too long. Give me the crystal thorn, Seagryn, for your own good! Or I'll take it from you and crunch your bones in the bargain."

Seagryn wrestled with the temptation to take his tugolith shape. How easy it would be to spear this bear on his tusk! Yet he'd promised himself . . . His momentary indecision robbed him of the chance to do or say anything; when he didn't respond, the bear charged. His horse had had enough of this, and it burst out from under him, departing the area in a plume of leaves. Seagryn fell backward, and despite the thick cushion of fallen leaves, the object in his pack stabbed into his back. He scrambled immediately to his feet, but the bear already towered over him, reaching around him to seize the backpack in its forepaws.

Power, this would be a wonderful time for a miracle, Seagryn thought. He waited as long as he could, but when none came, Seagryn surrendered to his rage and became a tugolith. The pack broke off his back, and the bear reeled away, dodging the first swipe of that wickedly tipped horn on Seagryn's forehead. "Now!" Seagryn bellowed. "We'll see who eats whom!"

"Finally!" Sheth shouted, sounding relieved, and his bear shape—and Sheth—disappeared. Seagryn turned human and cloaked the bag so Sheth couldn't see it. Again Sheth was a bear and right on top of Seagryn. With a smack of his paw, Sheth sent his rival whirling through the leaves like a tiny tornado. Seagryn banged off a tree and fell into a pile of leaves. When he realized the bear was once more pouncing upon him, Seagryn grew huge again. Instead of digging in and ripping his flesh, the bear's claws glanced off his armor plating. But this, of course, left exposed once again the location of the crystal thorn. As the bear bounded after it, Seagryn struggled vainly to horn Sheth's legs. Then he was up and chasing, for Sheth almost had his human hands upon the backpack, and Seagryn knew the wizard's next move would be to disappear where he could not follow. The leaves at Sheth's feet burst into flame, forcing him to dodge aside. Seagryn dived past him, burying the sack and its contents under his chest. If he could only disappear as Sheth and Talarath did! Perhaps he could! He tried . . .

Darkness, total darkness, a void in which he hung voiceless and alone. And—nothing else. Nothing happened. He went nowhere. He felt nothing in his body. But what he felt emotionally made any physical pain he'd yet experienced seem a trivial inconvenience, for almost immediately he recognized what he'd put himself inside. The dark being that had engulfed him at the meeting of the dragon cult now embraced him again—or had Seagryn embraced it? One thing was certain—he'd not brought the gem cluster along with him. Wherever he was, wherever he was going, the Power's gateway had been left behind.

He was utterly lost. In that timeless emptiness Seagryn reflected upon the immensity of his own foolishness and his own failure. He'd known better! He'd trusted himself just this morning to the Power's control alone, but his temper had stolen his peace, and with it had gone his wisdom. He had shaped—or tried to. Was he *still* trying?

"How many times must I do this to myself before I learn to just let go?" He asked the question ruefully to the darkness, which made no response whatsoever. "Of course," Seagryn mumbled. "Why should you give any hints?" Then he leaned backward into the void and let himself fall.

"He's back."

It was Dark's voice. How ironic, Seagryn was thinking to himself, that one so full of light should have been given such a name. What had Amyryth been thinking? He opened his eyes.

"You see?" Dark said again, and Elaryl pounced upon Seagryn as he'd jumped upon the gem cluster just a few moments—hours? days?—before. She smothered his face with kisses, and

Seagryn remembered that other name Dark had used for his mother. Still, it was nice. He was comfortable. He was back.

"From where?" he gasped, sitting upright and carrying Elaryl with him up onto her knees. "Where have I been?"

Dark smiled enigmatically. "You don't know?"

"Have I—has my body been here?"

"You might ask yourself," Dark said sardonically, "where is here, exactly."

Seagryn looked around. He was back in the tree-castle! "How did I . . ." He stopped. Dark gave him an elaborate shrug. Elaryl still clung tightly to his neck. "And the Power's gateway?"

Now Dark frowned. "Sheth has it."

"But he still wants to use it as a weapon against the dragon!"

"Yes . . ."

"He'll be killed!"

Dark rolled his eyes. "You think I don't know that?"

"But—but—" Seagryn babbled to himself, unconsciously squeezing Elaryl back and crushing a satisfied grunt from her. "He'll have taken it to the Central Gate already! We're too late!"

"Well, no . . ." Dark said thoughtfully. "He's discovered by this time the same thing you did."

"And what's that?" Seagryn asked.

"That the crystal object can't be carried through the void. Seeing that, he's recovered your horse and is riding toward the dragon's lair."

"Now?" Seagryn grunted, a mental map forming in his mind as he calculated their comparative distances from the pass.

"As we speak." Dark nodded.

"We've got to go!" Seagryn shouted. "Load the horses!"

"They're loaded already." Dark grinned at Seagryn's surprised expression. "Why so shocked? Remember—we've been expecting you!" Within moments Seagryn, Dark and Elaryl rode the last three horses at a breakneck pace toward the pass that much of the old One Land had already begun to refer to as Dragonsgate.

They heard the battle before they saw it. They'd ridden all night, and all three took the light glowing in the east for dawn until it started flashing. It pulsed—a rhythmical beating as regular as that of a heart. Then it disappeared, and moments later they heard the terrible roar of a bear, answered by the double-throated scream of the dragon. Then the explosions began.

Seagryn sorely missed Kerl. He urged this weary mount to run faster, but it couldn't. Its energy was spent. The temptation to take his tugolith shape grew stronger with every distant war cry, but this time Seagryn resisted it—the cost was just too high. Instead, he silently begged the Power for some miracle—but none came. And somewhere in the eastern night the titanic battle continued.

At last they were headed up the sharp incline into the pass. As dawn finally did shed its light upon the scene, they saw devastation everywhere—charred trees, ripped up by the roots, scorched cliffs, and boulders scattered in the roadway. Then they heard a scream high above them and looked up in time to see the dragon spread its wings and plummet from the sky like a falcon dropping onto its prey. Seagryn could bear this no longer. He jumped from his horse's back and sprinted the last few yards into the Central Gate . . .

Standing on his hind legs, the bear reared back to meet the dragon's plunge, the crystal thorn clutched in his forepaws and raised above his head. Just when it seemed certain that each head would tear a gaping hole in the bear's shaggy flanks, Sheth leaped nimbly forward and spun around, bringing himself right up under the beast's heart as it swooped by. With perfect timing, the wizard slammed the point of the object upward and in . . . then bounced helplessly aside as the cluster of gems shattered into its six original pieces. Not a one of them pierced the dragon's scales—not one. And in a maneuver Seagryn would not have believed physically possible, the two heads glided back beneath their shared body, causing it to flip over as gracefully as a fish. In a flash, before Seagryn could lift a hand to help, the two heads had each seized a part of Sheth. With a sickening rip, they sheared the wizard in half and bore the pieces aloft.

There was very little blood. Somehow that made it even more chilling, and Seagryn felt what remaining strength he possessed after the long day and night draining out through his rooted feet into the soil of Dragonsgate. Truly Dragonsgate—for without question, this place now belonged to Vicia-Heinox.

Elaryl and Dark had finally caught up with him, and each grabbed him under one arm and steadied him. Strange—he hadn't realized he was toppling over, but now he noticed the numbness in his legs. "Sheth," he murmured as they heard the dragon screeching its triumph from somewhere in the sky.

"You couldn't have done anything," Dark said, and received a glare for his trouble.

"The Power could have!" Seagryn snapped back.

The boy didn't flinch. "The One Who Will Not Force us did all that could be done," he murmured—and Seagryn knew Dark was right.

"Yes," he said finally. "Yes, the Power did. But Sheth refused . . .'' The results of that refusal lay scattered over the floor of the pass, sparkling in the slanting sunlight. ''The pieces—we'd better get them.'' Seagryn started forward, then stopped. The dawn's light also glinted off something coming up through the southern mouth of the pass.

''A caravan?'' he cried in alarm. ''Now?'' Behind him he heard Dark cackle.

''My wedding party, come to seek me out!'' the boy said, and Seagryn whirled around to face him.

''What?''

''It's Uda and my mother-in-law, come to take me home. Oh, don't worry, Seagryn,'' the boy added in more subdued tones. ''I told you already—no big wedding for me!''

Seagryn heard in that moment the obvious reason why. Vicia-Heinox came screaming down out of the sky. After such a prolonged battle, wasn't the dragon certain to be hungry? Seagryn pivoted slowly to watch as the beast suddenly furled its wings and floated the last few feet to the canyon floor. It was looking at the sparkling objects scattered all around.

''Elaryl! Dark!'' Seagryn whispered. ''Follow me!'' As he scrambled toward the far wall of the pass, Seagryn debated the question of magic once again. Why not cloak them all from view? Perhaps his brush with the dark presence yesterday had been an accident—perhaps it wouldn't happen again. Perhaps that dark force resided only in the Marwilds and never visited this high mountain pass. Certainly Sheth had put up a valiant magical struggle here—and apparently the Power was not interested in providing miracles today! Finally, the Power's gateway was lost—shattered into half a dozen fragments, two of which the beast was now holding in its mouths. Why not use magic after all? And yet—something prevented him.

In any case, they apparently would be able to bypass the beast without needing magic. It appeared to be absorbed in the glistening objects. Seagryn hastened forward, determined to prevent the caravan from coming any farther. And when she spotted him, the leader of the group angled her palfrey toward him.

''Kerily!'' Seagryn shouted when she came within earshot. ''Turn around!''

''I'll do nothing of the sort!'' the woman called back to him. ''Is that my runaway son-in-law behind you? Bring him here!''

Seagryn saw Uda now, riding behind her mother. But while Kerily threw an imperious gaze down at him, Seagryn saw that her daughter stared, gaping, at the dragon. She always had been a sensible girl . . .

"Kerily, turn your caravan around and get out of here! The dragon is right over there, and he eats caravans like this for breakfast! Turn around! Get out of the pass! Go!" he pleaded.

Kerily, however, wasn't moved. "I know perfectly well where that dragon is. You may not be aware of this, Seagryn, but my family has worked out a—relationship—with the dragon. Now where's my son-in-law? Dark! You come here!" She pointed to the ground at the foot of her horse, and Seagryn looked around in amazement as the boy slunk forward, his carefree demeanor fleeing in the face of her commands. Elaryl came up beside him and put her arm around his shoulder as Dark continued on past them.

"Dark," she murmured. "You don't have to do this . . ."

"Oh, yes, I do," the boy shot back without looking at either of them. His face wore a dutiful expression.

"Where have you been?" Kerily began. "Have you any idea what your sudden departure has done to my daughter, my household, and to myself—?"

"Mother!" Uda snapped. Kerily cut off as Uda slipped to the ground and ran forward to grab Dark around the neck. "I'm just glad he's all right! You are, aren't you?" She checked solicitously.

"I am." Dark nodded, then turned to look back at Seagryn and Elaryl and winked. Both of them relaxed. Of course—the boy knew what he was doing. He'd lived through this all before!

"Very well, then," Kerily muttered, fluttering a hand in a gesture that seemed to say she forgave the boy as long as Uda did. "The important thing now is to insure you don't run off again. You," she said, pointing at Seagryn.

"Yes?" he frowned.

"Marry them."

"What?" he gasped. "But there's a dragon right over—"

"I told you." Dark grinned. "No big wedding!"

"You mean you want me to—"

"Go ahead!" Uda pleaded. Then she rolled her eyes toward the dragon and added, "Quickly . . ."

Seagryn looked at Elaryl in confusion. She said nothing—she merely shrugged and walked around behind Uda and Dark, unbelting her tunic on the way. She kneeled behind them and bound his right ankle to her left, then stood up and nodded at Seagryn.

He looked at Dark inquiringly. "You want this?"

"Of course." The boy smiled. "I never had any problem with being married to Uda. I—" He glanced over at her. "I love her. Have since the first moment I saw her . . . in my dreams.'' Then he looked back at Seagryn and added, ''Which actually occurred when I was six, though I did manage to block it out for a few years.''

''But I thought you were running from—''

''It was the wedding I dreaded and all those endless, horrible plans . . .''

Seagryn saw Kerily frown and decided to plunge into the ceremony. ''You've chosen to be bound together at the feet,'' he mumbled quickly, wishing he could sneak a peek at the dragon, ''to link your paths together in the bonds of wedlock, to knot your destinies from this day forward. Hobbling one another, walking on three legs instead of four, you are nevertheless also supporting one another, dependent upon one another. I declare you linked before this assembly and before the Power. Now untie them, Elaryl, so we can get this caravan *away* from here!''

As Elaryl struggled to untie the knot she'd just made, Seagryn looked back over his shoulder at the beast. His heart leaped into his throat—it was gone!

But where—

A shadow passed across them, and Seagryn whirled back around to stare up as the twi-beast settled into the dust not twenty feet away. Both heads looked directly at him! Each mouth held a sparkling sliver of diamond, and now the Heinox head put his gem down in order to speak. Despite his terror, Seagryn found himself marveling at the wonderful dexterity of the beast's lips . . .

''Seagryn,'' Heinox began—so he had recognized him.

''Yes?'' he responded, his mouth dry.

''I've eaten Sheth.''

Seagryn swallowed—hard. ''Yes?'' He couldn't think of anything else to say. What else could one say of the passing of the greatest powershaper from the earth? Besides, Seagryn was remembering the size of the teeth beyond those dexterous lips . . .

''Watch,'' Heinox ordered. Then he picked up the crystal he had set in the dirt and tossed it into the air. Before it came down, Vicia, too, had tossed his crystal skyward—and the two necks twined together and each caught the other's crystal. Again each head tossed up the crystal he held, and the necks untwined and caught them again. The dragon was juggling . . .

''Juggling?'' Seagryn mumbled, and looked at Dark. The boy smiled back. ''Juggling,'' Seagryn said to himself again, and he looked back up at the dragon. ''Yes,'' he murmured. ''And very well, too . . .''

"Why, that's marvelous!" Kerily shouted, and the dragon appeared to smile. "Have you thought of appearing in public?"

Seagryn whirled to look at the woman, astonished. "This is a *dragon*, Kerily! Not an animal act!"

"Oh, I don't know," the woman murmured, watching the sparkling stones ascend and descend. "Of course, we'd have to remodel the concert hall to get him into it—"

Seagryn heard a gulp above him and looked back up at the dragon. Heinox wore a perplexed expression. Vicia, still holding one of the stones in his lips, regarded his other head with unmistakable contempt. And one of the stones was missing. Vicia dropped the diamond he held back into the dust and snarled, "Now why did I have to do *that*!"

"I don't know," Heinox responded honestly. "It just happened . . ."

Vicia swooped down to Seagryn, causing him to leap backward several yards. "I swallowed one," the beast snarled, his huge eyes wide with frustration. "Where can I find more of these stones?"

"Ah—ah . . ." Seagryn stammered, suddenly seeing a new possibility. Had the dragon not noticed the other fragments scattered about the pass? If he could get the dragon to fly away, perhaps there would be a chance yet to rescue the remaining pieces and reassemble the gateway! "An island—that way," he said, pointing to the northwest. "There's a sea in that direction, and an island right off the coast. This stone came from that island," he said, pointing at the fragment Vicia had dropped in the dirt. "I've been told there are piles of such stones there!"

"Piles?" Vicia cried enthusiastically, his eyes aglow with greed. "Piles!" he shouted to Heinox, and grabbed up the stone and shot skyward. Seagryn had time to blink twice—and the dragon was gone.

"How many did we recover?" Seagryn asked Dark, and the boy held up the two he had.

"Four, counting these." He held them out before him, and Seagryn took them and stored them in the bag with the others. Then he turned, looked at the prophet, and sighed. "Go ahead," the boy murmured. "You do ask, and I do tell you."

Seagryn nodded. "Is there any point to this? Do I even need to try?"

"Oh, yes," Dark said emphatically. "I told you long ago that this plan would succeed. Ultimately."

"You're certain of that?" Seagryn challenged.

"Absolutely," Dark said. "And much of that success depends on what you have yet to accomplish." He made no mention, however, of what that might be, nor just how long it might take . . .

"Where are you going now?" Seagryn asked.

"Off to the woods someplace." Dark shrugged. "Uda says they own a shack near here where we can spend a few weeks in peace. Of course, you know what this family means by the word *shack*."

Seagryn did indeed. It would doubtless turn out to be a palatial estate in the trees. In the trees . . .

"And you're going back to the tree-castle," Dark informed him.

"I am?"

"You and Elaryl."

"But it belongs to Thaaliana—"

"Not really. It's almost winter, Seagryn. Lamath is in a shambles, true, but there's nothing you can do about it until spring. Besides—you can't very well just leave Jocelath there with Paumer, can you?"

"I guess not." Seagryn smiled at the ground. The idea pleased him. He'd wondered what that fortress in the trees would look like covered with snow. Then he looked back up at his friend. "And when will we meet again?"

He saw something pass across Dark's face, some memory of fear or pain or evil—but then it was gone. "When the time comes." The boy smiled. "Don't worry." Dark took a long look over at Uda, who stood beside her horse talking with her mother, then looked back at Seagryn. This time the expression on his face was easy to read—wedding night nervousness. "Wish me luck," he mumbled, and he walked away, pausing to give Elaryl a parting hug before rejoining his new wife.

Elaryl looked at Seagryn, her eyes sparkling. "Husband." She smiled. "Are we ready to go get Jocelath?"

"We're ready," he answered, and he hoisted her up onto her horse's back, giving her an affectionate pat in the process.

"I dread this ride," she murmured, rubbing the spot he'd just patted in anticipation of its coming ordeal. "I wish we could just close our eyes and be there!"

"Careful, my darling," Seagryn warned her with a smile. "Such wishes have been known to come true!"

As they rode down out of Dragonsgate Pass toward the west, Seagryn reassured himself by counting the points of the diamond pyramids in his bag. He was already planning how they might replace the missing two . . .

✕✕✕✕✕✕

GLOSSARY

altershape: The animal shape taken by a wizard when he or she
so chooses. The animal form taken reveals something of the
wizard's personality or desires.

Amyryth: The affectionate mother of Dark the prophet, and a
spiritual giant in her own right.

Arl: A warlike state located in the mountainous region southwest of the Central Gate; its capital sits upon a promontory
in the Arl Lake.

bearsbane: A title given to anyone who has slain a bear.

Berillitha: A female tugolith who gave her life to save Seagryn—and thus became part of the twi-beast.

Bourne: The Lamathian village where Seagryn was born.

Chaom: Leading warrior of the army of Haranamous and chief
military advisor to Haran. A large, careful man not given to
revealing his feelings.

Dark the prophet: An adolescent with a gift of foreknowledge
so exact that his name is already legend. Other than that, a
normal youth.

drax: A three-sided table game played throughout the old One
Land, usually with wagers on the outcome.

Elaryl: Blond bride of Seagryn and daughter to Talarath, well meaning and spiritually astute, in addition to being very lovely.

Emeraude: A large green cat inhabiting one of the spice islands in the southern sea.

Fylynn: A female jester in the court of Haranamous. In love with Sheth.

Garney: The small, self-important Keeper of the Outer Portal for the old One Land, or Remnant. Single-minded in his sense of duty.

Haran: King of the land of Haranamous, which bears a part of his name.

Haranamous: A coastal state rich in culture and farmland, located south of the Central Gate and bordered by Pleclypsa and Arl.

Imperial House of Haranamous: The royal palace of the dynasty of Haran, brought to life centuries earlier by the wizard Nobalog.

Jarnel: Prince of the Army of Arl and a representative to the Conspiracy from that warlike state.

Jocelath: Maid—and best friend—to Elaryl.

Kerl: A stolid, stalwart, gray horse meaning much to Seagryn.

Kerily: Wife to Paumer and mother to Uda and Ognadzu. First and foremost, an artiste.

Lamath: "Land of faith," the large coastal land located north of the Central Gate, ruled as a theocracy by the Council of Elders.

Marwand: A nonstate composed of bands of fierce, independent warriors battling Arl or raiding into Lamath. With no real borders, but roughly occupying the Marwilds.

Marwilds: A vast, sparsely settled forest land to the west of the Central Gate occupied primarily by Marwandian raiders and wizards.

Merkle: A "digger" dwelling with others of his race underneath the Remnant.

megasin: An ancient power, able to shape rock with her will and craving human companionship.

moosers: Hooved herd animals domesticated to provide meat and milk.

mudgecurdle: A furry creature looking just like a rabbit, but ejecting a horrible stench when startled. Also an epithet meaning *traitor*.

Nebalath: A thin-faced wizard of some years, long the covering powershaper for the land of Haranamous. A friend to the Imperial House.

Nobalog: A long-dead wizard who brought the Imperial House to life and taught it to converse with wizards.

Norck: Captain of *The Norck Stork*, a free-trading vessel on the southern sea.

Ognadzu: Hostile son of Paumer the merchant. Fled his father's house and started his own sinister enterprise.

Paumer: The most successful merchant in all the Fragments of the old One Land. An organizer of the Conspiracy, now unable even to organize his own family.

Pleclypsa: A warm, sunny land to the south of Haranamous, bordered on three sides by the sea and populated by merchant types.

powershaper: Anyone gifted with the ability to shape the powers, but classically only those who, among other talents, can change into altershapes.

pyralu: Enormous, deadly insect, taken as the symbol of the Army of Arl.

Ranoth: Wise, diminutive leader of the Council of Elders, the ruling body of the Land of Lamath.

the Remnant: Name of the underground kingdom maintaining the ancient dynasty of the old One Land.

Ritaven: A pleasant village on the eastern edge of the Marwilds.

Seagryn: A powershaper regarded as a traitor by all the world.

Sheth: The foremost wizard of his time. Secretive, charming when choosing to be, irresponsible despite great talent, and occasionally cannibalistic. Altershape, a huge black bear.

Talarath: Tall, dour memeber of the Council of Elders of the Land of Lamath and father to Elaryl. Difficult to please.

tugoliths: Enormous, horned creatures from the far north able to carry on human conversation at the level of toddlers. Called *Northbeasts* by the Marwandians.

twi-beast: The name bestowed by Sheth upon the two-headed dragons of his manufacture.

Uda: Youthful daughter of Paumer the Shrewd. Bright and ambitious. In love with Dark the prophet.

Vicia-Heinox: A two-headed dragon made by Sheth and loosed upon the world by Seagryn.

Wilker: Foppish, posturing bureaucrat within the Remnant, bearing the title of Undersecretary for Provincial Affairs and a member of the Conspiracy.

Yammerlid: Childhood enemy of Seagryn, sworn to vengeance.

About the Author

Robert Don Hughes, the son of a Baptist pastor, was born in Ventura, California. He grew up in Long Beach and was educated in Redlands, Riverside, and Mill Valley, gaining degrees in theater arts and divinity. That education continued, and he finished a Ph.D. in missions, religions, and philosophy in Louisville, Kentucky.

He has been a pastor, playwright, teacher, film maker, and missionary and considers all those roles fulfilling. Besides the Pelmen the Powershaper trilogy, he has published several books of short plays and presently teaches communications and mass media. His two passions are writing and football—not necessarily in that order—especially in October. He is married to Gail, a beautiful South Alabama woman who loves rainbows and fill his life with them. They lived for several years in Africa, where he did missionary work. They now live in Louisville, Kentucky, with their daughter, Bronwynn, who was born in Africa.

Most of all, Bob likes people. The infinite variety of personalities and opinions makes life interesting. The sharing of faith makes it worthwhile.